**LEABHARLANNA CHONTAE NA GAILLIMHE
(GALWAY COUNTY LIBRARIES)**

TM

Acc. No. F127,202   Class No. ✓

Date of Return	Date of Return	Date of Return
- 3 JUN 2005		
E 5 JUL 2005		
E 2 AUG 2005		
2 7 OCT 2005		
1 0 OCT 2008		

Books are on loan for 21 days from date of issue.

Fines for overdue books: 10c for each week or portion of a week plus cost of postage incurred in recovery.

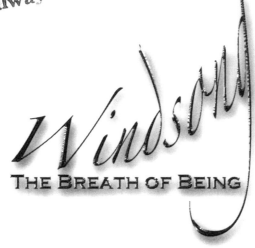

THE BREATH OF BEING

ROGER J. DERHAM

Wynkin deWorde

2 0 0 4

Published in 2004
by

**Wynkin
deWorde**

Wynkin deWorde Ltd.,
PO Box 257, Galway, Ireland.
info@deworde.com

A CIP catalogue record for this book is available from the British Library

ISBN: 1-904893-03-1

Typeset by Patricia Hope, Skerries, Co. Dublin, Ireland
Cover Design: Roger Derham
Cover Production Coordination: Design Direct, Galway, Ireland
Printed by Betaprint, Dublin, Ireland

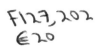

ACKNOWLEDGEMENTS

Most importantly to Brenda, David, Heather and Nicole for their support in the difficult days.

In Istanbul: to Füsun Arsan, in particular, for her friendship and interpretation and to M. Ugar Derman, for his expertise; and to both for guiding me through the alleyways of the Ok Meydani and Turkish calligraphy.

In Dublin: my sincere gratitude extends to the Director and staff of the Chester Beatty Library museum. When I embarked on this project in October 2001 they were unfailing in their courtesy to me; helping me gain an insight into the nature of the ancient manuscript purchase business as it existed in the 1930s. Later, as the museum and its workings became the basis for the structural support of the novel, some concerns were expressed because of sensitivities within the museum with regard to events in the recent past. I hope that everybody associated with the museum will recognise that these past events pale into insignificance against the distinct possibility of future problems, particularly in the light of current political and religious differences.

My special thanks also go to Susan Corr for leading me gently through the science of paper conservation and to Ken Bruen in Galway and Tom Kennedy in Copenhagen for encouragement when the going got tough.

I also wish to thank the poets Bejan Matur and Negar for permission to quote from the English translations of their work and to Coleman Barks for permission to quote two verses of his translation of Jelaluddin Rumi's *Like This*.

Finally, to Valerie Shortland: her editorial skills and reason make it is easy to work when such attention to detail is always available at your elbow.

"Time was when every epic had its tempest: winds were the divinities of the Mediterranean."

Predrag Matvejevic • *Mediterranean. A Cultural Landscape*

"When lovers moan,
They're telling our story.
Like this.
I am a sky where spirits live.
Stare into this deepening blue,
While the breeze says a secret.
Like this."

Jelaluddin Rumi • *Like This*
(Tr.: Coleman Barks)

The only Art is living Life, the alternative, artifice.

Windsong
THE BREATH OF BEING

Sirocco

BEING THE BEGINNING

"A beginning has no becoming into being."

Plato • *Phædrus*

"Being is not a problem for common sense
(or, rather, common sense does not see it as a problem)
because it is the condition for common sense itself."

Umberto Eco • *Kant and the Platypus*

Flanagan feels, hears his breathing race in short galloping bursts and is certain he sees a horse in the distance. In trying to capture the image he forces his eyelids to open and close like a camera shutter but the horse disappears into a distant fog. He rubs his eyes, massaging them into focus. At the far end of the room, a computer sleep-light blinks, and alongside the computer a package, delivered earlier in the day, sits unblinking. Jerome Augustine Flanagan – Jaffa to those who remembered the light-filled schooldays of his childhood more than him but also to his friends and rivals, in the adult and very twilight world of the rare manuscripts trade – wakes up feeling dreadful. Not just dreadful but also very disturbed and disorientated. The air around him is heavy with humidity and he feels suffocated by its pressure. The dream that had woken him had been all too real, too immediate.

His eyelids close again and in the blackness he hazily recollects the dream's beginning: him hitch-hiking at a crossroads; being picked up by a circus truck driven by a cackling clown; arriving at a fairground attraction, a tunnel of distorting mirrors, and

1

then slowly, ever so slowly, it dawning on him that he was watching himself and was also being watched from within his reflection by a curled-up, tadpole-eyed, ochre-veined, marble-skinned being of a thing, contained within a sac that floated around his dream like a speck in his eye. As he moved backwards and forwards in the dream the thing inside the sac changed and distorted, acquiring and losing definition as it filled and emptied from his reflection; the light surrounding the sac pulsed bright and dim and a whooshing sound blew up and down the tunnel, making noises like somebody whispering his name.

With increasing clarity of recall Flanagan then remembers stretching out to press a hand against his reflection and the sac suddenly sucking him in. And then he was the being on the inside looking out; at first there are two of him, then four, then eight . . . and then feeling the spasms start up and at their most intense sensing a pain, like pain of separation. And then there was the horse with four or five tails – a nightmare.

'Christ!' he says aloud, opening his eyes wide and touching his face for reassuring orientation.

He feels clammy, knows he has been sweating, and wonders if he smells of this. His clothes stick to him like membranes. The slug-ash ghost of a half-smoked Syrian Al-Hambra cigarette trails across the ashtray, its filter stub guillotined to the glass table. He resists the urge to light up another and unfurling from the large sofa, looks at his watch, focusing hard on the dial. Two hours he's been asleep, he reckons. Must have needed it, he reasons, feeling an intense urge to empty his bladder, the spasms that woke him beginning again. Standing, he picks up the ashtray, the unfinished pizza slice, now cold, and the near empty beer bottle, now warm, and carries them with him towards the kitchen.

Some time later, his grey-flecked sandy hair wet from a needed shower and a mug of dark-roasted Java in hand, Flanagan carefully descends the small set of steps that lead down into the living room of his ground-floor apartment. He is wearing his favourite silk kimono gown over a bare chest and baggy, oriental-style pyjama pants. There is a chill in the room, and he feels a sense of intrusion. He hesitates for a moment, steadying his hip against the steel handrail and tightening his grip on the mug. His eyes scan along the length of the room, past the reproduction Georgian fireplace and the tall unit made from mountain ash, which houses his stereo system and CD collection, towards the double-glazed patio door at the far end where a large, polished writing table is placed across the entrance. His eyes scan the magnolia-coloured walls, checking. The framed pictures are all in place: the original page CCLVII from the 1493 Nuremberg Chronicle showing Constantinople; a 1714 Homann map and panorama of the same city; and the drawing of an Irish fiddler caught in the full flow of his music.

Reassured somewhat, he relaxes and crosses the room to the writing table. He stands close to its edge, tapping with an agitated finger against the peach-coloured wood before searching beneath the scattered books, catalogues and layers of paper that float on the table surface like Sargasso seaweed. Finding what he is looking for he angles the remote control back over his shoulder to aim at the stereo, selects the second track and waits for the music.

Infrared music – night-vision music, he thinks.

On the table in front of him, the pale-pink flowers of the house-bound orchid, *cymbidium* – purple-blotched invitation, yellow-velvet vulva, cobra-like tumescent hood and sticky sweet depths of it – glimmer in the moonlight; the light of the moon, the light of Jupiter's moons under a March Gemini, looking serene and satisfied. A cadenza light, the moonbeams bring their own music, filtering into the room on a cool breeze that whistles softly through a half-open patio door. Beyond the door and the small garden, he hears the sound of the ocean that the apartment block overlooks. Govi's *Magellan's Beat* starts up on the CD player, quietly. He half-turns with the remote control in hand, gun-slinging it into the quietness.

On the liquid display it is 23:45, near the end of the second watch since sunset. And what a sunset it had been, he remembers, the dying embers of the day bouncing off the red wind – the dust-laden Sirocco that had brought the humidity and his dreaming. Earlier he had watched the windsurfers, attracted by the unseasonable warmth, appear like mayfly on the waters beyond the patio and chase the wind. It is music to steer by, he thinks tillering up the volume: the music of the wind.

Panpipes like siren squalls drift across the room and the ocean of his imagination. Suddenly the guitar sounds and he senses the sea-change: a pitching ship and the strains of halyard, sail and mast beating close to the wind's direction. Then gradually, a plectrum rudder has the ship and orchestra reaching away again, sails full of guitar liberation. Flanagan sits down to type. The laptop boots up and waits. And he waits, and waits, fingers hovering. Nothing happens! He drafts on the coffee and lights up a cigarette, drawing deeply on it.

To the right of the screen, the neatly packaged parcel lies unopened. He had immediately recognised the scratchy writing of its sender, its fragility, its anger and he felt afraid of that anger.

To the left of the screen, a yellowing newspaper cutting from last year's war: the image of an old man in Basra lifting a child; a child wearing a purple cardigan and green trousers; her little arm outstretched, clutching at life; her right ankle shattered, rendered of skin and sinew to abattoir bone; stripped useless, he thinks, by another type of liberation on a dog-day for the dogs-of-war. He wants to reach out to her. As if writing something would bring her back, him back, bring them all back. Exhaled smoke swirls around the computer. In his mind's eye there's a vortex, a black hole sucking back on the words, an anti-matter of what matters. The old man in Basra, is looking down at the face of the little girl, furrowed disbelief etched in his own. The very effort, the futility of it, drives Flanagan's head into his hands and he looks at the orchid, and the picture, and the keyboard, through the cracks between fingers.

He notices – senses – the bottle of single malt from the Isles and reaches out across the table. And the glass; unwashed, he smells the peat off it. His muscles twitch. It's an effort just to lift the bottle. He remembers how his own father shook as he reached out for a bottle – the bottles that were denied to him at the end. A miserable, sad and lonely end. He pours the whiskey slowly, stiffly, and tastes the bog off it.

He closes the lid of the laptop and reaching for the parcel pulls it towards him. He tears away at the paper until revealing an old calfskin-covered book, a computer disc in its case, and a folded piece of paper. He coughs suddenly, eyes opening wide, stubs out the cigarette and lifts the book. He recognises the frayed flaps and woven horsehair tassels.

'Jesus!' he says aloud, as he lays down the book and picks up the folded paper. He flattens it out and reads:

Dear Jaffa,

I am sorry but I was afraid, so afraid. For Rio, you and me. I wanted to protect us but that is no longer possible. My fight is over and it is a poisoned "arrow" that wings its way back to you.

The disc is Rio's, a diary of sorts, I think. She told me about it before she . . . I thought it might help and I took it. I needed to know, wanted to understand, about you and her, her and me . . .

In the end I couldn't read it, the possibility of hurt, hurt too much. I wish I could forgive you.

I wish I could forgive myself.

Mac

Flanagan's hands shake so much cigarette ash fans across the table. The letter flutters to the ground beneath his feet, landing face down. He leaves it there, hiding from its accusation and the difficulty in picking it up. He replaces the calfskin-covered book in the torn packaging and pushes it to one side. He sees a vague reflection from the shiny surface of the laptop and remembers K's concern regarding truth: *the reflection presenting two moments of thought, objective and subjective: two alternatives to existing.* Whatever way you look at it, Flanagan realises, objectively or subjectively, outwardly or inwardly, being or becoming, truth is a vanishing point. And reflection, *he hopes,* is just an approximation.

Lifting the lid, Pandora's lid, he suddenly thinks, and waits for its azure beginning.

MISTRAL

"Mention (Hud) one of 'Ad's (own) brethren:
Behold, he warned his people about the winding Sand-tracts:
but there have been warners before him and after him..."

The Qur'an • *surat al-ahqãf* (The Sand Dunes); 46, *v.* 21

1

THE EXCHANGE

"The scent of these arm-pits is aroma finer than prayer,
This head is more than churches or bibles or creeds."

Walt Whitman • *Leaves of Grass*

There is a gentle whirring of the disc reader, a slight pause and
then the disc icon appears and just as quickly departs through
virus protection before reappearing; sterilized. Flanagan double-
clicks on the icon, his joule of a finger defibrillating its inertia, he
thinks, half-smiling, remembering his own stiffness on the
treadmill of the clinic the previous day. The icon brings him, and
her in a way, back into orbit in what soon will be, he realises, *his*
emergency room. There is a further short delay and then the
contents box opens, pulses, and the screen changes to display a
box within a box. Like looking at his heart trace, he realises. A
sinus rhythm, the specialist had reassured, normality in the
signals. And then the patient waiting, his patient waiting for the
word: sorry.

There is one folder within the box: *The Armpit Diary*. He
looks at the name and twitches his nose. A personal diary, like
being itself, he had long ago agreed with Eco, is a multi-laned
highway in which you may travel in any direction but always

towards eventual dead-ends. "Amorphous stuff", the sign man from Bologna had written of the *continuum of the content*, an everything and a nothing, eluding determination. Thinking of determination, Flanagan wonders whether diaries warrant names, like cats or dogs, or imaginary friends. What if it were his, what would he do?

The question distracts him from proceeding to open the diary and he stares at the screen. He sees that the *Chapman* file from yesterday is still saved to the desktop and wonders why? But he knows! With all that has happened, and is about to happen, he has experienced – has exhibited – a terrible urgency to tidy up his affairs and going through the old computer files, one by one, was part of the process. *Chapman* was one of yesterday's tasks and should have been read and deleted. He must have missed it, or got tired. Flanagan doesn't want to fall behind in his schedule and is annoyed with himself: a patterned failing. He double-clicks and waits.

It is an old file, from about three years previously, containing reference material he had gathered to help track down a manuscript sent by Ralph Waldo Emerson in the mid-1800s to an English publisher called John Chapman. The commission, he remembers, had come his way from Justine, the wife of an extremely rich Turkish businessman; a collector of Americana – a collection which included Justine, the Kentucky-bred, Yale-educated, arm-decorating lawyer-wife. Not being his field of expertise, Flanagan had little enthusiasm for the commission, but needed the money and promised to help. Justine had pestered, and pestered him, as if finding that particular manuscript was the only thing in the world that would make her husband happy or satisfy him.

God she was beautiful, Flanagan remembers, with the perfect body, hair and smile of a collectable. 'What a sad smile you have!' he had observed, at their very first meeting. And a short time later, asked of her, 'How does a collectable move beyond the avarice of the collector?'

'Are you any different,' she asked. 'Is not the freedom you offer not a greater cupidity? A greater deception even?'

A fragile, beautiful woman frozen in a vacuum of emotion,

Justine had transferred her fixation; offered herself in a moment of romantic fantasy and then had lain there, eyes shut, crying from the necessity of it.

Flanagan takes a deep breath. He had started, he noted looking at the first page of the file, as he always did, with an explanation of a word and coincidences, trying to give himself a focus, a purpose. *Chapman: the old English for a barterer.* The name, he decides, is as good as any for a diary: an exchange between the inner and outer self.

He moves his finger over the mouse-pad again, closes the *Chapman* file and places it in the trash. He then returns to the Armpit file, opens it, waits and then click-adjusts the zoom, to 150 per cent enlargement; easier on the eye, he thinks, if not on the soul. A date and time appears in a muted header at the top of the page but she has still typed the date and its title, in big block capitals. He scrolls quickly down. Only a dozen or so entries, all in January, most long. Not ever having kept a diary, beyond his brief notes concerning appointments, at first glance it's not what Flanagan imagined. He had, for some reason, presumed one-line locations, perhaps two-line gossip or three-line observations, and some occasional underlined insights; all random, discontinuous, freely associated; all possibly dangerous; *all possibly full of shite.* But not this, he realises. "There are things that cannot be done (or said)" he remembers Eco wrote in *Kant and the Platypus*.

'Or undone,' he says aloud.

What had Rio planned for this, he wonders and then wonders again as to why she had stopped so soon? Should he intrude? Did he have a right to intrude? Did Mac have the right to force that intrusion? His eye catches the horsehair tassels just visible through a gap in the parcel wrapping. He resists the urge to start at the last entry, and returns to the beginning:

Armpit Diary,
January 3:
First thoughts for the New Year: my birthday coming up and a promise to keep a diary, and to keep to the diet I've started.

Why? The diet, I think, is a marginal need, a few pounds here and there, all on my butt, but necessary for a sense of well-being; my sense of well-being. And the diary? A formula for thinking about something else, anything else, except eating!

We had decided, amongst the staff in the museum, that for Christmas we would all give each other a book as a present, a book that each of us thought would be appropriate for this time in the other person's life. Phyllis Andrew gave me Erin Pizzy's *Food for Sluts* in which food, the microwave, and even the fridge become the focus of Pizzy's "seething rage", her isolation, her attempts to understand, her love and loathing of food . . . perhaps even her love and loathing of life. A definite resonance in that for me! Going through a crisis? Write a cookbook! Want to provoke a crisis? Try following the instructions!

Mac gave me Walt Whitman's, *Leaves of Grass*. American be-longing he called it.

Never thought about food much before, at least not in the erotic sense, but recently the new diet has precipitated a weirdly enhanced sense of smell. It doesn't dominate – what does in my life? – but does impact intensely every now and then and is always, nearly always, linked to a sense of *déjà vu*. Last night, for instance, I dreamt about eating food cooked by the body's own heat, food marinated in the juices of passion, eaten there and then, after love. Real food that would soak up the juices like croutons or freshly baked soda bread; that would taste of the senses, every last morsel savoured from the table of someone's chest or the small of their back. A sexual sushi counter complimented by aperitifs from the hollows of a lover's ear, by champagne bubbling from his mouth and nostrils, by wine from a cupped upturned palm, or by cognac from a puckered navel. In the dream I could smell each sensation, each vapour, each fleeting image. I'm not sure whether this was a memory or a fantasy; as time goes by they increasingly resemble one another.

Why? I wonder. I'm as fussy about the scent of cleanliness as the next person and stale sweat is the most potent antidote I know. But in those moments, those very immediate and selfish post-coital moments when all other senses are satisfied, it is my nose that cries out for more and it is in the aroma of a man's armpit and its testosterone haze of salinity and satisfaction that it is sated. I like to bury my head like a rutting animal and inhale deeply, like cocaine almost, bringing me to a high, sometimes to orgasm again, a private intense orgasm, which is not for sharing.

God, I'm hungry again. My need to fill in time between mouthfuls of food is the real reason for beginning the Armpit Diary. And between lusts too perhaps! Walt Whitman is responsible: *The scent of these arm-pits is aroma finer than prayer . . .*

Last time I tried writing a diary was 17 years ago, during those long months spent hiding out with Jack in Eleuthera; chasing by day the bonefish of Cat; chasing at night rum after rum; breathing in its sweet jasmine air and looking south over the blue, blue Caribbean, wondering what if. I wanted to be Rosita Forbes, near whose house at Unicorn Cay Jack has his: to be free in the forest of forgetfulness, roaming wild on forbidden roads to Samarkand and beyond. The diary didn't survive the energy required for dreaming.

Forget that crap! No second-guessing, Rio. Using a computer to write one is different though. A leap of faith almost, the words not being an indelible truth: too easy to revise, to spell-check . . . to soul-check. At least not until that truth is burnt! Mission statement: Stay true to yourself Rio and stay on the diet!

Went out with Mac and some of the others from the museum on New Year's Eve. Too much to drink; me and a thousand others, and we danced the night away suffused by the very particular mixed aroma of hormones and vomit. I behaved myself . . . just. Never got to bed. Talked into doing a charity swim in the sea, without a wet suit. Bloody cold and I still haven't recovered. Laid low but, alas, not laid. Séamus was away until yesterday skiing with his family, his wife, she who shall remain nameless, being there as well. Telephoned once or twice to wish me Happy New Year from the top of some mountain or other. Said he misses me, needs me. Wants to do things to me. Wants me forever and ever. Promises more time together in the coming year. I'll believe that when it happens. Going up to our secret place tomorrow to meet him.

Thinking about his aroma all the time, now. . .

Flanagan looks up, wondering whether he should continue.

'Shit,' he says aloud, cursing Mac for forcing this intrusion, this judgement. He remembers arguing with him about the nature of judgement, and what Eco wrote about the platypus and the fact that when it was first discovered, Kant was already going senile, and that, by the time it was decided that the platypus was an egg-laying mammal, Kant had been dead for 80 years and that if Kant had been able to venture his opinion, Eco argued that his opinion would have been shaped by reflective judgement, and that because the platypus had *bildende Kraft*, a capacity to begin, it had a capacity to be. It had its own place in the scheme of things.

Just like the diary!

Alanna liked the smell of his armpits after making love as well, he suddenly remembers. "The last real smell of a modern man" she called it. And "The last anything of modern man, who has all but lost his wild grace" she had then emphasised for his benefit.

The taunting of her remembered words haunt him.

He suddenly thinks of John Chapman again, the physician and publisher-owner of *The Westminster Review* in the 1800s. The same John Chapman who was a serial collector of mistresses not to mention his association and possible affair with George Eliot – Marian Cross nee Evans – his editorial partner. He moves the pointer, recovers the file from the trash, and opens the *Chapman* file once more to search amongst the assorted articles he has saved. In scrolling down he sees his coincidence notes about other men called by the same name and thinks even more of its use for a diary.

Perhaps because of his audience of one, his *iBook* and its being – Douglas R. Hofstadter's notion of *i-machination* – that he was reminded of John Chapman a.k.a. Johnny Appleseed, the nursery man of lore exchanging seedlings for hospitality and a chance to preach. That took i-magination, he thinks. Or perhaps it is because of another John Chapman, author of *Memories and Milestones*, thumping with single-handed indignation – having burnt one hand so badly, in despair at striking an admirer of his future wife, it necessitated amputation – in 1912 on the anniversary of a Negro lynching in Coatesville, Pennsylvania to an audience of two.

'Diaries are also indignant,' he whispers.

This particular concept bothers him. He wonders how much indignation is ever needed to do what must be done. Flanagan suddenly gets up from the table, crosses the room to the CD rack and searches. Finding what he his looking for he places it in the player. The song is haunting and he now thinks of that other Chapman: Mark, the killer of John Lennon and of *Double Fantasy*, the album Chapman had Lennon sign for him earlier in the day, before returning in the evening to wait with a gun in his hand and a copy of J D Salinger's *The Catcher in the Rye* in his pocket. Flanagan wonders about the multiplication of fantasy and sings along with his own emphasis to the song, '*I-magine all the people . . .*'

Returning to the computer he looks again at the two underlined passages, and smiles. Neither would, of course, help him track down the manuscript but this was his way. He also was a collector and the passages were a brief reward. Like many more, forgotten but recorded somewhere, they are part of what he is; purloined moments of insight and reflection; siphoned indulgences to his own being. He scrolls down to another entry: John Chapman, the publisher, had also kept a diary and in it had described some of his feelings for Eliot. Two lines of that diary had caught his attention and he had recorded them:

I dwelt also on the incomprehensible mystery and witchery of beauty. My words jarred upon her and put an end to her enjoyment.

Rio had reacted in that way, Flanagan thinks.

His eyes drift upwards to where her diary waits, its title and content muted on the screen's background, and then back again to his, own words. Coincidence holds little mystery, or mystique, for him anymore. He is an illusionist who has suddenly lost that magic, that sense of amazement and become disillusioned. He sees where he had flagged the same Westminster Review's savaging under Chapman's editorship – in a display of hypocritical prudery – of the poetry of Walt Whitman's *Leaves of Grass* in 1860: *a naked savage has often a wild grace of movement that a civilised man can hardly possess, but certainly not display.*

Alanna had wanted a wild grace, he remembers. Flanagan puts his hand to his throat, feels along its length, wondering why there is no pain, just difficulty. In contrast to Rio and Alanna, in his dreaming, in his breathing, he is afraid of food and movement. But not for very much longer, he reminds himself.

2

BILDENDE KRAFT

"When the song of one's self is coming all
of a piece, page after page, an attic room and
chamber pot do not insult the soul."

Lewis Hyde • *The Gift*

Flanagan lights a cigarette and returns to the screen. The notion of reflection bothers him for in his dream it had sucked him in. What if, the universe shakes when he shakes, not in a chaotic way, but as a result of the *bildende Kraft*, the formative force? He had long argued with Mac that everything is a reflection of everything else, that indeed the whole of time and space is double-helical, reflecting the DNA of the smallest living thing, the beginning and end of themselves, the beginning and the end of all nature; galaxies linked as the nucleic-acids are linked; curved time bending as the helix bends and that the expansion and separation of the universe is a reciprocation of the expansion and separation of the helix in the smallest thing; to divide, to create, to be a template, to renew, to breathe within ourselves: reciprocation. The universe is us, we are the universe, he had argued. When I breathe, it breathes. When I shake it shakes. When I die it dies.

'What a load of bollix,' Mac had said.

Flanagan begins to read again, wondering who is messing with his helix.

17

Armpit Diary,
January 6 – dawn:

It really sucks! Don't feel much like remembering but perhaps this will help. *I've started so I'll finish.* Also armed with a large bar of chocolate to help force-feed the misery.

All of the emotions and the might-have-beens of the night before, the unfinished night, followed me down the laneway from the house in the mountains, the secret place where Séamus and I had got together again. By the time I reached the exit I felt hedged in by the brooding silence of the May-waiting hawthorn. Letting the engine idle, I lowered the window and listened out into the darkness. Directly ahead, beyond a crumbling wall, the headlight beams disappeared into a black hole, the nothingness of a harvested swathe through a forest of grim pine.

Some birthday present!

Other than a freezing wind that rustled through the upper branches of the trees no other sounds could be heard. As I listened for traffic coming around the corner I had to smile, if only for a second. After our New Year's swim, when I told him, in general geographic terms, of my plans for the weekend, Mac had taken great pleasure in warning me to 'Watch out for kamikaze farmers in the mountains. Those risible sons of Wicklow screaming *Nora, Nora, Nora,* as they negotiate bends in methane-fuelled tractors they got from Santa Claus.' Satisfied that one of them was not about to ambush me I eased the jeep forward onto the narrow road that tracked around the edge of the mountain, instantly shattering the heavy quietness of the early hour with the rattling, rolling metallic groan of the laneway's cattle-grid.

A few minutes later however, shortly after beginning the steep descent, I began to second-guess myself, and wondered whether I should turn around and head back for the house; to confront Séamus, to say what I had not said; to exchange words like body fluids, loudly, passionately. *To break his balls!*

Being honest, the sex was rough, welcome and long overdue. And yet, it was not like before, like when, exhausted and satisfied, I would hum, purr like a cat almost, then turn over and have him scratch my back. After only ten days absence, there seemed little between us. Both of us taking what pleasure the sex brought, but giving pleasure if only to sustain our own. There was nothing in the frenzy to wish for it again and in the silence that followed I thought about food and he of God knows what. Séamus always has a twenty-minute or so period of withdrawal from me after we make love, like he wants to run away, pretend that what had just happened never happened: Séamus and many of the married men I have known and loved. It is then they are at their most vulnerable, most guilt laden. It is a good time for pissing them off.

Séamus, to be fair, had tried attending to my needs, had tried to harmonise our reasons for being there but this time I had an overwhelming sensation of him simply melting away. And he had used the C word. I don't know why but I hate the way he grunted it out, aggressively, like he was still negotiating a mountain . . . or a way out. I told him so and in the prolonged post-coital dysfunction that followed, to further annoy him, I asked whether he was going to leave his wife. I really did want to shatter his reality.

'I like things the way they are,' he replied in a smug fashion, satisfied with his performance – and by implication, I should be as well.

'Then I might ring her,' I said matter-of-factly, flicking his nipple with my finger, before continuing, 'She probably wonders why I haven't for so long.'

F will remain nameless for it is easier to sleep with, *to fuck*, the husband of an unacknowledged existence. Like the dodo or woolly mammoth there is a history there, a footprint on this earth, but to all intents and purposes she has been hunted out of my existence; declared extinct; nameless. I'm sure she knows that I exist, as most women instinctively know when their man is somewhere else in his mind. The difference being is that finding me, *naming me*, becomes all-important. Me, the something feral in the bush, the shadow, the scavenger, brought out into the open for a reckoning. What to do about the "man" becomes a secondary concern. The reaction might be immediate but, for most, the determination is delayed, calculated, chewed upon, rationalised. I know this, having been there before. F did not deserve all this grief. Who does? A conservator at the National Library generously invited me to a house party when I first arrived in Dublin so I could meet most of the other conservators in the city in a social setting. Séamus and F were there when I visited. He was a brooding handsome predatory presence whose sense of being completely resided in his crotch. I couldn't keep my eyes off him and when he rang me a week later, he knew I'd say yes.

F had always remained unspoken-of between us, the secret amongst secrets. Panic registered in his face. 'Don't you dare,' he shouted, slapping my finger away, and then trying to apologize.

I had no real intention of phoning her, but at that moment I wanted to hurt him. I have no call on Séamus, nor do I want his full time attention and would settle for what we had: the stolen moments, the afternoons of sex, the occasional night away. But the bastard now wanted space, now wanted his freedom from me whose only desire is freedom.

It's strange how you assume people will behave in a certain way. Tressa Hughes, my cleaning lady, told me how she once took a job working for a couple where the man was a paraplegic. 'A walking bastard', she'd called him – having assumed because he was paraplegic he would be pliant and grateful for her help – on account of his continual obnoxious behaviour.

Anyway back to my escape from the mountains. Shortly after leaving the laneway and heading down the hill I began to feel angry. I swerved, crazily, into the small lay-by, where star lovers and star-crossed lovers often came to gaze at the night sky, and each other, free from the dazzling lights and intrusive eyes of the city far below. I really needed – need – some of that magic. Pulling up beside the boundary wall, my eyes focused eastwards to where the faint line of the dawn horizon was being rapidly smudged by a gathering storm; the dark, low-slung, snow-laden clouds were being pushed landwards by the bitter-cold wind. Napoleon and Hitler were defeated by that same wind. *Stepped* on. Séamusgrad was a defeat for me.

I continued watching, engine and thoughts idling; fingers tapping against the knob of the gear stick, hovering, hesitating; eyes drifting to look back through the rear view mirror, back up the hill; feet pressing and depressing the brake pedal, until finally, with an almost involuntary shake of my shoulders, I accelerated away again, down the hill, towards the city.

'Screw him! Bastard doesn't know what he is missing out on,' I shouted.

Or does he?

By the time I reached the awakening suburban flatlands, the clouds had swept in from the sea and began to dump their load. It continued to snow heavily throughout the remainder of the journey to the centre of the city, but I paid it only passing attention until stopped at a traffic intersection controlled by redundant but functioning lights.

'Walk, don't walk. Go, don't go,' I said to the lights while waiting there, watching the sky.

Suddenly, and for no other reason than I needed to, as I always did in times of rejection – mine or others – I thought back to the exact moment in time, when as a fugitive child I first became aware of the mystical envelope of dawn snowfalls: a morning long ago, in Grandpa Dawson's lodge nestled high amongst the pines of Colorado, where even before I could see, hear, touch, smell or taste the new day, I could feel the sublimation and sense the muffling silence.

My lips stretched into a quivering smile as the memories flooded back. There had been many other snow-filled dawns after that first one, when my Norwegian grandmother would come to me and together we would watch the flaking sky. Nan Greta had intuitively understood their impact. 'Fear not, child,' she'd said in Eddic undertones, 'Dawn snowfalls are important in the balance of things because they hide the movements of the spirits of the winter nights.'

'What are spirits?' I asked.

'Lost souls riding the wind, whispering,' she replied.

That was on my sixth birthday and it was little better than

yesterday's, my thirty-sixth. 'Do you know who my father is?' I asked Nan Greta for the thousandth time, hoping to catch her out.

'I've told you, child. I never knew him and your Mom would never tell me his name.'

'Does Grandpa know?' I asked once – and only once.

'No!' she shouted out, as if in pain. 'And you are never, never to ask him. It upsets him too much.'

I'd cried and cried. She came and held me.

'He was a musician from the islands. Jamaica I think, that's all I know. That's what upsets your Grandfather. He was another islander. He was long gone before you were born,' she answered yet again, with artic dismissal.

The bastard! Making one of me. I fantasise what my reaction will be if I ever meet him. What do you say to a child whose skin contrasted so much with the white, white snow of the mountains, that she could never hide? I want the bastard to know what pain he has caused . . . and what all of the other bastards have caused in his stead.

'When will Mom be coming home, Nan?' I asked, again and again.

'Soon child,' she answered, always apologetic for her missing daughter.

'When?' I insisted.

'When she's stopped running away,' she said sadly, listening for the spirits in the snow.

It was shortly after my sixth birthday that they found her, my manic-depressive mother, the fairy godmother of good intentions; the chain-smoking, chain-fucking, chain-promising sad girl – she was only 23, thirteen years younger than I am now – strung-out and strung-up in Wichita Falls, of all places. Grandpa went down from the mountains to identify her body. A mountain of strength, rock-like, he came back from Texas a crumbling man. With my first decent pay check I replaced her headstone and had inscribed on it *She has stopped running away.*

I haven't.

'I was never confused when you were there, Nan,' I said aloud to the changing lights, touching the small, gold, hammer-shaped pendant that she had given me on my eighteenth birthday. I had to bring my hand quickly back to the steering wheel in order to negotiate the sharp, right-hand turn at Jury's Christchurch Inn and avoid a bread van. Had to pull over to answer my cell-phone: a text message from Mac, about croissants.

Strange that, the American terminology, *cell-phone* and its message about being boxed in, entrapped, contained. I once read *Discipline and Punish* by Michel Foucault, the French social scientist and Professor of the History of Systems of Thought. He wrote of the technocratic notion – and the danger – of the human body, and by extension society in general, as an object to be controlled and manipulated by technology but that in order for this technology to work its supposed "transformation and improvement" on a docile population then the individual members of a society must be disciplined. This discipline, subjection, would only be effective if those individual members are organized and enclosed by a defined space, the *Grid*. Once established, the *Grid* would then ensure the distribution of individuals who are to be rewarded and those who are to be disciplined.

On television recently, I saw a class of kids being asked by their teacher to explain what a box is. The answers in the beginning were reasonably normal; *a packet, Miss; a square envelope, an empty brick, a place to hide in*, but then began to get more bizarre as the options were used up until one kid at the back, fidgeting in front of the cameras, put up his hand.

'Yes, Tommy. What do you think a box is?' the teacher asked.

'It's a place waiting for something to happen, Miss . . . really bored like.'

The Grid *is* boring. But there is an obvious solution, and it's already here, I reckon – a fulfilment of the promise of those priests of the Technocratic Age. Ensure that there are enough satellites and that everyone in the world has a cell-phone then they can be in the *Grid*, and have them pay for that *happening* believing it to be a worthwhile state of being – happiness.

In Ireland they are called *mobiles* but it is a freedom in name only, and way overpriced.

Another memory. But then, what are memories? What is their structure or purpose? No longer ideas but idealisations, a circuitry of chemical imprint, laid down one on top of another like vertebrae, integrated into function, until the height of being is reached, until the brain's capacity – a being's capacity for being – for layers, is exhausted. Short-circuited at random, or sometimes deliberated dredged, memories spark to live again in my dreams of living; past the blood-brain barrier, they seem to leak out as I get tired – or rejected – to affect my breathing, my heart . . . my soul.

Right now it seems all the memories of past birthdays are being dredged. My mother's death near my sixth, the Thor locket given to me on my eighteenth by Nan, shortly before she also died, and yesterday's *happiness* with Séamus – yet another death in the family. And then there was David . . .

. . . David Stein, the psychoanalyst I went to see at college because of my surfacing memories; who gave me *Discipline and Punish* for my twenty-first birthday, along with Foucault's three-volume *History of Sexuality*. He wanted to help me, he said. '*Déclenchement,*' he called it. 'Use sex to release you,' he advised. Allowing him to lead me, and then me him, he and I explored every possible avenue to establish our own history, to jerk the sexual-triggers, to explore the limits of the pain I could experience – had experienced. In the end I realised I liked my memories and fantasies to remain separate. I did not want them to become fused like the pursuit of pain and pleasure I shared with David, so similar they no longer served as reference points. In the end I stopped equating pleasure with that pain, and unwilling to submit to it any longer, found it pathetic that he was.

It did not end there, unfortunately. Seven months later a midwife in Quebec advised *la déclenchement italienne* to get my long-overdue labour going and the words immediately triggered an apathy, a state of non-being. Where is she now, that child of my being, I wonder, 15 or so and by now almost a woman.

And the memory escapes to trigger tears. Enough for one night.

Watching you, watching me, Flanagan thinks, remembering the dream that had woken him earlier. He downs a malt quickly and sits there until the silence in the room suddenly reverberates. Getting up he goes to the CD cabinet, searches for Van Morrison's album *Inarticulate Speech of the Heart*, places it in the player and waits for the music. Soon "Celtic Swing" is swirling around him with its conscience of memories and then "Rave on, John Donne" begins and Flanagan returns to the computer.

That child, that nameless child, should be told, he decides, but how? Is it his responsibility to interfere? He opens up a file containing instructions for his solicitor and adds another clause before closing and scrolling to the next of Rio's entries.

3

GOSSAMER WINGS

"What we believe is our love, our jealousy, is not one indivisible, continuous passion. They are made up of an infinity of succeeding loves, of different fleeting jealousies that, because of their unbroken numbers, give the impression of continuity, the illusion of unity."

Marcel Proust • *Un amour de Swann*

Armpit Diary,
January 6 – mid-morning:
By the time I turned into the cobbled access road that would take me past the State Solicitor's Office to Dublin Castle's Ship's Gate – misnamed, I'd been informed, by a long-ago error of transcription and distance from the river from the original Sheep Gate – the main storm had already passed overhead, waning to leave a steady drizzle of orphaned flakes fluttering down in its wake. Like crystal gossamer wings they shimmered briefly in the alkaline chrome glow of the street lamps before settling on the fresh white blanket that now covered the road surface.

Snowfalls in Dublin, I had been told the previous Friday in Mulligan's, while catching the weekend forecast on the bar's television, in an uninvited shower of particulate words by a counter-clinging, weather-beaten, weather-watching, weather-vane citizen-poet, are temporary in their impact and despite the promise, quickly coalesce into melting pools of brown-gritted

27

clumps. A bit like my relationships, I thought then, but excited all the same at the prospects – my hopes – for the coming weekend in the mountains.

No bloody forecast could predict those, I think now.

Distracted by Joe Cocker's "Unchain My Heart" on the jeep's CD player, I braked late to stop at the gate security post. From a distance, the barrier appeared to be up and, encouraged by this unusual lack of obstruction, I had maintained my speed. It was only as I reached the archway I suddenly realized that most of the barrier was, in fact, missing, and that in fact a small stump remained, horizontal and defiant.

Screeching to a halt, the jeep skewed slightly as the locking tyres fought for grip. There was a lone guard on duty, shivering in the doorway of the small wooden garden-shed that functions as the security post. He withdrew a little, trying to avoid being sprayed, waiting for the jeep to come to a standstill in front of the barrier. He's new, I thought, not recognizing him. He looked at me, as all guards and their ilk in Ireland have looked at me since coming here – a black, half-black anyway, woman, driving a large jeep. Had to be into drugs or prostitution, they'd assume. I've been pulled over by the police so often now I'm thinking of having a card made up: Rio Dawson. *White powder and black blowjobs a speciality!*

Whether I am half-black or half-white depends; the colour changes with my mood. Of mixed race, in apartheid terminology; mixed up in my own. My blackness or whiteness was never an issue when I was small and alone. I was a princess and I adored me. Today was a half-black day and I felt victimized; by Séamus and by this shithead of a guard with prejudice in his eyes.

He first looked closely at my parking permits for the University of Colorado displayed on the front windscreen and then, with a pursing of his lips, leaned backwards to mockingly admire – in the peculiar Dublin way – the left-hand drive imported model of the Defender. He started to walk around to my driver's side before he suddenly seemed to think better of it, reversed his steps and officiously tapped a long handled torch on the glass of the passenger side-door window. I wanted to stick the torch so far up his . . . I lowered the window and had to stretch across the distance between us.

'What happened to the barrier?' I asked, holding up my identity card.

He inspected it carefully, inspected me, the card again and then shook his head in patronizing bemusement. 'Some fecking black . . . foreign *eejit* coming out from a reception in the Castle last night took it home as a bleeding souvenir. Lodged in the windscreen of his brand new Merc, it was. Blind drunk, he was, but with bleeding diplomatic immunity from some African arsehole with a shit-notion of nationhood,' he growled, then nodded once at the card and waved me through.

'Loose observations like that could get you in trouble with your superiors,' I said crossly.

'Listen lady, you asked the question. Right now my *superiors*, as you generously refer to them, are warm above in the castle while I freeze my balls off down here. Would you like to drive on through please.'

It was a demand not a request. Closing the passenger-side window, I waited for him to lean back through the security-post doorway to press the button that raised the mechanical barrier and then watched as the stump rose with an almost embarrassed jerking snap-to-attention. I gently accelerated the jeep forward to follow in the fresh tracks of earlier arrivals. Behind me, I noticed in the rear view mirror, the blue-faced guard continued to stare, and waited until I had negotiated the narrow, pillared entrance into Ship's Gate Lane before retreating back inside the shelter of the shed.

I pulled into my designated place, in the staff parking lot that the museum shared with the Customs and Excise staff, and left the engine, and its warming heat, to run, listening intently to the last part of a news item on the radio. It was 7.40am and the temperature outside, according to the dashboard display, hovered just above freezing point.

Suddenly, there was a loud thud on the roof of the car, which caused the entire chassis to shudder. An agitated shadow hovered outside my driver's door window. I startled with the fright of the interruption and took a few moments to calm before partially lowering the window to see the ruddy face of Cormac McMurragh gloating in at me through the gap. Dressed in a down-lined parka jacket, with only a blue-red nose and a frosted moustache visible through the puckered hood, he looked, I thought, like a lost Antarctic explorer. A wind-whipped flurry of snow squeezed in past him to catch me full in the face and even less amused I had to fumble in the dashboard storage space for a paper handkerchief.

'Christ Mac! You spooked me! Don't do things like that!' I said angrily.

'Hah! Hah! Gottcha girl!'

'It's not funny. I'm still half asleep,' I hissed, wiping my face. Noticing that some of that morning's very hastily applied make-up appeared on the paper, I adjusted the rear view mirror to check on the damage done.

'I gathered that. You nearly drowned me in slush near the gate,' he said sarcastically.

'I'm sorry, Mac. I didn't see you.'

'Or the barrier, it seems! But sure, don't worry about it. Having an excuse to scare the bejasus out of you made it all worthwhile. Come on! Let's grab some coffee before it's brewed to tar. Did you bring the croissants?' The face in the puckered hood smiled.

'Yes. I'll be with you in a second. Let me fix my face,' I pleaded. I really was embarrassed that I might have soaked him when the jeep skidded near the security gate.

Poor Mac, my confidant, the 40-something black-haired Connemara man, battered by this city, and the need to earn a living as the head of the photographic and reproduction unit at the museum, is banned from driving and walks the four miles from his home to the Castle every day, regardless of the weather. He'd head back to the wilds in the morning if he could. Has a plot in the local cemetery already picked out, he's told me, right alongside his family and relatives. 'To annoy them in Hell,' he'd explained without smiling.

Shutting up the window again, I turned off the ignition, replaced the lipstick in my bag and pushed the car door open. Stepping out, I immediately shivered in the damp cold air that burrowed through my clothes.

'A bit of a nip in the day. Eh!' he said, half-turning to half-smile at me.

I returned a weaker smile before realizing I had forgotten my gloves, 'Blast it! God, I wish I were back in Colorado. 20 below and it's not half as cold as this!' My breath hung in the air.

'No humidity and even less humour in some of those parts! Sure you're better off here, Rio. Winter only lasts about a week.' Mac grinned before trundling off through the slush.

The redbrick-paved roadway that is Ship's Gate Lane, with its imitation standard gas lamps, falling snow and the twinkle of still present Christmas tree fairy lights just visible behind frosted windows, reminded me of a scene from Dickens, or at least TV's versions of Dickens. All that was missing were ragged-dressed urchins throwing snowballs at pot-bellied, top-hatted toffs, I thought, and was wary of Mac duly obliging. He didn't and somewhat disappointed I watched him walk on ahead, huddled and hugged against the sheltering edge of the building.

As we rounded the Clock Tower and made for the glass-panelled doorway of the entrance foyer I drew up alongside him. 'But, the damp lasts most of the year, Mac. I'm rotting away in my townhouse. Have builders in Ireland never heard of insulation?'

We reached the door and he stood back to pull the glass panel open, allowing me to go in ahead of him.

'That inner-city regeneration development, or townhouse that you so grandly call it, Rio, was once part of a Victorian tenement, housing probably three or four families. They will always be damp, both with atmospheric moisture and the tears of past misery.'

'Thanks for that, Mac! I'm enough of a sociopath in the

mornings without knowing that history is against me as well,' I said, giving him a small dig in the midriff.

'My pleasure.'

'Good morning, Joe,' I called out.

'Good morning, Dr Dawson, Mr McMurragh. A day for bleeding penguins out there!' Joe Reilly, a heavy-set figure, with a drooping moustache, uncurled and raised his bulk above the counter like a large walrus to welcome us.

'Yes,' we both agreed, shaking off the snow. We must look like penguins, I thought, unbuttoning my long cashmere coat.

'Did you watch the John Wayne movie last night, Dr Dawson?' Joe asked enthusiastically.

I sometimes regret giving him a selection of Zane Grey novels for Christmas. He is sure that I am one of *them* – a Western fanatic, Trekkies in rawhide and stirrups. 'No,' I replied truthfully, my own version of the Alamo the previous evening had been enough trouble. 'Was it good?'

'One of the best! *True Grit*.'

Joe, the night security guard, would be soon off-duty and heading home. I find him an unnecessary servile and melancholic soul but not, I think, in any obvious self-destructive way; in the self-destructive way I had seen in other men with such a melancholy; men like my grandfather – and Mac at times. Black bile, I thought, removing my coat. How apt for the bitterness that eats from within. Joe's repeated complaints of the fact that all cowboys called "Joe" were usually killed in the first five minutes of any Western movie had long since lost its quirky appeal.

I know all about the impact of names, I wanted to tell him there and then, and also how I had wanted to lose my own first name, Babette, as soon as I was able. My mother's name; a mother in name only; a mother who deserted me, who had left me in the mountains, and who died in a seedy hotel before I could confront her with my anger. Only Jack, my guardian angel, my mother's brother, the man who is the father I never had, still calls me Babs, and he is wandering around Miami, already moaning about his fifth and most recently acquired wife.

'Stay single, Babs. It's more mirage than marriage!' he'd said, yet again, during our last telephone conversation.

Mind you, at 36 years-of-age it is the only advice of his that I have ever followed, although (Dear Jack, I really mean this. You don't owe me anything. I have *always* made my own choices!) I am more than grateful for the trust fund he established for me in less fraught times, allowing me the freedom to pick and choose the places and conditions I live and work in; free from the money haemorrhaging fallouts of his nuptial and alcohol-fuelled implosions; free to run away whenever things closed in around me. Today it was from a cottage in the Wicklow Mountains, but equally it could have been Quebec or the memory of my mother, I guess.

'Come on Rio. The others are in the café.' Mac had shed his coat and boots and after retrieving and donning on a pair of loafers from his knapsack, deposited the wet items on the counter of the foyer cloakroom.

'They'll stink the place out Mr McMurragh.' Joe Reilly shook his head as he watched the puddles of melted snow get ever bigger on the marble floor.

'I don't think there will be many visitors today, Joe. The place will be quiet for a change.'

'Yeah. I suppose.' He shrugged as he searched for a mop and bucket amongst the shadows. Not a job for a frontier marshal.

'I think Joe would be happier if we never had people coming to the museum,' Mac whispered to me as we headed for the museum café.

At that point I looked up to see the director of the museum, Professor Aengus FitzHenry, staring down at us from the second-floor walkway that connected the exhibition area to the museum's offices. I gave a small wave. 'He's not the only one, I think,' I whispered back.

'What?' Mac asked in a distracted way, not noticing FitzHenry.

'Forget it. Let's have that coffee,' I said, as FitzHenry disappeared from view.

A blast of heat, generated by the steaming coils of the large cappuccino machine and warming bodies, met us at the door of the café. Phyllis Andrew, the Islamic and Middle Eastern Curator; James Somerville, the Far Eastern Curator and Joyce Holden, the Western Curator were already present, their hands wrapped tightly around large mugs. All looked up as we entered and smiled a welcome.

Joyce had been away for eight weeks – a hysterectomy. She looked up and admired my recently acquired tan.

'Where were you, Rio?'

'My bathroom,' I admitted, laughing. 'Good for attracting licking dogs if not men,' I whispered, pulling out a chair and resting my satchel on it. Joyce and Phyllis smiled.

'Nice shoes,' Joyce said, looking down at the ankle length, stiletto-pointed Christmas present to myself.

'Thanks,' I said. Probably cost the same as a hysterectomy, I thought.

'What do you think, Rio,' Phyllis asked.

'About what?'

'Joyce wants to apply for a disability sticker on account of her recent loss of body parts.'

'Best parking slots in the country' Joyce said.

'If you say so yourself,' Mac said.

'Don't forget to mention that when I called up to see you in the hospital, in your private "womb with a view", you were swilling champagne to a welcome loss!' I reminded her.

'Still. It should count as a disability, at least for parking purposes,' Joyce defended.

'Post menstrual depression,' Mac suddenly added and we all burst out laughing.

My colleagues are good people, and great to work with.

All of this went way over James Somerville's head, of course, so I slowly, teasingly, drew out the bag of croissants and passing it under his nose placed it in the centre of the table while Mac headed for the counter.

'Two mugs of black coffee please, Mags,' he roared, good-naturedly, rubbing his hands together.

'Janey, Mac. Yous were fierce lucky to get those.' Mags the café manager spoke in her thick Liberties accent as she nodded towards the table where the croissants were being greedily grabbed. 'Our own supplier rang to say that they might not be able to deliver today. Lazy sods! One fecking bit of snow and the whole shagging country grinds to a halt. Where did Dr Dawson get them?'

'Rio! Mags wants to know where you got those?' he roared again, unnecessarily, across the room.

'The small French bakery near Christ Church,' I replied.

I like Mags Golden; six children and already three put through university, nothing seems to be too much trouble. It was she who arranged for Tressa, her sister-in-law, to come and clean the townhouse that I rent and now, increasingly resent for its coldness. Mac's earlier comments hadn't helped, particularly as there are some nights when I swear I hear a child's crying coming from beneath the floorboards. There are still four months to run on the lease.

'They do some lovely pastries, Mags. You should consider getting them to supply the café.'

'I might. Better than the shower who couldn't get their arses moving this morning. Thanks, Rio. I'll talk to Ahmed about it.'

Ahmed al-Akrash, the good-humoured Syrian chef-proprietor of the café in the museum, already had his trays of stuffed vine leaves, dates and sweet baklava laid out for the day's customers.

Mac brought over the mugs and, after sitting down between Joyce and myself, began to load his own with sugar. We watched with cringing horror as scoop after scoop was added. He blithely ignored our disapproval as he snatched at the last croissant and began dunking it in the coffee.

'Almonds would have been nice. Shit!' He slurped his words, cursing as a small piece of the pastry broke off and flopped back in to float on the surface of the coffee.

'You're a pig, Mac!' Joyce Holden squirmed as she watched him retrieve it with a teaspoon. 'How did Marie ever put – God, I'm sorry, Cormac.'

35

'Don't fret, Joyce. In fact Marie and I are on better terms apart than when we were together for ten years. Things are looking up between us since I stopped drinking.' He smiled as his finger dived in for another piece of the drowning croissant.

'How long has that been, Mac,' Phyllis asked.

Mac never talked much about his life away from the museum and I noticed that the others were all suddenly and intrusively attentive.

'Two years, eight months, two days, seven hours and about five minutes, but who's counting. I still need this sugar rush in the morning otherwise my hands shake too much,' he answered good-humouredly.

'Your metabolism must be rightly compromised McMurragh,' a voice pronounced. James Somerville, although born and bred in West Cork, spoke with the clipped and what Mac had once described as the *anal defensive* acquired accent of a returned Oxbridge educated academic. 'I remember a former colleague of mine in Delhi named Ralph Phipps, a good man on Tamil manuscripts, who had a similar problem. His liver was –'

James's penchant for gloom-laden anecdotes irritates nearly everybody and I was delighted at the sudden cessation caused by Aengus FitzHenry's entrance through the door of the café.

'Who the hell knows anyone called Ralph Phipps?' Mac whispered.

'Good morning Aengus.' Phyllis Andrew was the first to greet FitzHenry.

'Folks,' he said, in a summonsing way.

'Jasus! I hate it when he uses that word. FitzHenry is definitely not a folksy person,' Mac whispered again, between mouthfuls of sodden croissant.

I smiled conspiratorially.

'What were you saying, Mr McMurragh?'

'Oh! Just that it was a pity there were no croissants left for you Prof. It was merely a guilt response on my part. I occasionally still have them,' Mac spluttered.

'I've already breakfasted thank you. Anyway I wanted to

remind you all about the meeting on Thursday. 8.15 sharp. There is a lot to cover and Brigadier Crawford has to be away by 10.00. Be there on time, please,' he demanded.

Like guilty school children called to the headmaster's office for possible punishment we all watched FitzHenry turn on his heel and head for the stairs. The lazy breakfast mood was broken. I listened as Mac, a good mimic, repeated FitzHenry's command. Joyce joined in giggling out loud as we stood up and began to clear the table.

'Leave it lads! I'll do that.'

'Thanks, Mags,' Mac said for all of us.

'Blast it!' Phyllis was jerking at the control lever of her wheelchair. 'I think the battery is flat.'

'Let me –' Mac was moving to help when he was suddenly interrupted.

'*Its ok, Mr McMurragh*. Let me do it.' Joe Reilly had come into the café and pulling back on Mac's sleeve barged his way past to take control of the situation. 'I'll give you a push, Miss Andrew. The damp must be shorting it. Your spare battery is hooked up to the charger in my office and I'll arrange for one of the day staff to change it later.'

'Thanks, Joe. You're so sweet.'

I noticed how Phyllis gently touched Joe's hand as she smiled back up at him. Mac had also seen and he winked at me as we left the café.

'What's going on there?' I whispered to him as we reached the bottom rung of the first flight of steps.

'Heh! Listen! They're both consenting adults, whatever that means, but give me a few hours and I'll have the dirt.'

I laughed at his roguish grin. 'I bet you will too.'

'Do you mind if I dash ahead, girl? '

'Sure! You go on, Mac.' I watched as he pounded up the stairs, suddenly noticing that he was wearing odd socks and wondering for a moment how he was really doing on his own.

By the time I reached the first crosswalk I could see that Joe Reilly was manoeuvring Phyllis towards the ground-floor lift. He had managed to position himself so that James Somerville was excluded and forced to take the stairs. James was still annoyed as he joined me on the crosswalk.

'That man, Reilly is impossible. I plan to have a word about him to Aengus. Don't you agree, Dawson?'

'I wish you'd use my first name, James.'

'It's an old habit m'dear. No offence meant.'

'None taken . . . but do try.'

'What do you think of Reilly?' James Somerville was not to be distracted as he stiffly climbed the second flight of stairs beside me. Reaching the top we watched the lift opening onto the landing and then the smiling Joe Reilly push Phyllis in her wheelchair towards her office. Hey ho, Silver! I thought, before turning to James.

'Joe's wife died from multiple sclerosis a number of years ago. I think he feels very protective towards Phyllis,' I answered, trying to keep my voice low.

'Must say, didn't know that. Nevertheless, the man should know his station. Don't you agree Dawson?' James Somerville was not about to make any such effort.

'Listen to yourself James! The Raj has gone, join the present world.'

'There is no excuse for not maintaining standards, Dawson. After you, m'girl.'

I glared at him as he stood back to allow me pass.

For the remainder of the morning and afternoon I was busy with unpacking and cataloguing a crate delivered over from the Beatty collection at the Military Museum in the Curragh. Then home, supper and this. I'm exhausted.

Still thinking of food and sex. Last week I told Phyllis about my erotic food dreams on the new diet. She laughed and quickly followed up her Christmas present of Pizzy's *Food for Sluts* with a birthday gift of Radhika Jha's book *Smell*. The book is open beside me and a line catches my eye: *The smell of the paste made me feel hungry and satisfied at the same time.*

I feel the same about armpits.

One more call. Jack is still not home. I'll try again tomorrow.

4

NEMESIS

"I've been accused of having a death wish but I think it's life that
I wish for, terribly, shamelessly, on any terms whatsoever."

Tennessee Williams • *Sweet Bird of Youth*

Lighting another cigarette Flanagan thinks of Joe Reilly's wife with
multiple sclerosis, and of Phyllis Andrew in her wheelchair, and of
Tressa Hughes' paraplegic 'walking bastard', and of himself. He
knows he would not be a good invalid, and dreads not being able
to control his own destiny – to communicate that destiny. He
recalls a television reviewer once referring to the omission of the
obvious in dialogue as the 'dead hand' that hovers unseen over all
good screenwriting. Would there be anyone left who would hold
his dead hand, who would instinctively understand his obvious
wishes, and who would deal a real hand to those wishes? Exhaling
Flanagan scrolls to the next entry:

Armpit Diary,
January 9:
Things change. Thank God for work. *Love's labours lost in
labour's love.* What a day, what a great couple of days. The
meeting this morning was something else!

Mac and I met first thing, as usual, for coffee. Ahmed al-Akrash was there and in great humour. He wants us to come to a party in his house next month, a celebration of his first year in business at the museum. I've never been to his house before. In fact Ahmed says little to me, or to any of the other women working in the museum. Mac says the house is austere, hermitic almost. No family. I said I'd think about it. Makes bloody good baklava though and I wonder what the food in his house would be like.

At precisely 8.16, with adolescent, smirking precision, we marched into the museum's boardroom. Well I almost skipped, trying to contain my excitement. The polished oval table glistened warm beneath the dark, wood-panelled ceiling of the room as I took a seat next to Mac. Near the doorway, at the far end of the table, sitting in the place normally occupied by FitzHenry, was a thin man of about 70 with hollow cheeks, a short-cropped military haircut and sad, sunken eyes, which were nearly obscured by large, unkempt eyebrows. The same eyes were watching my every move and this made me a little uncomfortable, as I had never been formally introduced to Brigadier Crawford. Since arriving in Dublin I have seen him once or twice, always on the periphery, ghost-like, at museum functions. He is the remnant survivor of a once powerful brewing and publishing dynasty, and as the Chairman of the Trustees of the Museum is entitled to sit in on the monthly meeting of the heads of department.

Mac, in his inimitable way, informed me, very shortly after arriving, that I was now working in only remaining institution of medieval Dublin, as the Chester Beatty Library, despite a modernization of its constitution in 1997, was not owned by the people of Ireland but belonged, in law, to the Trustees. As I watched our *leader*, in a country check jacket a size too small for him, take an unfamiliar seat to the left of Crawford, his deferential body language gave every acknowledgment of this fact. The buttoned jacket was squeezing out a thin smile, like toothpaste.

'Brigadier. I think you know everybody here except perhaps the young lady next to Mr McMurragh at the far end of the table.'

'Young! I like that,' I whispered to Mac. 'Perhaps I was wrong about Aengus.'

Mac was somewhat distracted tinkering with his computer and didn't catch what I said. He leaned towards me to speak. 'What did you –' but then stopped his question short as FitzHenry glared at him.

'Brigadier Crawford!' Aengus barked. 'Let me introduce you to Dr Rio Dawson, our paper conservator, on secondment from the University of Colorado.'

'Hello, m'dear. I've heard good reports about you and the work that you're doing. Welcome to *the Library*.'

Like in my conversations with FitzHenry, Brigadier Crawford did not intend referring to the Chester Beatty Library Museum as a mere museum. It was *the Library*, no more, no less. His tone was patronisingly cold and disinterested, yet the old dude was smiling warmly.

'Thank you, Brigadier Crawford. I'm enjoying the experience.'

'Can't say the same for the rest of us,' Mac grunted under his breath. Joyce, who was sitting to his left, began to giggle.

I suddenly felt as if I was back in grade school with Brent Anderson putting spiders in my pencil case. Brent Andersen, the designated taker of my virginity – most of it – in the back of his father's pickup. I haven't thought about him for ages. Used to bully me in high school as well until, one day, I stood up to him and asked, 'Do you pick on me because I'm black?' Without batting an eyelid he'd replied 'Jesus H Christ no. I do it because yar a pain in the ass.' That decided it for me. He was to be the chosen one, the cherry picker. He later became the designated big-hitter for a minor-league baseball team until killed by a pickup crossing a road in Salem. Thinking of those fumbling moments so long ago I blushed, but was relieved to see that FitzHenry had not noticed. He was too busy sorting his papers into a neat pile and he began to speak without looking up.

'In fact, Brigadier, Dr Dawson's work is an additional and *late* item,' he growled, before continuing, 'to the agenda for this morning but *I* felt it important enough to include. Perhaps you could get us started Dr Dawson.' FitzHenry, finally satisfied with the order he had imposed smiled down at me over the rim of his reading glasses.

'Certainly. Cormac would you mind?' I took the opportunity to give Mac, and the memory of Brent Anderson, a kick under the table.

'*Ouch!* Of course not!' Mac stood up and walked with feigned limp towards a console panel mounted into the wall.

'Are you all right Mister McMurragh? You're limping.' I suppressed a smirk as FitzHenry enquired.

'No it's nothing, Prof. Old war injury.'

'What war is he talking about, Director?' I had to look towards the roof as Crawford asked earnestly of FitzHenry.

'I was speaking metaphorically, Brigadier. The abuses of time and early morning stiffness.' Mac tried explaining as he glared back at me. For a man who is so often at the centre of so much banter, he hates direct attention and instantly knew he was digging an even bigger hole for himself.

'Oh! I see,' Crawford said in a disappointed tone.

'Abuse is the right word,' James Somerville mumbled.

'Shut up, James,' Joyce hissed at him.

'Might we carry on?' FitzHenry was losing patience. I couldn't stop my head from nodding vigorously, yet again amazed at how, since arriving in Ireland, such surreal episodes seem to bubble up and then just as quickly evaporate.

Mac dimmed the room lights and the roof-mounted projector flickered into action. He stood there for a moment until satisfied with the focus before returning to the table and his computer to double click on one of the file icons displayed on the screen menu. There was a slight pause, as the programme loaded, before a picture of the Museum's copy of Durer's *The Knight, Death, and the Demon* scrolled into view. I decided to remain seated while speaking.

'*The Knight, Death and the Demon*, sometimes referred to as *Nemesis*, is one of several Durer prints bought by Chester Beatty. It is representative of his genius years as an engravist and the museum is very fortunate to have a number of high quality Durer engravings, from the "Apocalypse" and "Passion" series all of which were thought to have been catalogued, remounted and reframed in recent years.'

'What do you mean *thought*, Dr Dawson?'

'As you are well aware Brigadier Crawford, the Chester Beatty Library collection is very extensive and the greater proportion of it still remains in storage. Part of my remit is to carry out a condition survey of those items in storage to ensure that no damage is occurring and that the storage conditions are appropriate.'

'I'm sure the Brigadier is intimate with the responsibilities of your position, Dr Dawson. Please get to the point.' FitzHenry didn't make eye contact as he said this but leant sideways to whisper something in Crawford's ear. The old man smiled down at me.

'For the last two days I have been unpacking a crate that has not yet been catalogued, due to untimely death of the previous Director, and yesterday morning at the very bottom of the crate came across an old Silander storage box which former director, Professor Symmonds had just begun working on. As you know we have stopped using this type of container for storage but this particular box had apparently been included amongst the militaria bequeathed by Chester Beatty to the Military College Museum in the Curragh . . . I hope I pronounced that right.' I was relieved to see that Joyce nodded. 'After Prof Symmonds' death it was returned to the Curragh and has only recently been brought back here for us to complete the cataloguing.'

'Thank you for the itinerary! Please move on, Dr Dawson,' FitzHenry growled.

Mac giggled and I flared.

'Please go on, Dr Dawson,' Crawford said quietly.

'The Silander box contained four eighteenth century copies of

Mamluk books on military training and weaponry, which are of moderate rarity and value. The box itself was in very poor condition and disintegrating and I was about to send it for disposal when, by chance really, I noticed that there was a small square of ground-wood mounting-board stuck flush against one of the broken sides of the box. The board came away easily and on turning it over I got a very pleasant surprise.' I tried to keep a note of triumph from my voice while waiting for the slide change.

'It's another Durer, is it not?' Crawford asked as he looked at the screen.

'Possibly, Brigadier. We cannot be entirely certain. In the small shield on the bottom left you can see a date but although there is space for it, Durer's monogram is missing. It's a metallic engraving dated 1518, is on paper with the "Pitcher" watermark and is typical of Durer's style. I suspect it's probably a first proof of a new engraving and that the signature would only finally have been engraved when Durer was satisfied with the result.'

'What's it about?' Crawford was leaning forward to get a better look as he spoke. 'I don't recognise it.'

'That is not surprising, Brigadier as . . . and this is the exciting part, there is no other known Durer in existence with this composition. However, Joyce is more of an expert than me on Durer so perhaps she will be able to clarify the situation for you . . . us more.'

'Go ahead, Dr Holden.' FitzHenry re-imposed his control of the agenda.

'As Rio has pointed out, I do think it is a first proof and that alone will make it very unique. For some reason the engraved metal plate must have been lost or destroyed shortly after this imprint was taken. The subject is the Holy Spirit depicted as an advocate between mankind and God. The next slide will help explain it a bit more.' Joyce waited until the slide of an enlarged area of the engraving appeared. It showed an open book in the central figure's hand with the Greek letters "Παρακλητοσ" spread across the pages.

'Is that a word, Dr Holden?' Crawford asked.

'Yes. They –'

'The Greek letters spell out *Paraklitos*, Brigadier,' another voice interrupted loudly. 'The *Paraclete* is an appellation for the Holy Spirit, which occurs only in the Gospel of St John. It means an advocate, intercessor or occasionally a comforter.'

James Somerville had jumped in with the information, anxious to demonstrate his classical training. Joyce's face flushed; a roosting hen disturbed and I immediately glared at him, an opportunist fox. I had told all of the senior museum staff of the discovery, and by now they would have worked this out for themselves. I decided not to let him away with his rudeness.

'I'm sorry that Dr Holden was *not* able to finish what she was saying but I know she is preparing a thorough report which will be circulated in the next day or so.' I slowly took my eyes off James Somerville and half-turned to look at the projected image on the wall. 'Unfortunately the engraving is in poor condition. Despite having been in the dark the acid from the ground-wood board has leaked through to stain the paper and there are also some mould spots.'

'Is it repairable?' FitzHenry asked.

'Yes, Director. However, there is one other item of interest, if you can bear with me. This is something that only came to light late last evening and I haven't had the chance to tell you about it before now.' I watched for FitzHenry's reaction knowing that he was not a man to have information dispersed before he'd had a chance to censor it.

He hesitated for a moment but then, after a quick look at his watch, relented. 'Be brief, Dr Dawson. Please!'

'Sure. We have on loan at present, with the hope of purchase, I might add . . .' I looked at Crawford with pleading eyes. '. . . a newly developed forensic diagnostic camera from Art Innovation in Holland. This camera is able to photograph through the full range of infrared, ultraviolet and visible wavelengths. It was Mac . . . Mister McMurragh who spotted something in the UV images which might be a problem.'

'What problem, Dr Dawson?' Brigadier Crawford had put on glasses and was staring intently at the projection screen.

'It will become a little more obvious with the next slide Brigadier. Thanks Cormac.' At that point I pushed back my chair and standing up, walked slowly – sashayed – towards the screen as the image changed. The Halle Berry of conservation, I briefly imagined, thrusting my hips, loving the drama. Who ever said conservation was a frigid endeavour. At that moment all I felt was a *frisson*. (Thanks Andre!) An area of the original photograph had been isolated and enlarged. The slide showed the faint outline of writing. 'If you would concentrate –'

'I'm sorry, Dr Dawson. You're a big girl and in the way a bit. Could you move further to one side?' Brigadier Crawford asked in a matter-of-fact way.

Mac coughed loudly, his face contorted by a stunted laugh.

'Big, the old weasel called me big, the bastard,' I mumbled, blushing self-consciously before moving to the side.

I remember that Andre, the Frenchman, used to call me '*beeig*' as well but eventually found competing with my height in public annoying and I tired of his joking reference to our otherwise enjoyable lovemaking as climbing. He was my first, and only, experience of a French lover, and now I am not altogether sure that lover is an accurate description of what we had going. To my mind French women are high maintenance and French men aim to please. When you pout or push them away it spurs them on, no means maybe, disdain invites ardour. But it's just a game, a challenge. The more exotic and unobtainable I pretended to be the more he pursued. Andre was a gourmet and I was a truffle – and the pig got me in the end and tried to devour me . . .

I suddenly realised that the others were waiting for me to continue and moved as deep into the shadows of the wall as I could. 'Sure. Sorry. If. . . if you would concentrate on the area just behind where the Holy Spirit or *Paraclete's* left ear is, you will notice the reason for our concern.' The red laser dot was behaving like a firefly and I forced my hand to steady.

'It's writing . . . Arabic I think. Arabic writing, obscuring the lines of engraving?' Phyllis Andrew was first to speak.

'Exactly, Phyllis. I'm not sure whether the paper is just thin at this point or whether ink has leaked through to stain the paper.'

'Are you saying that there is Arabic writing on the back of the engraving, Dr Dawson?'

'I don't think so Brigadier, because its not reversed writing. I suspect that the writing is on the layer of paper that was used between the engraving and the mounting-board. I think the ink from this is staining through onto the engraving, and suspect it might be an organic iron containing ink, which has oxidized. As a consequence I think we will have to deal with the engraving and the backing-paper as a co-determinate procedure.'

'What do you propose to do about it?'

It was Crawford who continued to question me. I couldn't make out his face in the glare of the projection. 'Remove the engraving from the mounting-board and then carefully try and moisten away the intervening paper. The mounting-board may have to be taken down in layers.'

'Is there a danger in that?'

'Yes, but if we don't act now the oxidization could get worse. In addition, if the ink used is for example iron-gall ink, this becomes very acidic in time. We will have to coat it with barium sulphate to raise the pH and prevent any further damage.'

I was – am – sure on this point. The mould and staining should be easy to correct and future storage conditions will hopefully prevent any further deterioration. To emphasise that confidence, I moved back to the console, raised the room lights, turned off the projector and winked at Mac as I retook my seat. A drama-queen on her throne.

'I meant *any danger* to the intervening paper or co-determinate, as you so elegantly put it, Dr Dawson. What if this *co-determinate* is parchment?' The ex-army man asked – interrogated – in a slightly sarcastic tone.

I realised then that Crawford was very much aware of the hazards of separation procedures. It was a very astute question and I flushed with the embarrassment of knowing that I hadn't really considered that the intervening leaf might be parchment.

'I'm sorry, Brigadier,' I blustered, trying to avoid the drop. 'I did not mean to gloss over the potential of that particular possibility. If it is parchment then we will have to be very careful and would use controlled humidity only. Any contact with water and the parchment becomes irreversibly translucent and we could lose any hope of deciphering the little writing that's present.'

'Are you competent in forensic investigative techniques of paper and parchment analysis, Dr Dawson . . . or should we contact the British Museum?' Crawford persisted.

The old bastard, he wasn't letting go. But I deserved it and searched for a reply. 'Yes, Brigadier. *I am!* I have trained both at the FBI in Quantico, and also in Japan. I'm an accredited forensic expert in paper conservation.'

'That's very good.' Crawford's features remained passive.

'Where might this Durer have come from?' FitzHenry, trying to lighten the adversarial mood, turned to James Somerville who was also the Museum's archivist.

'Most of the Durer's in the Museum were purchased in New York but I am not able to find any correspondence with regard to this one.'

'Is that unusual or just incompetence?' Crawford barked.

'He's going after everybody,' I whispered to Mac.

'Pre-senile tension,' Mac whispered back.

James Somerville bristled. '*No.* Of course not. Many dealers sent items on approval to Chester Beatty. There is sometimes no information of what he accepted or what he sent back.'

Mac and Joyce winked at each other, delighted by James' defensive indignation.

'I see,' Crawford said quietly.

'What should we do so?' FitzHenry eyes were still fixed on the blank projection screen.

'I think, Rio . . . Dr Dawson should go ahead and remove the mounting board while documenting everything carefully. By all means get an expert opinion on the writing but it would be a disaster if there is any further deterioration.' Joyce Holden was adamant in her assessment.

Aengus FitzHenry looked around the table for objections and

when there was none nodded towards me. 'Very well then, Dr Dawson, you may proceed. By the way, thank you for your diligence Mister McMurragh.'

'Pleasure Prof,' Mac purred.

'How much is it? The camera?' Joyce Holden asked loudly.

Good girl I thought.

'About €32,000.' Mac tried to hurry the words.

'That's very expensive.' Crawford shook his head.

'But worth it!' I almost shouted.

'Perhaps, but let's move on to the original items on the agenda. We'll discuss the camera another time,' FitzHenry said as he, almost reluctantly, pulled a single piece of paper from his neatly stacked pile and handed it to Crawford. 'I've had an e-mail from Jerome Flanagan in Istanbul. He writes that he has come across an unusual fragment of a thirteenth century Ptolemy's Geography and is offering it to the Museum.'

'What's unusual about it?' Crawford sneered as he plucked the sheet from FitzHenry's hand. The old man was handling the paper as though it were contagious.

'It . . . it has books three to twelve included,' FitzHenry said with the voice of an earnest schoolboy seeking parental approval. 'With the Agathodaimon endorsement but, of more importance, it also has very detailed marginal notes in Maghrebi script.'

'We *must* get it, Aengus!' Phyllis Andrew spoke for the first time in the meeting.

'I think so too. I'll contact him and ask that he brings it here.'

'*You will do no such thing, FitzHenry!*' Crawford slammed down his fist with surprising force. Everybody startled as they felt the table jump. 'The Trustees of *the Library* will have nothing to do with Jerome Flanagan.'

'But, Brigadier,' FitzHenry pleaded.

'*Nothing*, I tell you! Good day to you all,' Crawford rasped as he suddenly stood up and then briskly left the room.

After a moment of stunned indecision Aengus FitzHenry got up and followed after him. The others remained at the table, saying nothing, fully expecting FitzHenry to return. When this didn't happen James Somerville eventually went to the window that overlooked the Dubh Linn garden. The snow had stopped falling and he reported that he could see the gesticulating figures of FitzHenry and the Brigadier standing near the ornamental pond, involved in a passionate debate. He turned back to face the rest of us. 'I think this particular meeting is over. We should go about our work.'

We all nodded sombrely. James offered to push Phyllis' wheelchair and Joyce followed them out from the room. I hesitated and sat looking at Mac until he got up to leave.

'What gives, Mac? Who is Jerome Flanagan?' I asked.

'Dr Jerome Augustine Flanagan used be the Islamic curator in the museum. A genius and brilliant Arabic scholar but . . .' Mac's voice dropped to a whisper.

'But what?'

'A bit unconventional for the staid precincts of the museum. There was a clash of egos with the Director and it ended in tears. You know how it is, the *hego* or *igo* ultimatum. The Prof won out.'

'With Aengus? I don't believe it.'

'No! With old, the now dead, Prof Symmonds, FitzHenry's predecessor. Your silander box man.'

'What happened to him?'

'Heart attack while driving. In Turkey of all places. Why do you ask?'

'No. Not Symmonds. I meant to Jerome Flanagan.'

'Oh!' Mac sounded relieved for some reason. 'He went freelance and has become the Indiana Jones of rare manuscripts.'

'Why the vitriol from Crawford.'

'The usual. Money and pride.'

'Explain.'

'About three years ago Jaffa –'

'Jaffa?' I asked.

'Jerome Flanagan's nickname! Jaffa sourced an important Persian book of miniatures and out of a misplaced sense of loyalty first offered it to the museum, at a reasonable price. With their usual procrastinating pace, the Trustees dithered over the cost, so he sold it to the Metropolitan instead, and for a far greater sum. Crawford was doing the negotiation on behalf of the Trustees and he was blamed for throwing away the opportunity. He has never forgiven Flanagan for it.'

'How long has he been gone from the museum?'

'About five years. We keep in touch though. I could arrange a blind date for you if you're interested. Jaffa's a great man for the women; likes them tall, like you.'

'Don't go there, Mac! I had enough from Crawford.'

'You're such a *big girl* m'dear.'

I could only laugh at his accurate mimicry of the Brigadier. 'Bastard.'

'Do you want me to arrange a date?'

'Thanks but no thanks, Mac. I can sort out my own social life,' I said hurriedly, knowing immediately I didn't sound convincing enough.

'Yeah . . . right. What happened to the stud I met with you last week? Séamus something-or-other, the cattle dealer. Weren't you heading off to the mountains with him?'

'Its none of your business, Mac.'

I was angry, angry with Mac for probing and with myself for caring. The stud, as vague a reality as Mac had implied, was already a figment of my past, yet another brief interlude left behind in a love nest of thorns, high in the Wicklow mountains.

'A cattle prod for your thoughts.'

'Not funny, Mac.'

'I'm sorry, Rio. I mean it. What happened?'

'I'll . . . I'll tell you about it some other time. I want to get going on the Durer. It's so exciting.'

'Riveting. I love watching damp spots dry, Rio. Its such a Zen thing!' Mac said as he pretended to kick-start a motorbike.

'Sarcastic bastard!' I pouted before leaving the boardroom and making my way to the small laboratory I could hide from the world in.

Then home, food and this. Two large bourbons as well! Mac

phoned about an hour ago and I told him about Séamus. Though full of sympathy he seems happy at the outcome. A short time later there was a text message on my cell-phone from Séamus, saying 'gdby' – not even bothering to fully sign off on me. I forwarded the message to Mac.

Message back from Mac saying 'fuk de bollix!'

Erased Séamus from my phone's memory – and the smell of his armpits from mine. Texted Mac, 'Never again!' A full declaration of intent.

Bull, I'm already available. Always have been! Dyslexic vibrations on a 'g' string. Must ring Jack.

5

ODD SHOES

"Perhaps nothing,
Nothing, can alter the truth of me,
I am earth's dream,
A sleeper ending his sleep
Will see when he wakes,
Real darkness beyond."

Bejan Matur • *Yeryuzunun Dusu* (Earth's Dream)

His fingers twitch. Flanagan scrolls back to re-read the last two pages and then decides to quit. Closing the laptop he stoops down, picks the letter from the floor and places it underneath the computer. It is 4.00 am and his eyes hurt. He has some difficulty draining the dregs of the malt. He thinks about and then decides against another cigarette before crossing to the CD storage unit. He searches for and pulls out Ry Cooder and Manuel Galbán's, *Mambo Sinuendo*, places the CD in the machine, selects the tenth track and waits for "Secret Love" to begin.

He switches off the lights. Unsteady in the darkness he nearly trips taking the steps before leaving the living room door ajar so that he might hear the music waft across the narrow hallway to his bedroom.

Teeth washed he lies in the bed, naked beneath the sheets of fresh cotton, probing with his tongue a large nerve-dead cavity plugged with the mint toothpaste and looking wide-eyed at the blank canvas of the ceiling. It is illuminated by a projection of moonlight flickering through the branches of the plum tree outside the bedroom window. As Cooder's riff on the last track, "María La O", fades, he remembers when Mac called him in Istanbul:

His mobile phone had vibrated and thrilled in his pocket as he climbed the small set of steps up through the Gate of the Engravers that would bring him into the courtyard of the booksellers. He opened the flap, checked the number on the caller-display and held it to his ear.

'Mac! It's good to hear from you. How are you?'

'It was there all the time, Jaffa. Symmonds –'

'What?' he interjected before furtively looking around him. Nobody to overhear. After the brazen soliciting of the leather-laden pimps of the Grand Bazaar and adjoining streets, the courtyard of second-hand booksellers, which had conducted its business just to the side of the Beyazit mosque since the early eighteenth century was an island of relative peace in the sea of bedlam that is the market quarter of Istanbul.

'Listen! It was there all the time! Symmonds must have missed it when he went through the contents. No wonder we never found it.'

'I see.'

'See my arse. Where are you?'

'Where am I? Oh. Istanbul. Working hard, don't you know, trying to turn a dollar. How did you –'

Mac spoke for a few minutes; he mainly listened before hanging up. He then entered the Kitabevi Kaabiz bookshop at the top of the steps. Once inside, a heavily built man, with a well lived-in face, grey unruly hair and a light dusting of cigarette ash and dandruff on his shoulders stood up to greet him.

'You are welcome, Jaffa, my friend.'

'I got your message, Ismâil. What is it you have for me?'

Ismâil Ibrahim, the proprietor of the bookshop, first barked an order to a young assistant – who immediately darted from the shop – before fixing him with indignant and bulging eyes. 'Have I not always been honest in my dealings with you, Jaffa? Was not the Ptolemy proof of that? Are we not partners?' he wailed, extending his arms.

'Of course. Excuse my rudeness, Ismâil. I've had no reply to my e-mail on the Ptolemy and it worries me somewhat. I thought that they would have learnt a lesson by now and jumped at the offer. I may have to look elsewhere for another buyer.' He said wearily as he slumped into a small chair, covered by a high quality but very worn Kashan *kilim* rug.

'Do not worry, Jaffa, my friend. Allah will provide. I have come across something of even greater value which I think will remove all fatigue from your heart.' Ismâil had consoled, slapping him on the shoulder before retaking his own seat.

'What is it?' He asked with more caution than was necessary.

Ismâil's assistant returned at that point carrying a large, bubble-lined envelope and a small, artist's portfolio case. The bookseller took them and after unzipping the portfolio carefully extracted seven or eight plastic transparent pockets. Each pocket contained a sheet of loose-leaf paper, which appeared quite fragile and on which there was faded but beautiful Arabic script. The bookseller then held up one of the pockets, in tender triumph.

'This!'

'Let me look. Shit!' As he reached across the table to take the plastic envelope the muscles in his left hand started cramping and he was unable to grasp it. The envelope floated to the ground.

Ismâil bent down and retrieved it.

'It's happening more often,' Jerome said trying to rub the stiffness out of his hand.

'Did you go to see my friend?' the bookseller asked.

'Tomorrow. I've made an appointment. Probably nothing. Vitamin lack or something! Pass me the envelope.'

The cramping eased after a minute or so and he was finally

able to prise open the envelope, and inspect its contents carefully. The paper was of high quality linen-rag manufacture, Italian probably, and appeared in reasonable condition, with no evidence of rust or mould. He then looked at the penmanship and frowned. The language of the writing was not Arabic but Ottoman Turkish, he realised, and his ability to read this was poor.

Ismâil had smiled knowingly. 'Would you like me to read what it says, Jaffa?' the bookseller asked as he reached for another folder and pull out a loosely bound series of typewritten pages. He fanned these in Flanagan's direction. 'I've gone to the trouble of translating it for you, putting in punctuation, capitals and inverted commas for direct speech.'

'Please.' He had smiled thinly as he handed the sheet of linen paper with its densely packed lines of calligraphy back. He had watched as Ismâil replaced it with the others in the portfolio case before starting to read the typescript. This, he had known then, was going to cost him dear –

Finally Flanagan's eyes fully close and sleep overwhelms him. A very short time later, beneath the leaden lids, his pupils began to move rapidly from side to side, as if searching to focus on the flickering images. He dreamt in colour as he always did:

'It is dated 1080AH, approximately 1669 years after the birth of Christ, and is a letter composed by one *Iskender Aga Sidanli* to his son. It has quite an interesting story to tell.'

'Go on!'

'Patience, my friend! Time will reveal all. Would you like a coffee?' Ismâil smiled indulgently.

'Please.'

'Turkish or Nescafe?'

'Turkish, medium sweet,' Jerome answered as he pulled out a box of his favourite *Petit* brand of small Sumatra cigars made by Nobel in Denmark. He offered one to the bookseller, who declined in favour of a more pungent cigarette, before lighting up the cigar and tasting its bitter smoke.

' *"To Heki, my beloved son"*,' the bookseller began, '*"In the hope that someday you will read this and come to know your father. Judge me not harshly for I loved your mother and you more than life itself and willingly give that life to protect you from its harsh –* " '

'Sentimental! Why is it of such interest?' Jerome asked in a distracted way as he accepted the coffee from the bookseller's assistant.

'Why, you ask? Because, my doubting Irish friend, Iskender Aga Sidanli was one of the greatest calligraphers of all time. You know him as *Karabatak Iskender Aga*.'

'*Karabatak*, the cormorant?'

'Exactly. Shall I continue?'

'Please do!' Jerome inhaled impatiently on his cigar.

' *"It was early afternoon on one of the last ten days of the month, that the Christians name April and others Nisan, in the one thousand and seventy-fifth year since the Prophet Mohammed – Praise be upon his name – had abandoned his clansmen in Mecca. I was eighteen years old –*" '

'Abandoned? That's an unusual word to use,' Jerome exhaled as he interrupted.

The bookseller looked up with patient eyes. 'Jaffa, my friend. Despite your expertise, there is much of the nuance in Middle Eastern terminology you have yet to appreciate. It is better to use the word "abandon" rather than "flight" to explain the *hidjra* of the Prophet, because, as my expert and orthodox friends tell me, the Arabic verb *hadjara* means a deliberate breaking-off-of-relations-with, or emigration from one's tribe, rather than fleeing from an enemy or danger. The predominant emotions of *hadjara* are loneliness and elation, not cowardice and fear; a crossroad of opportunity not impasse; a familial disruption as old as time. The Glorious Prophet was not running away but moving towards something better and to do this he needed to *abandon* his tribal ties.' Ismâil drew deeply on his cigarette. 'A little like your self, Jaffa.'

'With respect, Ismâil, would it be possible to give a summary of the letter? I can read it again later.' Jerome grunted, stung by the observation, as he lifted the small cup of black sweet coffee that bookseller's assistant brought in on a small tray.

'Of course my friend! The letter begins with a description of the times, and the trouble that the Ottoman's were having with Count Nicholas Serini, *Serinogli*, of Croatia, the trouble with the new *Chmil* or leader of the Cossacks, Yuri Boganzade and the internal difficulties in the city which had caused the Sultan Mehmet Han to remove himself to Edrine. It then goes onto describe the circumstances how *Iskender Aga Sidanli* first met his future master Abazade Effendi, a Vizier of the Divan and a personal friend of the chief minister Fazil Pasha Koprulu; how Iskender was taken to the Koprulu library to be trained in calligraphy by Abazade, who like Fazil Pasha was a student of Dervis Ali, the honoured successor to Seyh Hamdullah, the greatest calligrapher of them all.'

'Very interesting,' Jerome said with little interest displayed in his voice.

'I think you will find the next section more so, if I might read it.' Ismâil pulled out the third page and searched for his starting point.

'Sure.'

' "*Abazade Effendi explained that I was to become his pupil because he had been informed of my skills as a linguist, calligrapher and archer. I told him I would rather join the army to fight, as I was anxious, as all young men are, my son, to prove my valour on the field of battle. He asked me at that point how long I had been in the school and I told him that I went there when I was eight year-of-age and that my family were Christian. I told him about my grandfather, your great-grandfather, my beloved son, and his people who were followers of Nestorius the Christian and who were employed as interpreters in the Divan of the Shah of Persia. I told him how my own father, your grandfather, became a valued administrator in the house of the Emir of Sidan, in the Sanziack of Saphet and how it was the Emir who sent me to the Sultan's palace as part of a tribute payment. 'And you are now content to be a Muslim instead of a Christian?' Abazade asked. I simply said yes with my eyes.*

He then asked me about my facility in calligraphy and I told him that before being taken to the city that my father, your grandfather, had begun to teach me the sulus and nesih scripts as well as an old kufic type known only, in those times, to my grandfather and my father. In the palace school they wanted us to concentrate more on the divani style so the others suffered. Your great grandfather died in the conquest of Baghdad, my son, but my father, your grandfather still lives in Damascus. Allah be praised. I told him all this and then asked him why I was being brought to the Koprulu library instead of to the new palace at Odout Pasha, near Edrine. He said to me, 'You, my clever and alert young friend, are to be trained here by me and under the patronage of Kopruluzade rather than the Sultan. That is where the power in the land now lies. That is both yours and my destiny.'

I waited there . . ." ' The bookseller paused as he searched for the next page which was not in proper sequence, blaming, with his eyes, everyone in the shop except himself.

'There is a point to this, is there not Ismâil?' Jerome held out his cup to the assistant; relieved to have an excuse to leave the shop.

'Be alert, my friend. The next part is most important,' Ismâil scowled as he searched for the next page: ' *"It was at that point, my son, sitting in the dusty unfinished library of Kopruluzade, that my destiny, your destiny, all our destinies changed forever. 'Read the colophon', Abazade Effendi instructed as he handed a very old and fragile calf leather-bound book, with horsehair tassels for closure, to me for inspection. I opened the cover and held the book upwards to the light from a nearby window and as I read, tried to keep the surprise from my face. The pages were made of very old parchment and were coloured with age. There was little in the way of decoration and it was written in an old script similar to the kufic type of my grandfather, which my own father had begun to teach me before I was sent to the palace school and I was able to understand it. The colophon was written in the religious script of my grandfather: the letters of the Syriac Christians. It was a very old book filled with verses from the Qur'an, but very beautiful in its simplicity.*

I remember the words as if they were burnt on my forehead: This is the kitab al-dhikr al-Rûh, the Book of the Warnings of the Messenger Spirit, in whose ear the white dove revealed the Infallible formula for happiness, the secret of which lies within these pages." ' Ismâil read the lines with feigned indifference before looking up to watch for his visitor's reaction.

There was a prolonged silence before Jerome suddenly stood up, a look of wild excitement on his face.

'Jesus Christ, Ismâil. It exists! It god dam exists. I knew it,' Jerome shouted. He paced the floor of the shop before stopping in front of the bookseller's desk. 'Where did you get these, Ismâil? I must know!' He leant forward and made a sudden grab for the loose pages.

The old bookseller, with surprising speed, slammed his hand down on top of them. Dandruff, dust and ash fanned in all directions.

'Not so fast, Jaffa, my friend. Now that I suddenly have your interest you will favour me with some patience. Please sit down.' Ismâil failed in trying to suppress his satisfaction as he watched Jerome meekly withdraw his hand and retake his seat. 'Let me finish it first. Where was I? Oh yes. Iskender goes on to relate his emotional confusion of surprise and fear when Abazade gives him the signal that he, like Iskender, is one of the *Mu'shirin*; a secret Sufi and semi-Christian lodge that existed within the palace school. Iskender writes his son that he suspected a trap and that he was being tested as part of the Sultan's plan to eradicate secret lodges.'

'What was the signal?' Jerome asked quietly. He had been waiting for a moment like this for many years and needed to confirm the authenticity.

The bookseller searched down the page. ' *"The true secret is with us"*. That was the password.'

'Read the full section please, Ismâil,' Jerome asked, scenting a fake and needing to be sure. The words and the sense of the words were important in this assessment.

'If you insist,' Ismâil said with a knowing smile before returning his eyes to the page: ' *"Abazade Effendi said, 'I will be your pir or teacher in many things including the journey through those last two gates. From me you will finally learn the Secret but along the way you will also learn to be fully proficient in each of the six main calligraphy scripts as well as the* **ilm-i-abjad,** *the science of the letters. You will learn to prepare and cut your reeds, to size and burnish your paper, and to make your ink of soot and gold. You will watch how the tanners prepare the leather, how the binders bind, how the paper makers prepare their pages, how the illuminators pluck the neck fur of white kittens for their brushes, how ink colours are extracted from what is all around you. Finally, as an exercise to strengthen and steady your hand, you will learn to fly your arrow further than ever before or what you thought possible. You will learn to make your own bow and pick the pine for your arrows as well as from where to pluck the peacock for your flights and how to weave the silken threads of their loosening. By the discipline of these paths and the final gates of the Mu'shirin you will know the Spirit of the Truth. From intelligence and will your soul will be found. You will know everything because you will know what is superior.'*

I was very overwhelmed, my beloved son, by all these events and even more so by what followed. It was at that point that Abazade Effendi said he was giving me a new name, the name that you now carry. He said he would call me Karabatakzade, the black arrow of the cormorant: the arrow that disappears and then suddenly appears again. I liked my new name as Abazade explained that it was a question of unity in spirit and action and I accepted. I was still unsure, however, why he was willing to grant me my freedom and I asked him about this.

'Ah that,' he said as he stroked his beard, a beard you could lose yourself in, and looked at me, 'Because you will be the next guardian of this book.' He pointed to the leather-bound book I still held in my hands: The Book of the Messenger. 'It is the only

one in which the Secret is recorded. The warnings or the al-dhikr of the Messenger are hidden in the understanding of the secret letters of al-Muqatta'at. That is its power and its glory. You will learn how to uncover the secret but that is a lesson for another day. Are you prepared to learn?' he asked of me and I agreed.

That is the story, my son, of how I came to meet the great and glorious Abazade Effendi and touched the Book of the Messenger Spirit for the first time. My destiny from that day on was determined and I want you to understand that, my son. It is . . ."'

'Go on,' Jerome said,

'The letter ends there, abruptly. The other pages are missing,' Ismâil said apologetically as he handed the last loose page over for Jerome to look at.

'Shit,' Jerome groaned.

'It is a very important document and very rare given the personal nature of it.' Ismâil tried to be positive.

'Forget the personalities! Of more importance it tells us that the Book of the Messenger existed in the mid-seventeenth century. Don't you realise, that is almost a 700 years after its last previous reported reference. Where did you get these?' Jerome leaned over the desk and picked up the rest of the pages. This time there was no obstruction.

'From the personal papers of Leon Arsan, a book dealer in this market in the 1930's. It seems he sent a number of the pages to an intermediary in Cairo who was instructed to show them to a collector.'

'Who?'

'Why, Chester Beatty of course, at his winter house in *Bait al Azrak* in Egypt. Leon Arsan was a friend of Behir Nushet Bogac, Beatty's guide in Istanbul.'

'I don't believe it,' he almost shouted.

'Listen, Jaffa. I'm hungry. Why don't we go and have something to eat?'

Jerome looked at his watch, shook his head. 'I'm sorry Ismâil. I'm meeting Alanna at 9.30. Tomorrow? We can meet here at say . . . 6.00.'

'That is fine by me.'

'Good. I better be going.'

'Jaffa.'

'Yes.'

'A word in your ear, my friend.' As he said this Ismâil stood up and directed him by the arm to the doorway of the shop, pausing to whisper out of earshot, 'Be careful there . . . with Alanna, I mean.'

'What do you mean?'

'She is not a friend of the military.'

'What have you heard?'

'They dislike her politics and are almost certainly watching her . . . and you too. Just be careful.'

'I will. Thanks Ismâil. See you tomorrow.'

'*Insha' Allâh*, Jaffa my friend. *Insha' Allâh*.'

Flanagan sits up in his bed, as if still living the dream. Half asleep and half awake he imagines that the shadow cast on the bedroom wall by the moonlight, the cadenza light, is Mac. The shadow mouth, in profile, moves, speaking to him:

Supine dreams
Rendered prone
A paralysis of
Being:
Being alone.

The shadow loses its substance, as if afraid, and the wind causing the rattle of the plum-tree branches against the window eases off. At that moment he is fully awake. 'Jesus,' he whispers, feeling his heart pound and skin moisten. He switches on the light, picks up the clock, and looks at it: 6.30. His hands are cramping again, locking around the clock. He is unable to leave it down. '*Nothing can be done*,' the Turkish specialist had said. '*We can do nothing*,' the Dublin specialist had said, giving him nothing. Alanna had once given him a card with poetry by a

Kurdish poet written on it. The card sits on the bedside table and he re-reads the words:

Perhaps nothing,
nothing, can alter the truth of me,
I am earth's dream,
a sleeper ending his sleep
will see when he wakes,
real darkness beyond.

He remembers all. He remembers the pain and embarrassment of coming home from school and seeing his mother drunk for the first time, with a man who was not his father – the first of many – standing behind her, equally drunk, fondling her breast with a dead smile on his face. He remembers Kundera's Franz: a twelve year-old boy walking the streets with a mother wearing odd shoes. He had never wanted to hurt her, but did, just by noticing.

'Why are you here, Jerome?' his mother had asked as she lay dying.

'I need to confront my dreams,' he had replied.

Still holding the clock Flanagan clumsily switches off the light with his free hand, closes his eyes on the darkness, sinks back on the pillow and lets a deeper level pull him in.

6

AL-RÛH

"Thereon descend angels and al-rûh by
the command of their lord with divine
decree concerning every matter."

The Qur'an • *surat al-Qadr; 97 v. 5*

"He is the answerer. What can be answered he
answers, and what cannot be answered he shows
how it cannot be answered."

Walt Whitman • *Leaves of Grass*

It's nearly midday when Flanagan wakes again, thinks of the dream again, and promises himself a better day – what's left of it. Getting up from the bed, he stretches stiffly before walking to the window. There is a blue, blue sky and the burst of brilliant light causes him to sneeze. He notices the unusually early appearance of small flowers on the plum tree that is planted close to the bedroom window.

'Plum conception,' he says aloud, promising, because it's a self-pollinating variety, to help it later with the small artist's brush he keeps for the pollen transfer. Felicity Fellows suddenly rounds the corner on her way to the shops. She is of an indeterminate age and cute with it, he thinks, feeling a morning erection coming on. She stops to look at the plum tree, does with her fingers what he

65

had intended with his brush. He is now fully erect. She looks up from what she is doing, *looks* at him and smiles. He jumps back, pulling all into the shadows, suddenly aware of his obvious nakedness. He leaves a visible hand to wave her on her way. Or bring her back, he hopes for a moment before heading for the bathroom.

An hour later, he could hear the outer door of the communal atrium opening and the footsteps bypassing the elevator bank. He pulls on the handle of his door and steps out, safe in the plan of going to retrieve his post. He has waited patiently for the opportunity, hoping she would return. Her back is to him as she inserts a key in the deadlock. Bag of shopping at her feet; ready meals – meals for one – some fruit, a bottle of wine and a bunch of flowers visible through its opening. She turns, a dancer's movement of the hips, he thinks.

'Hi,' she says.

'Just going for my post,' he says, sticking to the plan.

'Sure,' she says with a smile, turning back towards her door.

'Listen. I'm sorry about earlier. I was half asleep and forgot I had no clothes on.'

She has a mischievous smile and her green flecked eyes flash with amusement. 'I noticed,' she laughs.

He blushes. 'We've never had a chance to talk about what happened . . . or anything really, I'm never here . . . I was wondering, if you are not doing anything later, whether you would like to join me for a drink.'

'Sure. That would be – shit! Bloody door!' She leans heavily against her door to force it open. It creaks before surrendering to the pressure. She almost falls in but once inside she turns again to look at him. 'Sorry about that. The wood has expanded and keeps sticking. They were meant to fix it today.'

'It's done that as long as I remember,' he says. The noise had always bothered him. He picks up her bag of groceries and hands them to her. Their fingers brush off each other for a moment. Plum conception, Flanagan thinks.

'Thanks,' she says taking the bag, Her expression changes. 'Did you know that I knew her?'

'Who?'

'Rio.'

'No . . . I mean how?'

'I'm also a conservator. We met once or twice through work.'

F, he thinks. *Fuck*, he almost splutters out. 'Is . . . do you have a husband called Séamus?'

'Yes, but we've recently separated.'

'I'm sorry to hear that.'

'I'm not.' She pushes against her door to close it but then stops. 'How did you know my husband's . . . his name?'

'I'm not sure. Perhaps . . . perhaps Rio mentioned it to me.'

'Why would she do that? I didn't know her all that well.'

'Because of my line of work I like to hear of people with certain skills and I might have extracted the information out of her. Your husband's a cattle-dealer, if I remember correctly, and you work in the National Library. That association intrigued me, when I heard it, wondering how you two met up. I tend to latch onto seemingly irrelevant stuff like that.' He hoped he had got away with it, away with his easy facility for lying.

'Very impressive, Jerome . . . I think. Anyway that is one association that you can now erase.'

'I will,' he said. She hesitated at the door and he saw what he thought was the beginning of a tear. 'I'm sorry to have upset you, Felicity. I only make those mental notes about families and stuff so that I can find an approach to charm favours out of people.'

'Does it work?' she laughed.

'Sometimes! The drink later?' he asks.

'Sure, Jerome. I'd like that.'

'Great.' He holds out his hand and she takes it. She has long fingers: pianoforte fingers, he thinks, good for playing and pollinating.

'I'll see you,' she says.

'Did it not put you off?' he suddenly wonders, looking around the corridor.

'What?' she teased. 'Your display earlier?'

He smiled but then became serious. 'No. I mean what happened here. Did it not put you off the building? The apartment?'

'No! The opposite, if anything. Do you think that's weird?' she asks with a very direct stare.

'No,' he says, thinking yes. Stick to the plan, he reminds himself. 'We'll talk about it later, perhaps.'

'Perhaps,' she says.

'Until later then, Felicity. Anytime you like. Suit yourself. I'll be in.' He turns and retreats into his own doorway.

Plan accomplished – almost.

'Jerome,' she says, smiling.

'Yes.'

'Your post.'

'Oh right! Thanks. The excitement got to me,' he blusters, moving to plan B, the Danish plan: *He who flatters gets.*

'You're easily excited, but thank you all the same,' she says, laughing the words sweetly before closing her door.

It is late afternoon by the time he is able to sit down at the computer and boot it up. The room, the apartment had had to be cleaned first, the bedroom in particular. He thinks about sex and the possibility of sex. He wonders if he can still manage it. The last time was with Alanna and that . . .

The desktop screen appears; like an angry father, waiting, demanding an explanation. Flanagan double clicks the diary file and scrolls:

Armpit Diary,
January 10:
With an absence of visitors, due to the continued bad weather, the museum beat along to a purposeful pulse of its own. A Dan Fogleberg song is playing on the small, compact disc-player that perches precariously on top of the drying cabinet, at the far end of the lab.

'*Listen to the rhythm of the falling rain, telling me just what a fool I've been,*' I hummed along – badly – to its chorus while retrieving the copper-bracketed, Japanese paste-bowels to begin preparing the week's supply of the wheat-starch paste used for the repair and remounting of damaged engravings and prints. The boiling, skimming, cooling and sieving of the paste is a once a week chore and takes about 20 minutes. Early in my training my Japanese paper-conservation instructors always insisted that the paste making was the true beginning of the preparation of the mind for the tasks ahead. 'Work with nature and it will work with you,' they insisted, keeping me in a kneeling position, my height bothering them more than tradition.

Not when applied to humans, I think now.

I can still picture those same instructors, and their single instruction about some task for me to do, their expectation, and then the silence as they watched. The continued silence, a gift of their learning passed on, praise for the receipt of that gift inappropriate. I never knew what they thought about my work, for them it was what I thought that mattered. Also their almost priestly reverence as they retrieved and handled the very precious – and very pungent – paste, which they insisted, was to be reserved for the most delicate and worthy of works: *the secret*, their emerald stone. Like products of medieval alchemy the paste was prepared and then buried for up to a year before use and the patience of waiting for those Japanese conservators was everything.

Thankfully, the weekly paste suffices for routine work and doesn't smell. In any event, I suppose, I am never in one place long enough to prepare, bury and retrieve the special paste. Love perhaps but never paste.

'*Rain won't you tell her that I love her so . . .*'

At the far end of the room, the Durer engraving and the intervening paper layer to which it was attached, were finally sitting on a blotter mount inside the hooded humidifier. Separating the paper layers from the mounting board had proved easier than anticipated, as only a minute amount of glue had originally been used for attaching the corners. I was able to achieve this first separation by cutting close to the surface of the board, with a surgical scalpel. Freed from the board, humidified air generated by the moistened bottom leaves of the blotter mound then began the work of separating the engraving from the intervening paper layer. Water is the slowest of all solvents but it is also the safest. It would take a few hours before the glue bridging the engraving and the backing paper began to expand. Be patient, I reminded myself, before setting the lab's alarm clock.

A soft hissing sound drifted through the silence left by the last song on the disc and I stood up to change it for another, George Benson's *Absolute Benson*. "The Ghetto" started up as the door opened and James Somerville sauntered in. I noticed, with mild amusement, how his face twitched in disgust as he dodged through the debris of my paste making.

'Hello, Dawson,' he said jauntily.

'For the last time, James! Call me Rio,' I demanded.

'Right. Sorry. Rio then.'

James has a problem with intimacy, but then so do many of the Irishmen that I encounter. He, of course, doesn't think of himself as being like other Irishmen. Needs a spell in a humidifier to separate the layers.

'What can I do for you, James?'

'I just popped in to see how you were getting on with the engraving.'

'I've managed to separate it from the mounting board but its still in the humidifier. I'll be taking it out in a few hours. You're welcome to come back then if you like and watch.'

I hoped he wouldn't. James really irritates me at times.

'No thanks. I'd only be in the way.'

'Of course you wouldn't.' I almost coughed as the words came out.

'It's a very interesting find. Very interesting indeed.'

'Yes it is. You must explain something more about the *Paraclete* to me, some other –'

'As a word . . .'

I could only watch his face light up as he assumed my interest was an immediate invitation to explain.

' . . . it derives from the Greek verb *para-kalein* meaning "to call to one's side". As I mentioned this morning it is a description of the Holy Spirit that only appears in the Gospel of St John and is therefore somewhat unusual. John's Gospel records that Jesus promised the disciples that he will ask the Father to send another *Paraclete* in His stead, to be with them always and that this presence would be both the messenger *and* the Spirit of the Truth. The other interesting facet of this description of the Holy Spirit is that it is very much akin to that of the Qumran covenanters, to whom the *Paraclete* was the Angel of Light advocate, who will overturn the judgment of the evil Angels of Deception and will bear witness for the disciples in front of the Father. If this is a Durer, I suspect that he might have engraved his interpretation of the *Paraclete* as a response to the schism prompted by Martin Luther's posting of his 95 theses against the established church in 1517.'

James looked towards where the speakers belted out Benson's "El Barrio". It rushed through the room.

'Was Durer a supporter of Luther?' Despite myself, I was interested in what he had to say.

'We don't think so, but he did come to admire his intellectual capabilities. Durer was a moderate and the schism would have upset him. This engraving was perhaps his response, a call to help to the Holy Spirit to become the advocate in the dispute.'

'Why do you think there are no other prints?'

'Durer met Luther shortly afterwards at a Diet called to discuss the matters of contention and may have become sympathetic to his views. Perhaps he changed his mind or regretted implying in the engraving that Luther was an Angel of Darkness who needed to be overcome by the *Paraclete*. I suspect the plate was probably destroyed. If this engraving does turn out to be a Durer it will provide a fascinating window on his feelings towards the schism as well as being almost a unique find.'

'That's very interesting, James. Thanks.' I genuinely appreciated his knowledge. 'I'll be very careful.'

'Right. Glad to be of help. I'll leave you to it Daw . . . Rio. See you at lunch.'

'Bye, James.'

I waited for the door to close behind him before returning to my work. Outside, the snow had begun falling again and the room grew dark as the light was smothered. I had just begun running water into the stainless steel-jacketed soaking basin, which occupied the same corner as the hooded humidifier when the telephone suddenly started ringing. After crossing the room I tried to keep the irritation, at yet another interruption, from my voice as I answered the wall mounted telephone.

'Hello. Conservator's lab.'

'Rio. I have an inspector from Health and Safety on the other line. It seems we have been a bit remiss lately, although I can't imagine how. He wants to know if there are any redundant solvents or solvent mixtures in the storage cupboard ready for disposal.'

Aengus FitzHenry sounded equally exasperated; this type of banal enquiry was way below his dignity and his level of responsibility.

'In small quantities only, Aengus. There is about 30mls of a Toluene and isopropanol mixture, 20mls of Isoctane-ethanol and diethyl-ether mixture and a small amount of chloroform, that the French conservator who was working here in October used for varnish removal. It can be disposed of, if you like, as I don't use any of it.'

I had done a quick check this morning when getting the materials for the paste. It is a habit.

'Hold on a sec!'

He put me on hold. Elevator Enya musak played, clashing with Benson's "Come Back Baby" in the room. I waited for some time, imagining FitzHenry (penultimate level, or so, of civil-service pay scale) negotiating with the inspector (midway down the scale) on the other line.

'Rio.'

'Yes, Aengus.'

'He said that he is very busy and would prefer to drop in

around the 30th to pick them up. He will also collect both Decembers and January's atmospheric passive diffusion samples so they can be analysed. Is that ok?'

'Sure. I'll have them ready.'

'Thank you.'

'No problem.' I was about to put down the phone when he spoke again. He sounded more hesitant and less sure of himself.

'Rio.'

'Yes, Aengus.'

'I'm sorry about yesterday and the way that the meeting broke up. It must give a bad impression of the Library to a visiting colleague.'

The Library, I think. 'Don't worry about it, Aengus. Every institution I have ever worked in has its personalities and conflicts . . . I do think however that the camera would be a good purchase.'

'Ha! I don't feel that sorry, Rio but I promise you I'll think about it. How is it going with the engraving?'

'I was just about to check on it when you telephoned.' I knew I sounded annoyed.

'Right. I understand. You best get on with it. I'll drop by later, if you don't mind.'

'Leave it for a –'

The line went dead, he did not wait to find out whether I minded or not. I stared at the receiver for a moment but didn't replace it its cradle. I knew that for those next few hours I could not afford to be interrupted and after activating the "Do not disturb" corridor display-light lifted the saucepan and began pouring its contents into the sieve.

The separation process took longer than expected and it was nearly 3.00 in the afternoon when I finally finished. I felt very hungry but there was something I needed to do first. I tried a number of extensions with a similar result before my fourth attempt was answered.

'Auditorium. McMurragh speaking.' He sounded breathless.

'Mac. Can you come up here?' I said a little too brusquely, irritated by the delay in finding him. Mac sometimes used the auditorium and the blackout capability of the public projection theatre to photograph large manuscripts. I should have tried there first.

'*Is that you, Clarice?*' He imitated Hopkins' rasp to perfection. 'Imagine having a trained FBI agent in our midst. Golly gee. I missed you at lunch, I wanted to discuss eating some of our colleagues.'

'Very funny! I was busy as it happens. Are you able to come up here? Soon?'

'Give me five minutes and I'll be there. Is there a problem? You sound funny.'

'No. No problem. I just need your professional help.'

'Shit! And I thought you had developed a sudden, and not altogether surprising, hunger for my body.'

I have to admit, that there have been moments, usually alcohol fuelled, when this thought had crossed my mind. Mac despite his alcohol problems in the past is a good looking man – in a lived-in sense – and fit from all that enforced walking. I have wondered what it would be like, the two of us together.

Not today though! 'I lost my lunch-hour not my sense of taste, Mac. Get up here . . . please.'

Replacing the phone and waiting for him to arrive I became fascinated by what was happening in the courtyard below the laboratory window. Small tornados of snow were being whipped up by a strengthening wind in the narrow confines of the courtyard to hover like will-o'-the-wisps for a moment, before travelling for a short distance and suddenly collapsing in the open space of the nearby road. When he eventually pushed open the door I hardly noticed.

'Hi Rio. Your knight in shining armour is here. Dragon food!'

'What? Oh hi, Mac. I deserved that.'

'Did you finish with the separation?' He walked right past me and towards the humidifier in the far corner of the room.

'Yep! It went very well. Come and see.' I called him back to the drying rack and pulled out the top tray. 'Careful though, they are a bit fragile.' I had placed the two square pieces – the engraving and backing, both about A4 size – from the separation process side by side on a layer of absorbent Japanese tissue paper that rested on the knotless nylon mesh of the rack. He noticed.

'I see you managed to recover the intervening paper fully intact as well. Well done.' I flinched protectively as Mac touched the corner of the square on the right.

'It's not paper, Mac. I hate to say this but Crawford was right. It is very fine parchment, and you can just make out the writing.' I did hate to acknowledge it.

'God bless your eyes. It's very faint.'

'I know. I want you to photograph it across the entire spectrum before I try to enhance the writing.'

'Enhance! What do you mean Rio?'

'Mac. I had a quick look at the stain on the reverse of the engraving and I definitely think the ink used was a vegetable tannin and iron mixture. I want you to photograph it particularly in ultraviolet.'

'The engraving?'

'No, the parchment.'

'Why? Surely the engraving deserves more attention. It could be a unique Durer.'

'No could be, Mac. It is!'

'How do you know?'

'Look there, with this.' In a smug but suitably restrained triumphal flourish I handed him a magnifying glass, lying *conveniently* near by, and pointed to a spot on the reverse of the engraving.

'It's . . . *it is* his monogram but not printed.'

'No, it's probably in a light charcoal pencil. Added afterwards.'

'It could be a forgery.'

'I risk my reputation that it isn't.'

'What reputation?'

I gave him a thump on the shoulder. 'Very smart. Now let's get back to the parchment.'

'Why?'

'It intrigues me. Ok! The engraving is almost certainly cut and dried from a forensic point of view but the parchment appeals to the detective in me.'

'Why?'

'Because, as he pointed out in the meeting, James could find no reference to the Durer in the correspondence. Given its unique nature I'm very surprised that Beatty never mentioned it.'

'Perhaps he never saw it.' Mac shrugged his shoulders.

'That's possible and that is why the parchment is so important. Because of its intimate association we might be able to use it to determine the provenance of the etching.'

There was a sudden tension in the air, like a fast approaching thunderstorm.

'I would like an intimate association,' Mac said suddenly, with bolting intensity, but without looking at me. 'At least, what I mean to say is that I like being here with you, Rio. Just the two of us. No bollixes like Séamus what's-his-name, who wouldn't know the prize they are letting go of. Would you ever . . .' His voice faded away as angry, misting eyes diverted to the etching.

'Sorry, Mac,' I said, trying to call a halt. It was the best I could manage.

Although not surprised by this turn of events, the passion rattled me. In truth I was dreading the moment but had thought I would get some warning. Unlike those times as a child on Eleuthera, when watching a storm far out to sea, guessing the direction it would take. The wind would rise and a perimeter of light would appear on the water just ahead of the dark cloud shadow, a brilliant light rushing ahead, telling me to take shelter, warning me. Mac's timing caught me out. Often he would look at me with a smile and unsaid thoughts and I would smile back, screwing up my face to jokingly banish those thoughts. Sometimes, however, I'd catch him looking at me in an intensely possessive way, and he'd turn away like a spoilt child with something close to the anger I saw now, in his eyes. I was never sure whether he was annoyed with himself for having being caught or with me for catching him. Either way they were awkward moments, which were never fully resolved. Now, with Séamus out of the way, I was –am – worried that he was about to spoil our friendship by asking me out on a date, asking me for a decision.

At that moment Mac lost his nerve, retreated. 'Yeah. I see what you're getting at. Is there anything to go on?'

'Yes.' I tried to keep the relief from my voice.

'Which is?' he asked with a quizzical look.

I gently lifted the edge of tissue paper covering the parchment with a blunt ended wooden forceps to show him. 'Look here, Mac. There is . . . darn!' At that moment the telephone rang and I wanted to ignore it. It kept ringing.

'Do you want me to get it?' Mac asked.

'No,' I said, a little too brusquely. He smarted. Leaving down the paper, I walked across the room to answer.

'Yes,' I said, not bothering to hide my annoyance.

'Well hel . . . lo to you too,' a voice drawled and slurred down the line.

'Oh. Jack. I was going to ring you later.'

'Were you. That's goo . . . good. An uncle likes to . . . to hear from his . . . his only godchild.'

'You sound tired, Jack.' He sounded drunk, I thought, forcing a smile for the benefit of Mac who was watching me closely.

'That's one . . . one way of describing it Babs.'

'How's the curvaceous Sara Lou?' I asked in a conspiratorial voice. Sara Lou Hubble Dawson, Miss Oregon Runner Bean Queen 1990, was the 30-something, sub-pectoral enhanced, silicone illusion that Jack had taken for a fifth wife. All four topics, suitable for a conversation between them, had apparently been exhausted by the second day of their sudden and bourbon floated Reno nuptials but to his credit, Jack Dawson had persisted.

'I'm fi . . . fine but I think my hearing is going.'

'Why do you say that?'

'When Sara Lou says 'I love you', it increasingly sounds like *I got you*. We . . . we're rapidly running out of pages with colour pictures, so I give us about two more months.'

'That's a rotten thing to say. It's your own fault, Jack.'

I cringed at his offhand assessment of his current partner yet still sympathised with his plight. We are too similar. I have met Sara Lou just once and had to listen to her complain for the whole time that we were together that Jack just did not understand the benefits of paying for her to get Botox injections and would I help convince him.

'Is she there with you? Let me talk to her.'

There was a long pause and all I could hear was his heavy breathing.

'I . . . I lied Babs . . . about the two or three month thing. Sara Lou's go . . . gone . . . and good riddance.'

'Oh Jack.'

'No problemo, kid. It was bound to happen sooner or later. I'm out celebrating.'

'Too well by the sound of it.' I looked at my watch. It was about 10.00 am in Miami.

'Listen. Gotta go, Babs. Ring me soon.'

'Jack. Listen –' The line went dead. 'Shit!' I leant my head against the wall staring at the receiver in my hand. What advice could I have given him, what help? I fare little better in my own relationships. A meeting of Bore Easily Anonymous, Jack in the chair perhaps.

'Are you all right, Rio. Any problem?' Mac, the anonymous of another kind of high, asked concerned.

'No.' I lied as I always lie. 'But thanks for asking Mac. Now where were we? Oh yes.' I walked back and continued where I had left off by lifting away the tissue paper. 'Look at the bottom of the parchment . . . there.'

Mac bent over the laid-out parchment and immediately saw, what I had also noticed first, that in one corner, written in French, in what appeared to be lead pencil, were two sentences and a signature. He read them aloud, slowly, '*Karabatakzade Aga circa 1669. Note mention of kitab al-dhikr al-Rûh – Leon Arsan, Kaabiz Kitabevi, 1931.*'

'What do you think?' I asked.

He looked up at me, suppressing enthusiasm – thinking back, the tone of his voice was reluctant, blocking even. 'Almost certainly a dealer's note – but I suppose that's something to go on.'

'Please indulge me on this, Mac. I want to be able to read the parchment. It might fluoresce and the tannin-quenched areas will show up dark.'

'The whole parchment sheet looks like it's tannin or lake stained. What happens if there is little or no fluorescence?'

'Then I will spray the parchment carefully with an iron-gall ink and gum Arabic mixture.'

'Iron-gall ink. Where will you get that?'

'I have a ferrous sulphate enriched concentrate of sumac leaves and Chinese oak galls from my time in Japan. If I prepare and spray on a strong solution of the ink with added gum Arabic the tannin will be rapidly absorbed onto areas where tannin ink has been used previously. The gum Arabic and rapid drying will prevent absorption onto other areas of the parchment. We can then photograph again across the entire spectrum.'

'Isn't there a danger in that?'

'As a conservator I would say yes because you can turn the parchment into rawhide with too much moisture but as a forensic necessity I would say it's worth a shot. Remember, I'm trained!'

'If you say so, G-person! You're so big and brave.'

'I'll have my Agency friends take you out, permanently, if there are any more of the *big* jokes, Mac.' I couldn't help but laugh and leant forward to kiss him on the cheek.

You never know the moment when friendships change. For good or bad, it's sudden, unexpected and all that has gone before changes forever. I think, no, I know, this was one of those moments. For some reason the line, always a fine line, had been crossed and he blushed profusely. An Irish blush, the kind that envelops the whole person. Vulnerable. Transparent.

There was a silence, an adolescent silence, between us. What to do about him? Solid, sound Mac, not dangerous – to me at least. But to him? Soul buddies almost. Wanting a whole lot more. Needing a whole lot more. Anything that happens between us would almost be a gift on my part, an unfair gift, refusing further reciprocation.

I turned back and busied myself replacing the tissue layer over the parchment.

'When will you know about the ink?' he eventually blustered.

'Two or three days.' I looked at him and it was my turn to bluster knowing that he had already suspected that I had already taken a small piece of the parchment, with a sample of the writing, for analysis – as conservators we are loath to admit that this occasionally has to be done; a secret of the trade, a secret lie. 'I've sent a sample of the ink writing to the spectroscopy laboratory in Abbotstown, and have also taken a small piece of the parchment for dating purposes.'

'Right,' he winked at me, composed again. 'I'll get the camera set up. Bring it down when it's dry.'

'There's one other problem, Mac.' I had been hatching a plan and it was now time to put it into action.

'What is it, Rio?' he asked suspiciously.

'Phyllis Andrew, left after the meeting and is away until Friday week. I don't know anybody else who reads Arabic around here. I would like to get the parchment translated as soon as possible. Do you by any chance . . . eh . . .know someone who –'

'Oh you cunning cow! I know what you're getting at.'

'What?' I felt my face redden. Mac had seen straight through me.

'Jaffa Flanagan! You want to meet him.'

'He reads Arabic doesn't he?'

'And people just as quickly. In your present state of desperation I'd say you'd resist for at least five minutes.'

I looked at him, holding out a mirror in my eyes, in my smile. He understood and nodded. Some day it might happen between us.

'Will you set it up?' I asked.

'Sure. I know . . . I mean, he . . . he could be away. He's always travelling in pursuit of material but I'll try him on his mobile. I might get lucky.' He stopped briefly at the doorway, a nervous thin smile on his face.

As the door closed behind him the smells from the café below wafted through the lab. I winked at my reflection in the glass of the extraction hood before finally succumbing to the aromas and the hunger pangs they induced, and headed for the ground floor and the food I could already taste.

Thinking about it again now, Mac's hesitation when I asked him to set up the meeting bothers me a little. I sense he knows exactly where Flanagan is but for some reason changed his mind about saying it straight out. Jealous? I must ask him about that tomorrow . . .

No answer from Jack's phone.

7

A LOVE SUPREME

*"'I love you' is a phrase one says while knowing
its truth and its untruth simultaneously."*

Victoria Griffin • *The Mistress*

Flanagan leans back against the chair and looks at his watch.
Nearly 5.30. He needs to go out to the local shop to pick up some
tonic and soda water. Might run into Khalid, once a nuclear
physicist in Baghdad, now a grocer in Dublin. See if he has any
news from home. Perhaps ginger ale as well. He wonders what
drink is Felicity Fellow's poison, guesses gin or vodka and plans
to have enough of it.

He opens the file with his own appointment diary and scrolls
to 11 January. There it is, his entry: *Phone call from Mac: further
info on parchment they uncovered. Note in pencil mentioning
Karabatakzade and Book of M. Leon Arsan confirmed as being
involved, 1931. Connection to Beatty? Meeting arranged with
Rio Dawson for following Monday in Dublin. The 14th. Hairy
Lemon, 12.30. Meeting with Ismâil, Sahaflar, 7.00 pm.*

He scrolls back up to the previous entry: *Meeting Alanna.
Four Seasons. 9.30.* He looks at the words and his hands shake.
She had never looked more beautiful; more fired up, he

remembers, having called him out-of-the blue after nearly six months of silence. As she came into the hotel foyer it was like the first time he had seen her in the village high in the mountains of Corsica, as they stood beside each other mesmerised by the weaving procession of San Nicolo. They had touched briefly back then, bare arm on bare arm, and electricity flowed. It flowed, from him; yet again as they sat down to eat in the hotel restaurant. Alanna, her eyes of opal black framed by flaming red hair, was so alive she'd hardly touched her food, excited by the prospect of getting an interview with General Orhan, to question him about the information – *the dossier* – she had stumbled upon, a dossier that she subsequently hid away for safekeeping, both afraid and exhilarated by its contents. The dossier she then told him where to find, that she wanted him to retrieve and take out of the country. 'They are watching me too closely. I cannot take the chance. If I mean anything to you, Jaffa . . . if I meant anything to you, please do this for me,' she pleaded. He had hesitated, tried to caution her, told her of Ismâil's warning and asked her to be careful, asked her to back off for a while. 'I am a Kurd, Jaffa but this is my Turkey, my reality,' she shouted at him. 'Why don't you go home and close your eyes and heart?' were her departing, angry, words before she left him sitting there.

It was the last time that he would ever hear her voice except for the brief message left on his answering service . . .

Nobody should see this and certainly not Jack, he thinks, scrolling back down to the entry concerning Mac. It's too damaging and would be difficult to explain. Jack Dawson will want answers; will want to know about how much Mac and he – or he alone – shared responsibility for what happened. I need to be very careful, he thinks, suddenly pressing the delete button and then again when the programme questions him, second-guesses him – parallel lives.

Arvo Pärt's "Com Cierva Sedienta" is playing on the CD and he reads aloud from the sleeve notes, '*Cuando pienso en estas cosas: When* I remember these things, *Doy rienda suelta a mi dolar:* I pour out my soul in me.' Leaning back he tries to remember:

The meeting with the bookseller had taken place as arranged. Ismâil Ibrahim had a quick look around the, by now, deserted courtyard of the book bazaar before tucking the envelope and portfolio case under his arm and locking the shop door. He then linked his free arm through that of Jerome and together they descended the small set of steps to exit through the Gate of the Engravers. A biting, cold wind tunnelled down the narrow street.

'Where shall we eat, Jaffa? I'm hungry,' he grunted.

'You're always hungry. How about the Rumeli Café across the road from the Hôtel Nomade, where I'm staying.'

'Why? What's wrong with the apartment in Beyoglu?' Ismâil asked defensively.

'That cousin of yours has no taste. I have the decorators in and the paint fumes give me headaches. I only go there at the moment to deal with my mail and telephone messages.'

'I see. The Rumeli will be fine. It's warm in there and it's a bitterly cold evening,' Ismâil grunted again as he shivered in the cold wind.

'I think you're holding something back from me. What is it?' Jerome asked as they jostled for room on the street with de-camping sellers and homebound students from the nearby university.

'All in good time, my friend! All in good time. Let us eat first. I hate ruining good food with a rushed story,' the bookseller cautioned as they reached Divanyolu Cadessi and hopped on a tram that would take them the short distance down the hill.

They got off at the Firuz Aga mosque, crossed the tramway-tracked road and walked the short distance up the narrow adjoining Ticarethane street to the café. Inside there was a roaring fire in the corridor chimney and Ismâil stopped to warm his hands before climbing the narrow stairs to a table Aaron had reserved for them on the first floor. Once they had ordered their food Ismâil prized open the envelope and extracted a typed manuscript which was different in its binding to the one he had read from earlier. He handed it to Jerome. It was written in French and dated 6 June 1931.

'What's this?' Flanagan asked as he began to read.

'I am not entirely sure but I think, based on the manuscript I've already translated for you and other information available to me, I think it's a background story Leon Arsan wrote about Karabatakzade Iskender Aga, and the times he lived in.'

'Why?'

'I'm not sure. Perhaps it was a way to enhance the value of the document he already had and which he could use to touch on the history of the Book of the Messenger. I suspect he either used it, or planned to use it, as a coded means of inviting interest in the letter of Karabatakzade he already had possession of.'

Ismâil finished speaking as a plate of stuffed vine-leaves and small grilled fish arrived. He began eating immediately.

'Does it contain any relevant information?' Jerome asked.

'You tell me. Your French is better than mine,' the bookseller spluttered with a full mouth. 'I only came across all of these documents five days ago and my attention was directed to the letter.'

Jerome picked at his food as he turned his attention to the typed pages. He read through it once silently before returning to the beginning. 'It's written in the first person, almost as if Arsan was trying to imitate the style of the letter.'

'Or create a forgery, perhaps,' Ismâil added as he began his second course, a large chicken-meat kebab. 'To be translated and written into Ottoman Turkish later.'

'Perhaps.' Jerome nodded his head.

'What does it say?'

'Do you want me to read it to you?' Jerome asked, knowing inevitably the answer would be yes.

Ismâil grunted, his mouth full.

'Oh, very well! I hope it's worth it,' Jerome growls.

The bookseller shrugs.

Jerome began, reading through a paragraph carefully then returning to the start to give his translation, ' *"I felt like a thief in the night as I moved towards a large storage chest that occupied one corner of the small workshop attached to the Köprülü library. I had not been in the workshop for nearly a year, it seemed from the layers of accumulated dust neither had anybody else. I watched the fine particles of this dust bellow up through the beams of early morning light before sliding back the small bolt that secured the chest lid. A memory of happier days in the workshop came back to me and pausing for a moment, a silent prayer escaped my lips for the departed soul of my friend and master, Abazade Effendi.*

At that point a cold chill suddenly made the hairs on the back of my neck. Abazade Effendi had been killed by falling masonry, three years previously, at the Panigra bastion of the castle of Candia when he had accompanied his friend, the Great Vizier Fazil Ahmet Pasha Köprülü, on the campaign to finally end the interminable siege of Candia in Crete. Despite his martyr's death at the site of a glorious victory I regretted that our time together had been far too short. I had grown to love him as a son would a father. Before leaving for Crete, Abazade Effendi had arranged for me to complete my calligraphy training under his own former master, Dervis Ali and I had duly received my iscadet diploma. Our association also had other benefits as Dervis Ali was also a great archer and had welcomed me into the Archer's tekke near the Ok Meydani, the Field of the Arrows. It was the comradeship of the lodge that determined my decision about my future following the death of Abazade Effendi.

Because of the friendship of the Vizier Fazil and Abazade Effendi, the Vizier, on his return from Crete, offered me either the custodianship of the Köprülü library or the position of an Aga in his own personal guard. I knew by then that I would prefer the company of soldiers to the isolation of the library and had willingly accepted the captaincy. I truly enjoyed being a soldier and prayed daily that my friend and master in paradise would not judge me too harshly for turning my back on the glory of the letters to wield a bow instead . . .

By now I had an increasing sense of danger in the deserted library, as if someone was watching. I leant down into the chest and extracting a thick bundle of parchment leaves that were tied together with a string of cotton. Then, after ensuring once more that I was still alone in the workshop I lifted a false panel that disguised a secret compartment in the bottom of the chest. From here I removed a thick leather-wrapped parcel before replacing the panel and closing the chest.

Moving quickly to another container on a nearby bench, I left down the parchment leaves and the parcel and selected four reed shafts from the upright clay pot to fashion the pens for my work. I knew that these particular reeds had been buried in dung for up to two years and as I rolled them between my fingers, admired the burnished colour and felt their hardness. I also knew that like the reed shafts I too had grown hard; in the dung heap that was the political manoeuvring of the Sultan's court. Abazade Effendi had often warned me of this possibility and how, I wish now, I had listened and learnt the lesson more.

'This is long enough and smooth enough for a flight arrow,' I whispered while admiring one of the reeds and looking down its length. A dove disturbed by my voice hopped along his ledge. I smiled at the bird's unease as I felt it also. The sense of unease was everywhere in the empire. People were cautious. The Sultan Mehmed Han, known as Avci, the Hunter, had recently issued a ferman, from his encampment at Larissa, ordering that his own half-brothers, those that remained imprisoned in the cage of the palace harem, were to be executed by strangulation with a silken rope. To me, although I did not agree with the killing of the innocent princes, it was not an altogether unexpected demand of the Sultan. He was just continuing the practice of his predecessors in removing rivals to the throne, particularly when his own queen, Gulnus, had given birth to a surviving son. Others, were not so understanding. Over 40,000 of Istanbul's citizens gathered on the Ok Meydani to object to the order being carried out. I knew however that it had been the Sultan Mehmed's own mother, the Valide Sultana Turhan, who had seduced the Janissary Aga

and who, with his help, had incited a group of Janissaries to storm the palace and free the princes. The Viziers thorough and secret police anticipated this plan and the Janissaries were captured.

I reflected on how I had executed these men on Vizier Fazil's orders, impaling them without hesitation. I watched them die slowly at first and then quickly as the sharpened bamboo stakes had finally penetrated from their bowels to their hearts. 'They were misguided and stupid,' I murmured as I ran my finger over the ends of the reed shafts to test their strength, 'to listen to the entreaties of a woman.' I reflected for a second before adding, 'But no more stupid than I'.

I never had much time for the love of a woman as my needs could, and were, satisfied by readily available slave boys and the intermittent bounty of a victorious campaign. But that had all changed a year previously, when I saw Roxanna for the first time. Standing alone in the library, all danger seem to be forgotten as I closed my eyes and thought of those of my beautiful Roxanna and the memories of how my heart had leapt when she had finally agreed to elope with me from the house of the Sultana Sporcha, a house where the slave-girls were picked for their grace and beauty and forced to dance and entertain paying guests of the Sultana. I remembered the very moment when Roxanna told me she was carrying our child and the joy I felt coursing through my entire being when she recently gave birth to our son, a fine son called Kasim, now ten weeks old. Our love had also brought great pain and danger, as the Sultana Sporcha was still looking for her missing slave. Nobody must know where she is hidden, from the clutches of that devil-woman.

Leaning against the chest I sighed as I pondered on the power of a Sultan's command. How it would be to have that power. Reaching into my pocket I recovered a scroll of paper, which had lain hot against my chest. This was the berat or imperial order that had arrived from Larissa yesterday. Unravelling the scroll as I held it up to the light, I once again admired the stylised turgha seal of the Sultan that adorned the top of the letter and which incorporated the words:

Shah Mehmed Han, son of Ibrahim Han, the ever victorious.

To one side of the turgha, in a decorated window, written in the Sultan's own hand, was the hatt-I humayun order of the sultan:

Let my illustrious decree be put into effect; beware of opposing it.

I felt my heart miss a beat. 'Do you hear that little dove? A message in the Sultan's own hand to me, Iskender Sidanli: Let my illustrious decree be put into effect: beware of opposing it. You won't oppose it, will you small bird?' I laughed as I began to read the scroll again, the writing in the main of formal celi divani style of one of the court calligraphers, and a poor calligrapher at that:

We confirm on Karabatakzade Iskender Aga Sidanli, the tax-collecting rights previously granted to Abazade Effendi from his properties in the Bergos district. Furthermore, we do hereby commission from the same Karabatakzade Iskender Aga Sidanli, a student of the renowned calligraphers Abazade Effendi and Dervis Ali, whose work pleases Us greatly, and who is also a captain of Our champion, Sadrazam Kopruluzade Fazil Ahmed Pasha's archers, to execute a hilyeler **with the description of the glorious Prophet Mohammed by his son-in-law, Ali. The work shall be done on the finest parchment stained with the colour of pomegranates and bound in the leather of calf. Monies shall be provided from Our treasury for the purchase of first wash lapis lazuli blue and the finest yellow and green gold leaf to adorn the beauty of the words. It shall be executed in the sulus and nesih scripts and if this work is pleasing to Us and to Allah then further tax-collecting rights will be grant –" '**

'Let me look at that!' Ismâil interrupted.

Jerome passed over the paper and watched the bookseller examine the writing while picking at some of his food. 'What do you think, Ismâil?'

'I have no doubt that this is a made up story but it is almost certainly based on original source material. Material that is now gone unfortunately.'

'Why do you say that?'

'It would have been together. Never mind. Finish your reading.' The old bookseller shrugged as he handed the sheet back.

Jerome obliged, ' *"The berat had been dated almost a month previously and I knew that I would need to get working on the commission soon. 'But not today, little dove, not today! Too much to do.' I murmured while picking up the bundle of parchment leaves, the leather bound parcel, and the reeds from the chest lid.*

The following day was the day when all the best archers would hold a competition on the Ok Meydani and I was determined to gain the embroidered silk for the longest flight. My arm had never been stronger. My abide monument stone would mark the Field of Arrows with the prowess of that arm and I would be this year's champion. It was my destiny. 'After that nobody will oppose me! Today I will be your champion, my sweetest Roxanna and together we will find Paradise,' I whispered while taking one last look at the workshop. I needed to hurry as a boat was waiting to take me up the Golden Horn. I needed to prepare my arrows." '

Jerome stopped reading, pushed away his plate of uneaten food and lit a cigar. He didn't feel hungry.

'Not much there so far,' Ismâil volunteered.

'No. The rest of it is much of the same.' Jerome shook his head in exacerbation.

'You don't know that. There might be clues. Go on!' Ismâil encouraged.

Jerome began reading aloud again, ' *"On the following day, the afternoon sun had moved to my back by the time I had climbed up the steep hill from the jetty at Kasimpasa. As I reached the steps of the shooting platform there was a favourable wind coming from the sea to gently lick the flags that fluttered in the courtyard of the archer's tekke, high on the hill at the southern end of the Ok Meydani. Ahead, on the gently rising plain I could just make out the monument stones of previous years champions. The target for this year's competition was to be*

the Puta-Tobra idol to the northeast. The target lay about . . ."
What's this word? And what are these idols he mentions?' Jerome
pointed out a word on the typescript to Ismâil.

'Its pronounced as you see it. *Gez.* It's a unit of measurement,'
Ismâil explained. 'In reality the Puta-Tobra was one of three
statues taken from a Christian church by Fatih in 1453, after he
captured the city, and set up in the *Ok Meydani* as targets for
archery practice.'

Jerome returned to his reading, ' *"The target lay about 1200
gez away on the small hill that overlooked the Piyale Pasha
mosque. Looking around at the remaining men on the platform I
knew my turn would soon arise and so it was time to select my
equipment and do the pisrev exercises to prepare my arm and
concentration.*

*My bow was smaller than those, which I use for warfare,
measuring between its nocks, the distance from my right armpit
to the tips of the fingers of my outstretched left hand. It was a
composite reflex bow, the core of the three sections made of
maple and Cornelian cherry. The belly and handle had an overlay
of birch wood and buffalo horn but giving its strength were the
pasted layers of battered sinew of wild deer using the fish glue
made from the mouth lining of Danube sturgeons. This particular
bow had been seasoned for a year before the tillering and
stringing took place and now as I checked its strength and
flexibility was happy that the heating in the conditioning box for
the previous four days had achieved its desired dryness. The
shoulders or kasans of the bow were decorated on the inner side
with taliq script calligraphy of my own. On the upper one I had
inscribed 'Would that this arrow burn itself in the heart of Omar,'
and on the lower, a favourite quote of Abazade Effendi from al-
Bistami: 'al-kamil al-tamm – the perfect and complete'. The silk
woven string was taut against my pull and nodding my head,
both in homage and satisfaction, I slung the bow over my
shoulder and headed for my place. I was content with its
suitability. The bow was, in our family's language, a keman
kajani, or a strong bow.*

I could see Abdul, my servant, whom I had sent on ahead earlier that morning, rushing towards me. Abdul was a mute but we communicated in the sign language of the mutes that I had learnt in Fazil Pasha's household. He was excited. He informed me that my main rival had shot 1030 gez so I knew I would have to be at my best. I chose three arrows, all of which were made of pine, measured half the length of the bow and had carved tips of bone. I next tested the resistance of the nocks which were made of antelope horn and which ensured that the string would be held. Two of the arrows had flights made of eagle feathers but for the third I had decided to use a little of the parchment I use for calligraphy. When this particular arrow flew it whistled, the sound made by the air flowing through holes drilled in the tip. This was a chaush or messenger arrow adapted for the test of distance. A small drill of gold had been inserted near the nock to change the balance and as I tasted the wind I knew that this arrow would be my champion.

Soon it was time. I walked slowly to the firing mound. The wind rustled in the nearby trees. It felt a little more humid than it had been previously and I knew then that its direction was swinging to the southeast. Unslinging the bow I chose the chaush arrow and rested this in the grooved silar arrow guide that was strapped to my left arm. Slowly I gripped and un-gripped the belly until comfortable with the hold. My hands were dry. I nocked the arrow on the silk string and gradually drew back on the string with the siri-mahi zihgir or thumb mounted draw ring made from a shark's tooth. When the string reached my right ear the arrow tip no longer was visible at the belly but lay withdrawn inside the silar. My left arm held rigid as I fought against the power of the bow and the urge to release. The watching crowds quietened, but I waited and waited.

I knew it would come. A slight squall ruffled the hairs at the base of my neck and I understood. Rotating about fifteen degrees to take aim at the solitary western wall minaret of the Piyale Pasha mosque in the valley below I then raised the elevation until satisfied with the angle. The squall was now lifting the thin cotton strips woven at right angles into the silk thread. Suddenly I knew it was the right time, my thumb released and the arrow flew from its hold. The string sang and the soaring arrow whistled in its assent. 'Fly kalam! Fly my messenger. Fly on the back of Allah's breath,' I whispered as I watched the arrow soar higher and higher into the sky before it finally crested to begin its descent. This was not as abrupt as the people around me expected and the arrow seemed to take wings and glide further and further into the distance. The crowds began cheering as they saw the destar bozmak or signal turban being thrown in the air to indicate the arrow has landed safely and its distance could be measured. Ten minutes later Abdul came running breathless up the hill waving his hands. For most of the crowds these were just the wild movements of excitement but for Abdul and me they were a voice, a language. 1090 gez was the signal . . .

I knew then that I was the champion. For a moment I thought of how this feat would bring great honour to me, to the archer's lodge and to my regiment but then I thought of Roxanna, my beautiful Roxanna. She would be waiting for me in our secret place and tonight our pleasure would know no limits. I smiled broadly and bowed to the cheering onlookers before accepting the embroidered handkerchief of the victor. I also made sure that Abdul had retrieved the arrows and bow of my glory before turning and melting into the departing crowds that now streamed away from the Ok Meydani."'

A silence descended for a moment and hovered over the two men.

'What is it, Jaffa?' The bookseller asked.

'It finishes at that point,' he eventually, and unnecessarily, said as he signalled to the waiter, ordering a beer for both of them.

Ismâil declined in favour of a coffee.

'What are *gez* measurement units?' Jerome asked as the beer arrived. He pulled out a small Turkish-English dictionary he always carried in his pocket and searched for the word. 'It says here *gez* means a plumb-line or back-sight.'

'Now it does but in the old days it was a measurement, like a cubit, and was, as far as I understand, about five feet or two paces, just short of a yard and three-quarters,' Ismâil explained.

'Impressive arrow flights,' Jerome said as he calculated the distance.

'Yes, some of the *abidesi*, the old competition monuments on the *Ok Meydani*, record distances of 1000 *gez* or more,' Ismâil agreed before adding, 'Poetic licence I suspect, measured as a walking distance up and down the hills of the *Ok Meydani* rather than as the crow flies over a flat piece of ground! As far as I know modern tests with old Turkish bows suggest a flight distance of about 850 yards.'

'Not much help for our problem,' Jerome said after pausing to sip his beer.

'No. At least no clues to its likely whereabouts that I can sense.' Ismâil shook his head in a disappointed fashion but then smiled. 'However . . .' He pulled another typewritten page from his pocket and handed it to Jerome.

'What is –'

'Read it. It's the final page. I think you will find it interesting.'

Jerome obliged, ' *"However, in the blindness of my joy, I did not notice the two green-turbaned azap soldiers, from the garrison of the prison of Rumelia Hisar, who hurried to follow in my footsteps. They –"* Shit. Jesus!' Jerome stared at the paper. Underneath the typescript was a handwritten note: *Silander 402-A, Curragh. October 1998,* and the signature of old Prof Symmonds.

'Interesting eh?' Ismâil smiled.

'No wonder the old bastard wanted me out of there. He was after it himself. How did you come across this?'

'Let's say, your friend Professor Symmonds accident was almost certainly no accident. This and the earlier document I showed you were recovered from his car before they –'

'They?'

'You know whom I mean.'

Jerome nodded.

'By a local, who came upon his car in an isolated area. Stole the briefcase and luckily sold its contents onto a fence, a man I have dealings with on occasions . . .'

'Jesus. This is dangerous ground.' Jerome lit another cigarette.

'Very much! By the way how did it go with Alanna?'

'We fought. She stormed off.'

'I see. Probably for the best.' Ismâil looked relieved. 'What should we do about the Book? Where to next?'

'I don't know. But . . . Perhaps there might yet be another avenue to explore. An unexpected and strangely coincidental one.'

'What do you mean, Jaffa?' the bookseller probed.

Jerome explained about his earlier phone call from Mac. When he finished the old bookseller smiled.

'*Insha' Allâh! Insha' Allâh*, my friend. That might be the original material that Arsan had on which to base his story, and which he sent to Beatty to entice him with regard to the Book of the Messenger.'

'I wonder if Beatty ever saw it?' Jerome pondered aloud as he got up to stretch his legs.

'What? The Book or the letter your friend has seen in Dublin.'

'Either, I suppose.'

'Who knows the secrets hidden in dead men's hearts?'

A loud knock on the door brings Flanagan back to reality. Its nearly 6.00 pm. Felicity Fellows is early, or eager, he hopes. I need sex badly or even bad sex, he thinks, remembering to place the newly released re-mastering of Coltrane's *Love Supreme* on the CD player before going to answer the door.

'Hello,' he says expectantly before focusing and stepping back in surprise. '*Jack!* Jesus. I wasn't expecting you so soon.'

'Disturbing you, am I?' Jack Dawson pushes past him, alcohol fumes wafting in his wake.

'No. Well yes. I'm . . . someone's coming in a little while.' He waits at the door, holding it open.

'Nooky, huh. You don't waste time do you, Flanagan?' Jack's

voice at first is brittle, bitter. Then hard, 'Who is the unfortunate victim?'

'Listen, Jack. I'm not in any mood to deal with this now. Nor are you. Tomorrow would be better. Give you time to sober up. Say around 10.00. Ok!'

He watches him hesitate for a moment. Unsteady in both emotion and stance.

'No, Flanagan. We'll sort it out now.'

'Fuck off, Jack. Get out,' he shouts holding the door open.

Jack Dawson grunts, looks for a confrontation but then seems to think better of it. As he exits past him through the doorway, the door on the other side of the hallway suddenly opens. Felicity Fellows is standing there, checking on the commotion. Jack Dawson sees her.

'I hope its not you he's waiting for, maam.' He turns and looks back at him, a sneer ripping his features. 'Because this . . . this *gentleman* here is one sorry bastard and will bring you nothing but pain.'

She says nothing but he sees that her face says it all. They watch in silence as Jack Dawson tacks his way out the building.

'A bit worse for wear,' she says, watching.

'Yes. I'm very sorry about that. Listen! I was just about to pop out to buy some mixers. I will not be long. '

Her eyes flicker, unsure.

'About . . . about tonight, Jerome. I'm . . . I'm afraid I have to cancel. Something urgent has come up. I hope I have not put you to any trouble.'

'No. I understand. Some other time perhaps? We should talk about it.'

'That would be nice. . . I must rush.'

'Sure. Goodnight Felicity.'

Her door is already closed. Nice but not likely, Flanagan thinks, closing his own door behind him.

I opened my mouth, and nothing came out. Coltrane said this, he remembers. The morning after he played his tenor sax in Antibes on 26 July 1965 and the chant-silenced version of "A Love Supreme".

8

THE THREE-CORNERED LIGHT

"Now, you cannot ask a man to meet a ghost,
because ghosts are not to be counted on."

Oliver St John Gogarty • *Sackville Street*

Coltrane is discarded – leaving before the applause – and
Flanagan puts on Joe Cocker instead. Plays it loud: rocking head-
banging loud. Hears Felicity leave. Good grace to pretend she is
actually going somewhere, he thinks. There might be a chance
after all. Later perhaps he'll listen for her coming back, step out,
nonchalantly invite her in. She'll . . .

He silently curses Jack Dawson and drinks three single malts
quickly to fuel his annoyance. By the third his stomach burns and
he makes himself a supper of yoghurt and PepAcid and waits for
the pain to go. The computer is still on, and in the distance he
sees its pulsing light. With a lit cigarette and a fourth whiskey in
hand he goes towards it.

Jack will question me and I need to be ready, he thinks,
reaching the table. Rio's diary boots:

Armpit Diary,
January 15:
I'm writing this in Belfast's Jury's Inn. *Deadly quiet* – Irish

expression, as if quietness is a condition only of the dead. Came up to my room after dinner and not bothering to go down again. Undressed, I sit in bed, laptop on my lap. It's warm like a hot water bottle. Read recently about somebody's penis being scorched by a computer. 'A lap-dancing injury and will probably get *condensation* for it,' Mac had quipped.

Back to me. Met the famous – infamous – Jerome Augustine Flanagan yesterday, at a pub on Stephen Street. *The Hairy Lemon* . . . What a name! I sat in the panelled snug by the window waiting for him. Across the road is a bigger bar called *Break for the Border*, and I was just thinking of doing the same when he finally arrived, almost an hour late, introduced himself with the briefest of apologies, 'Sorry. I'd a doctor's appointment. Took longer than expected.' Nothing trivial I hope, I wanted to say in half-jest, annoyed by the waiting around, but decided against it. He asked me to move to the far, less visible, end of the pub.

I obliged . . . too easily. And Flanagan knew it. He smiled at me before heading for the counter. I watched as he waited and paid for our coffees. He, I noted then with a slight feeling of disappointment, was not very tall but, on the credit side, had a welterweight boxer's build and to compliment this a slight shuffling gait, like a fighter's movement in the ring. I guess he is about 45 or so, however, with only the slightest hint of grey flecking in his abundant sandy hair, it is hard to be sure. He was wearing a cream, well-creased, linen suit with a blue, linen shirt underneath. And sneakers! Ugh!

Some men, Jack and Grandpa Dawson included, might age but they don't get old – unless they have to identify dead daughters or acknowledge their mistakes. 'It's in their eyes,' Nan Greta once declared in words of cautious admiration. 'Men age first in their eyes and some never lose the sparkle; never get old.' Even at a distance I could see that Flanagan had dangerous eyes. They were scanning the perimeter of the room as he walked, momentarily locking onto someone or something that caught his interest. I watched as his focus turned to a blonde woman sitting at a nearby table and who had been, quite obviously, making the same appraisal of him as I was.

As he neared the table I moved sideways to make room for him. He seemed to either miss or deliberately ignore the invitation and instead, leaving the coffee cups down, half-turned away from me to ask the blonde woman if he could take one of the unoccupied chairs at hers.

'Sure, as long as *you* bring it back to me though,' the woman purred.

'Bitch,' I hissed while sipping the froth of my coffee. He smiled as he pulled over the chair and sat down with his back to the window and the street.

'What did you say?' His voice was soft and teasing.

'Oh . . . rich. The coffee is rich, just the way I like it,' I blurted.

'I thought you might. The coffee is excellent here.' He looked around the room. 'Atmosphere is everything. Don't you think?'

'Yes.'

It was already mid-afternoon and most of the city's late-lunchers were already back at work. Apart from the blonde woman, who persisted in lazily fluttering her availability in Flanagan's direction at every possible opportunity, we had the pub to ourselves. I reached down and retrieved my artist's portfolio case and rested it on my lap, waiting for him to move our coffee cups to one end before opening it and carefully laying it on the table. Inside, protected by transparent plastic envelopes, were the pictures that Mac had taken of the parchment that morning, and subsequently developed. I had worked continuously on it over the weekend and as I thought, the best results were obtained after a tannin soak in a weak solution of oak gall. Three of the photographs detailed a beautiful and finely defined script and, more than pleased with the end results, couldn't hide the smile of satisfaction as I rotated the portfolio to orientate the photographs in Flanagan's direction.

I was less pleased as he ignored them and continued to stare at me. He kept staring in silence until frustration – annoyance –

got the better of me. Enough of this, I'm not that desperate, I thought, deciding not to indulge him in the game. 'What do you think?' I demanded, nodding towards the photographs.

'Tell me about you, Dr Dawson.' He continued to stare. Not blinking.

'Rio. My name is Rio.'

'Tell me about you, Rio.'

'Why? What has it got to do with the photographs?' I was losing the staring game.

'Nothing. I just like what I see in your eyes and I would like to know more. It's not a condition.' His mouth creased into a slight smile as he broke off his stare and looked down at the portfolio. He slowly began to draw out one of the photographs from its plastic envelope. 'I'm more than happy to look at these for you and give you any help I can.'

'You're serious aren't you?'

'Yes!'

'I could lie.'

'You might skirt certain issues but you won't lie.'

'How do you know? My eyes?' I mocked.

'They are beautiful . . . but no, Mac told me!' He laughed with a gentle teasing laugh.

'The traitor!' I laughed with him before launching into what Jack calls my well-rehearsed "talking to strangers" resume, when I can be anybody I want, and often am.

'I think you skimmed over pages five, ten, eleven and 27,' he mumbled as I finished, his eyes drifting away.

'What do you mean?' I reddened at being so quickly found out.

'Despite all the information, I now know even less about you. It's like camouflage. The colouring has hidden the detail.' His eyes locked onto mine again, and he waited.

'For example?' I snapped back.

'Well, let me see. I know what you liked about hiking in the jungles of Borneo but have no idea about what you liked about the person you went with.'

'That's personal.'

'Damn right it is. . . and a much better basis for interaction, if you don't mind me saying,' he said in a distracted away as he began to carefully inspect the photograph he had chosen.

'You have a lousy chat-up technique, Flanagan,' I said suddenly.

He looks up. 'Is that what I'm here for?'

'No!'

'Good. Because I'm terrible at it.'

I looked at him for a long time, a mixture of irritation and apprehension welling up inside. 'I don't want you to think I'm a pushover,' I finally said, defensively, instantly regretting I had said it at all.

'I wouldn't dare.' He smiled briefly before returning to his examination of the photograph.

'I'm ex-FBI, you know?'

'I know. Mac told me.'

'Good, because if I reveal any of my real self to you, my real secrets, then you know I'll have to kill you.'

'Some things are worth dying for, Rio,' he said in an eerily sincere way.

'*Tres gallant, mon cher.*' I blushed.

'*Mon plaisir, mademoiselle.*'

'What about you, Dr Flanagan?'

'Jerome, please or Jaffa, if you'd prefer. My close friends call me that.'

'What's your story, Jerome? Mac only gave me the briefest of hints about your somewhat mysterious life.' I was a little annoyed that he was holding back and hadn't taken the opportunity to lean into the space I had created for him.

He seemed to hesitate for a moment before once again, this time slowly, raising his eyes towards me. 'I'm single, reasonably solvent and available –'

'That's a *cheap* shot, Flanagan. Whatever Mac might have said, I'm not that desperate,' I flared, leaning forward to snatch the photograph from his grasp. It was me who had made myself available and he had thrown it back in my face. But why so aggressively, I wondered. 'What's with the heavy come on, Flanagan? Are you always so forward . . . so tactless?' I asked.

'You're right, Rio. I'm sorry. At this moment in time I feel in such a hurry about things and don't want to create misunderstandings or play games,' he said with obvious honesty.

'Why? Do you not like games?' I asked, trying to lighten the atmosphere.

He hesitated, looked away over my shoulder towards the window. 'Games are all I know, Rio. It's reality that I don't deal with very well.' He pulled the photograph away from my reach, distracting me from what I wanted to ask. 'For your information, Mac said very little about you. He seems quite protective, almost as if warning me not to mess with you. What I meant to say is that I would like to tell you my story. I cannot think of anyone else in my present that I could say that to. It's a lonely admission.'

'It's also a very quick appraisal of my willingness.'

'I tend to do that, I'm afraid.'

'I see,' I mumbled, somewhat appeased. Jerome Augustine Flanagan, I realised, was an enigma – no more than me I suppose – and I was finding making a judgement about him difficult. The blonde woman had finally surrendered the floor but as she left, raised an eyebrow. I couldn't help returning a slightly smug smile.

Flanagan didn't, or didn't appear to, even notice. 'This is a very interesting letter, Rio. Is it still permitted to call you by your first name, now that were enemies,' he said, in a very considered fashion.

'Adversary is sometimes more interesting, Jerome. There is less bullshit.'

'And often more enjoyable in the cessation of hostilities. We should get on well with each other as we seem to be equally curious about one another.'

'That's a nice way of putting it.'

'Its an old Bedouin saying, probably originating from the observation of how a new camel would fit in with an established desert caravan and where to place him in that caravan.'

His warm smile disarmed and I held out my hand for him to take. It was a firm handshake and he let it continue for just the right length of time. 'Do you like the desert, Jerome?' I asked.

'Yes. I think Rosita Forbes once put it the best.'

'Rosita Forbes?'

'An adventurous traveller and writer of the 1920s.'

'I *know* who she is?'

He looked at me, strangely, as if suddenly impressed. 'Do you? How? I mean not many people do,' he questioned.

'Typical man,' I said. 'Putting indulgent, or even masturbatory, layers between you and the outside world. Layers waiting to be peeled back so that you are finally impressed. Are you?'

'Have you read much of her work?'

'A little.'

'How did . . .'

'I'll put you out of your misery, Jerome. Jack has his house near where she lived at Unicorn Cay in Eleuthera.'

'Jack? Eleuthera?'

'Did I not mention him in my resume.' Even this short time later I couldn't remember what version I'd given.

'No.'

'Jack's my uncle, and guardian angel. I often go to stay there. Eleuthera's an island in the Caribbean. In the '30s it was the hang-out of a group of very independent women writers.'

'I see,' he said, nodding his head.

'What was it you were about to say about her?' I asked.

'Forbes once wrote that when you were two or three days into the desert all smells and perfumes of your previous existence disappear and all you can smell is the aroma of the sand, unadulterated by flower or wind.'

'And the occasional camel!'

'Perhaps,' he said, frowning at my flippancy.

'I'm sorry,' I said. 'I did not mean to break the spell.'

'I think I'd be waiting a long time for a spell of mine to work on you Rio Dawson. I get carried away sometimes. In truth the smell of the desert is the aroma of solitude. I go there to get away.'

'From what?'

'Myself, mainly. Do you ever get that lonely that you have to seek out a greater desolation.'

I hesitated. 'Sometimes, but for me it's the high-mountains and powder-snow of the mornings.'

'Mornings are important in solitude,' he said.

'Why?' I asked.

'It's the light, the peculiar light of a new day. The Bedouin call it the three-cornered light, referring as it does to the light of the sunrise coming through the slit in their tents. It's a cold light, equally as cold as that on high mountains; illuminating but not yet warming; a light for your soul not your body. Somehow it gives a definition to the solitude.'

I sat and watched him for a moment, uneasy and easy at the same time. 'It's a very romantic description,' I laughed.

'I used to know a poem about it. Not all that romantic.'

'Recite it for me. Please,' I encouraged.

'No. Not now!' And his eyes drifted off again, somewhere else.

'In that case Jerome, if you could come out of your tent, or wherever you've suddenly disappeared to, perhaps you might get on with explaining about the letter. Are you able to read the Arabic?'

He smiled, a thin smile, and returned to the business in hand. 'It's not Arabic as it happens, Rio, but Persian and in a very fine *nasta'liq* script at that. The writer is, was a calligrapher of some considerable merit,' he remarked, looking closely at the page. He continued to inspect it for some time.

'Well?' I asked, impatiently.

'After Mac's call I was so looking forward to seeing this.' Jerome waved the photograph in the air. 'Now that I have, I'm both relieved and disappointed in a way.'

'Why?'

'Oh! It's just when Mac told me that you had found a document possibly written by one Karabatakzade Aga, I was half expecting the document to be something else.' He paused for a second to gather his thoughts.

'What do you mean, something else?' I asked, a little puzzled.

'Oh, sorry . . . what I meant to say, Rio, is that I expected the document to be written in Ottoman Turkish. In a way I'm relieved it's in Persian, as my Turkish is not that good, yet also am a little bit disappointed because it is a personal letter.'

'What do you mean?'

'I was hoping it might be a court or state document, given the quality of the script. Do you want me to read it to you?'

'Oh yes. Please do.' The excitement in my voice was too obvious.

'It begins, "*To my dearest father*".' Flanagan kept his voice low as his finger scanned the words from right to left, ' "*I am so sorry that I have not written to you for such a long time because so much has happened and I need to explain the events that have overtaken me. A year or so ago I fell in love with a beautiful woman called Roxanna. My love for her has been both my salvation and the cause of my destruction. In her I have become the Perfect Man, and together we have produced a son, Kasim, who has the stars and the moon on his head, and your eyes.*

In the midst of all this happiness sadness has now descended. When I first met Roxanna, she was dancing for my entertainment, in the house of her mistress the Sultana Sporcha, the brothel-owning former wife of Sultan Mehmed Han's late father Ibrahaim Han. Despite the devil-woman's threats Roxanna refused to be a harlot and a more virtuous person you would never encounter. I was made aware, when we first met, that her grace and beauty had been denied to the Royal harem by the Sultana Sporcha, who had refused Sultan Mehmed Han's demand on the grounds that Roxanna was a virgin and a freewoman. Yet, the same devil-woman dismissed my own offer of marriage saying that Roxanna was in fact a slave of her house and therefore not free to marry. Both lies were used to ensure that Roxanna would remain in her house of entertainment to lighten the gold-bearing pockets of her guests.

In the end my heart would not stand us being apart and so Roxanna and I eloped. We managed to remain hidden but recently, in the midst of the joy of winning the archery competition on the

Ok Meydani, I relaxed my guard and was followed to our secret place by spies in the employ of the devil-woman. Because of her lies to the Sultan about Roxanna she feared being caught in the web of her own deceit and having finally discovered our whereabouts reported me to the Sultan saying that I deserve death for my defilement of His rightful property.

So it is to be, my dearest father. In the presence of Fazil Pasha, my patron since the death of Abazade Effendi, I have received the order for my death and for Roxanna and Kasim to be taken into the imperial harem in Odout Pasha. I don't welcome this death but it is to be. Fazil Pasha has allowed me the time and freedom to write this letter and to settle my affairs. My faithful friend Abdul, will deliver this letter and also a letter for my son that I wish you to guard. Give it to him when he is old enough to understand.

I have given Abdul freedom from his bondage but take him into your heart and house and he will explain more than I can write here in the short time left to –" '

At that point Jerome abruptly stopped reading and looked at me, a slightly puzzled look on his face.

'Is it finished?' I asked. 'Why did you stop?'

'Phyllis would probably have been able to read this. Her Persian is quite good. Why didn't you ask her?' he asked.

'I've left a copy for her, but she is away until tomorrow. Anyway, as you already pointed out, I did want to meet you, intrigued as I was by what Mac had told me and . . .' she paused.

'And what?' he asked.

'. . . the rumours about you that still linger in the dark passages of the museum.'

'I see. Are you always so conniving?'

'Sometimes.' I blushed.

'Are you intrigued?'

'Too early to say, I'd say. Curious is strong enough for now.'

'I'll take what I can get.'

'Is the letter finished, Jerome?' He seemed very hesitant to continue.

'Not quite,' he eventually answered before returning to his reading. 'But the next five or six lines are in a very old script that I cannot decipher. It changes again towards the end. ' *"I have taken care to hide it in the meadow of my sweetest victory and there you will find its flowering. Count out the hidden numbers of **our messenger spirit**, and pace those numbers starting in a line from the Puta-Tobra idol to the. . ."* ' He looked up. 'It finishes at that point, but there would have been a second page.' Flanagan suddenly sounded annoyed.

'How lovely. How sad?' I ignored his tone as I thought of the doomed lovers. 'When was it written?'

'1080 years after the Hejira, 1669 in our calendar.'

'Do you think it is by Karabatakzade Aga?'

'Almost certainly! Karabatakzade Iskender Aga Sidanli, to give him his full title, was a student of Abazade Effendi and his family were originally scribes to the Persian Shah, hence the unusual letter in Persian. It would have been his father's first language and the natural medium of any communication between them.'

'What do you think he is referring to when he said he hid something in the meadow of his sweetest victory?' I took out my small notebook and began to write some notes.

Suddenly he leant across and held my hand. He said nothing for a moment but when he did, his voice was sharp and direct. 'Where's the *mus'ir*, Rio?'

'The what?' I was puzzled by his stridency. 'What in God's sake are you talking about?' I said pulling my hand from his grip.

He held up the photograph he had been examining and, turning it to face me, pointed to the bottom left hand corner. 'You know very well what I'm talking about Rio. The *mus'ir*, the pointer or catchword, or if you prefer, the *rakib* or watchman, is missing. This is an unfinished letter by master calligrapher and by force of habit there would probably have been a *mus'ir* in the bottom left hand corner to be repeated as the first word on the next page. The photograph is unclear but there looks like a defect in that area.' He tapped at the surface before angrily questioning me. 'Did *you* remove it?'

'Eh!' I felt my face going red.

'Did you Rio?' His tone was less strident but reminded me of how my grandfather would confront me whenever he suspected me of sneaking tadpoles or wounded animals into the house.

'Yes.'

'For your ink and paper analysis I suspect.' He probed and I nodded. 'Is there a photograph of the original with the *mus'ir* in place?' he demanded.

I watched as he pulled the other photographs from their envelopes and started examining them carefully. 'No,' I said truthfully. 'The corner where the catchword was written had been bent back on itself like a dog-ear. The piece of parchment came away almost spontaneously as I straightened it out so that is the piece I sent for analysis. I had done this before Mac did the pre-tannin soak photographs. It was the most distinct sample of the original ink, probably preserved from fading by the fold back.'

'Did you copy the word?'

'Of course!'

'Where is it? In your office.'

'Why all the questions?' I asked.

There was a sudden edginess to his voice, as if he was afraid of something. 'Where is it, Rio?'

'In my apartment, stuffed into a book I'm reading at the moment.'

'And the original parchment?'

'In the small "work in progress" safe at the lab. I'm planning to remount and frame the parchment on Saturday.'

'Why not tomorrow?'

'I'm leaving on the early train for a conference in Belfast. I'm there until late on Friday.'

'That'll be ok, I suppose. You'll need to make the *mus'ir* copy more secure though. You must hide its whereabouts.' He leant back in the chair and pulled out a packet of cigarettes from his breast pocket. He proffered the packet to me. '*Al-Hambra*. Syrian. They're quite mild.'

'No thanks,' I declined. My only nicotine indulgence has been the occasional mid-sized cigar when with Jack, his Cuban-exile friends and some serious cognac. I waited for Flanagan to light and inhale the first pull of the cigarette. 'Why all the questions about the parchment, Jerome? You sound worried about something.'

'I am, Rio. I was wrong about the value of this document. You don't realise what you have here.'

'What do you mean?'

'If I'm right, the parchment, and what it implies, could be dynamite.' He held up one of the photographs and waved it in front of me. 'It also places you in very great danger. Who else has seen these?'

'Mac of course! No one else. *What danger?*'

'Are you seeing anybody at the moment?'

'What's that got to do with it?'

'Are you?'

'Yes . . .' I protested defensively before continuing in a "so what" tone, 'Well no, as it happens.'

'Right. I want you to ring Mac and get him to come to your apartment tonight. Does he know where it is?'

'Yes, of course he does!'

He had a half-smile on his face.

'For your information Mac is a good friend but why all this concern? What danger?'

'Good. Tell him to bring all the negatives and any other prints he has.' He ignored my question to look at his watch before continuing. 'Listen its nearly 4.30. Ring him now and I will see you later. There is something I need to do first.'

I watched as he got up. '*You* don't know where I live, Jerome?'

'That's not a problem. Leave here at precisely 5.00 and head for your apartment. I'll be following you.'

'What's all this precaution for? *Tell me now* or I won't be going anywhere!' I demanded to his disappearing back.

'Please trust me, Rio,' he turned and mouthed from the doorway.

Before I had a chance to press him further he was gone and with him, I realised, went one of the photographs. I picked up my cell-phone and started to dial. It was a few minutes before I got through to Mac and another ten before I had convinced him to meet me at the apartment.

At exactly 5.00 I left the Hairy Lemon and pausing at the door looked up and down the street for a moment. There was no sign of Jerome Flanagan. I shook my head and pulling my coat in against the biting wind began the twenty minute walk that it would take me to reach home on Bride Street; one of the small streets close to St Patrick's Cathedral.

Stopping when I reached the road junction close to the old Iveagh Baths, I looked around once more. There was no sign of him but some of the early vagrant arrivals waiting to be admitted to the night hostel, on the opposite side of the street, eyed me suspiciously. I walked on up Bride Street with an increasing sense of unease that only evaporated when I saw Cormac McMurragh waiting at the front door of the apartment.

'Took your bleeding time!' he moaned.

'I'm sorry about all this, Mac. It wasn't my idea.' I brushed past him and inserted the door key. Once inside the small hallway I disabled the alarm system and we started removing our coats.

'Your FBI training might attract you to the shadow world that Jaffa inhabits, Rio but it does nothing for me. Where is Omar Sharif anyway?' Mac asked, his back to the unclosed door.

'Right here, you big gobshite!'

We both turned to see him standing in the doorway. He was looking back towards the street. 'All clear,' he murmured before stepping in and closing the door behind him.

'Phew! What a relief. I can now sleep easy in my bed knowing that the world is your safe mitts, Jaffa.' Mac winked at Rio, 'Will I put on some coffee?'

'Sure, Mac. You know where everything is. Jerome and I will go on into the lounge.' Jerome stood somewhat awkwardly in the hallway and I wondered if he was jealous of Mac's familiarity. I enjoyed the view. 'This way, Jerome. Make yourself at home . . . as well.' I moved towards the doorway that led into the lounge.

'He will. Have no fear on that score, girl,' Mac grunted before disappearing through a narrow doorway that led off the hallway into the kitchen.

'I'll bring this if I may.' He picked up the portfolio case from where I had left it down.

I looked back. 'Sure. Thanks.'

He followed me into the lounge, which is an L-shaped room. Along the longer axis, an old stable house in its tenement days but now incorporated into the refurbished building, the ceiling has been allowed to ascend to the pitch of the roof. I had fully intended the room to be minimalist: a white-walled, pine-floored, modern anonymous-future type of room. But then the floorboards started creaking – crying out at night. With each episode I rushed to hang something of my past, as if trying to dampen the cries. There was an old fly-fishing rod over the fireplace, some large montage photographs of Colorado and even a Navaho woven rug.

Jerome Flanagan looked smaller against the height of the room. He came to where I stood on the lowest rung of the spiral staircase that leads to the balcony walkway, which overlooked the lounge. I saw his eyes were taking in everything.

'Nice apartment,' he said. 'What have you got up there?' He pointed towards the balcony.

'A master bedroom with an en-suite shower and toilet, a second bathroom, and a smaller guest bedroom,' I answered stepping off the rung and moving towards the glass-topped dining table – my office. 'I'm sorry, Jerome, I should have asked you. Would you prefer a drink instead of coffee?'

'Thank God. For a while I thought this was going to be a dry, Puritan household. You never know with some Americans.'

'Whiskey or bourbon? Ice, water, soda?' I smiled, ignoring the jibe.

'Whiskey. Unadulterated please.'

'Sure. I'll join you.' I knelt down to open a small drinks cabinet that was situated beside a connecting door to the kitchen and knew that he was watching as my short dress concertinaed. The hem rode up and the waistline curved down to reveal the small of my back, I could feel the draft. Joyce told me the other day that many of her daughter's friends, now go to the teenage discos wearing the shortest skirts possible, and no underwear. Bushing they call it. I smiled as I thought about this while shouting into Mac, who was busy in the kitchen, 'Mac. Bring in some ice as well.' Standing up I held the bottle and tumblers in one hand as the other straightened my skirt.

'It had a certain appeal the way it was?' He smirked.

'Is that also a *puritan* observation,' I asked, pouring our drinks.

The door swung open and Mac came in with a tray of coffee mugs, a cafétière and napkins. Where did he find those, I wondered. He looked at me and then at the already poured glasses of whiskey. 'All of this effort wasted, it seems,' he whined as he placed the tray on the small table in the centre of the room. 'Shall we get on with it?' he demanded, sitting down with anonymous frustration.

I joined him on the leather-covered settee and Jerome took the remaining single armchair, pulling it closer to the table. He placed the portfolio at one end, accepted the whiskey glass from me before turning to Mac. 'Have you got the prints and negatives with you, Mac?' he asked while sipping the whiskey.

'Sure. But why all this cloak-and-dagger stuff?'

Jerome left down his glass and unzipped the portfolio. He then retrieved the photograph from his pocket that he had taken with him from our meeting earlier and held it up for a moment, waving it, threatening with it. 'Because of this . . . These photographs and the parchment are likely to place you *both* in great danger.'

'What the fuck –' Mac spluttered some of his heavily sweetened coffee across the table. A bit exaggerated, I thought, using a napkin to mop up the drops of spray.

'What do you mean, Jerome? What is so dangerous about an old parchment letter?' I leant forward to take the photograph from him. Our fingers touched for an instant and he offered no resistance.

'After I left you in the pub, I faxed this to a friend of mine who could decipher the lines written in the very old script. As I suspected it was an old *Kufic* script and they mention the Book of the Warnings of the Messenger Spirit, the *kitab al-dhikr al-Rûh.*'

'What are you on about?' Mac asked in a bored tone.

'Read those lines to us.' I handed him back the photograph. 'So Mac and I know exactly what's happening. I sort of filled him in on the rest of it over the phone.'

'Very well,' Jerome agreed as he looked at the photograph. ' *"There is one other important task that I need you to undertake, my beloved father. The true Secret is with us, the muserin, my father and I must discharge my duty. The kitab al-dhikr al-Rûh, the Book of the Warnings of the Messenger Spirit, trusted into my care by Abazade Effendi, must now become your responsibility."* '

'What is the Book of the Messenger Spirit, Jerome?' I sipped the whiskey and settled back in the chair. Mac was fidgeting beside me.

'It's the Holy Grail,' he said quietly.

'It's the. . .' Mac began, but seemed to change his mind. 'What do you mean, Jaffa?'

Jerome looked at both of us for a considerable time before answering. He suddenly seemed nervous. I was worried he might stop, and wanting him to continue gave him a smile of encouragement.

'As you are aware the revelations of Mohammed were initially dispersed in early Islam by the *kurrã'* or "reciters" and at the death of the Prophet in June 632ce, there was not in existence a definitive book or written collection of the revelations in the form of the al-Kur'ãn or Qur'an as we know it now. The gathering and compilation of the oral renditions resulted in about four or five slightly different written versions all of which were then suppressed by the third caliph, Uthman around about 650ce, when he commissioned an official edition. One of these early versions for example, attributed to one of Mohammed's secretaries, Ubaiy b. Ka'b contained two extra *suras* or chapters.'

'Explain it to her . . . to us about the Messenger book, Jaffa.' Mac leant forward, looking at his watch. He blushed slightly.

'You must understand that for many devout Muslims the

115

Qur'an is the word of God in revealed form and therefore unaltered in textual perfection since the revelations. However within the editorial compilation of the first official version some *ayat* or revelations were abrogated, or substituted if you like, at the intervention of Allah for something "better or similar", a possibility allowed for within the Qur'an. In most cases both the abrogated version and the substituted verses are retained, however there is strong evidence, particularly from al-Titmithi in his *Kitab al-Tafsir*, one of the six major works of authentic Islamic tradition, that some verses were omitted altogether. Rumours have persisted from earliest times that a collection of traditions known as the *kitāb al-dhikr al-Rûh*, written down by one Abu Dharr al-Ghifari, a *kurrā* known as the Fifth Muslim, who as Al-Tabari reported was sworn to secrecy by Mohammed, might contain the key to understanding the mysterious letters, the *al-fawatih* or *al-Muqatta'at*, seen at the beginning of 29 of the suras. For many scholars the letters are nothing more than prompts used to help the early reciters or *kurrā* and then retained in the written version. But for others, scholars and mystics alike, these letters are considered to be a pathway to the hidden treasures of eternal Truth placed within the Qur'an by God.'

'Mufti Flanagan and the Curry-Pots. Has a certain ring to it, don't you think, for a tribute band,' Mac interjected.

Jerome ignored him. 'The Arabic word for the Messenger Spirit, *al-Rûh*, has its origins in the word for wind or breath, as does spirit in Latin and Greek but in the Qur'an it was also used to define an intermediary and advocate spirit. More importantly the *Rûh al-Amin*, the Spirit Faithful to the Trust, and the *Rûh al-Qudus*, the Spirit of Holiness, are used as epithets within the Qur'an to point out the freedom from error or blemish in the Qur'an by the former and the Divine protection afforded against all tampering by the latter. Abu Dharr himself was reported to have clashed with Uthman over his intended compilation of the Qur'an and later, from very shortly after Uthman's death, there were whispers from Kufa that the *kitāb al-dhikr al-Rûh* had been placed in the keeping of Ali's secretary by Jirayr b. Abdullah al-

Dayali, the man who had buried Abu Dharr, and who, despite his master being deposed from the Caliphate in 658CE, had it still in his possession at the time of Ali's assassination in Kufa in January 661CE.'

'If it did exist, what happened to it?' I asked.

'It was supposed to have been seen in Baghdad in 885ce but then disappeared.'

'What's so dangerous about it?' Mac seemed genuinely intrigued.

'Some say that the supposed "missing" *ayat* from the official version, those seized upon by the Shi'at 'Ali party and since then by Shi'a in general as an official Sunni attempt to obliterate the importance of Ali, Mohammed's son-in-law, were to be found in it. Others have concentrated on *ayat* mentioning the very Christian idea of a Holy Spirit, or what St John called the *Paraklitos*, and how these Christian beliefs needed to be quickly expunged from an official version that extolled and encouraged the virtues of an emerging militant, and to a large extent, anti-Christian Islam.'

'The what?' I asked before I could stop myself.

'Did you not tell him about the engraving, Rio?' Mac slurped his coffee as he spoke, his eyes probing.

'Tell me what?' Jerome asked.

I hadn't mentioned the engraving to him.

'I have to say, I'm not all that keen on too many more surprises.'

'The parchment was found hidden behind what we think is a new Durer etching. The etching is engraved with the same name you just mentioned, the *Paraklitos*.' I stood up, walked to the dining table and recovered a picture of the engraving. I gave it to Jerome.

'Very interesting,' he dismissed – in a tone, thinking back on it now, which suggested he was not all that surprised.

'Why,' I asked.

'As I mentioned earlier there was mention of an intermediary spirit or advocate in earlier versions of the Qur'an and this is the direct transcription of the meaning of Paraclete. After 750ce or so

117

orthodox Islamic scholars taught against the concept of an intermediary between man and God and so the notion of Paraclete was changed, with a few linguistic assumptions to *Periklitos* or "praiseworthy", and from this a deduction that the promised Paraclete mentioned in John's Gospel was actually Mohammed, which is derived from the Arabic *Ahmed* meaning praiseworthy. Thus the sensitivity about any early writings which might contradict this view.'

'I still do not understand about the danger it's meant to put us in,' Mac persisted.

'For over 1,000 years the Book has been rumoured to still be in existence but this . . . this letter, is the first evidence that I have ever seen to possibly confirm the fact. It is the Holy Grail, if you will forgive the contradiction, of Islamic collectors like myself but if found and its contents verified then it could possibly open up huge chasms in Islam. The fundamentalists would never want it to see the light of day.'

'Then why bother?' I asked.

'The challenge,' Jerome said in a serious tone.

'Indy Flanagan and the Book of the Messenger! I can see the movie already. Brad Pitt perhaps?' Mac spluttered again.

I could not help smiling causing Jerome to glare.

'I wish I could be so flippant,' he said sarcastically. 'This is dangerous ground, Rio. *Deadly* dangerous!'

'What are you implying?' I asked, disturbed by his intensity.

'There are well supported rumours that "sleepers" have been put in place around the world by one or other of the ultra-orthodox Islamic sects to keep a watch for the Book's reappearance and to do everything to recover it if it does surface. They will want to find it first and destroy both the evidence and any person known to have seen that evidence.'

' "Sleepers" waiting for a book that probably no longer exists! You're mad, Jaffa. I mean it.' Mac laughed out loud.

'Think back to 11 September and the Twin Trade Towers, Mac. Those al-Qa'ida pilots were "sleepers" and for a less obvious ideology than the fear of something totally undermining the foundations of their faith. All faiths have their "sleepers" to protect the orthodoxy of those faiths.'

He had finished his whiskey and I stood up to refill it. I noticed while he was talking that he had great difficulty in keeping his eyes off my legs and this time I did not readjust the pulled-up hem.

'I'm hungry. Let's order in a Chinese meal,' I announced from the far end of the room.

'Listen Rio, I'm sorry. I thought I could stay longer, but I must get home as, Paul and Pip are being dropped off at my place by Marie at 7.00. Some sort of emergency in her schedule! She rang me just after you,' Mac said as looked at his watch. 'In fact I'll probably have to call in sick tomorrow to look after them. I'd better get going.'

'Before you go, Mac, did you bring the negatives and all the other prints?' Jerome stood up.

'Sure but –'

'I want you to give them to me.'

'No way!' Mac was adamant. For my benefit, I sensed.

'Listen.' Jerome threw an arm around Mac's shoulder and led him towards the door. 'My car is nearby and I'll give you a lift home. I'll explain on the way why this is so important.'

'I'll call you in the morning, Rio.'

Mac hesitated, inviting me to come towards him, to say goodbye. I stayed where I was and called out after him, 'Give the kids a hug for me,' blowing him a kiss. For some reason I had not wanted to oblige, not with Flanagan watching as intently as he was.

'Right,' Mac said, upset, before finally leaving.

I could hear them arguing, but then relaxing to whisper to each other. They were almost half way down the small front entrance pathway when I rushed after them. 'Hey you two! What about me? Leaving me in the lurch like this.'

Jerome turned and walked back to where I stood in the doorway. He smiled as he whispered out of Mac's hearing. 'Order the Chinese and it should get here about the time I get back. I'll pick up some wine as well. Would that suit?'

'Oh! Yeah. Sure. Excuse me.' I pushed past him and reached

Mac as he sat into the car. He looked up at me. There was hurt in his eyes. 'I'm sorry, Mac, ' I said and kissed him on the lips.

'Be careful with him,' he said.

'No fear,' I replied, closing the car door on the now smiling face. Like a child, I thought.

'Red or white,' Jerome asked as I went back into the house.

'Both . . . either,' I said.

I'll finish this tomorrow. Need some sleep.

Flanagan scrolls back to the beginning and rereads this entry. He smiles at Rio's description of him catching the other woman's eye in the *Hairy Lemon*. And of *his* eyes! Dangerous she called them, and he knew this to be true . . . in the past. In the past he could make eye contact with any woman he desired – hunt with his eyes as he hunted manuscripts – giving nothing away until closing in. And the quarry would respond, seeking out his eyes with hers. He would wait for the moment of release, that brief moment of eternity when the pupils would dilate and the hunter and the quarry were as one, with a unity of purpose, reaching an immediate understanding, pursuing the inevitable.

That seldom happened any more, as hard as Flanagan tried. The woman in *Hairy Lemon* had dead eyes, permanently dilated, seeking not release but obliteration. Whereas in the living, their eyes would find him, pity him – dismiss him. It was as if his told them he is already dead . . .

9

SERENDIPITY

"The constitution exhibited by every being is an intermingling of subjugation and being subjugated, of action and passion. After the mixture is produced there is a state of readiness for life . . ."

Katib Chelebi • *The Balance of Truth in Choosing the Most True*

Flanagan looks at his watch: 11.30. He feels the spasms start up and heads for the toilet. After finishing he has difficulty closing his zip and looks at his reflection in the bathroom mirror. 'Some lover you'll be,' he says aloud thinking about Felicity. He returns to the living room, goes to the CD cabinet and pulls out Eric Clapton's *Pilgrim*. Exchanging discs on the player he selects the eleventh track and by the time he is sitting at the computer Clapton is singing, '*he needs his woman . . .*'

Armpit Diary,
January 16 – Belfast:
Conference today was good. F was there but I avoided bumping into her. No sign of Séamus with her, thank God. Another early night so back to the Armpit, and that first night with Jerome Augustine Flanagan!

The deliveryman from the Typhoon take-away and the returning

121

Flanagan must have arrived about the same time. I could hear their voices below the bathroom window. Naked and dripping wet I opened the window quietly. Snow was falling again and their breath hung in the air. Prepared for the possibility of being caught in the shower I threw down a key that bounced off Jerome's shoulder and onto the ground beside his foot. I didn't wait for him to look up and retreated back into the bedroom, anxious to attend to an unmade-up face. When I did finally make it down the spiral staircase, some ten minutes later, I was surprised to see that the leather-clad delivery-boy was still standing, somewhat forlornly, in the doorway. I could hear Jerome moving about in the kitchen and suddenly realised that he hadn't offered to pay.

For no accountable reason I glared at the delivery-boy, blaming him for letting Flanagan get away with it.

'Don't take it out on me, Miss. I'm just the fucking messenger,' he glared back.

While I rummaged in my purse for the money, I remembered one of Nan Greta's more basic bits of advice: 'Avoid tight-fisted men, Babette. Life is difficult enough without having to account for every pair of new shoes.'

Jerome came back into the hallway as I apologetically closed the front door behind the well-tipped delivery-boy.

'You look gorgeous, Rio.'

It sounded like he meant it and I said nothing about payment for the food as he followed me into the lounge. Perhaps he assumed that because I had approached him about the parchment, everything else was my call. He was a consultant after all, giving his time for free, or for what he could get . . .

Thinking back. I was in a dangerous mood. My time of danger though – pre-menstrual; hair held up in a loose bun by a large clip and wearing the turquoise coloured cocktail dress that the sales assistant had said, was a outfit on the very edge of decency. He had opened two bottles of wine opened, the white, already on ice. My annoyance melted with the sight of his choice of Cloudy Bay. He's not that mean, after all, I compromised – how easy it is to compromise, contemporise.

'Thanks, Jerome. I like the choice of wine.'

'I hoped you would. Sit down and I'll serve you some food.' He held out a glass of the wine, which I took and began to sip as I watched him share out the food.

'You'll make somebody a fine wife, Jerome,' I giggled, enjoying his slight embarrassment as we began to eat.

He said he was unattached. I wondered if he was ever married. Mac hadn't said. 'Have you ever been married?' I asked straight out.

'No, never felt the need. You?'

'No,' I replied, truthfully.

The meal and the two bottles of wine were quickly disposed of as he told me something of his life story. I wondered what version it was. He didn't seem uncomfortable with my touching his arm, for a moment, when I wished to clarify a point. I had to restrain myself from making too many physical interruptions as I listened to his side of his dispute with the Museum.

'It's in the past now and I've moved on,' he assured me. 'However, depending on sourcing rare Islamic texts for a living is a bit like being an old-time gold prospector; some years are good, some are bad, but all of them are exciting.'

'I bet,' I said, instantly attracted to that excitement.

'And now the possibility of finding the Book of the Messenger!' he said, clapping his hands together before leaning forward and kissing me on the lips, lightly, friendly. 'Thanks to you.'

I stood up from the dining table, its surface strewn with empty containers, feeling a little unsteady. 'Wow. That wine was powerful. A mean mule's kick,' I drawled in my best western accent – Joe Reilly would have been proud. Poor Joe – while walking giddily to the sofa and plopping down into its welcoming softness. I loosened my hair free and tossed the clip in his direction to crash against his back. Good shot, I thought, good signal. And he knew it.

He turned, smiled, picked up the clip, stood up and followed me across the room and leant in to kiss me, if you call a gentle brush of my lips a kiss, before sitting down beside me and taking my hand, touching my fingertips.

'You really are a very beautiful woman, Rio,' he said.

'Thank you kind sir,' I said fully expecting – inviting – more.

He looked at me for a moment, a lost look, before handing me the clip. 'This is yours, I think.' He smiled.

His hesitation grated. I was not in the mood for games. I knew instantly. 'Who is she, Jerome? I thought you were *free and available*, to put it bluntly.'

'Her name is Alanna. We have known each other for many years, lovers on and off, loving each other on and off, over those years. We are now off, for good it seems, since a week ago. I didn't match up to her expectations . . .'

'Is that a warning?'

'Perhaps.'

'What happened?'

His eyes drifted away, out of reach. 'Alanna is married to a politician in Ankara. They live separate lives, but are Kurdish and very tribal. They will never divorce. She has long been a crusading journalist for a large Istanbul paper and recently has increasingly questioned the continuing influence of the Turkish military in what purports to be a modern democratic country seeking entry to the European Union. She wanted my help and I . . .'

'What?'

'I declined, hoping it would stop her.'

'Why?'

'The military is Turkey. Most of the papers are in their sphere of influence. At the very least she will probably lose her job, but could also end up in jail or worse. I don't want to see that happening. I even asked her to seek a divorce and marry me, hoping it might afford her some protection.'

'And?'

'Don't know. She stormed off. I've not been able to contact her since.'

'Is she Muslim?'

'Yes, and devout with it. Why would that matter?'

'I just wondered . . .'

He laughed. 'About her and me, getting it on.'

'Yes,' I blushed.

'Kurdish women, even in secular Turkey, are formal and reserved in public. It's part of their upbringing, their education. However in private, all that constraint is removed and their exuberance, their real passion, is released and spent on the lucky man, or woman, they love.'

'Do you miss that?'

'It's been a long time. Politics has become Alanna's passion.'

'Out of practice so?'

'Yes. Despite what Mac may or may not have said about me to you I'm a serial monogamist. Something needs to click . . . beyond the obvious.'

'And is it?' I asked.

'What?' he teased.

'Bastard!'

He laughed again. 'Yes of course it is, you are very beautiful.'

'But?'

'Don't get me wrong, Rio. I love sex and am as predatory as the next man but . . . It's what I said earlier today. I'm lousy at chatting up people and therefore wait for something to happen, knowing that it will sooner or later. I make myself available yet have an uncanny knack of then talking my way out of opportunities presented. Sometimes I wish I could be more direct, passionate even. Tell a woman, 'I'd like to fuck you right now. Oh and do you mind if we leave the talking 'till later.' Most men seem to be able to do that! I can't, and so wait for it to happen. Wait for the woman to take the initiative.'

'Are you nervous, my big, brave manuscript hunter?' It was my turn to laugh as I moved in close.

'Try me,' he said turning, our faces just inches apart.

Perhaps it was the wine or perhaps it was the need to eradicate Séamus but I did want to try and imagined a furious, hungry tongue entering my mouth and elsewhere.

Andre, the French climber, was the last good tongue in my life. He would stay down for ever, probing, circling, asking of me clockwise or anticlockwise, pronouncing it as '*cock*wise' or 'anti*cock*wise', exciting me to the point of explosion . . . indulging himself. Sometimes I wished he would just fuck, just give of himself, not gift himself on me. He hated talking. Mac calls a good tongue a 'Cunning Lingus' but then I'm certain he would not like me describing it, or the possibility of it: not with his friend, Jaffa at any rate.

Flanagan's hand moved down towards my thigh to trace his finger along the skin and my pelvis began to shift in response. I was ready to go again.

Suddenly, the telephone shrilled, and I had to lean across him to pick it up. I caught him with the flying elbow of my automatic swivel to answer and he let out a muffled yelp. With one hand on the receiver I delayed answering as he squirmed from under me and I tried to apologize. It was to no avail however as he was already heading for the kitchen. The phone continued to ring and I reluctantly picked it up.

The Grid calling! 'Jeez, Babs. You took your time. Were you asleep.'

'Not quite, Jack.' I knew I sounded breathless but made no attempt to hide it. My pelvis was still moving. Time for *discipline and punishment*.

'Christ, Babs. I'm sorry. Bad timing as usual. I'll ring back in the morning.'

'No it's fine, Jack. You always somehow knew when I was fooling around.'

'I know. I'm sorry.'

Jack sounded lonely and also a little drunk. More than me at any rate! I calculated that it was about 7.30 in Florida as I watched Flanagan saunter back into the room. He indicated that he was going for another drink.

'Do you want one?' he whispered.

I covered the mouthpiece. 'It's Jack . . . my uncle.'

'Your guardian angel?'

I nodded.

'Babs! Are you there?'

'Sorry, Jack. I was distracted.'

'Spare me the kinky details but tell me what's been happening with you. How's it going with the parchment?'

I telephoned Jack yesterday to tell him about it.

'Good. Exciting really. I was going to ring you again tomorrow with an update. A man . . . Dr Jerome Flanagan, who used to work in the Museum, has been very helpful.' I wonder now whether I should have told him of Jerome's concerns.

'I delighted for you. Is that who's with you. A home run on the first date eh.'

'Don't be so lewd.'

'I'm sorry, sweetheart. You deserve the happiness.'

'Thanks.'

There followed a prolonged silence when all I could hear was his breathing. I sensed he wanted to say something but didn't know how. I had to help him. 'Spit it out, Jack, whatever it is that's on your mind.'

'I could never fool you for long, Babs but you're right. I'm planning on making some changes myself.'

'What do you mean?'

'Sara Lou telephoned me from her mother's. In all honesty I don't think she and I will be able to patch things up. She's bored and wants to move on.'

'I'm sorry to hear that.' I couldn't help smiling at the historical irony of his assessment.

'That's only part of it. I've decided to sell the firm, Babs. Jake Jago has organised a management buy-out and the price is good. I'd like to travel a bit . . . perhaps even move to Europe. Whadddaya think?' he slurred.

'Christ, Jack. That's a bit of a . . .' I hesitated, searching for the right description and wondering whether he was in full control of his actions.

'Wow! Are you sure?' I asked. It was all I could manage.

'Yes. That's why I rang you. The deal was signed today and will be notified to the exchange tomorrow. My only other real love has also left me.'

Whoa, I thought. I'm not going down that road . . . again.

'Don't be so morose, Jack. I've never left you. You know that.'

'I know, Babs, but . . . Listen I'll ring you tomorrow when my head is together more.'

'Jack,' I said quietly, worried about him.

'Yes, Babs.'

'Are you ok?'

'Sure. No problem. I might even try the position on page 90 without Sara Lou tonight. I'll consider it my celebration. 'Night Babs.'

The phone went dead and I stared at it for a moment wondering whether to call him back. I decided against it as Jerome returned. He sat down and snuggled in close.

'You deserted me?' I cooed with invitation.

'Is there a problem?' he asked.

'Jack is thinking of coming here.'

'What does he do?'

'Jack started his working life as a Colorado State Trooper, switched to the FBI and after ten years left to establish his own security and industrial intelligence firm. It grew quickly and eventually gained a stock exchange listing and it was with some of the proceeds of that listing that he established a trust fund for me. Although a lousy husband, Jack is a good employer and delegator. In recent years he has relinquished operational control to a man called Hank Jago, like him, a former FBI agent. The firm has continued to expand and by now is about the third biggest in the United States. There is a management buy-out on the cards and Jack is seriously considering it. His 51 per cent holding is worth a considerable sum.'

Jerome nodded then leaned forward and picked up the photographs from the coffee table. 'I can't stop thinking about these.'

'Doesn't say much for my attraction,' I pouted.

'On the contrary, it says everything, Rio. I really am very concerned. I've a bad vibe about these.' He touched my face lightly with the back of his hand before putting his arm around my shoulders, drawing me in.

'Read it again, Jerome.'

'No need to! I've written it out for you.' He handed me a foolscap page with neat but small writing.

I had to focus hard. 'Who was the Sultana Sporcha?' I asked.

'She was one of the mad Sultan Ibrahim's junior wives who, after the Sultan's execution, was married off to an elderly general. After his own, some say hastened, demise she opened the equivalent of a geisha house for the entertainment of the elite in Istanbul. According to the letter Roxanne was one of those geisha girls.'

'And the Ok Meydani?'

'The "Field of the Arrows", or archer's shooting range on the high ground on the northern side of the Golden Horn. It was the site of public gatherings as well as competitions for the longest flight. No longer there of course. Its demise hurried by artillery in the eighteenth century and the squatters of the nineteenth. It had a number of distinctive traditions however. The targets of the original space were known as "the idols" and the winning distances of famous archers were marked by large stones, some of which were still standing in the late eighties holding up clothes lines and the like.'

'Idols?'

'Yeah. The Turkish for a cross or idol is *Put*. Like the mentioned *Tobra*.' He pointed to the bottom of the letter.

'I don't understand.'

'The so-called "idols" were probably statues of the crucifixion taken from the Byzantine churches when Constantinople fell in 1453. Sultan Mehemmed the Conqueror had them carried up to the *Meydani* and set up as targets. There was *Puta Ebrisi* to the north, *Yaaf* and *Nesr* and *Tobra* to the east, *Aymaish* and *Hekim* on the south side, *Pelenk* to the west and *Pish* was to the north-west.'

'And you think the *mus'ir* will tell us which target the letter writer was telling his father to walk towards in order to retrieve the Book.'

'Exactly! Have you got it?'

I found that his hold relaxed alarmingly quickly, almost

pushing me off the sofa. 'Sure,' I said with an annoyance as I uncoiled, stood up and headed for the kitchen, where I had left Jha's *Smell,* the previous evening when preparing a meal. The book was not immediately visible but after searching around for a moment finally found it had slipped down behind the microwave unit. My face drained of its colour when I realized, as I flicked through the pages, that the folded piece of paper with the copy of the catchword was missing. I held the book upside down, shaking it angrily, as I returned to the lounge.

'It's gone. It's bloody missing.'

'Are you sure?' He stood up and took the book from me.

'Yes I'm bloody sure. Who would have taken it? Only I . . .' I stopped and looked at him.

'Only you, what?' he enquired gently, trying to placate.

'I was going to say that only I had been in the kitchen but then I remembered you were, and so was Mac for that matter.' Language and lunacy, I suddenly thought.

'Where did you find the book?' he asked.

'Behind the microwave!'

'Hold on a second.' He brushed past and went into the kitchen. I could hear him moving around and it was only a matter of minutes before he returned, brandishing the folded paper in his hand.

'Where did you find it?' I asked, relieved.

'It must have fallen out of the book and slipped under the microwave base.' He smiled as he waved it and then walked away from me, towards the better light in the dining area, unfolding the paper. 'We've got it. It's *Nesr,* the target on the south west side of the Ok Meydani. Logical really, it would be the closest to the waterfront of the Golden Horn,' he shouted excitedly before going to the fireplace and setting alight to the paper. He continued to watch it burn on the grate as I joined him.

'Why did you do that, Jerome?'

'No one else must know, Rio. It's too dangerous. Do you understand?'

'No! Not yet, if you must know. Tonight was so nice it's hard to sense any danger lurking in the shadows.' It was nearly 2.00 am and I felt that the passion of earlier had completely evaporated. Relieved in a way, I got up, walked to the table and picked up the copy of the letter that he had written out for me.

'*Was?*' he asked from behind.

'What are the "*muserin*" that the letter refers to?' I ignored the demand, not even turning to look at him.

There was silence for a moment, frustration hanging in the space between us.

'That's a very interesting word, Rio because it confirms that this letter definitely refers to the long lost Book of Warnings of the Messenger.'

'Why? What's the connection with writer of the letter?'

He came up from behind me, to rest his hand on my hip. 'Around the time this was written, because of the fusion of Christian and Islamic beliefs in the Imperial schools and also the influence of Sufism a number of strange sects developed. The *Muserin,* and another group called the *Chapmessahi*, believed Christ to be the God and Redeemer and that Mohammed was the Holy Spirit promised by him. The book of the Warnings of the Messenger may have been supposed to, *or was*, supportive of these beliefs. Obviously these would have been seen by the Sunni orthodox theologians as completely heretical and dangerous, hence the supposed "sleepers" who wait and watch for its reappearance and . . . hence the danger to you. They will stop at nothing to retrieve it.'

His hand was moving down, but I somehow sensed his heart was no longer in it. He looked exhausted.

'Talking of "sleepers", I'm suddenly very tired,' I said with a forced yawn, turning towards him, hoping he would take the hint.

He laughed and leant forward to kiss me. 'Yeah! We can worry about that tomorrow. Meantime let's go back to where we were at.'

'And where was that?' I asked, pulling back.

He began to kiss my neck. 'You are almost impossible to resist.'

'Almost!' I hissed. 'What do you mean?'

'Listen, Rio, I'd travel with you to Belfast tomorrow but there is something I need to do here urgently. It's important for your safety.'

'Tell me.'

'The less you know the safer it will be. Trust me?'

'Trust you? I'd rather know what you are planning.'

'That's for tomorrow. Right now I'd rather. . .' He moved in closer, his fingers pulling at the silk of my panties. He seemed to be having some difficulty getting a hold and his fingers felt clumsy, uninviting. It was as if he was trying hard to meet my expectations, not his. Also, and weirdly, there was now a strange odour coming from him, mixed in with the aftershave. Not from his breath but from his skin. It had a slight whiff, like that from day or two-day-old wet grass cuttings. Not the matured peat-smell of malt or heath which I love but the early scent of that decay and I pulled back from him.

'Not so fast, Jerome Flanagan! I'm not that easy and you'll have to earn my trust. You may stay here tonight, if you want . . . in the spare bedroom but we'll take things slowly on the personal front. Right now I want to sleep. Remember I have to leave early.'

'But before . . . eh, your uncle rang? You were so . . . You seemed to be enjoying yourself.'

'That was then, Jerome. Spare bedroom or nothing.'

'It amounts to the same thing,' he said with a generous smile and both of us were laughing as he let me pull him playfully up the stairs. He tripped near the top and I noticed it took a little time for him to stand up. The wine was getting to him too, I thought. We kissed goodnight at his door: a thank you, first-date kind of kiss. Strangely, he looked relieved.

Some hours later, after waiting for the door-opening creak of my bedroom that never came, I heard him slip quietly from his room and out of the house. On the floor outside my door he had left a single sheet of paper with a poem written on it:

The Pillars of Ubar

Into the empty quarter:
Rub-al Khali.
Empty, pitiless.
Cleansed
Red-eyed tracks
Travelling amongst the fortunate people,
To Shabwah
And beyond.

And the three-cornered light awakening
So strong as to take your breath away

With Afiah b. Nasr al-Shabatini:
The last of the Uzza.
Morning star, sacrificed.
Moving, mounting
Searching
Following the scent of precious trees,
To the pillars of Ubar
And beyond.

And the three-cornered light awakening
So strong as to take your breath away

There follows:
A khamson wind.
With Hud, the warner.
To swallow, drown
In seas of silica silence
All the people of 'Ad,
In Atlantis,
And beyond.

And the three-cornered light awakening
So strong as to take your breath away

Dear Rio,
We need to be very careful!
Jerome.

When I woke again, mid-morning, the paper was crumpled in my hand.

Couldn't have done it if I tried, Flanagan thinks, and then wonders what time it is. He has difficulty focusing on the dial of his watch and settles for looking at the display on the CD player. 02:12 it announces, then 02:13, 02:14, 02:15. . . He continues watching, mesmerized, feeling his pulse, counting to see if he can predict the moment the new minute will arrive. He holds his breath in concentration. His pulse rate changes and he loses the rhythm of his count. The clock continues to change at its own pace: 02:18, 02:19, 02:20 . . .

'Fuck that!' he says aloud, exhaling, pulling his eyes away.

10

THE WATCHMAN

"A strange spark flashes in the eyes,
a strange word slides into the song,
the soul, rising itself with the dawn,
does not know about its night to be."

Negar • *Disenchantment*

Reaching for the familiar ground of the malt he hesitates mid way through spinning its cap off and changes his mind. Ground coffee is required instead, he realises, a caffeine concentration of wits. He heads for the kitchen, ladles a double helping of Java into a cafétière and waits for the kettle to boil. Once prepared, he leans against the breakfast counter, gulping down the coffee before refilling the cup and returning across the room to the diary.

Jack is always getting in the way, Flanagan thinks, running point between Rio and the world, his world. He wonders about their attachment and the silence of that attachment. Almost a conjugal silence he had thought that night in the hotel; so little need to say anything between them and yet so much unsaid between them, between all of them.

He waits for an announcing creak of the apartment building's front door but it doesn't come. Felicity Fellows is not returning, he finally decides, rubbing his eyes. He scrolls down to check how many entries are left and decides to keep going. Jack

Dawson is bad enough drunk, but sober he'll be lethal, he reasons.

'I need to understand everything,' he says into the silence.

He scrolls down, glancing quickly at two short entries. The one for January 18 reads: Back from Belfast. No word from Flanagan. Bastard! Mac rang, wants to come over. I put him off. He thinks I'm with Flanagan. Hangs up not believing.

He skips over the accusation, remembering an article he'd read recently about how George Gamow's predicted cosmic radiation, the Universal *noise* from the Big Bang, was detected after all possible elements that might account for that *noise* were eliminated, including the "white dielectric material" – birdshit – scrubbed from the antenna dish. *Bastard!* She called me. Bullshit, he thinks, brown dielectric material confusing the *noise* of his imploding universe. 'Bring it back,' he tells himself, sipping the coffee. Azure dielectric material:

Armpit Diary,
January 20 – morning:
What a shit day! It started with a loud and persistent knocking sound that woke me up. I looked at the clock. It was nearly midday and I had been asleep for the best part of nine hours; too much to drink after Mac's telephone call. The knocking noise got louder.

'Right. Hold on. I'm coming,' I shouted, throwing off the covers and moving to the window. Below, in the street, a white police patrol car was parked against the kerb, its engine running. I opened the window, but just enough to stick my head out. Standing at the front door, was a uniformed policewoman. 'Hello,' I called down, my tongue moving like sandpaper in my mouth.

'Dr Dawson?' The policewoman looked annoyed.

'Yes.'

'Would you come down ma'am. I need to talk to you.'

'About what?'

'Just come down please and open the door.'

'Sure.' I closed the window, straightened up, turned and stubbed my toe against something hard. 'Shit. What's that doing there?' I said aloud, looking down to where the combined telephone-answering machine and its handset lay scattered and unconnected to each other. Jerome's poem lay beside them. I must have knocked it off the side table during the night and not realised it. I bent down, lifted the handset and listened. There was the low hum of an engaged signal and the low-battery warning light was flashing. Replacing the handset on the machine, and the machine on the table, I checked that the line was working before donning a towel-robe and going downstairs.

'Please come in,' I said as brightly as I could. 'What's the problem, officer?'

'We need you to come to your lab in the museum, Dr Dawson. We have been trying to contact you since 10.00,' she said with a clipped, impatient emphasis.

'I'm sorry about that. My phone was off the hook. I must have knocked it over in the night.' I offered pathetically. 'What's up with the lab? There wasn't a fire or anything was there.'

'No.'

'Then what.'

'Dr Dawson, please get dressed quickly and come with us. Everything will be explained when we get there. I'll wait in the car for you.' The policewoman turned on her heel and left.

I watched her get into the patrol car before closing the front door and it was another ten minutes, and a quickly taken shower, before I joined them. Without a word we sped the short distance, with siren blazing and against the flow of traffic, to Ship Lane. This time the repaired barrier of the security gate was already erect and as we pulled in I saw that there was a tremendous amount of police activity all around the Clock House building.

There had been recent rumours of an impending, unscheduled visit by former US President, Bill Clinton to the museum and I now thought that all staff had been called in on their Saturday off to be in grovelling attendance. To the Irish, he is still the real President and the full trappings, if not the protocol, of a State Visit would be afforded him.

'I'll kill Aengus.' The words slipped out before I could stop them.

'What did you say, Dr Dawson?' The young policewoman looked sideways at me as the car skidded to a halt.

'Look at all the activity. I'm annoyed with the Director for not letting me know there was an important visitor coming. The lab is in a mess.'

'You're right there,' the policewoman growled.

'What?' I was taken aback by her tone.

'Please come with me, Dr Dawson.'

The policewoman stepped out of the car and waited for me to do the same. We headed for the front entrance and it was only when I saw the blacked-out windows of the Silk Road café and the fluttering yellow tape, of a crime scene exclusion area, blocking their way that I suddenly realised that something terrible must have happened. As the policewoman held up the tape for me to duck under, a tanned, dark-haired man came forward to meet us.

'Dr Dawson, I'm Detective Inspector Flatley of the Garda Central Detective Unit in the Phoenix Park.'

DI Flatley was taller than me, and had eyes that were so brown, I noticed, they were nearly black. Wearing a well cut and very tight fitting black suit, a bright-pink tie and pale-blue shirt, and pointed, highly polished Italian shoes, he didn't strike me as very Irish nor of any image I might have had of an Irish police detective. 'What's going on Inspector?' I asked accepting his proffered handshake, which was firm.

'We're here investigating a possible homicide,' he said, brusquely, releasing his grip.

'Did you say homicide?' I asked, confused.

'Yes. I need to ask you a few questions. Please follow me.'

I meekly followed him around the corner of the foyer entrance and into the first room of the restaurant. Through a connecting doorway I saw an ashen-faced Mac sitting at another table being questioned by another, heavier built, man. He looked up briefly as I passed. I was shown to a chair with my back to where they were sitting. DI Flatley sat down on the chair opposite, his face impassive.

'What's going on, Inspector? Please tell me.'

'Somebody may have been murdered here last night . . . in your lab as it happens. We're trying to piece it all together. When were you in the lab last?'

'*What?* Who for God's sake?'

'A Mister Joseph Reilly, the night security guard.'

'*Christ no!* I don't believe it.' I felt my stomach heave. 'I'm going to get sick. Excuse me.'

I got up and ran across the marble floor of the atrium, jumping over the ornamental pool in the hurry to get to the ladies toilet. The policewoman who had collected me from the house followed, to stand near the cubicle door as I retched, annoyed by the need to do so. It was a few minutes before I felt well enough to return to the restaurant where DI Flatley was waiting with two cups of coffee.

'Sugar.'

'No. Thanks.'

'When were you last in the lab, Dr Dawson?' Flatley asked, opening his notebook and resting it on his knee.

'About 2.30 pm Tuesday! I had a meeting in the afternoon and went straight home from there. I was in Belfast until yesterday. At a meeting. Took the evening train back. You can check, if you like.'

'I have,' he said, flipping over a page. 'Alone?'

'What?'

'Last night. Were you alone at home?'

I could hear Mac's distinctive slurp behind me. 'Yes,' I said, blushing.

The policeman noticed. 'Anybody call to the house?'

'No.'

'What about Tuesday?'

'What about it?'

'Anybody call to your house then?'

'What's that got to do with it?'

'Please answer the question Dr Dawson. We are trying to establish everybody's movements for the last week or so.'

'Why?'

'It's what we do.'

I relented and answered his question. 'Yes, two people did. Mac . . . Cormac McMurragh and Jerome.'

'Jerome . . .' DI Flatley did not look up as he flicked through the notebook until reaching a blank page, '. . . that would be Jerome?'

'Dr Jerome Flanagan! He used to be a curator in the museum.'

'I see,' he said, writing it down. 'Any telephone calls.'

'When? During the entire week?'

'No. Last night,' the policeman asked, in a tone which suggested he already knew.

'Yes my uncle. About midnight.'

'A bit late!'

'Not for him. He lives in Florida.'

'I thought that Dr Flanagan was staying in the house.'

'No he's not,' I said, a little too emphatically.

'I thought he was with you.'

'Who told you that?'

'Something Mr McMurragh said,' Flatley mumbled, flicking back to another page.

'That was on Tuesday last. I told you. He and Mac . . . Cormac McMurragh were with me.'

'Until what time.'

'They left at about 7.00.'

'You were alone all night so?' Flatley's eyes were sizing me up, testing me.

'No. Dr Flanagan came back for dinner.'

'I see and what time did he leave.'

'About 3.00 or 4.00 in the morning.' I couldn't stop my face going red.

'Was that the last time you saw him, Dr Flanagan . . . the early hours of Wednesday morning?'

'Yes!'

'Any telephone contact since?'

'No!'

'I understand.' He almost smirked.

'*Well, I don't.*' I shouted back at him, annoyed with the process, the intrusion and the inference in his tone. I stood up. Heads everywhere turned to look at us. 'What's happened here? *Tell me*!'

'Take it easy, Dr Dawson,' he whispered as he leaned forward and touched my hand. 'Please sit down.'

He smelt of expensive aftershave, Issy Misake, I thought, calming down a little and retaking my seat. 'I will if you start explaining.'

DI Flatley studied me for a long time before answering. 'The body of Mr Reilly was found in your lab. The deceased will be removed to the morgue shortly but it's still not a pleasant sight. Tell me, apart from the routine security patrols which he usually made at . . . let me check,' he flicked through his notebook again, ' . . . at midnight and 6.00 am would there have been any other routine reason for going into your lab. Would, for example, he be doing something for you?'

'No. Why do you say that?'

'Dr Hanratty, the Assistant State Pathologist, has determined that his death took place roughly between 2.00 and 5.00 am, no sooner than that at any rate. The last person to leave the building was Phyllis Andrew at 02.00.' He paused for a moment. 'Why would Miss Andrew have been working in her office so late?'

'Phyllis, Dr Andrew, is the Islamic curator. She has been away all week in the States and perhaps was catching up on some work. She'd have still been on East Coast time. It's not that unusual for some people when they come back. Why don't you ask her?'

'We will when we find her.'

'What.'

'Oh. Nothing serious. Her neighbours said she left early this morning. By taxi.'

'I'd left her a message yesterday about something that I'd been working on.'

'We know. We found it in her office . . . let me see.' The

detective pulled a clear plastic bag from his jacket pocket. Inside Rio could see that there was a single piece of paper; the writing on it was her own. DI Flatley began to read it. ' "Dear Phyllis, I hope you had a good trip. Please destroy the letter I sent you for an opinion. I'll explain later. Love Rio." I thought you said you went straight home yesterday evening.'

'I said I got home about 11.00. I called into the museum on the way from the train-station to pick up my mail, and that is when I left the message for Phyllis . . . Miss Andrew.'

'So you were in your lab?'

'No. The mail collection boxes are in the foyer. Joe Reilly let me in and I left straight away again without going up to the lab. I was very tired.'

'How did he seem?'

'Fine.'

'And Miss Andrew?'

'No. Phyllis wasn't there then . . . at least Joe didn't mention it. He offered to slip my note under her door.'

'What is the letter you mentioned?'

'Oh. Nothing important. Some . . . museum business,' I said defensively.

'I see,' DI Flatley said with a click of his tongue. After a moment of contemplation he spoke again. 'On a different note, Joe Reilly and Miss Andrew were very close, weren't they? ' He asked in a nonchalant way as he folded up the plastic bag containing her note and replaced it in his pocket.

'Yes, they were good friends and whenever Joe was working nights, Phyllis would often stay in to talk with him. It's so sad.' My eyes filled with tears as I spoke my thoughts out loud.

'Yes. That's what Mister McMurragh said.' DI Flatley smiled, a thin sad smile, reminding me of Flanagan. 'Would you mind coming up to the lab with me, Dr Dawson? You have to be careful not to touch anything but I would value your help. See if anything is missing; that sort of thing. I'm looking for a motive. The deceased's body is at this moment being taken away so the scene is still fresh.'

I cringed at the word and had to fight hard against the waves of nausea that suddenly washed over me. 'Sure.'

'I gather you have an association with the FBI. You've probably been to many of these scenes?' Flatley enquired as he walked alongside.

'As it happens, Inspector, I have not. My work was always lab based although my uncle would sometimes describe some of his cases when I was growing up.'

'Was he a policeman?'

'State Trooper then FBI.'

'I see,' he said with another click of his tongue. 'I'd like you to put on a pair of crime-scene overalls and gloves. You don't have a latex allergy do you?'

'No,' I replied, searching Flatley's face for any hint of unwarranted intrusion.

We soon reached the top floor landing, stopping to put on the overalls at a spot from where I could see an animated Aengus FitzHenry entering the foyer below. Alongside a fingerprint technician was dusting the doorway that led to the lab corridor and slightly irritated by the disruption protested loudly before pushing it open with the end of his dusting brush. We entered the corridor and turned into the laboratory doorway.

'*Oh God no!*' I suddenly screamed.

'I'm sorry about that,' Flatley said in annoyed fashion as we had to retreat again to allow the gurney with Joe Reilly's body on it pass out. One of his hands had released and had slipped out through a small tear in the body bag.

I shivered. The familiar was no longer familiar. I felt disembodied, as if walking in an alien space, observing it from a distance. Its sanctity seemed desecrated and destroyed, dirty and in need of a cleansing wind.

'This way Dr Dawson.' Flatley led me to the far end of the room. There was a large crescent-shaped board with writing on it being held up by another detective.

'DI Flatley.'

'Yes sergeant.' Flatley spoke down to another detective who

was on his hands and knees in front of them searching around in the shadows beneath the sink.

'Look at this.'

'Show me.'

The sergeant moved to one side and Rio could see a small square piece of paper on the floor. It had writing on it.

Flatley hunched down to examine, without touching, the paper more carefully. He read it aloud, '*Dear Rio, I've done what you asked. By the way the Watchman translates as the "idol of Hakim", the judge. Love P.* Do you know what she meant?' he asked.

My head was spinning. Phyllis had translated the word as *hakim* and not *nesr* as Jerome Flanagan had done. What's he up to? I wondered.

'What's a "Watchman"?' Flatley persisted.

'The linking word between the end of one page of a document and the start of another, usually used as a guide to the binders, so that the proper page sequence would be maintained,' I answered automatically. Suddenly my hand came to my mouth. Oh Jesus . . . Flanagan lied, I thought as my stomach heaved again. I wobbled before leaning heavily against a workbench.

Flatley had a concerned look on his face as he stood up to hold me. 'Do you want to sit down?'

'No thank you, Inspector. I'll be ok in a minute.'

It was at that moment I noticed the slightly sweet smell, which was drifting through the lab. I looked around and then noticed the pink, frothing liquid that filled the jacketed water tank. I moved forward for a closer look.

DI Flatley spoke softly, 'Joe Reilly was found slumped on the floor beneath the tank. He had copious frothing liquid coming from his nostrils and mouth. Drowned probably. Held down into the bath.'

'Oh dear God,' I said, horrified by the thought. 'But it's not deep enough!' I protested.

'It is if you're concussed or drugged and your head is held down. I'd say he was carrying that letter to you when he collapsed and that the letter fell from his grasp and lay hidden from view under the sink.'

'God! I'm going to retch again.' With that I turned and vomited into a small hand-washing sink beside the tank. Straightening up I accepted a handkerchief that he offered. 'I'm sorry Inspector.'

'No harm done. It's a distressing scene for you. We should go.'

'Yes . . . no. It's not just the scene. There is something else.' I was sniffing the air again.

'What?'

'That sweet aroma in the room! Do you smell it?'

'Yes, I think so. Is it somebody's deodorant?'

'I have a very keen sense of smell, Inspector. It's not perfume it's . . .' I broke off and went to the middle section of the lab where the small solvent cupboard and over night storage safe were located, side-by-side. Their presence was obscured for security purposes by a false panel on the wall. I depressed a small lever and the panel slid to one side. The solvent cupboard's door was open. 'Inspector. Come here please!' I called out.

'What is it, Dr Dawson?'

'The solvent cupboard! It's been opened.'

'What of it?'

'There was some chloroform in there.'

'Chloroform! Why on earth would you have that in here.'

'It is sometimes used for removing old varnish in picture restoring. It was due to be disposed of on Monday.'

'I see. Why such security measures?' Flatley examined the sliding panel.

'The security is for the night-storage safe. It is really a lockable, modified drying cabinet where small items I might be working on can be safely deposited overnight, or at weekends, without having to return them to the main vaults or leaving them lying about. Small items have a habit of disappearing from museums.'

'And the solvent cupboard?'

'It was easier to position them side-by-side when remodelling the building. Both need the same controlled humidity and air extraction connections.'

'And the safe. What's in there?'

'God. *The parchment!* I'd forgotten all about it,' I bent down and started to dial in the combination of the safe. I suddenly thought of the fingerprint technician. I looked up at Flatley. He nodded for me to go ahead, as I still wore the latex gloves. The safe opened. It was empty. I almost knew it would be. 'They're gone,' I said wearily flopping back onto the floor.

'What are?'

'A Durer etching and an old parchment letter that I was working on. They are *both* gone.'

'You mean stolen?'

'Yes . . . I suppose so.'

'Were they valuable?'

'Priceless . . . oh my God.'

'Do many people know about the safe and the cupboard? Their location and security codes?'

'God. I don't know. Anybody who has ever worked here I suppose. At least anybody who has worked since the Library moved to this location. Oh my God!' I felt myself getting dizzy again and tilted forward to lean against the safe.

'Right. Let me help you up, Dr Dawson.' Flatley placed his hand under my elbow and helped me to my feet. 'I'll get the technical lads over here and we'll go downstairs again and you can give me a description of the etching and the parchment and also detail who, currently, has access to the lab. Before we go out however, is there anything else out of place?'

I had difficulty taking my eyes away from the empty safe but eventually looked around as he requested. The rest of the lab was the way I'd left it on Tuesday afternoon, only it wasn't. It was changed forever.

Outside fresh snow was beginning to fall again and I wanted to rush forward and open the window and let it blow in; to cover over me; to hide me.

Flanagan scrolls quickly on:

Armpit Diary,
January 20 – afternoon:
After FitzHenry and DI Flatley had left the conference room, I sat

staring up at the blue sky through the nearest window. Mac was opposite, fidgeting, his face in shadow. Each of us, I thought, nervous; waiting in silence; anticipating the explosion that would surely happen when FitzHenry returned. It was not long in coming. The door swung open and looking up I could see that his face was already a flaming, incandescent red. He stood at the head of the table, visibly shaking, a labile volcano looking down its length at us, saying nothing, threatening everything.

'Aengus. I –' I began, trying to deflect the eruption.

'Dr Dawson if you don't mind,' he interrupted, with magma spittle that showered over us. 'I would like you to remain silent for a moment. I will come to you shortly. First, I want some answers from you, Mister McMurragh.

'Prof! Honestly. There is nothing linking me to the theft or the murder. How was I to know that Ahmed could do something like this? I was simply in the café having a coffee and had the pictures with me when he came over and asked me about them. He seemed genuinely interested and I saw no harm in it.' Mac protested, moving his hands around like a small child.

'You should not, *should not* have discussed confidential Library business with a man running the *café*!' FitzHenry shouted, the veins on his temples almost distended to bursting point.

'But Prof –'

Mac was flustered and I felt sorry for him.

Together with FitzHenry and Mac, I had spent three hours with DI Flatley going over our individual statements and trying to piece together what had happened in the days prior to the murder. I gave an account of the work with the parchment; Jerome Flanagan's involvement; the story of the Book of the Messenger; and finally had explained to Flatley about the concerns Flanagan expressed with regard to the significance of the parchment to orthodox Islam and his theory about "sleepers" waiting in the shadows. At one point I was just about to bring to Flatley's attention the discrepancy between Phyllis's and Jerome's version of the "Watchman" word when Mac suddenly mentioned he had shown some of the photographs of the parchment to Ahmed al-Akrāsh, the proprietor of the Silk Road Café in the museum. This had brought the first noticeable flicker of genuine excitement to Flatley's otherwise impassive features.

The policeman had then explained that Ahmed al-Akrash had not been seen since the afternoon of the murder, had not come into work the Saturday morning and that the café manageress, Mags had not heard from him. A neighbour returning from the night shift in Guinness's Brewery thought he had last seen him leaving his house in a hurry very early on Saturday morning and enquiries with the Syrian Embassy in London were equally worrying. Neither they nor the authorities in Damascus had issued a current passport or exit visa to anybody called Ahmed al-Akrash.

'I don't believe for one moment Flanagan's tall tale of "sleepers" waiting for a mysterious book to suddenly reappear after hundreds of years,' FitzHenry continued. 'The Durer is *missing* and, DI Flatley agrees with me on this, that is far more likely to be the motive of the robbery and murder.' He spoke in a sarcastic tone as he paced across the top of the room.

'Putative Durer, Aengus!' I said, annoyed with his attitude.

FitzHenry suddenly stopped pacing and glared down. 'From now on I think it would be better if you addressed me as Professor or Director, Dr Dawson. How could you have put my . . . our work here in the library at so much risk by involving yourself with the likes of Jerome Flanagan?' He took some pains to emphasise the involvement reference.

I glared at him, my own volatility releasing. 'How dare you make judgement on, or assumptions about, my personal life FitzHenry! It's none of your concern,' I shouted, feeling my face redden.

'As it happens, it is very much my concern.' FitzHenry's voice hardened to a superior sneer as he sat down. 'Your personal involvement with Flanagan has led to property of the Library going missing and puts our reputation at considerable risk.'

'Jerome Flanagan would have had nothing to do with the

murder and I think you are jumping to conclusions. In any event, only a week or so ago, if I remember correctly, you were prepared to be *involved* with Flanagan in trying to acquire the Ptolemy, only for Brigadier Crawford to slap you down.' I stood up, wanting to leave when the thought struck me. '*Is this where this is coming from?* Are you lap-dogging for Crawford?' I was fuming and like a trapped animal would fight my way out if required.

'Sit down Dr Dawson. I was in fact talking about the photographs that you and McMurragh kindly supplied him with. I gather from Inspector Flatley that they are all gone; taken the night he was with you. I also understand that Flanagan needs to account for his whereabouts since then. You're not enough of an alibi it seems. Pity.'

DI Flatly had informed us before he left that the police were reasonably certain Flanagan had caught a connection to Istanbul on the Saturday morning, about the time Joe Reilly's body was discovered. The Turkish police had been informed that he was wanted for questioning but they held little hope of finding him in a city of twelve million people. 'Istanbul is a city full of the disappeared,' the Turkish Chief of Detectives had said to Flatley.

'I've had enough of this bullshit innuendo. I'm leaving.' I picked up my bag.

'That's a good idea.' FitzHenry was nodding his head with a resigned look on his face.

'What do you mean?' I asked, suddenly disarmed by his vacant stare.

'Brigadier Crawford contacted me only ten minutes ago on behalf of the Trustees and I appraised him of the situation. Your contract with the Library is to be terminated forthwith, Dr Dawson and we would like you to leave straight away. The Garda technical bureau are not finished with the lab so you will have to come back at some stage for your belongings. I'll take your security swipe-card if I may.'

I was too stunned to speak and in a dazed fashion lifted the ribbon-held card from around my neck and slid it down the table to FitzHenry.

'You too Mister McMurragh,' he said without looking up.

'Wha . . . wha . . . what do you mean Professor?' Mac stuttered.

'As a full time employee you are suspended without pay and your future with the Library will depend on a full review of your involvement. I suggest you contact your union representative for advice on this matter.'

'That's bloody typical of you FitzHenry! Isn't it?' I had recovered some composure but was not going to back down. 'Whatever about me, suspending Mac is not warranted. He only brought the photographs to my house as a favour to me. We have not even buried Joe yet and you want to pile on the bodies. Because of past problems in the museum, the almighty bloody Library, you want to make us scapegoats for deficiencies in the very expensive, and much hyped, security system you sanctioned. It's a typical bloody overreaction on your part.'

Aengus FitzHenry stood up. 'I'm sorry our association has ended this way but it's your own fault, Dr Dawson. I will arrange for one of the security men to accompany you off the premises. Good bye!' He was gone and I turned to look back at Mac.

'I'm so sorry, Mac.'

'Jasus. It's enough of a blow to drive a man back to drink.'

'You wouldn't?' I said, genuinely worried.

'Nah. Even if the worst came to the worst a man with my skills will have no problem getting work. It's not a problem. The stuck-up gob-shite!'

'I'm so sorry,' I said.

'Flanagan is a bollix,' he said with real anger.

'I thought you were friends,' I said surprised by the intensity.

'We are. We go back a long way. Did you know we were at school together, at a boarding school in Dublin? Me up from Connemara, him flying in from Kuwait like some exotic bird – his father worked in the oil industry. Only children, the both of us and an unlikely pair, even then, fair and dark, surface and deep. When his parents separated and his mother came back to live in Dublin, he stayed on in the school. For some reason he preferred it that way as he and his mother didn't get on. Jaffa was always a selfish bollix. Calculating and loving himself, and himself alone, in the way that calculating men do. Brave with it though, brilliant mind, very few loyalties in his life, except me for some reason. Stuck by me when I left the seminary and –'

'*The what?*'

'The seminary. A place where they train you for the priesthood.'

'I know what it is? What were you doing there?'

'Chancing my arm, really.'

'For how long?'

'Nearly six years! Went awol before my ordination.'

'A crisis of faith?'

'No, it was lust. I'd met Marie and she got pregnant. Jaffa was my best man.'

'Jesus!'

'He later got me a job in the museum. Told them I was a top-notch photographer when I could hardly spell Polaroid. He could charm the pants off a nun, but a bollix all the same.'

'I'm sorry to have got you into this,' I said.

'I don't give a shit about the job, Rio.' His voice quivered. 'It's you I care about and the thought of you and Jaffa getting together is tormenting me. I love you, Rio. There I've said it. I love you.'

There was a long silence. I reached out and touched his hand.

'I know,' I said softly.

'*What?*'

'I know how you feel about me. You don't hide your feelings very well.'

'But you and Jaffa?'

'Nothing happened between us, Mac.'

'Then you and I . . .'

'I don't know, Mac. What does one say to a best friend who has suddenly declared his love? I like you but I want us to remain friends, or some crap like that. I'm no good at this. It changes everything and nothing. I want to run away and not deal with it. That's *my* real skill.'

I stood there looking at him not knowing what else to say. A

151

chasm had opened up between us. He wilted before my eyes. Flanagan had betrayed us both and I would get him for it.

Mac read my mind.

'What'll you do, Rio? Go after him.'

'Yes.'

'Then this might be helpful!' Mac reached into his pocket and pulled out a roll of film. 'This was the last roll of film I had installed in the camera on Tuesday morning. I had only taken two or three images of the parchment and engraving with it before you took them back from me to lock away, so I hadn't bothered developing the entire role. Given our new circumstances I plan to get a few copies made. I'll give you a set and also one to the police. FitzHenry can go and fry himself!'

'Mac that's fantastic! Do those images show the writing clearly?' I wanted to hug him, but somehow I felt a barrier between us. Everything had changed.

'Yeah! Thanks for speaking up for me with FitzHenry but it was my own fault.'

'What do you mean?'

'I shouldn't have shown the photographs to Ahmed and I shouldn't have set you up with Jaffa. I knew you would find him attractive. It was like I was testing you, us, or least the fantasy of us.'

'Listen Mac! I make my own mistakes.'

'Jaffa would have had nothing to do with the murders, Rio,' he said quietly.

'No, of course not! I know that. Jerome's intensity fooled me. The truth be told, he's far more interested in going off chasing after some bloody book than in me. He used me . . . us and I will make him pay for that. Whatever it takes! I'll get the bastard.'

'I am sorry,' he said, obvious relief washing over him. 'Anyway, the police might get him first.'

I said nothing for a while until the thought could no longer be contained. 'Mac. You really don't think he had anything to do with it, do you? From our conversations he seemed to have all the information he needed from the photographs.' I suddenly felt very unsure.

'No! But if he doesn't get back here soon and answer Flatley's questions, Brigadier Crawford will be quite happy to have him made the prime suspect.'

'Serve him right!'

'Rio?'

'Yes, Mac,' I said, knowing what was coming.

'Could I call over to you tonight?'

'No, not tonight. I'm really tired.'

'Yeah.' Resignation. 'Tomorrow then?' Another test of the notion of us.

'Yes Mac, I'd like that. Call me around 6.00 first though.'

A smile, a strange smile from Mac and we parted, each to collect our belongings before leaving the building. He didn't wait to talk to me again and I saw him heading off home, walking as usual, head down into a biting wind.

It will be ok, I think. I owe him that much, an easy gift to give . . .

Jack rang. All arrangements in place. He'll be here soon.

11

THE UPRIGHT WAY

"Detach thyself, be *hanifi*
And from all faiths' fetters free."

Mahmud Shabistari • *Garden of Mystery*

'Shit,' Flanagan says aloud, re-reading to be sure.

He feels a sudden pain wrap around his temples, rise to a throbbing crescendo then release for a moment before settling to irritate the back of his neck. His vision blurs for a second and this worries him. Rubbing doesn't help so he stands up and heads for the kitchen where he finds the Spanish alchemical paracetamol tablets – the ones that always work – and gulps them down.

There is noise in the building, that of the click of high-heeled shoes approaching his door. He looks at his watch, still finds it hard to focus on the dial: 3.25 am. 'She's coming back,' he whispers to his reflection in a hanging saucepan. He drops the saucepan to the floor with a clang, to let her know he's still here, awake; he waits for *her* to knock, wanting her. The footsteps stop, there is a grunt, then a creaking groan and then . . . giggles. More than one voice, Flanagan realises, as silence returns to the corridor when the laughing door closes.

Serves him right, he thinks, thinking he was doing Felicity Fellows a favour, even just by asking. She on the other hand, had not lied to him, and did have better things to do. Not Jack's fault after all. This time!

'Shit,' he says aloud, thinking of Jack.

'Shit, shit, *shit*,' he repeats, thinking of Mac and Rio.

Returning to the table, Flanagan decides on a single malt and the Coltrane trio again; Islay and Antibes; peat and performance: double helpings of both. Mac's puppy-dog opportunist seduction of Rio had played out before his eyes; and I'm the bastard, she thought! Mac had never told him.

Didn't fool Flatley though!

His brain computes, an enigma decoding of himself. The pain is easing. Lights a cigarette and draws deeply. Decides to stand: be *hanif*, the upright way. No more idols. He bends down and exhales his smoke at the mouse, testing how slight a movement will enable the screen. *Rûh*, the breath, the wind, he thinks. Like a spinnaker, the screen fills and pulls him away:

Armpit Diary,
January 21:
Woke late, midday or thereabouts. Drank to keep my misery, my annoyance company. Joyce Holden called over around 3.00 in the afternoon. She was visibly upset at the state I was in.

'I'm so sorry about what has happened, Rio. Aengus is being very unfair.'

'Doing his job, I suppose. I did break the rules,' I said. 'He shouldn't have suspended Mac, though.'

She looked at me for a few seconds, and then shook her head.

'That's what I wanted to talk to you about.'

'What do you mean,' I asked.

'About Mac. Marie rang me, very upset.'

'Marie?'

'His wife . . . ex-wife. We have remained friends.'

'Of course.'

'It seems he called round to the house when she was at work. One of the kids was home from school and they got in an argument over nothing. Mac hit her . . . hard it seems. The −'

'Jesus! He loves those kids. Wouldn't do anything to hurt them.'

'The child was devastated, and very distressed. Locked herself in the bathroom. When Marie got home Mac was still there, curled-up at the foot of the stairs, crying like a baby. Marie said she was frightened. It was like old times.'

'Old times?'

'When Mac was drinking, he used to get violent. One the major reasons for their separation.'

'Christ!'

'When that did happen he was served with a barring order and denied access to the kids. It got to him so much he threatened suicide . . . attempted suicide –'

'Suicide!'

'Took a combination of Valium, paracetamol and whiskey. Only for Jerome Flanagan he would have died.'

'Jerome?'

'Yes. He found Mac and brought him to casualty. Stayed with him as his stomach was pumped. Afterwards got him signed into John O'Gods. Set him on the road to recovery. Attended AA with him as well. The whole deal.'

'I never knew.'

'How could you?'

'Does FitzHenry know?'

'Don't think so. Happened during old Prof Symmonds time here, in the museum I mean.'

'I don't know what to say. Where's Mac now.'

'Marie said he left the house, went off into the night.'

'Shit.'

'I just wanted you to know. If Jerome gets in touch tell him.'

'I will.'

'Also . . .'

'Spit it out, Joan.'

'I know you and Mac are close, maybe closer than close. He worships the ground you walk on.'

'Nothing has happened between us.' I was surprised that somebody else had noticed, yet should not have been.

157

'Be that as it may . . . be careful, Rio.'

We talked for another hour or so and then she left.

The phone rang at 6.00. I didn't answer it, couldn't answer it. I turned off the lights in the house and pretended I wasn't there. It stopped ringing after midnight. Eight messages in all from Mac. Nothing from Flanagan!

Flanagan shrugged and scrolled to the next entry.

Armpit Diary,
January 25:

Jack arrived late yesterday, worse the wear for all the first-class pampering he'd had and I immediately put him to bed. Withdrawing quietly from his room I found myself hesitating, suddenly feeling a strange desire to linger. With one hand on the handle of the half-closed door, I looked back into the room and found my thoughts being transported to something that happened in December. It's hard to believe it is only a month ago now.

While browsing with Séamus in the pre-Christmas bedlam of the second-hand market, I picked up a book by a French writer called Daniel Pennac. Opening a page at random I began to read only to have to put it down again, to be swept away by the tide of Séamus' interest in a woolly hat for his ski trip. Later I returned to the same spot but the book was gone and no one in the bedlam quite knew where.

At that moment, for some strange reason – if there are ever strange reasons – in the closing of the door, those briefly glimpsed lines of Pennac resurfaced as I watched Jack flop, exhausted, onto the clean sheets and plumped up pillows of the second bedroom.

'*The Coot was a Pole who'd been spat back up to the surface by a flatulent mine-shaft,*' I said quietly.

'What did you say Babs? Who's the Coot?' asked the six-o-clock shadow from the darkened room.

Jack, I thought, looked – after his late evening, and much delayed, flight arrival from Miami – as if *he* had been spat out from an even darker hole. 'Nothing, Jack. Go off to sleep. I'll see you later,' I called back through the narrowing gap before closing the door as silently as possible.

It was much later, some five sleep-hours later, when I heard him shuffling around upstairs. After a piping hot shower and endless gargling, he finally made it down to the lounge. I like that Jack is still a handsome man; a man whose dancing green-blue eyes never fail to shine for me whenever we meet, despite all that has happened between us. It is an exclusive response that annoyed Nan Greta when I was small.

He clapped his hands together after kissing me on the cheek. 'Right! Down to business, Babs. What in God's hell sort-of-mess have you got yourself into?'

'Sit down, Jack and have something to eat first. After that I'll tell you all about it, or at least as much as I understand.' I pointed to a chair before moving into the kitchen to fetch the Costa-Rican coffee and type of blue-cheese sandwiches that he liked; that I like. 'Would you like some wine . . . or beer,' I shouted from the kitchen.

'No thanks . . . just coffee. I'm swearing off the booze for good.'

'And matrimony?' I couldn't help asking as I brought in the tray.

'That too,' he said with a smile. 'All the good women run away.'

I said nothing as I entered and just watched as he ate in the silence, hurrying to finish his food. Finally, after starting his third cup of coffee, he looked over at me, wanting, telling me to begin. He listened intently, the only reaction being a slight facial twitch whenever I mentioned Flanagan's name. Pulling out a penknife he began to pare at a small piece of wood he recovered from deep in the same pocket. I smiled at this as whenever he needs to concentrate, Jack whittles. It is an enduring image from my childhood and it felt good, and warm.

'Lets go over the facts again, Babs. What time did –'

The shrill of the telephone suddenly interrupted.

'Shit. Sorry, Jack. I should have left it off the hook. It's probably Mac.' I went over, picked up the mobile unit from the lounge table and answered in an irritable voice, 'Hello.' The caller introduced himself. 'Oh. Hello Inspector Flatley. What can I do for you? Any word on Phyllis?' I asked.

I shook my head in Jack's direction. He looks puzzled as I suddenly broke into a beaming smile. 'That's *great* news, Inspector,' I shouted. 'Sure. Come on over. Jack, my uncle is here.' Hanging-up I almost danced to where he sat.

'What's up, Babs?' Jack frowned, still puzzled.

'*They found it!* They've found the Durer engraving. Flatley is bringing it here for me to identify.'

'Where?'

'He said he'd tell me when he got here. Isn't that great news?'

'Yeah. What about the parchment? Any news on that?'

'No!' The waltz abruptly ended and I slumped into a chair. 'He did say he had some other news.'

'I wonder . . . nah, it doesn't matter,' he grunted.

'What, Jack?' I looked at him.

'I wonder why he is bringing it here instead of asking you to come down to the station. It's a little bit unusual where evidence is concerned. I was just wondering why.'

I shrugged, not really caring as he became silent again, continuing to whittle. It was almost 20 minutes later when the doorbell sounded. Jack suddenly got up and headed for the kitchen.

'I hope I'm not intruding,' Detective Inspector Flatley said as he shut the door behind him and followed me back into the lounge. He had left his overcoat on and carried a small briefcase, tucked tightly under his arm.

'No. Of course not, Inspector. After all that's happened this is a welcome visit,' I said, turning to face him.

'I hope so.' The detective frowned as he opened the briefcase and pulled out a cellophane envelope. 'Is this it?'

My hand trembled as I peeled back the envelope join and extracted the etching. I then held it up to the light to check the watermark before inspecting the front and back surfaces of the small rectangle of paper. 'Yes it is. *Yes it is!* See there Inspector.' I pointed to the area of oxidised writing on the back. 'That confirms it. Thank God. Where did you find it?'

Around that time Jack must have come back into the room behind me and he and the Irish policeman were probably eyeing each other territorially for quite a considerable time before it became uncomfortable for both of them and a loud cough from Jack distracted me from the etching to introduce them.

'Oh! Sorry you two. Inspector Flatley this is Jack Dawson, my uncle. I'm sorry I don't know your first name, Inspector.' He has very dark irises and a small mole just below his left eye.

'Gerrit,' he said quietly as the two men smiled, and moved towards each other to shake hands. The Irish policeman shrugged his shoulders a little in response to my all-too-obvious bemused expression. 'My mother's choosing.'

'It's a nice name, Inspector,' I said sincerely.

'Thanks. Most of the lads call me Gerry.'

'I prefer Gerrit,' I said, too quickly and a little too possessively.

'You, at least, pronounce it right, Dr Dawson,' he said.

'Rio,' I said. 'Please call me Rio, Gerrit, but don't get confused when Jack calls me Babs. It's a childhood pet name I've nearly discarded.' I held out my hand to take Jack's, warning him with a squeeze not to start arguing the point: not now at any rate. 'Why don't you take off your coat and sit down Inspector . . . Gerrit. Surely you have time for a drink.'

'Sure! Coffee if you have it. Black please.' He slipped out of his coat and laid it neatly across the armrest. The mohair suit he wore underneath was of an indigo hue. I liked its sheen of communication.

'On duty eh! Commendable,' Jack ventured.

'No. I don't drink much, Mr Dawson,' Detective Inspector Gerrit Flatley said flatly, as he looked at the older man. 'Coffee is fine just now.'

'Call me Jack please, since we're all cosying up so much,' Jack said, grinning at me.

I glared at him, let go of his hand.

'Talking of duty, Jack,' Gerrit Flatley said with slight annoyance. 'I've been asked by my superiors to extend you every courtesy. You still have friends in very high places in the FBI!'

'I am only here as an uncle, supporting Babs through a difficult time,' Jack said as he put his hand around my shoulder and pulled me in.

'Gee, Uncle Jack! I didn't know you cared,' I teased sarcastically while secretly wondering how the detective would handle the situation. Jack had done this blocking, "over my dead body" routine to boyfriends of mine for as long as I can remember and suddenly I blushed, before squirming from his grip.

Gerrit Flatley smiled. 'If it was as simple as that, Jack I could well understand your concerns, but, my contacts in the FBI assure me that you are not a man to ever remain uninvolved and that you have a wealth of experience and expertise that might help in the case.'

'Does that bother you?' Jack challenged, admitting.

The late-afternoon light was fading fast and afraid to miss any of the expressions of the sparring men I turned on two of the large pottery lamps that dominated either end of the room. I was enjoying the antler bashing too much.

'No.' The Irish policeman's answer was adamant and unstrained. 'But if you get any leads or information I'm to hear of it at the same moment in time. Is that understood, Jack?'

'Yeah. Sure, Gerry.' Jack knew then that he would be able to work with this young detective. 'Babs mentioned that you had other news.'

'Jasus, I nearly forgot. The pathologist Dr Hanratty has completed the post-mortem examination and has suggested – it's preliminary, you understand, that Joe Reilly died following a sudden and massive myocardial occlusion . . . a heart attack. There was no evidence of assault. He must have been surprised by the intruder–'

'Or perhaps surprised them and rushed into the situation,' I interrupted.

'Perhaps, but in any event the most likely scenario is that he had the heart attack and collapsed into the water bath. I am . . . our unit is to remain on the case however until the whereabouts of Phyllis Andrew is established.'

'That's good,' I said too quickly.

'Speaking of the spirit of co-operation, Gerry there is something I want to show you in the kitchen,' Jack said. 'Come on thru'. If nothing else it'll get you closer to the coffee you were promised in any case.'

'Watch it,' I said, reddening.

Jack smiled at me before turning to the policeman. 'Has Babs filled you in on the whole story, Gerry?'

'As far as I know . . . yes. Yes, she has.'

I was still glaring at Jack for the smart comment about the coffee, but the look turned to one of bewilderment as I followed the two men into the kitchen. 'What's the big mystery Jack?' I asked.

He moved immediately to the microwave unit, lifted it from its position and placed it down, further along the granite worktop. He pointed to the cleared space. 'Babs told me that Flanagan said he had found the piece of paper with the copied word from the bottom of the parchment underneath the microwave. Look at the dust, Gerry. It's undisturbed!'

Flatley nodded in agreement.

'But why would he lie?' I mouthed the words, already knowing the answer.

Jack nodded angrily, upset for me. 'He found the paper with Babs' copy of the catchword on it all right but not when he said or where he said. He needed to be sure but once he had the information he then was able to relax into a knight errant role later on. Girls keep falling for knight-errants. Don't they Gerry?'

I ignored the jibe; too busy looking at the dust, resisting the urge to wipe it away. 'The bastard! He would have only had about a few minutes at most though.' I was angry but in truth it was directed more at my feelings of stupidity.

'Time enough,' Gerrit added, unhelpfully.

'I also suspect that the catchword . . . What did you say Flanagan called it? *Nesr*, was a deliberate false trail and that the word Phyllis Andrew worked out for you, *Hakim*, is the right one.'

'Any word on Phyllis?' I asked.

'No. Unfortunately,' Gerrit replied.

'Are you worried?' I knew he was.

'Yes.'

'Do you think Jerome Flanagan really has anything to do with the robbery, Gerrit?' I asked before turning away to fill the kettle hoping that either of the men would not notice the hurt in my eyes. 'He already had most of the information he was looking for.'

'I don't know, Rio, and that's why we need to question him. Even if he is in Istanbul, we should have heard from him by now. The robbery and possible murder was well publicised and it would be in his own interests to make contact as soon as possible.'

'You two go on back in. I'll . . . I'll bring the coffee,' I stuttered. My voice was breaking and both men hesitated for a moment before acceding. Policemen both they were examining the etching with policemen's zeal when I joined them. 'Where did you recover it from, Gerry?' I asked.

'There was a problem with staffing in the State Pathologist's office and Joe Reilly's post-mortem was only carried out yesterday. The etching was found lying against his stomach deep under three layers of clothes.'

'That means –'

'Watch it!' I interrupted.

Jack had pushed back his chair in an excited jump. The tray in my hand rattled as I left it down. 'I'm sorry, Babs.'

'Its ok, Jack. Go on.'

'Phyllis Andrew and Joe Reilly were good friends,' Gerrit Flatley continued. 'She signed out of the museum at 2.00 am. She's wheelchair bound, right! Imagine for a moment that when she came to the museum and found your note she might have asked Joe Reilly – did he have the combination of the safe?' he asked looking at me.

'No. I don't think so. Phyllis did though,' I said.

'Yeah!' Jack said enthusiastically. 'She might have asked Reilly to get the etching and parchment for her from the safe. Suppose a little later, when she was finished with one or both of them, he was bringing them back when he realised there was someone in the lab and managed to hide the etching before – he would have seen that as his priority. And then the intruder probably went looking elsewhere and came across Phyllis Andrew . . .' he hesitated, looking at Gerrit.

'It's a possibility, Jack. That's why we need to find Phyllis Andrew,' Gerrit summarised, in a way that only policemen can.

'Unless of course there were two or more intruders,' Jack said, nodding his head.

'There is also that possibility but we have found only one type of alien clothes fibres on Reilly.' Gerrit then turned to me. 'By the way Rio, traces of chloroform were identified in Phyllis Andrew's office. Would she use it for her work?'

'No.'

'I see. Then . . .'

'That one intruder may have overpowered her and taken her away,' Jack finished what Gerrit was thinking.

The policeman nodded.

'But why wouldn't the murderer have searched for the etching?' I tried not to think of Joe's miserable death or of Phyllis missing somewhere.

'The parchment was the real objective all along and he got that.'

'And Ahmed al-Akrash, the Syrian?' Jack asked.

Jack, Rio, saw was beginning to take notes.

'Our prime suspect.' Flatley smiled at the ex FBI man. 'Disappeared from the face of the planet but we'll track him down.'

'I feel so responsible. I must do something.' I looked at each man in turn.

'We will, Babs. We'll go to Istanbul sweetheart. Follow the trail of Flanagan.' Jack reached out to console.

'Then you'll need this.' The policeman pulled out my blue American passport, which I had been forced to surrender.

'Thanks, Gerrit. I'm no longer a suspect so?' I said flippantly, taking it back.

'No. You're not as it happens. There was some blood swabbed from beneath Joe Reilly's fingernails, which tested as group A. Neither he, Phyllis Andrew as far as we can ascertain, nor you have that type so he must have grappled with the intruder at some stage. We have sent everything for DNA analysis.' Gerrit was courtroom-serious in his cold summation.

'What about all the others working in the museum? Have they been blood grouped?' Jack asked.

'Yes. About 42 per cent of the Irish population are group AA or AO and the breakdown amongst the museum staff is similar. We can only really use it for exclusion not inclusion.'

'I know that Gerry. Tell me who else was group A.'

'That's confidential to our enquiries and to the people involved, Jack. I'm sure you'll understand.' Gerrit blushed a little as if uncomfortable with his answer.

'So much for co-operation. Listen Gerry.' Suddenly there was a hard edge to Jack's voice. 'This was certainly an inside job, on that we're agreed right?' Flatley nodded. 'In that case Babs is in danger and I want to know who can be excluded from my concerns. If you don't see the reason in this then you'll get jackshit help from me. Comprendez!'

'Very well. We don't know about Ahmed al-Akrash, given the lack of documentation concerning him, but five of the part-time and full-time museum staff are group A. Mags Golden, the manageress of the café, Brigadier Crawford one of the Trustees, Aengus FitzHenry the director, Cormac McMurragh the photographer and Brian Foley one of the other guards.'

In place of sense there was only numbness. 'And Flanagan?' I asked.

'We also have a problem there in obtaining any sort of record.

Jerome Flanagan is either incredibly healthy or incredibly careful about leaving a spoor. In fact, this is something I need to talk to you about Rio. Did -' Gerrit Flatley looked towards Jack, hesitant about continuing.

Jack Dawson nodded knowingly and stood up. 'I'm just going to grab some fresh air. I want to look around the back laneway before it gets too dark.'

He winked as he left.

'What was all that about, Gerrit?' I asked, puzzled.

'I felt a little awkward about asking this in front of your uncle. Did you and Flanagan use a condom?'

I immediately realised that he was looking for a sample of Jerome's semen for blood group and DNA analysis but still resented the intrusion. 'You mean did we have sex?' I asked defiantly.

'Yes. Did you and he have . . . penetrative sex?'

'No. There was . . . is neither penetration nor substance in my relationship with Jerome Flanagan,' I said with a bitter conviction.

His eyebrow lifted slightly. 'Good . . . I mean fine.' I thought his discomfort endearing, old-fashioned. 'A great pity though.'

'I'll remember to demand a sample next time I'm a suspect.' I began to laugh. 'Would you like some more coffee, Gerrit?'

He also started to laugh and its deep timbre carried the mood of the room before it. Jack returned and was relieved at the atmosphere between us. Gerrit noticed the fly-fishing rod hanging over the fireplace and asked about it. Jack obliged. 'Babs caught her first bonefish with that rod. Be carefully Gerry what she hangs up there next.' They both laughed about this and at my embarrassment.

'I must get along, Rio. Thanks for the identification and the coffee.' Gerrit pulled on his coat.

'Thank you,' I said.

'I'll keep in touch,' he said, looking at Jack. 'With you both,' he added looking at me.

I walked him to the door and watched until he had disappeared around the corner. Nice man. Uncomplicated. Good-looking with it! He held onto the etching as it was still in the chain of evidence. I did not mind, as long as it had been recovered and definitely thought that things were looking up then Aengus FitzHenry arrived shortly afterwards. I was upstairs and from the bedroom could hear Jack giving him a very frosty reception. I delayed as long as possible before coming down. FitzHenry was still standing and looked furious.

'What do you want FitzHenry?' Jack demanded loudly he saw me coming down.

'I'm used to my title being used Mr Dawson,' he blustered.

'What do you want Dickhead,' Jack obliged.

'Easy, Jack. I'm sure Professor FitzHenry has a good reason for being here,' I said standing close to Jack.

'I thought Inspector Flatley would be here. I received a message that they recovered the etching.'

'They have and they are holding onto it as evidence. He asked me to identify it and also about the conditions it should be stored in. I obliged on the museums behalf, free of charge.'

'I see. Thank you?'

'A lot more loyal than you fucking were,' Jack growled.

'My hands were tied Mr Dawson. The trustees demanded it. Somebody had to be held responsible.'

'And you decided it should be Babs . . . Rio. Why not you? Ahmed al-Akrash was, I understand, employed directly by you. Did you not check him out? Where did you hire him from?' Jack was being the policeman.

FitzHenry was caught off guard. 'That . . . that is none of your business. I don't discuss the museum's hiring practice with strangers.'

'You were happy to discuss my firing with all and sundry,' I said.

'I'll do what I please, Dr Dawson.'

'Goodbye then, Aengus. I'd like to say it was a pleasure working with you but you will understand if I don't,' I said with icy control while moving towards the door.

FitzHenry suddenly looked uncomfortable with his dismissal. 'Listen Dr Dawson . . . Rio. I am ready to apologize for my hastiness, to you and to Mr McMurragh. I would like you both to return to work.'

'I'm not sure Aengus. My uncle and I are planning to go to Istanbul and I will take some time there to think about it.'

'Istanbul? Are you meeting up with Jerome Flanagan?'

'If we are it's none of your business?' Jack growled.

'Why? What do you know? What does he know?'

'About what Aengus?'

'Oh . . . the Book.'

'I thought you said the Book was bullshit. You certainly didn't give it much credence when you were firing me.'

'Suspending, to be accurate. Which is now lifted. I hope we can forget this little contretemps between us. We have the opening of the Anglo-Danish exhibition in two weeks and I hope to use the occasion to announce the finding of the Durer.'

'*Little*! For God's sake Aengus, Joe Reilly is dead and Phyllis is still missing. That is not *little*. How can you be so unthinking? The opening should be cancelled.'

'That is most unfortunate, I know, but the Library must carry on. Dr Andrew would have wanted . . . would want that. I'm sure the police will soon sort it out soon. Now I really must go. Goodnight Mr Dawson.'

Jack simply grunted.

I opened the door to let him out. He was in a great hurry to leave. 'Oh Aengus,' I called after him remembering something. 'Talking about the museum. Do you have a key for the solvent cupboard?'

'*What?* Yes . . . why do you ask?'

'I have December's diffusion samples in a sealed bag inside my fridge. You need to bring them to the museum.'

'Why?'

'Isn't the safety officer coming first thing tomorrow to dispose of the solvents and collect the diffusion samples?'

'Oh right! I'd forgotten. Thank you. I'll look after it.'

'Fine. Hold on there,' I said, turning back, to retrieve the samples from the kitchen.

Accepting the bags, FitzHenry mumbled, 'I hope you'll come back. You are very conscientious. It's a rare commodity.'

'I'll think about it and let you know,' I said closing the door.

12

ANGELS

"Her eyes consumed the beauty of his light, moving slowly down his powerful body, the richly feathered wings, broad, elegantly flat torso, the lovely girded loins, long leanly muscled thighs and calves. Then she saw the feet . . ."

Thomas E. Kennedy • *Angel Body*

3.00 am. Flanagan rubs his eyes. One more entry, a short one! Did not want to bring her laptop to Istanbul; and that's why it ends, he suspects. Wonders whether there is a handwritten diary somewhere, she didn't mention it . . . nor did Mac for that matter. Keep going, he reminds himself, Jack is sure to arrive at an ungodly early hour. So what, he thinks. I'll confront the bastard. Most of this mess is his fault. He should have known better. Should not have taken Rio to Istanbul. Should have taken her away from here. Should not have ever been anywhere near her . . .

Armpit Diary,
JANUARY 29:
Getting ready for departure tomorrow morning. Busy all day. When Gerrit rang I had to dodge through the suitcases cluttering the hallway to get to the phone. His mood was light. 'Are you all set?' he asked.

'Yes, Gerrit. Listen, you don't need to bother taking us. It would be just as easy to catch a cab,' I volunteered, politely.

'It's no problem, Rio. I'll see you first thing in the morning. I wanted to have a quick word with Jack. Is he there?'

'Sure,' I said, not altogether pleased at being dismissed so quickly. 'Hold on I'll get him.'

I brought the phone to where Jack was sitting at the dining table. He had spent the previous evening and most of the morning calling in favours from his former FBI colleagues for their help in tracking down any information they could get on Flanagan and Ahmed al-Akrash. As Jack took the phone the doorbell rang and his eyes flickered anxiously for a moment, flashing a note of caution, before I went to answer it.

'One moment, Gerry,' Jack whispered into the phone as he waited for me to look out through slightly drawn back window curtains at whoever might be at the front door. I turned back and gave a silent, thumbs-up before heading for the hallway.

'Yes, Gerry. Go on. . . oh no problem.'

As I returned to the room the conversation ended.

'No Gerry, best say nothing . . . gotta go . . . see you in the morning.'

'Say nothing about what? What did Gerrit want?' I asked.

'Oh that. One of my contacts in the FBI had telephoned Gerry's boss seeking some clarification on what I was up to. I was telling him to keep it to himself. He also wanted to know if there was anything more he could do before we left. Police work I mean.' Jack grinned.

'Don't be crude. He's a nice man.'

'He likes you, Babs. Anyway you better introduce us.' Jack was smiling in my direction.

'What! Oh I'm sorry.' I moved aside a little. 'Jack Dawson, my uncle, James Somerville, the Western Curator in the Library.' I was still somewhat surprised by his unexpected appearance.

'How do you do, sir?' James Somerville leant forward, reluctantly offering his hand.

'It's a pleasure to meet you, Jimbo,' Jack said, extending his. It was a very brief shake and their hands seemed to withdraw quickly. From the corner of his eye Jack could see me trying to stop my face creasing in amusement.

'Please sit down, James. Would you like some coffee? I've no milk I'm afraid, as I've thrown it out. We're heading off very shortly.' I hoped he wouldn't.

'No thanks Daw . . . Rio. I heard you were heading for Istanbul tomorrow and I wanted to be as much help as I could.' James Somerville was blushing. 'I think you were dealt with in a very unjust and undeserved way by the Museum and I wanted to try and make some amends.'

'That's very sweet of you, James.' I smiled at him.

'What do you mean, Jimbo?' Jack seemed edgy and anxious for him to get to the point.

'I've tracked down the names of all the dealers in Istanbul that Chester Beatty sometimes bought from. They, or their inheritors, might be able to throw some light on the parchment's origins and perhaps give you a lead to its present whereabouts. If Jerome Flanagan has gone to Istanbul –'

'How do you know that, Jimbo?'

'I'd prefer, James if you don't mind Mister Dawson.'

'Sure. How did you know that . . . James?'

'There is little else talked about in the museum and little kept secret. If he has gone there, then there is a very good chance that that is where the parchment is by now. I am hoping . . . no, I believe he is following rather than leading, if you catch my drift. Cormac McMurr –'

'Right.' Jack interrupted. 'May I see the list?'

James nodded gravely as he opened his very old and very battered tan leather briefcase, pulling out three pages of neatly hand written notes and laying them on the table. 'Under no circumstances must anyone in the museum, particularly Aengus, know that I've done this. Is that understood Rio . . . Mister Dawson?'

'Sure,' they said in unison sitting down on either side of him.

James squirmed a little with the close bodily contact.

'What's this one here?' Jack asked as he pointed to one of the pages where there was a lot of underlining for emphasis.

James Somerville smiled. 'I think that might be your best bet but also a little frustrating.'

'Why?' Rio asked.

'There are three file entries relating to one Bay Arslan Nuzhet Bogac, a bookseller who had dealings with Chester Beatty, first as a guide to Beatty and his daughter in 1926 and subsequently, as a dealer between 1928 and 1947. One of the files is empty but is cross referenced with another in the archives.'

'Why is the file empty?' Jack looked at him suspiciously.

'A few possibilities. Sometimes it might have been only one page of correspondence or a bill of sale and it has been re-filed by mistake in a different folder.'

'And the cross reference?'

'Refers to another dealer called Malek Hakim, who brought a Qur'an to Cairo after the war for Beatty to look at. There is a letter to Beatty from this man complaining of his troubles with two or more other dealers in their attempts to get hold of the Qur'an. He calls himself a intermediary and said he was enclosing something by way of proof of his right to negotiate.'

'*Hakim*! But–' I blurted out before Jack quickly interrupted.

'That's very interesting, Jim . . . James.'

'And he refers to himself as a –' I started to ask before Jack interrupted again.

'Any record of this particular Qur'an? Did Beatty buy it?' Jack questioning was very business like as he looked at his watch.

'No record, I'm afraid Mister Dawson. As I've mentioned to Rio before that is not altogether unusual. Many of the files in the archives are just notes of the money involved and not the actual purchase details.'

'Are you saying, Jim . . . James, that this Malek fellow might have been an agent for another bookseller like say Arslan Nuzhet?'

'The cross-referencing points that way. However, you should realise at the outset that transactions with dealers of ancient and rare manuscripts is like walking into a hall of mirrors. Due to difficulties of provenance you can never be really sure of whom you're dealing with. Even though Nuzhet and Chester Beatty had a long-standing relationship, the Turk was more of an intermediary than source of rare books. Other dealers would use him to make a pitch to Beatty. Malek Hakim might just have been another cog further down the line,' James Somerville concluded with a smile.

'I'd love a photocopy of that letter.' Jack's fingers were playing with his lips.

'I thought you might,' James said with a satisfied air as he pulled a sealed, brown envelope from his briefcase. 'There is a photocopy of all the correspondence and also the addresses of all the dealers, in Istanbul at the time.'

'That's fantastic James. I could kiss you!' I put my arm around him and hugged. It caused James to shoot up in almost ballistic fashion from the chair.

'I . . .I'd better be going. I hope I've been of some help Rio and I do wish you the best of luck.' He had retrieved his bag and was already bolting for the door as he spoke.

'One more question, James. Is there no mention of a Hekim or Hakim on this list,' I asked without any undue emphasis.

'No. As I said, it was a murky world,' he replied.

'*Ça alors!*' Jack said with surprising accentuation.

'Please don't mention my visit to anyone.' James looked really worried.

'We won't. Thank you so much, James. Hold on and I'll see you out,' I said, getting up. I looked at Jack, in passing, and he had a wide smirk on his face, which was still there when I returned to the room.

'I think I would have better luck with James than you.' He laughed. 'I could practice my sensitive side and if his limp handshake is anything to go by, Jimbo is one dude who likes to keep a distance.'

'Don't be so cruel Jack. Irish gays are the most homophobic homosexuals in the world. You'd need a complete makeover.' I laughed back. 'It was very kind of him all the same.'

'Yes.'

'Why did you cut me off earlier?' I asked as I sat down beside him.

'This is in code, Babs. Somebody was alerting Beatty to the true nature of the Book. ' He pulled the copy of Malek Hakim's letter from amongst the enclosed pages. 'I bet you that Hakim is not even the true name of the dealers agent. There was no need for Somerville to know of the possible significance of the word.'

'*Melek* or *malak* means angel or God's messenger,' I added, suddenly realising what he was alluding to.

'I'm not completely ignorant Babs,' he said defensively.

'So do you think now that Jerome knew of this letter when he gave me the false name?' I had mixed feelings about the possibility.

'Perhaps. I don't know. He worked in the museum for long enough and has been looking for the Book, his Holy Grail as he called it. He probably came across the letter but ignored its significance. The 'catchword' or 'Watchman' you found sealed it for him and he already knows . . . or knows where to find out about this intermediary. He's after that Book of his, the parchment is of no further interest. We'll need to study this carefully. It might be our only lead to tracking him down.' Jack pursed his lips.

The doorbell rang.

This time Jack answered and walked back into the room with Gerrit.

'I'm sorry to intrude, but I called into say that I'll not be able to take you to the airport tomorrow, something has–'

'Phyllis?' I asked, hoped, dreaded.

'No word yet, I'm afraid.'

'That's good of you, Gerry.' Jack was almost pushing him out of the room again. I followed them out to doorway.

'If you run into any language or communication difficulties in Turkey give me a shout,' the detective offered, hesitating before getting into the car.

'Why? Do you know someone?' Jack asked.

'Yes. Me!'

'I don't understand,' I said, puzzled.

'Gerit is the Turkish for Crete. My mother was the daughter of a Turkish diplomat and she named me after the island where I was conceived when on honeymoon with my father, although in Ireland they added the second "r" on my birth certificate. Turkish was the first language I learnt. Have a safe trip.'

That's where his colouring comes from, I thought, as I watched his car speed off. 'Jesus! That's a turn up,' I said, turning to Jack.

'Yeah. Isn't it?' He frowned. 'Come on. Lets get some shuteye!'

Something was bothering me. I needed to ask him.

'Jack.'

'Yes.'

'Why did you really – No. It doesn't matter. Some other time.'

'Right,' he shrugged, and headed for bed. 'Are you coming?'

'In a while. I want to finish up some writing before we leave,' I said thinking of this diary.

Later the unanswered question bothers me again. Looking up, I see he has left his door open. It is a question for another time, perhaps in Istanbul. Perhaps never!

I wonder why Mac hasn't called back. No. I know why he hasn't. Left a message on his machine telling him where we are staying. Will ring him again tomorrow. Need to somehow . . . that night, ignoring him was a mistake. I know that now.

I don't do intense . . . or forgiveness well.

Right! Time to back up on disc and then bed. The thought of Istanbul is exciting.

13

THE CAVE OF MONTESINOS

"Tell me thy company, and I will tell thee what thou art."

Miguel de Cervantes Saavedra • *Don Quixote*

Flanagan reads through the last entry again. 'Fuck,' he whispers, relieved that Mac had not read the diary. 29 January, the date he remembers Mac said he was brought in for further questioning. They had left him out the following day, he'd said. Went on a bender, he knew now but back then he had believed him. He'd just arrived back at the hotel after a visit to Ismâil's specialist friend. Not wanting to be alone he had headed for the café across the street, looking for company. He was nursing his fear and a double vodka when Mac had phoned, ranting.

'I'm glad you're ok, Mac,' he said after listening until the rage finished. 'Though you do sound rough.'

'Where the hell are you, Jaffa?'

'Where do you think? Istanbul.'

'You've left a sorry mess behind you here.'

'What do you mean?'

'There's an all-points-bulletin out on you with Interpol. They think you are responsible for the robbery and Joe's death . . . and the disappearance of Phyllis. You're not, are you?'

'Both you and I know I had nothing to do with that.'

'Rio's seriously pissed off with you. She and her Uncle Jack are heading for Istanbul. He's some sort of a cop, I think.'

'Shit!'

'Yeah! Leaving me to wallow in it.'

'I'm sorry about that Mac. Once I have the Book I'll come back and explain . . . to Rio as well.'

'If she doesn't get to you first.'

There was a long silence, just the sound of our breathing. Across the road, beneath the hotel was a shop selling carpets. Two good-looking men sat outside preening themselves, waiting to ponce and pounce on any pedestrian who might show a half-interest in their wares.

'Like *Altisidora*!' He suddenly said, loudly, hoping Mac would remember better days: their schooldays and the drama enactment that had brought them together for the first time.

There was another pause but then at last it came.

'*Since thou, false fiend, When nymph's thy friend, Aeneas-like dost bob her Go rot, and die, Boil, roast, or fry, With Barnabas the robber* . . . Fucking apt all the same, ya bollix.' Mac's voice was brittle.

'You remembered, Mac. We did have some great times. Didn't we?'

'What's up with you, Jaffa? You sound weird!'

'Na. Just tired.'

'You and I both! Why are you pushing so hard for the bloody book? Do you think that you'll find that it really has some secret, the answer to the world's ills . . . or your own for that matter.'

One of the carpet sellers was looking at him intently, calculating. 'You and I know there are no secrets, Mac, just distorting mirrors. No, it's just something I have to do. . . . must do before . . .'

'Speak up, Jaffa. The line is shite.'

'Any chance of you coming out here, Mac? I could do with your company.'

'You're serious?'

'Yeah. I'll pay.'

'Christ. You must be desperate.'

'Dear Sancho. *Pardon me that I have brought upon thee, as well as myself, the scandal of madness . . .*'

Mac laughed, finally. 'Alive or dead! The bounty hunters ride again!'

'What do you mean by that, Mac?' he'd asked, wondering if his friend already knew.

'Nothing and everything, Jaffa! It's always been our way, you and I . . . you leading, me following, but with a duty to each other, to our purpose, our existence. The great thing is though . . .' Mac slurred to a stop, was silent for a moment then, 'The great thing is though, that to you and me, the bounty hunters of being, the reward is the same. Alive or dead, either way we get it.'

'You're right.'

'Bollix I am!'

'Get over here, Mac. I really need you.'

'I'm on my way. If only to protect you from Rio.'

'She's some woman, Mac.'

'The best, Jaffa! The very best.'

Flanagan cannot keep his eyes open any longer – and doesn't.

MELTIMI

*"In the fate of the 'Ãd there was another sign. We let loose
on them a blighting wind . . ."*

The Qur'an • *surat al-dhãriyãt* (The Winds); 51, *v.* 41

14

IDOLS

"On the surface, an intelligible lie;
underneath, the unintelligible truth."

Milan Kundera • *The Unbearable Lightness of Being*

The mobile phone shrills loudly beside him on the bench as he sits drinking water in the small park beside of the mosque. Flanagan has just turned it on with the intention of checking for messages but the water is a more urgent need. He has spent the best part of the last eight hours, since dawn, walking the warren of streets above the northern bank of the Golden Horn, created when the squatters had moved into the Ok Meydani in the early nineteenth century. The climb had taken him from the Koç museum on the waterfront up to the site of the old archer's lodge, in front of the Ok Meydani mosque, and then down the hill again into the valley. He feels exhausted. His hands are shaking. He gulps down the water and ignores the phone's shrill. It stops ringing.

To his right, to the northeast, on the next rise in the landscape is the Feriköy cemetery where he is convinced the *Puta Tobra* target-idol once stood. To his left, over the classically domed roof of Piyale Pasha mosque, back up the hill, is the Sinan Pasha mosque, the site where he determined the *Hekim* target to have been. He thinks through his calculations again and is even more certain. All the clues, he reminds himself, are in Karabatakzade's letters to his son and father.

He flips open his notepad and checks his notations one more time: *Our messenger spirit*, the calligrapher had written deliberately, to his father, as a coded message. The use of the emphatic '*Our*', Flanagan noted, acknowledged the family's writing heritage, a heritage which predated the family's use of Arabic or Persian but still had to be a northern Semitic language. It had to be if the *ilm-i-abjad*, the science of the letters, was to be used to find the spot. Aramaic-Syriac or Palmyran, Flanagan had written in bold red letters. In the older Biblical literature in Palestine, he knew that the Messenger Spirit, the Paraclete of John, was called *m-n-h-mna* in Syriac, or sometimes *munahhemna*, meaning 'the life giver'. Convinced of this, he had paced the distance derived from the calculation of the letter values of the *m-n-h-mna* word-root– a total of 196 *gez* – from the graveyard towards the Sinan mosque. This had placed him in the middle of the footbridge that crossed the Piyale Pasha Boulevard – a huge fucking motorway!

Sitting on the bench, looking back towards the footbridge Flanagan feels defeated. Concrete and bitumen have long covered-over the field of his dreams.

His mobile phone shrills again. This time he answers it.

'Ismâil.'

'Jaffa my friend. Where are you?'

'It's no fucking good, Ismâil. There is a huge bloody motorway exactly where the Book is most likely buried. It's a dead end.'

'Where are you?'

'Piyale Pasha mosque.'

'Let us meet. I have some wonderful news for you?'

'What is it?'

'Tomorrow my friend. I have no time now. There is much to achieve.'

'Where.'

'There is a good restaurant beside the Kariye mosque near the Edrine Gate. Midday?'

'Fine. But tell me the news.'

'Tomorrow, my friend.' The line goes dead.

Flanagan looks at the phone for a moment and then dials in for his messages. There are two: from Mac telling him he is coming to Istanbul and the other from Alanna. She has not contacted him since that night when they argued in the hotel. He listens. The recording is poor, he thinks she says she is in Izmir, is coming back to the city, and wants him to meet her with the dossier.

'Fuck the dossier,' he says aloud. Two small boys playing in the park are staring and laughing at him. He tries calling her back. There is no answer.

He stands up and walks towards the small garage directly ahead of him, across the small road that skirts the front of the mosque. There is a large poster on a nearby shop wall advertising a health drink. It has a Japanese archer taking aim, 60 or so in years, Flanagan estimates; his face deeply tanned and lined; eyes intense in their focused concentration. The archer's left arm, that holding the bow, is uncovered and is pearly white, with the skin colour and contours of a baby's arm, remarkable in its contrast, steady in its purpose. Flanagan looks back up the hill over the roof of the mosque towards the Ok Meydani and wonders whether Karabatakzade's arm was white.

He then turns his attention back to the garage. Three or four taxis are parked outside. They cannot be all in for repair, he thinks. One of them would surely bring him back to the city.

15

NIGHTINGALE

"Nightingales are put in cages because their songs give pleasure.
Whoever heard of keeping a crow?"

Jelaluddin Balkhi (Rumi) • *The Mathnawi*

They had arranged to meet at a restaurant famous for its
geographic location right on the Bospherous in Bebek – and for
its social visibility. The general's aide was waiting at the front
door as he pulled across the flow of the traffic, ignoring the
blaring horns, and stepped out to meet him.

'The General is upstairs, Colonel.'

A dark-suited attendant quickly sat in and drove the car away.

'Thank you, Captain.'

A brisk wind was blowing as the Colonel reached the glass
panel-doors at the top of the restaurant steps. He could see that
the General had declined the open terrace in favour of a table in
the far corner where there was a full view of the room. This
public display of endorsement, of patronage, on the part of the
General, was deliberate. It was the senior Army officer's exercise
of his status under Article 118 of the Turkish constitution, and its
power. This was *devlet*, the undefined notion of Turkish
statehood and the expected and fundamental duty of every
Turkish man, woman and child to subscribe to its obligation. An

obligation determined by the will of the chosen men like the General. The Colonel was now to be one of those men, a *Guardian*, and today was his ordination.

Colonel Mehmet Zorlu walked slowly, enjoying the moment. Men nodded towards him and women whispered to each other as he passed their tables. Soon all of Istanbul – all of Istanbul that mattered – would be talking of him. Approaching the General's table, he apologised for being late. The General smiled, indicated for him to sit down. A waiter held his chair.

Uncomfortable in the silence that followed, he concentrated on studying the menu – a redundant exercise, and Zorlu knew it! He waited and then watched as the older man ordered for both of them: *kadin budu*, the Lady's Thigh – ground meat, rice and eggs – for the General: *kilic siste* – swordfish – for him; and a red wine from Mamara called G.

The General, a heavy man in a dark-blue suit, exquisitely tailored to hide his paunch, pulled out a cigar holder and small guillotine from his pocket. He offered a cigar, but Zorlu declined, preferring a cigarette. The older man fingered the slight scar that ran down his temple before guillotining the tip of his cigar and slowly lighting and puffing on it.

Zorlu couldn't help but stare at his host's white-framed, manicured nails and the, very obvious, missing two fingers – the index and thumb – from the right hand. He already knew the full story of the General's fingers: a famous archer in his youth, he had mutilated himself, in despair at failing to qualify for the Olympics in Rome. It was the last time the General had failed at anything and that same brutality he now brought to bear on anybody else's failure to meet expectations. Colonel Mehmet Zorlu waited for the older man to speak.

'It is better here! More eyes, less ears.'

'Yes, General,' he agreed.

'Is it arranged?'

'Two special force units in place. Ready to go to Kirkuk on your signal. The targets have been identified. Unit 8200 and Mossad have been most helpful in this regard. It was Unit 8200 that tipped us off about Ocalan's aide and the woman arriving from Izmir.'

'We must prevent any immediate power base being established by the mountain Turks in the new Iraq.'

'And the Americans? What do you expect of them, General?'

'As always they confuse information with intelligence. They are out of their depth because their superior technology has dulled their wits. I give them six, maybe seven months, and then they'll pull out of their arrangements with the Iraqi Provisional Government. No more Vietnams. They have no stomach for body bags any more. We must be ready to move.'

'Yes, General.'

'That is why getting back that dossier is so important.'

A large puff of smoke drifted across their table. The waiter approached. Both men fell silent as their food was served. Every now and then another diner would approach their table and shake the General's hand. Each time, the younger man noticed the instant stiffening of four diners, two men and two women, at the next table. Alert, hands dropping simultaneously beneath the tablecloth, relaxing only when the pleasantries were concluded.

'I need *you* to handle this personally, Mehmet,' the older man finally said.

'Yes, General.'

'It is most important. That dossier must not get into the hands of the Americans or British. If they know of our true plans for Iraqi Kurdistan, or our arrangement with Baku, then it will cause great difficulty. We are not yet ready.'

'What of our own government, General?'

'*Motherfuckers*, all of them. We'll let them get on with fooling themselves . . . and the Europeans, that they have the power to determine the future of Turkey. Imbeciles. The military is, and has always been, Turkey. Have they not learnt that lesson? We have that power and we will exercise it when we see fit. *The true secret is with us*, Mehmet!'

'Yes, General. I'll see to it personally.'

'Good. How is your wife, my godchild?'

'In good health. Looking forward to our daughter's wedding.'

'And your son?'

'Starts in MIT in September, when his cadet training is over.'

'Does he plan to stay on in the military?'

'Of course.'

'Good. It is the only future in Turkey. You better go about the business, Colonel Zorlu, with my blessing, with all *our* blessings. Get back to me as soon as possible.'

The uniformed man watches from the shadows. The woman, early 40s he guesses, is slumped in a high-backed chair, her hands tied behind, naked and exposed apart from long dank blood-stained hair that covers her left breast. Hard to know what colour it really is, he thinks. Her head rests on her chest, moving sideways and back on the point of her chin. Tears flow down her cheeks, coursing clear streaks through the grease and grime that covers her face. A single arc light shines brightly in her face. In its glare, through half-closed and bruised eyelids, he knows she can just make out the shape of her tormentor, a bull-necked face in the sun. From somewhere else she hears, as they all hear, and reacts to the scream of a man. Its piercing agony penetrates the room.

He continues to watch, unbothered.

'In God's name, no,' she whimpers with the hoarse cry of a wounded animal.

'Give me the information I want and this will be all over for you.'

He watches her legs being separated and follows closely as the Captain's nightstick gets closer, pushing against her, penetrating her, higher and higher. Nice move, he thinks, feeling horny.

'*Tell me*,' the inquisitor shouts.

The nightstick is withdrawn, brought up to her mouth and pushed in.

'Taste your own cunt-fear, bitch!'

He hears a tooth break, sees her face distort. She can taste her own blood, he senses . . . and more. She starts to choke and tries to pull her head back. Then the vomit comes, shoots out of her. Bad move, he thinks. Starve them first, deny them water. No vomit to annoy.

'Bitch,' the inquisitor roars, covered in bile, lifting the stick to strike her.

'*Hold it*, Captain Remzi,' he orders. 'Clean the woman up and bring her back to her cell. She is no good to us dead.'

Later – how much later, she isn't sure. Outside she thinks she can hear the song of a nightingale: *lu lu lü lü li li*. Again and again, higher and higher. Must be near dawn she thinks. She is curled up on the floor of her cell. Beside her is a pot. She had tried to urinate but all that came was blood. The cold has made her skin blue and the bruising black. The door opens. A blanket is thrown down to her.

'Get up,' the same voice that had helped earlier spoke.

She just pulls tighter into a ball. Two pairs of hands lift her and sit her on a chair.

'This is not good for you. Your husband cannot help, your family cannot help, your fucking newspaper friends cannot help, nobody can help you. You are disappeared. Save yourself further pain by telling me where the dossier is. We know you have it. *Where is it?*'

She shakes her head. 'I don't know . . . what it is you want?'

'Listen. Your friend the devil-worshiper is dead. He was not as brave or as strong as you. Typical Kurd shit of a man. Their women have always been stronger and great fucks as well. Like to get it up the ass. But then you know that.'

'Please . . .'

'Don't think we don't know about all your screwing around. Fucking that Irishman. Fucking that hiristiyani filth. Fucking any mountain man with a dick bigger than his brain.'

'I don't know . . .'

There is a knock on the door. 'Colonel. The *hekim* is here with his drugs.'

'Took his fucking time!'

'Please . . .'

'Shut up bitch. Hold her down boys! I feel like one good ass-fuck before we scramble her brains. I want her to know what a man in uniform can do for her. I want her to feel the power of a 'Guardian'.'

'Please. Oh God . . .'

They met at the house hidden in the private estate on the heights above Bebek. The General was in the garden, pruning roses and did not look up as Colonel Zorlu approached.

'What happened,' he asked.

'She never broke. Died on the table,' Zorlu replied, wishing at this moment for some of the strength she had had.

'Fuck! I'm very disappointed, Mehmet. Very disappointed indeed.' The General turned to face his subordinate.

Zorlu could see the stumps of the missing fingers blanche. 'We have another possible lead, General. Her friend, the Irishman, is in town. I am having him followed. I am certain . . . I have information he knows something of the dossier. Who else would she have trusted?'

'How do we explain her death?'

'Easy. The two of them together, the Kurd terrorist and herself in a pit, made to appear like they were stoned. An honour killing.'

'Does the husband agree?'

'He does. The new de-criminalization of honour killings by the Government made it easier to persuade him to take responsibility. One or two years in a plush jail, money in the bank, in truth, his honour satisfied for her long history of betrayals. Re-election guaranteed. A good deal all-round.'

'Very ingenious, Mehmet.'

'Thank you, General.'

'And the dossier?'

'Give me two days. No more.'

'That is good. You must join us for lunch on Saturday. You and your wife. We, the incoming Council members and our wives, are flying to the house in Dilmun.'

'Thank you, Sir. I would be honoured.'

'And so you shall, Mehmet . . . if this works out.'

16

THE PERFECT SQUARE

"... for the purposes of the calculation one must measure time
using imaginary numbers, rather than real ones. This has an
interesting effect on space-time: the distinction between time
and space disappears completely."

Stephen Hawking • *A Brief History of Time*

Approaching from the Ayasofya Meydani direction, Flanagan
turns left opposite the Haseki Hamani, the baths built by Sinan
for Suleyman's Roxelana, into Tevikhane Sok. The *place of
custody*, he translates the name of the street silently while walking
alongside high, grim walls before entering the doorway of the Four
Seasons hotel and crossing the narrow lobby of the old, refurbished
prison. A large, thick-necked concierge stares at him, then moves
out, flashing his golden-keyed badge of expertise, and authority.
Times have changed but not the jailers, Flanagan thinks, shaking
his head, before stepping around the hulk to approach an auburn-
haired receptionist. He has been walking all morning and knows
he needs a shower.

'*Affedersiniz*. Dr Rio Dawson,' he asks, looking around. 'I
apologise but I don't know the room number.'

'One moment please.' She smiles back at him, dials with her
right hand, while the left pushes back a single strand of loose hair
behind her ear. This causes her name badge to move up and over
a firm breast: Fusun.

He notes her name, and also its declaration of English, Russian and French spoken. Istanbul; always a city of many languages, and many secrets, he thinks. Fusun is a very attractive girl with long fingers, manicured nails and a bloody big ruby on her finger. Way out of his league, he thinks.

'It is connecting, sir, please pick up the courtesy phone. Line 2.'

'*Tesekkur ederim*,' he says before picking up the phone.

'Hello.'

'Rio, it's Jerome.'

There is a silence then, 'You . . . How dare . . . How did you know where I was?'

'Mac told me.'

'Mac?'

'Did he tell you I came to Istanbul to find you. To have you arrested.'

'Yes.'

'Where are you? Hiding out somewhere like the sewer rat you are.'

'Downstairs. In the lobby.'

'Here?'

'Yes.'

'You've a bloody nerve,' she shouts. 'I am calling the pol . . .'

He holds the phone away from his ear. Fusun, the ruby toting receptionist, notices. Her name badge rides up. Shouting sounds much the same in English, French or Russian, Flanagan thinks: Dante's *vulgaris locutio*, Eco's simultaneous translation by angels. He tries to calm the situation.

'Rio. Come down stairs and talk to me. Give me a chance to explain. If you still want to inform the police, I'll surrender myself.' To you, he wants to add but doesn't.

Fusun's eyes widen. She looks at him and then at the concierge. He hears Rio's breathing, and then whispering with someone else.

'Rio?' he interrupts.

'I'll be down in five minutes. Jack's with me.'

'Right.' He puts down the phone. '*Tesekkur ederim*,' he says again.

The pretty receptionist nods and looks away.

A few minutes later he sees them. Rio and a man he assumes is Jack Dawson. The man looks angry, Flanagan thinks, watching him running point for Rio, whose head he sees bobbing above and behind. He is surprised. The man is as tall as Rio and has her colouring. For some reason he had expected him to be white. He doesn't know why he had thought this. He holds out his hand as the man approaches. 'Jerome Flanagan. You must be Jack Dawson. I've heard a lot about you.'

Jack ignores it and looks like he wants to hit him. 'Son of a bitch! What the hell are you playing at, Flanagan.'

The concierge is watching closely, waiting for a signal, an invitation.

'Nice hotel, Jack. Never could afford it myself but have eaten here once or twice. Great restaurant. Irish chef.' He tries to lighten the mood.

'Enough of your bullshit, Jerome! What did you want to say?' Rio presses herself between them.

He knows he looks less cocky, less sure of himself. 'Do you mind if we go somewhere private?' he asks.

'Why bother?' Rio is dismissive, her tone screaming, *screw the bastard.*

'Its probably a good idea,' Jack agrees, noticing the concierge's interest.

Rio relents and they walk by the restaurant and outside to what was once the inner courtyard of the old prison. What horrors would have taken place here in the past, Jerome wonders as he leads them to the stone staircase that leads to the hotel bedrooms – once the old cells – and sits on its lower rung. He touches a pillar that prisoners had carved their initials in – a matter of strange pride for the promoters of the hotel.

'You had better start explaining, and fast,' Rio demands. 'By the way, what happened to Mac? He was uncontactable before I left.'

'He was hauled in by the police for further questioning. I thought you knew?'

'I did,' Jack says quietly.

'What?' Rio is surprised and turns to glare at him.

'That time, back in the apartment. Gerry Flatley rang to fill me in. I didn't want you becoming upset so I decided not to tell you.'

'How dare you, Jack.'

'I'm sorry.'

The belligerence melts away from Jack, like a snake shedding skin. He's like a young child, Flanagan thinks, intrigued by the scene playing out before him: Jack wanting Rio's approval, afraid of her disapproval. For a moment she hesitates, as if wishing to pursue the issue, but then stretches out a hand and touches Jack's face, tenderly, indulgently. Something weird about this, he thinks, only half-suppressing a smile. Rio sees the smile, senses what his is thinking and turns on him. Her bitter annoyance spills out.

'Don't you dare make fun of this!'

Flanagan hesitates for a moment, calculates. 'Fuck off, Rio. And grow up.'

She feels it like a slap, reels back.

'Watch your mouth, you shit! You are in no position to . . .' Jack barks, but then appears to regret exposing himself, his inner self, so easily. A red mist descends. He lashes out.

Flanagan sees it coming, more of a slap than a fist, and the blow glances off the side of his head, but with enough force to push him back against the pillar. The impact is sharp, his nose making first contact. He thinks he hears a crack. For a moment there is no pain, just a sense of inner rebound. Then it comes. Furious. Blood flows, spurts.

'Fuck you, Dawson. You've broken my nose,' he shouts, but bends to his knees, hands over his face, in case other blows follow. His hand is twitching. He feels groggy, needs to collect himself, if he has to defend himself. They don't come.

'I doubt it,' Jack says, looking at the blood.

'Shit, Jack,' Rio says, and, to Flanagan's ears, sounding pleased.

Jack is looking down at him. He exhibits no remorse and looks like he wants to hit him again and finish the job but then decides against it. 'I'll go and get a towel. It's a long time since I hit anyone, and I'm little disturbed at the pleasure it brings. And pain,' he says, rubbing his knuckles. 'By the way, Flanagan. What blood group are you?'

'Why? Are you thinking of hitting me again?'

'Given half a chance! What blood group are you . . . in case you're unconscious or dead even?'

'Fuck off!'

'I'm serious Flanagan. Your blood group has a bearing on whether we help you or not. Either tell me, or I'll beat it out of you!' Jack Dawson said in an ice-cold tone.

He cannot be sure whether Jack is serious or not but answers. 'B Pos.' He reaches into his pocket for his wallet. Pulls out a laminated card. Shows it. 'They can have everything except my nose,' he snorts through a mouthful of blood.

'Right,' Jack says, ignoring the sarcasm and sounding somewhat disappointed.

Flanagan watches him climb the stairs and disappear inside the building. He looks at Rio. 'For some reason I did not expect him to be black . . . like you. He is very like you.'

Rio looks at him for a second, caught off-guard. 'Grandpa Dawson was from Montserrat. He fought with the British army as an expert radio-operator and was assigned to a unit working with the Norwegian resistance during the war. That's where he met my Grandmother.'

'Romantic stuff,' Flanagan remarks.

'Hardly. My grandmother's family had been ostracised, her father was a *quisling*, a collaborator with the Nazis. My grandfather understood the nature of prejudice, and its effects, given his experiences as a black man in a white army. He protected her from the retribution and, shortly after he was demobbed, they emigrated to Canada. He got a job as a park ranger, first in British Columbia and then later, after moving south, in Colorado. Jack is very like him whereas my mother was almost white, like my grandmother.'

'I see,' he says holding his nose nightly to stem the flow.

Rio sits down on the step beside him, tilts his head back. 'Tell me about Mac.'

'Why should I tell you anything?'

'Listen, Jerome, I don't give a shit about your nose. You had it coming. You lied to me.'

No sympathy here, he realises, just a broken nose, and pain. 'Is it displaced?' He takes his hand away. Tears and blood are mingling to flow down onto his shirt.

'No.'

'Do you think I had anything to do with the robbery?'

She hesitates for a second, thinking about her answer. 'No. What about Mac?'

'He was hauled in by an Inspector called Flatley. I think you know him.'

'Yes.'

Two other guests, a man and a woman come down the steps and have to step around them. The man is in his 60s – white shirt, red tie, tailored dark-blue suit, slicked back black-grey hair, and flashing a gold Rolex watch. The woman, 30 or so – bottle-blonde, tanned, pouting lips, black dress, impossibly perfect breasts, a diamond necklace disappearing between those breasts and clutching a gold-coloured, clam-shaped bag. They stop, look back, see the blood, and shake their heads.

'*Fuck off,*' Flanagan shouts at them.

'Come on. You better come up to my room,' Rio says.

He gets up, unsteady on his feet, holding his nose. They climb the stairs and take the left-hand corridor leading to her room where they meet Jack leaving his. He has a wet towel in his hand. He steps aside and insists they use his room. Flanagan holds the towel to his nose. He feels it swelling, but the bleeding stops. Rio brings him a glass of water and two painkillers from her supply.

'Whiskey would be better,' he says tasting the dilute blood in his mouth.

'Here,' Jack obliges, having poured it for himself.

'Go on about Mac,' Rio insists, accepting a glass as well.

'He was detained, and questioned. Not so much about Joe Reilly, because as you probably know the post-mortem has shown Joe had a heart attack, but in relation to the robbery and the disappearance of Phyllis Andrew.'

'And?'

'Mac had an alibi for the night of the robbery.'

'What?' Rio asks. Mac had said nothing about this.

'Angie Townsend, a daughter of one of the Friends of the Library! Works in the bookshop occasionally. Attractive.'

'What about *her*?' Rio demands, already guessing the answer.

Not in quite the way she thinks, Flanagan cautions himself, before deciding to continue. 'She has put herself through college, Philosophy and Economics. Now doing a Masters. Works as an escort to pay the –'

'*A fucking hooker*?' Rio instantly regrets her brutality.

'Mac has been availing of her services for a year or so . . . whenever he could afford it.' He remembers that Mac referred to Angie as his 'being counter' but does not say this. 'Nice kid, it seems. Had a conscience and came forward.'

'That's great.' Rio says lamely. And then her eyes narrow. 'And I was going to gift him . . . All men are the same. Bastards!' she says looking at him: looking right through him.

'Why did you run off, Flanagan? And why did you lie to Babs?' Jack sees the flicker of pain cross his niece's face and wants her to know that they are not all the same. He catches her eye, lifts his hand slightly, spreads the fingers back, and apologizes for them all.

She ignores him, Flanagan notices and for the moment men as a malignant species are all lumped together.

'I keep telling you that the Book, and what it represents, is very dangerous ground. Word will have got out very quickly. There would only be the narrowest timeframe of opportunity to try and track it down. I had to take that opportunity, to keep you out of it . . .' He looks at Rio, sees she does not believe him, ' . . . keep you out of danger.'

'Bullshit,' she flares. 'Why did you tell me the idol was *nesr* and not *hekim* and that –'

'Rio!' Jack wants to stop her.

'– you had access to a letter that would point you to a dealer who probably had the Book at one stage,' she continues.

'What do you mean?'

'Melek Hekim, the dealer's agent who wrote to Beatty in Egypt.'

'How did –' Flanagan felt stunned again, more so than from the blow.

'James Somerville showed it to us. It was easy to work out its significance.' Jack added, enjoying the second hit.

'Who else knows?' He is alarmed.

'Just us. Why . . . and please go way beyond your pathetic excuse that you want to protect us.' Rio is determined.

'You . . . you are right. Mac and I –'

'Mac?'

'I first heard about the Book along time ago, while sourcing manuscripts for the Library. In my time at the museum, Mac and I always worked as a team, trawled through every bit of information we could lay our hands on, looking for clues. Recently, a dealer friend, here in Istanbul, showed me two letters, one from the seventeenth century and one from the twentieth. Both gave credence to the existence of the Book and then, out of the blue, along comes your discovery of the parchment letter and a further clue to the Book's possible resting place . . . at least back in the seventeenth century. I wondered . . . and then was afraid.'

'Wondered what?' Jack asks, wanting to keep him on the defence.

Flanagan spends the next 30 minutes explaining the contents of the two letters that Ismâil had shown him and how the bookseller had told him that they had probably been recovered from the wreck of Symmonds' car and also about Ismâil's warning that the car crash not being an accident. He then concluded, 'Mac and I always thought that old Prof Symmonds, was after the same thing as us. It is likely he was cataloguing the old Silander box from the Curragh Military museum, the one that Rio worked on, and came across the letters but somehow missed the etching, and the letter that Rio found, in his excitement. He must have dashed off to Turkey in hot pursuit, almost certainly called attention to himself, and the Book, and then paid the ultimate price. Because the car and his belongings, including the letters, were stolen before those responsible for the accident could get to them a 'sleeper', Ahmed al-Akrash, was positioned in the Chester Beatty in case they resurfaced there, if for example the robbers tried to enter into a negotiation with the museum.'

'How do we know you're not bullshitting us?' Jack was trying desperately not to believe him. Flanagan could see Rio relaxing, letting down her guard . . . again.

'Come with me tomorrow. I have spent all day today on the Ok Meydani searching for clues, reaching a dead end. The Book existed in 1931, and it still exists, that I am certain of. It cannot be lost under concrete. I feel is presence all around me. There is something out there that I am missing which will point us to its present whereabouts. Leon Arslan and the mysterious Melek Hekim are the keys. I am meeting my friend Ismâil tomorrow. He has some further news. Come with me to meet him. Search with me.'

'Ok,' Rio said, flatly.

'What? He's fooling with you, Babs, with us.' Jack blustered. 'I don't trust him.'

Flanagan watches as she turns to Jack, calming him with her eyes, her smile. 'I believe him, Jack . . . at least I believe he had nothing to do with the break in. He's obsessed with the Book and now that were here surely it will do no harm to help. I still want to try and recover the parchment. We might hear something to help point us in the right direction. Get to see a bit of the city, as well.'

It wasn't this logic that made Jack back down, Jerome sensed, as he gave him one of his own shirts to wear, a Floridian colour explosion. As he and Rio left the room Jack warned him with his eyes. She walked him as far as the courtyard steps where he paused on the lowest rung, to smile at her. 'I am always having uncomfortable meetings in this place.'

'Alanna?' she asked.

He nodded and turned to walk away. The concierge was standing, waiting on the far side of the courtyard. Flanagan looked at the pillar, and its tortured names, and then around him, at the Square of Justice. He turned back to call to her when he was half way across.

'Did you know that the Pythagorean's equated justice, and its virtue of fairness, with the number 4. A perfect square: the product of two equal forces, good and evil, right and wrong, subjugation and being subjugated . . . reciprocity.'

'Where shall we meet?' she asked, quietly.

'The Church of St Saviour in Chora, the Kariye mosque. 11.45, ok?'

She nodded and was gone.

The hulk, on the other hand, and his perfect square jaw, followed him out through the lobby of the hotel. Flanagan stopped to light a cigarette before walking up the street. A short distance later, he felt nervous, as if other eyes were on him, tracking him. He turned around quickly, but could see nothing untoward: no shadows moving other than the bulk of the porter retreating from the doorway of the hotel, a mobile phone to his ear. He shook the unease off, putting it down to tiredness, and headed for the Hotel Nomade and sleep.

17

HAUNTING

"You reach a zenith of torment that is an extreme misfortune,
poisoned with some remaining hope."

Stendhal • *De l'amour*

'I needed that,' she says coming through the adjoining door
between their rooms.

He looks up. Her head is covered with a white towel, turbaned
wrapped, and wet patches of her dark skin shine like patent
leather through the silk of a thin kimono. He watches as she flops
into the chair opposite him, one leg dangling over the armrest.
The kimono falls away to partially reveal her crotch and almost
fully reveal her left breast.

'What's bothering you, Jack,' she asks, filing her nails.

He wants to tell her, wants it to be like it was before. He
remains silent. The intense silence irritates her. He watches her
become uncomfortable; cover over the fleeting breast; unravel the
towel and put it across her knees, pretending she needs it as a
base for her manicure.

'I just don't trust him, Babs,' he says.

'Or any man,' she laughs but then seems to regret the invitation.
'What should we do?'

'Be careful not to get out our depth . . . or into his.' Jack

Dawson hesitates for a moment, realising what he has just said. 'Flanagan knows Istanbul and could be leading us a merry dance. Don't get too close to him, Babs.'

'I won't. But I would like to recover the Book, and shove it up FitzHenry's ass.'

He laughs, understands. Her skin is black-velvet, glistening in the shadows. He thinks for a moment. 'The Book is Flanagan's obsession and little else will fill that need, apart from killing a little time. Even you!'

'I've told you, Jack. I've no intention of going down that road. Anyway you are a man of obsessions yourself.'

She holds up five fingers and smiles.

Only one, he thinks and wants to . . .

She gets up, one long leg trailing after the other. 'Did you notice how his hand shook, after you hit him,' she asks.

'Yes.'

'Fear?'

'Perhaps. Don't know.'

'Strange. Wouldn't have expected him to react like that . . . anyway, I'm off to bed. I want to see if I can track down Joyce Holden before I go to sleep. See how she is.' She leans down and kisses him on the forehead.

All he sees are her breasts.

'Good night, Jack,' she smiles.

'Good night, Babs.' He watches her open the door. 'Babs.'

She turns. 'Yes.'

'You look so like Nan Greta sometimes.'

She feels her chest suddenly tighten and she looks at him with suspicion. Had he forgotten so conveniently, she wonders, how he had . . . how they both had betrayed that love?

How, after her mother's death and Grandpa Dawson's breakdown, Nan Greta had arranged for her to stay with Jack in Eleuthera, at a wrong moment in time for all of them. Jack's first marriage had just ended and he needed love; she needed love, reassurance; a seven-year old girl and a thirty-seven year old man holding each other together. And each summer after that first she could not wait to be with him again, when they would have each other to each other for a month; Jack always careful to have his wives stay away. And each summer the sexuality between them developed further, never to intercourse, but she learned to make him happy, make him come, taste and breathe in the smell of him after he came. So much so she wanted more and more, never wanted it to end. 'Don't tell Nan Greta, he always begged when she eventually had to go home. 'Keep it our secret, Babs.'

This stopped the summer she was twelve, around the time she had her first period. She showed him the sheet from their bed and he looked frightened. Later, he said they should stop sleeping together. She was a woman now, now longer a child. He said he was afraid of her touch, her hunger, and her need to have him. She didn't understand why, she felt dirty. She rejected him after that until years later when her need surfaced again . . . his had never gone away.

Rio looked down at him. 'I never told her, Jack.'

His face flickered. 'I know.' His voice was brittle and tears welled in his eyes. 'I'm always here for you, Babs. Forever!'

'I realise that, Jack and I love you for it. Goodnight.'

The door closes. He gets up and listens against it for a moment. She always liked her own space afterwards, away from him. He hears her voice, muffled.

'Joyce. Thank God I got you. How are . . .'

He moves away from the door and checks his watch. 8.00 pm in Dublin. Lifts the receiver and dials.

'Hello.'

'Gerry? It's Jack Dawson.' Keeps his voice low.

'Jack. How's it going in Istanbul.'

'Flanagan turned up tonight. Came to see us at the hotel.'

'Jesus!'

'Yeah. Cocky bastard. I hit him.'

'Did you call the police? Do you want me to do it?'

'No. I . . . I don't think he had anything to do with the robbery, Gerry. He's just after that stupid book. I think you should call off the bulletin on him.'

'Are you sure?'

'Yes. Blood group B Pos. I checked. Much as I'd like to see him locked up I don't want to have it on my conscience.'

'Thanks for that. I'll do that right away. How's Rio taking it?'

'Fine.'

There is a silence for a moment, each man stuck in his own thoughts. Gerrit Flatley breaks it. 'Jack?'

'Yes.'

'About Rio! This is very old-fashioned . . . I was wondering . . .'

'About what?' Jack was instantly cautious.

'Do you think she would go out with me . . . on a date.'

'Jeez. I don't know Gerry. She's just come out of a bad relationship and with all that has happened . . . perhaps it's not a good time.'

'You're probably right. Anyway I'll be able to judge for myself soon-enough.'

'What do you mean?'

'I'll be in Istanbul myself tomorrow. A city built for romance.'

'*What?*' Jack shouted but then quietened to continue, 'What do you mean you are coming to Istanbul?'

'Everybody is on edge, Jack. Al-Qaeda is on the march again and the Brits are worried about Ahmed Al-Akrash. Seems he might have a *significant* past. On a tip off from the Israelis the Turkish police picked up two passengers, a man and a woman, off the ferry from Izmir. My contact in Istanbul thinks that the man answers to our friend Ahmed's description. They want me to go and check him out from our end.'

'What type of past?'

'I don't know. Terrorism most likely. What type of past do any of us have?'

'Yeah,' Jack answers tiredly.

'I have your mobile number, Jack. I'll give you call when I get in. Meet up for dinner perhaps, you, me and Rio.'

'Right. That's fine. I'll see you tomorrow, Gerry.'

'Goodnight Jack.'

He replaces the receiver, walks to the door and thinks about knocking. Babs is still talking, so he decides against it. Time enough in the morning.

18

THE UNCOUNTAINABLE

"Here, at last, is the definition of image, of all images: it is
that from which I am excluded . . . I am not in the scene."

Roland Barthes • *Fragments d'un discours amoureux*

The museum, although open, seems deserted by any other
visitors. After paying her admission fee Rio turns left to walk
along the outer narthex. She regrets now that she had not waited
for Jack, as there was something she wanted to say to him and
the quietness and splendour that surrounds her now would have
helped.

Getting up early she had left a note telling him where she was
going and that she would meet him later at the restaurant.
Having pointed out to a taxi-driver the place on a map where she
wanted to be left off, he had equated speed with potential
compensation and had screeched down the cobbled streets from
the Four Seasons hotel and out onto Kennedy Cadessi – against
the lights – before she had time to draw breath. Rounding the
Topkapi point he had finally slowed, momentarily, to negotiate
the hordes of commuters getting on and off the ferries at
Eminonu terminus before accelerating again and entering, with
abandon, the maelstrom at the intersection of Resadiye Cadessi
with the Galata bridge.

In what seemed like a kaleidoscope of colour and motion she watched with fascination as people, cars and bicycles loaded with goods surrounded them for a moment, before magically clearing in their hurry past to disgorge into the old city. Once through they followed the highway that skirted the Golden Horn and she had just begun to relax when the taxi suddenly veered sharply, across the highway, into the maze of small streets that climbed, narrower and narrower, up the hill towards its apex at Egri Kapi, the Crooked Gate, where she was very, very relieved to get out.

She had intended to head northeast along the last part of the old land walls but instead headed south. This was a different Istanbul and the poverty of ramshackle homes built against the old walls bothered her. In the small playground near the boarded up Tefukserai, the Palace of the Porphyrogenitus, which after the Conquest was both a zoo and a brothel she had ignored the stares of curious children before eventually finding her way to the Kariye mosque, no longer an active mosque but a museum; the repository, her guide book had said, of the finest Byzantine mosaics in the world.

And now she can only but agree with this assessment as she leaves the outer and moves into the inner narthex walking slowly to its limit to stand under the cupola at the northern end. She stares at the tomb of Demetrius Doukas Angelus Palaeologus.

'Hello Rio.'

She almost jumps before turning to the voice. 'Don't sneak up on me like that, Flanagan.'

'*Thou art the Fount of Life, Mother of God the Word, and I am thy slave in love.*' He is smiling.

'Get over it, Jerome.'

'I meant the inscription on the tomb,' he says pointing to the wall.

She didn't turn. 'I have a guidebook. I know what it says,' she lies, holding it up. The hastily bought, glossy English version of the Aksit selection available at the kiosk, omitted any such explanations.

'I'm sure that all men want to be your slave in love, Rio, given half a chance.'

'For all the satisfaction it has brought me,' she replies, truthfully.

'Whose fault is that? What do you demand of them?'

'That's it, Jerome. I perhaps do not know how to love but give myself willingly to loving. Men cannot deal with that "demand", as you put it.' She waits for him to reply and when he doesn't, continues, 'What about you? Do you always lie or are you just passionate about lying?'

Flanagan shrugs. 'I suppose this is as good a place as any to try and explain.'

'What do you mean?'

'Look up there, at that picture,' he says pointing to a mosaic on the west lunette beside where they stood. She notices how his hands shake and then seeing her puzzled frown how he quickly drops it, indicating with his eyes instead.

'What about it?' she asks.

'Those two scenes are from the apocryphal Gospel of St John: firstly Joseph taking leave of the Virgin to go about his business and then Joseph being angry with the Virgin on his return home, six months later, when he finds her heavily pregnant. How does one explain to someone else that a messenger Angel bearing the word of God made you pregnant and that you succumbed willingly to its intent, its message? A difficult moment in any relationship, wouldn't you say?'

'I'm no virgin, Jerome but I certainly do not like being lied to or deceived.'

'I did not mean to Rio. I truly wanted to protect you from any danger. Was not what happened to Joe Reilly and Phyllis proof of that?'

'No! You had left before the robbery was discovered. You dumped me and came here to chase the bloody book, to chase your apocryphal grail. . . since you're so fond of hidden imagery.'

Flanagan looks at her for a moment. 'You are right, Rio. In truth I don't give a shit anymore about the Book, or any other idea or aspiration, which seeks to provide a message or promise of future fulfilment. I owe the future nothing for it has done

211

nothing for me. I do owe the present something, my being, your being . . . Alanna's being.'

'Alanna?'

'She's in real trouble, I can sense it and I'm not sure what to do.'

'Are you responsible for her? I thought you and her were no longer attached.'

'No. But having loved each other once, there are conditions attached. Responsibilities if you like. That's what I meant earlier about being a slave to love.'

'I don't understand what you're getting at, Jerome.'

'Similar to the reasons for my marriage proposal to Alanna, I was worried for you. I felt something awful might happen and wanted to prevent it from happing to you. That is love, Rio, at least my kind of love, the responsible kind.'

'It's not my kind, Jerome. Never can be.'

'Afraid of responsibility?'

She ignores the challenge. 'How did you know about the danger associated with the Book?'

'I didn't at first. I had heard about its existence of course, but only in a gossipy way. Then Mac and I suspected that old Prof Symmonds was chasing something extraordinary. He was always secretive about it, but when he was killed –'

'Killed? Mac said nothing about that to me.'

'I suspected but Mac felt I was fantasising. In fact it's only very recently that it was confirmed for me. Anyway I knew that whatever Symmonds was after it held great danger. That danger excited me, drove me on to find out what he was after, and having found that, drove me on to find the Book. My Grail.'

'What's changed?' she says, looking back up at the mosaics.

'Me. It's no longer that important or relevant. I . . . Now I'm hoping that if Phyllis is alive, that if we get hold of the Book, we might be able to use it to negotiate. It must be the only reason for her disappearance. A bargaining tool.'

'Yeah sure! You . . .' She stops short and can sense his eyes boring into her. She hadn't thought about this possibility and wonders whether to believe him. She now suddenly realises that she had come to Istanbul for one reason and one reason only: to beat Jerome Augustine Flanagan at his own game. Nothing more or nothing less would do. To her shame she now admits that helping Phyllis had not figured into that equation. She flushes with the thought and hesitates before looking back from the mosaic to face him. *If he looks anyway smug*, she decides, *I'll hit him.*

She need not have worried. Flanagan turned his back and was making his way, through a throng of newly arrived Japanese tourists, towards the exit. She hurries to catch up with him. He pauses to look up at the *Virgin Blachernitissa and the Angels*, the mosaic over the inner wall above the entrance, the last mosaic to be seen before leaving the building.

He turns to her with sadness in his eyes and weariness in his voice. 'The inscription translates as *The Mother of God, the Dwelling-Place of the Uncontainable.*'

'The Dwelling-Place of the Uncontainable,' she repeats aloud, struck by his explanation, before following him out into the sunshine.

19

THE EAR OF MALCHUS

"It is to your advantage that I go away, for if I do not go away,
the Paraclete will never come to you . . ."

The Bible • John 16: 7, *Gospel of*

Flanagan follows Rio through the small side gate and down the
steps to the restaurant's garden dining area. There is no wind and
as the early afternoon temperature is unusually pleasant for the
time of year tables have been laid out in the open with white linen
coverings and single long-stemmed flowers in thin vases. Along
the high perimeter wall are olive trees and a creeping vine. Rio
smells the scent of the table flowers in the air as they approach.

Jack is already seated and glares up at them. 'Took your time,'
he growls.

'You should have joined us, Jack. The church is fantastic,' Rio
placates. 'Have you ordered?'

'I'm going to have the house speciality. Half-melons stuffed
with mince in a mint sauce. I've also ordered some wine.'

Before Jack has a chance to get up, Flanagan holds out a chair
for Rio, which is directly opposite to where Jack sits, with her
back to the entrance steps. He then takes the chair between them.
The waiter arrives and gives them menus.

'What time is this friend of yours coming?' Jack asks.

Flanagan looks at his watch. '12.15. He should be here by now.'

'Are you ready to order, Sir,' the grave-faced waiter asks.

'No. I am waiting for another – Oh. Here he is now!' The bitter smell of Ismâil's cigarette reached them first and Flanagan stands up to greet his friend, '*Merhaba* Ismâil.'

'*Merhaba* Jaffa, my friend. A good day for the time of year!'

Flanagan nods and indicates to Ismâil that he should take the chair opposite him. The waiter holds it out. 'Ismâil. May I present Dr Rio Dawson and her uncle, Mr Jack Dawson from Florida.'

Rio looks at him. Late 50s, tall, overweight, long grey hair, loose dandruff on the shoulders of an expensive suit, pale skin, beautifully manicured nails. She holds out her hand. The bookseller takes her hand, looks at her fingers for a moment, and then turns the palm prone to brush his lips off the tips. 'Enchanté, Mademoiselle. My friend, Jaffa never told me he had such a beautiful companion.'

'Merci, Monsieur Ismâil. Vous etês tres gallant,' Rio answers.

The randy old goat, Flanagan thinks, smiling. Jack Dawson coughs. The waiter is still waiting, holding out the chair.

'Excuse my manners, Monsieur Dawson, but I was blinded,' Ismâil adds as he reluctantly releases Rio's hand and shakes Jack's. 'I hear Florida is a beautiful place with a good climate. Good for old bones like mine.'

Flanagan sees Jack bristle with the 'old' implication and moves to diffuse. 'Sit down you charmer. What is the good news you have for me, Ismâil?'

The bookseller to the obvious relief of the waiter finally takes his seat. 'One moment, my young friend! Your impatience will kill you. You know I like to satisfy my appetites first and talk later.' Ismâil removes his dark-tinted sunglasses then reaches out and takes Rio's hand again, squeezes it, looks into her eyes. 'Young men do not know how to take their time. Is that not right mademoiselle? All moments like these should be savoured as if time was a whisper. Smelling, touching, tasting, are all blunted by loudness. Young men want to be surrounded by noise and miss the nuance, the passionate nuance, of whispered sensation.'

'I think Ismâil, if you were allowed, you would have me screaming,' Rio says releasing her hand and touching the bookseller on the cheek. She hadn't meant to say it like that, or even touch him, but that was what had happened. She liked beauty in men and the bookseller was no beauty. Yet she felt a charge between them, that electricity that always drove her on. It's his eyes she realised, hoping her interest had not been noticed. But the bookseller had noticed and smiled.

'You have cool fingers, mademoiselle.'

'What do you suggest from the menu, Ismâil? It's all in Turkish. I'm very hungry,' Rio says, smiling back at him for an instant before quickly dropping her eyes to the menu.

He sighs, taking the menu from her; an exaggerated sigh. 'My heart is yours, mademoiselle but,' he laughs loudly, 'My stomach is the chefs.'

At that moment the waiter returns with Jack's order. They all stare at a mountain of meat contained within a half-melon. Mint suffuses the air. 'I'll have that also,' Flanagan says, thinking that the mince would be easy to swallow.

Ismâil follows suit because of the ample proportions served, as does the woman, he notes. Because of the scent of mint, she says, smiling at him again. While eating he watches the two men, Jaffa and the American called Jack, and how they interact with the woman. She is laughing and gay and is teasing them, playing one off against the other, resting her hand on his for longer than necessary when she wishes to get him to take sides. Once or twice he feels her leg beneath the table touch against his and then pull away slowly. On the next occasion he responds with pressure of his own but with a look she tells him some other time. Not here, not now. He nods.

'Do you like intrigue, Rio?' he asks her.

He thinks he has me, she thinks, arching her eyebrows at the smiling bookseller before responding, 'What ever do you mean, Ismâil?'

'Istanbul of course! Here in this garden restaurant, this moment in time with your friends. Do you like the intrigue of it all?'

Jack doesn't like the edge to the question but cannot prevent himself from asking, 'What are you getting at?'

'Intrigue, the secret love affair of the moment before it is gone.' His eyes flicker mischievously.

'Or a plot to steal the moment, Ismâil!' Rio answers.

'Touché,' he responds, enjoying the game.

'Your English is very good, Ismâil,' Jack butts in.

'Thank you! In a former life I was an officer in the army. Spent many years on overseas assignment in both England and the United States.'

'You never told me that, Ismâil,' Flanagan says, genuinely surprised.

'You never asked, Jaffa.'

Flanagan sits back. Suddenly remembers the warning Ismâil had given him about Alanna. Tries to put it out of his head as they finish their meal. He is swirling wine about in his glass as he waits for Ismâil to pull away the tucked-in napkin from beneath his generous chin. When this finally happens, he leans forward trying to keep his voice steady, 'Come on Ismâil! What is the good news.'

The bookseller lights up a cigarette and smiles. 'I have found the Book. Well two books actually.'

'What,' Flanagan almost chokes on the wines.

'Where?' Rio asks.

'Once the letters of Karabatakzade came to light, I thought that the archery connection might help us.'

'Another thing you said nothing to me about that,' Flanagan mutters with suspicion. He is also annoyed that he hadn't considered it.

'I am sure there are many things you keep from me too, Jaffa. It is the nature of our arrangement. We have usefulness to each other. No more . . . no less.'

Flanagan sits back again, deflated. Jack is grinning widely and cannot resist taking the opportunity to needle. 'Better to keep your mouth shut, Flanagan and be thought a fool, than open it and have it confirmed.'

'Shut up, Jack,' Flanagan rasps, stung by Jack's opportunism.

'Take it easy you two,' Rio intervenes before turning to the bookseller. 'Tell us, Ismâil. I'm really excited.'

God, she's pulling his strings with that little-girl-lost voice of hers and fluttering eyes, Flanagan thinks.

'For you anything, mademoiselle.' Ismâil smiles and then continues, 'In the 1920s, under Attaturk, all of the old lodges were suppressed . . . the Mevlevi and Beçktasi *tekkes* and the like, mainly because of their influence on the military which he wanted to reform. I found out that an Archer's *tekke,* dislocated from the Ok Meydani to Eyup, still existed until that time and I was fortunate to be able to track down the son of the last *pir.*'

'*Pir.* What is that?' Jack asked.

'The leader, or *baba,* of a lodge or *tekke,* as they were known. Most were Sufi in orientation and the *pir* was responsible for the spiritual or mystical side of the lodge's activity. The Archer's lodge would be no different from that of the Mevlevi whirling dancers with layers of initiation and discipline attached, in their case, to the practice of the bow and arrow,' Flanagan explains, recovering his composure.

'Exactly, Jaffa! Through my contacts I learned that this man's son, was still alive and living in Eyup. I arranged to visit on the pretext of asking him if he knew anything further about Karabatakzade, but secretly hoping to find out if he had any knowledge of the Book and its whereabouts. It was a difficult job finding him. The house was very old and almost derelict but serving as the doorframe, remarkably, were two of the old *abidesi* distance stones from the Ok Meydani. He greeted me at the door and led me into a well-kept house. "I am Zergerdan Hekim" –'

'Do you hear that? His name was Hekim. There's the bloody connection with Beatty,' Flanagan shouts.

The bookseller frowns at the interruption.

'Please continue, Ismâil,' Jack says.

'Where was I, oh yes! "I am Zergerdan Hekim, son of Melek

Hekim and you are welcome. It is a long time since anyone has spoken to me of the Archer's lodge." This man was in his 80s, had a wasted left arm, and leg, yet he had a great dignity. "Karabatak, the cormorant, the silent arrow that once released would disappear in flight and then suddenly appear again, like the memory of the man you are looking for," he said to me.'

'Wow!' Rio exclaims, beaming encouragement at the bookseller.

'I told him of what we knew about Karabatakzade's life and how he had been betrayed. "One moment," he then said, holding up a hand and calling out a woman's name. This woman appeared from the back of the house and he whispered in her ear. "My daughter," he explained before she returned carrying a small chest. He then opened the chest with great reverence and lifted out an old book, its morocco cover decorated in beautiful gold calligraphy and the embossed engraving of an archer kneeling to Allah. He handed it to me. "That is the record of all the famous archers of our lodge up to the last of the Sultans. The history was handed down generation after generation and it was the responsibility of the *pirs* to record those histories. The pages age with their story but the binding and last few pages are my father's. Search for the name of your archer." '

Ismâil stops speaking, lights up another cigarette.

'Heck,' Jack says.

'Oh please continue, Ismâil,' Rio pleads.

'I found it of course—'

'And?' Flanagan could not help pressing.

'Our friend Karabatakzade was all that he seemed to us across the centuries: brave, skilled and loyal. According to the records, he died the death of a messenger.'

'What do you mean?' Jack asks first.

'He requested that he be killed by use of the *chaush* or messenger arrow. He wanted to hear its whistle in the air as his death approached.'

'Oh!' Rio groans with an involuntary sigh of concern.

'Dying from an arrow wound could be slow and painful. The

Sultan had his head gardener complete the execution swiftly once the arrow struck home. A significant benevolence in a time when death was often prolonged and its finality no doubt a very welcome pleasure.'

'A gardener?' Jack queries.

'The head gardener of the Sultan was also the chief-executioner,' Flanagan explains.

'Do you believe in execution for serious crimes, Rio?' Ismâil suddenly asks but keeps looking at Flanagan. He sees that his friend understands.

'Damn right,' Jack interrupts.

'Only for the executioners, Ismâil,' Rio says, noticing the pain in Flanagan's face.

'Go on with the story,' Flanagan demands.

'I closed the book and looked up at the old man. He had tears in his eyes as he spoke. "My father Melek Hekim gave me a proud name but I could never be the man he was," he said pointing to his wasted arm. "Polio. Couldn't hold or draw a bow." I did not tell him that his father most likely tried to sell the records of the *tekke* before or very soon after it was closed down. He held him in such obvious reverence it touched my soul to see an old man talk as if he still was a child at his father's knee but . . .'

Ishmail's voice falters and then fails him. He lights another cigarette and stares into the sky.

'But what?' Jack presses.

After a few moments of inhaling and exhaling deeply the bookseller takes up the story again. 'I began to make my excuses to leave but Zergerdan held up his hand. "Wait," he said. "I have something else to show you." He then lifted from the chest another book. It had leather bindings and there were horse hair tassels attached.'

'Jesus!' Flanagan shouts.

Ismâil smiles and shrugs his shoulders. 'I didn't dare breathe or show any emotion. I thought I would explode. Here was the Book, being handed to me.'

'What did you do?' Jack questions.

'Nothing. Just stared at it. I was afraid to touch it in case, like Jaffa, my hands would betray my anxiety.'

'What do you mean by that, Ismâil?' Rio asks, looking at Flanagan.

'He . . . he means I have a nervous fingering when I get excited about a manuscript,' Flanagan quickly bluffs while throwing a warning flash of his eyes at Ismâil. 'What happened then, Ismâil?'

How many secrets can you keep, Jaffa, Ismâil thinks before continuing, 'Zergerdan said, "I am an old man and will soon join the illustrious in the cemetery behind the house. These books were the most precious possessions of the *tekke*. All of the initiated archers are long dead and as I have no sons, only the daughter you have met, and so the living memory of the lodge dies with me. I've always hoped somebody would come for these before I die. To relieve me of the burden." '

'He gave them to you!' Flanagan stands up to pace around the table.

'Be sensible, Jaffa. He was old but not stupid. His daughter is unmarried and has looked after him all her life. He wants her to be taken care of. This was a negotiation. He knew the value of what he was offering.'

'Like his father!' Jack says.

'And,' Flanagan asks.

'$80,000 or thereabouts. For both books! A very reasonable price.'

'What is your cut, Ismâil?' Flanagan questions, suspicious again, before retaking his seat.

'The usual! No more no less. Just for the lodge's history book.'
'Why?'

'I want nothing to do with the Book of the . . . Messenger Spirit, Jaffa. See! I'm almost afraid to utter its name. Like our friend Zergerdan said, it is a burden. I have no desire to be a slave to that burden . . . or a victim –'

At that moment Ismâil's cell-phone shrills and interrupts.

'What do you mean by victim,' Rio asks.

The bookseller holds up a hand in apology as he listens to the phone. 'Excuse me a moment,' he says, getting up and walking towards the far end of the garden.

'Shit! Where would I get my hands on that type of money?' Flanagan says aloud with a worried frown on his face when the bookseller is out of earshot.

'Do you want the Book that bad, Jerome?' Rio challenges.

'I . . . no, no I don't,' Flanagan says truthfully.

'Are you not going to try and bargain him down, Flanagan?' Jack asks, genuinely intrigued by Flanagan's reaction.

'No, Jack. I'm not sure that it is that important any more.'

'Well I do,' Jack Dawson suddenly says.

'Why,' Rio asks concerned.

'Just business, Babs! This is a good deal and the sell-on value extremely high. Think of all those Saudi or fundamentalist Arabs, who are desperate to get their hands on the Book. In my book, to coin a phrase, they can have whatever it is they are afraid of, at a price. Let me at it, darlin'. This is my type of game!' Jack Dawson gets up from the table and walks to where Ismâil is standing. He waits for the bookseller to finish his telephone call, and then links his arm. Soon they are in animated conversation.

'I suppose it's ironic in a way,' Flanagan muses as he watches the two men haggle as if deep in the souk.

'What is?' Rio asks.

'Why did you come to Istanbul, Rio? It was hardly to corner me.'

'You're wrong about that, Jerome. I did want to corner you because you had lied to me. I wanted to see your eyes when you explained yourself. And I hoped in a way I could beat you to the Book, to get back at you.'

'You will win so. Looking at Jack he seems about to close the deal. He likes making your wishes come true, Rio. Doesn't he?'

'What do you mean?' she spits back at him defensively.

'He is very indulgent of you. Almost deferential! I suspect the only reason Jack came to Istanbul was to get me, to get back at me for hurting you. Did you see the way his nostrils flared and his eyes lit up? This is his opportunity to put one over me. Now the real Jack is coming out. He senses a collectable at a bargain price and is going after it. Way to go Jack!'

'There is nothing wrong with that.'

'When I was young, all my friends who were the go-getters, the property developers, the stock-market wizards and so on, were very attractive. They were in the game, wanted me to share in it, if I played to their rules, and both they, and the game, were exciting, something to be part of. I bought into it, lock stock and barrel. That is the main reason I left the museum. Now we meet up, infrequently it must be said because what drove us together now drives us apart, and we all seem sad. The more we acquired money, status and power the less we understood why we did so. The more we achieved the more frightening became what we perceived we had not achieved. It was automatic, without pleasure, without excitement. We could buy and sell souls at will not knowing what a soul was or could be.'

'And you're reformed I suppose,' Rio taunts.

Flanagan shakes his head slowly. 'No, in reality I'm not. I never allowed myself a choice in the matter. Too late now, to choose again.'

'Why?'

He ignores the question. 'What about you, Rio? What is your choice?'

'You mean you and me?'

'No. I know that's not possible although I would like to have tried,' he says honestly. Flanagan wants to say to her: I'm too neutral for you; I offer nothing for you to get passionate about because I have lost my own passion; I'm not a challenge because I've given up. He is unable to tell her. He does not want her pity . . . like with Mac. 'No. I was thinking of Mac. I should not have told you what I did. You know he loves you?'

'Yes,' Rio says quietly.

'What are you going to do about it? Shit!' At that moment Flanagan's hands are gripped by spasms and the wine glass he is holding falls to the artificial grass of the ground. He stoops to retrieve it, but has difficulty stretching out his fingers.

Rio ignores the fact he is bent down from the table to answer him. '*Nothing!* I have enough of my own problems without taking on Mac's. He's fucked up, angry about his life, with his existence and thinks by having me all that will magically disappear. I'm little different from that *hooker* of his. People like me don't provide solutions . . . distractions perhaps, never solutions. It's not just a colour thing but is everything about me. I seek refuge in the shadows but spend my live seeking light. Mac will douse whatever light there is. He can't help it. It's his way of being.'

Flanagan hears these last words as he raises his head back to table level, the glass finally in hand. 'But – Jesus!'

He looks up to see Cormac McMurragh standing behind Rio's shoulder. He looks pale and drawn, lips quivering as if he's about to cry. At the far end of the garden Flanagan sees that there is another man talking with Ismâil and Jack.

'Mac. How long have you been standing there?' Flanagan asks in a quiet tone.

Rio spins round. 'Mac. What are you doing here?' she flusters.

'Long enough!' Mac's voice was harsh. He moved around to take the seat vacated by Ismâil. He looks directly at Rio. 'Jaffa asked me to come. Said he needed a friend. I thought we could all be friends here. I had this notion it would be a magical time, that you and I could . . . I thought we were friends.'

'You are my friend.'

'Fuck off, Rio. I was standing behind you. I heard what you said.' He starts to stand up.

'Let's talk about this, Mac. Please.' Rio shook with emotion. 'I never meant to hurt you. I'm so sorry. Please sit down.'

Flanagan watches not knowing what to say or do. Mac hesitates for a moment but then relents. He pulls out a chair, noisily, and sits with his back half-turned to Rio. Flanagan decides to leave them together, gets up and heads for the far end of the garden where Jack and Ismâil are talking to the newcomer, a tall, dark-haired and good looking man. As he approaches them he hears them speaking Turkish and decides that he must be one of the bookseller's contacts. Jack looks a little excluded but suddenly brightens as Flanagan approaches.

'Flanagan, the very man! Let me introduce you to Detective Inspector Gerry Flatley of the Garda Homicide Division. You two have a lot to talk about.'

Flanagan's mouth opens. The good-looking man turns but does not offer his hand. He switches easily from Turkish to Dublin-accented English.

'You have lead us a merry dance Dr Flanagan. But thanks to Mr Dawson here you are not in as much trouble as you think.'

'What do you mean?' He barely gets the words out.

'Your blood group! I asked you about it in the hotel. It excludes you from the investigation,' Jack explains.

'Why are you here so, Inspector?' Ismâil asks in English.

'Our main suspect, Ahmed al-Akrash was thought to have travelled to Istanbul with a woman journalist. A couple matching their description were detained off the ferry from Izmir. I was sent to question them but on arrival this morning it seems that the man was not al-Akrash and that the couple were released into the custody of the military who wanted to question them on something to do with the Kurds. They were long gone when I arrived.'

Izmir – a woman journalist! It was too much of a coincidence. A dread flowed through his being. 'What did you say? Was the journalist called Alanna Savur?' Flanagan asks hoping against hope.

'I think so. Let me check.'

Flanagan watches as Flatley pulls out the small notebook, that all policemen seem to be born with, and flick through the pages.

'Yes. Alanna Savur. Do you know her?'

'You said the army picked her up this morning.'

'Yes.'

'Excuse me, I must go!'

'Where to?' Jack and Ismâil ask simultaneously.

'I cannot say but I will contact you later.'

'I've a good deal of questions for you Dr Flanagan. I'd prefer if you'd stay,' Flatley says evenly.

'I'm sorry, Inspector. I must go.' Flanagan was already racing towards the steps. He hoped they wouldn't try to stop him. 'Hold on to this!' he shouts, pulling his passport from his pocket and throwing it back over his shoulder. He doesn't wait to see Flatley bending down to pick it up nor look back at the noise coming from the other end of the garden.

Jack does. He hears Cormac McMurragh and Rio arguing loudly and turns. He starts to walk towards them. Then he sees a movement and hears Rio cry out. Her hand goes up to cover her ear. He starts to run. Mac is getting to his feet. His hand is raised, fisted this time, drawn back ready to strike again. Jack instinctively goes for his gun that isn't there. He screams out Rio's name. He . . .

Flanagan hails a taxi and tells the driver to take him to the ferry terminus at Yenikapi as quickly as possible.

20

MAUVAIS PAS

"Time slows and life extends beyond imagination . . ."

Joe Simpson • *One Life*

They leave the shadows of the trees and enter into the large open space. It is almost deserted. Flanagan looks at his watch.

The ferry journey had taken about an hour from the Old City and after it docked, he had quickly crossed the promenade to Buyukada's old square and joined the short queue for a horse drawn phaeton that would bring him up to the monastery. Most of those queuing were island locals, he noticed, returning from the city, laden down with bags of clothes and shoes and because of this lack of tourists the driver, bored with an unproductive day and sensing a foreigner's tip, was fully intent on taking him on the full Buyuk tour of the island's sights. After much argument they'd settled for the shorter Küçük route.

Circling the square they first passed the street where the summer residence of the Papal Nuncio to Turkey stood, mattresses and bedding being aired on its steps; and behind it to where the island's biggest mosque had been built. Flanagan smiled at the thought of Angelo Guiseppe Roncali, the future Pope John xxiii, being called to prayer six times a day. The late

229

afternoon air was cool but there was enough weak winter sunshine to make it tolerable and once they had passed the mansion where Trotsky had begun his *History of the Russian Revolution,* and the other clapperboard Charleston-like mansions that lined the elegant boulevard out of town, he was pleased to note that the horse increased its trotting tempo to move at speed through the winding avenues of tall trees that spiralled upwards around the mountain.

Nearly 4.00 pm, he notes, as they pull into the phaeton terminus at the base of the final summit of Yuce Tepe. Flanagan pays off the driver and begins the short but steep climb to the Monastery of St George. In the beginning he moves quickly but then feels a cloud of tiredness settle on him. The flagstones underfoot are slippery and he has great difficulty keeping his balance. Even putting one foot in front of the other is frustratingly difficult and he has to rest on two occasions to stop falling over. This worries and annoys him. He is used to his fingers and hands cramping with tiredness but his feet have never been a problem before. After twenty minutes of this effort he is finally relieved to feel the ground level out.

Flanagan stands in front of the main chapel of the complex and rests there for a few minutes before moving through its open door. He feels uneasy, wondering why there are no priests or penitents to be seen. Surrounding him and the entire complex, he notices, was a dense quietness, an eerie stillness that contrasts with the spasms in his hands. He eventually retreats from the church and walking its perimeter makes his way to the tea garden at the very apex of the summit. The restaurant is closed and the garden is empty of people.

Returning to the front entrance of the church Flanagan passes a row of flat tombstones – one with a skull and crossbones carving that stares starkly back at him – before pushing open the small side gate of the monastery complex and descending the steep set of steps to the first of the smaller chapels built into the side of the hill. He ducks his head as he enters and immediately turns to face the altar of dark wood and icons, the altar of Our

Lady of Blachernae. Moving close he stretches up and drops his hand into the narrow space above the altar frame. For a moment his heart stops, when he could feel nothing, but then he finds it and pulls the plastic folder towards him until he can get a grip and withdraw it over the frame and down into both his hands. He recognises Alanna's handwriting on the cover.

'Thank God,' he murmurs, tucking the slim folder into his bag and turning to leave.

He hears the footsteps first and feels a draft of wind. The hairs on his neck instantly prickle. He turns around slowly holding tightly onto the bag.

'That saves me, and you, a lot of trouble.' The voice is chilling, threatening.

'What do you want? Who are you?' Flanagan asks, frightened by the cold, dead eyes of the man opposite.

'Please step outside Dr Flanagan. This is not to be your sanctuary.'

'How do you know my name? Who are you?'

'Either you step out now or I will have you dragged out. Your choice.'

The two men look at each other for some time then Flanagan decides to obey and steps out into the sunshine. The man follows him.

'What is it you want?' he asks, looking up and seeing two other younger men standing near the top of the steps, grinning at him, one spitting towards were he stood.

'My name is Colonel Mehmet Zorlu of Army Intelligence and I want you to hand over the dossier, hidden in there by the woman.'

Flanagan spins round to confront the officer. '*What's happened to Alanna?* What have you done with her?'

Colonel Zorlu shrugs, dismissively, before coming and standing beside Flanagan. He looks out over the nightshade waters of the Mamara that are pounding the base of the cliff, far below them.

'Do you see that island over there, Dr Flanagan?' he asks, pointing to a small island in the distance.

'Yes.'

'That is Yassiada island, where Adnan Menderes was tried in 1961 by the Turkish Military and where he was held before being hanged on Imrali. He found out the hard way. We . . . the military are the real power in Turkey, Dr Flanagan and Menderes forgot that. He tried to deny the great legacy of Kemal and pander to the needs of minorities who wanted to see this great country destroyed. It is best that you don't.

'But you said your name was Zorlu?'

The soldier smiles, nodding his head, a harelip exposed momentarily before curling upwards again to bury itself under a bushy moustache. 'He was a relation. He trusted . . . was duped by Menderes. That was his mistake and he paid for that gamble with his life. I will not make the same. The dossier please.'

Flanagan wonders whether they carry guns, knew they did, thinks about making a run for it through the warren of the complex, and then realises he would have to choose – again.

'I know what you are thinking,' Zorlu says without looking back from the sea. The harelip quivers. 'This moment, this particular moment in your life, is what is known in mountaineering terms as a *mauvais pas*, Dr Flanagan. You have a decision to make. If you take the step, perhaps you will make it, but you also know that one error, one minute error of judgement will mean your long fall into hell, a death of splattering against the rocks down there, perhaps . . .' He then swivelled to fix Flanagan with his stare. 'Or you can pull back, not take the step, not take the risk, knowing that the climb is then over but you live to think about that failure. I have climbed many mountains Dr Flanagan, and know what I am talking about.'

Flanagan stalls for time, and information. In the soldier's eyes he sees that whatever he decides he is a dead man walking. Where is she? What had they done to her?

'Where is Alanna?' he demands again.

'The woman does not matter. She was a traitor to this country by trying to undermine its balance, its very delicate balance.'

'You mean your power and that of the Generals?'

Zorlu's eyes narrow. 'You have no knowledge of what it is to be a soldier, a warrior, or a leader of men. Power is exercised to instruct the ignorant. That is the *secret* of our effectiveness.'

The emphasis was blatant. '*Secret*. I know who you are now, Colonel. *The true secret is with us.* You are Muserin,' Flanagan suddenly realises and says aloud. He is unprepared for the soldier's reaction.

'*How . . .*' The colonel starts shouting but then quickly calms to a whisper, out of earshot of the men above, 'How could *you* possibly know about that?'

Flanagan knows he is clutching at straws. He knows he has to keep the bluff going. 'I know many things, Colonel Zorlu. I have made sure that if any harm comes to me this information will be passed to a senior politician in the Turkish government. Names, rituals, intentions, the lot! That is my power and –'

'One moment,' Zorlu interrupts, turning away to dial a number on his cell-phone and speaking in a low voice.

Flanagan watches him, watches the skin flush in the man's neck, until the call ends and he turns back to face him again. The eyes are murderous. He feels his hands begin to stiffen up and then spasm. The Colonel's image blurs and then comes back into focus again.

'My superiors do not give a shit for any secret obligations. But I believe in the legacy, I believe in the responsibility of the ages. Your knowledge has saved you for now Dr Flanagan, but only if you hand over the dossier.'

'But–'

'The dossier . . . now! Or you die where you stand. Those are the orders from my superiors, your superiors.'

He watches Zorlu look up to the men on the steps behind. He turns. They pull back their jackets to reveal holstered guns and begin to descend towards him. He reaches into his bag and withdraws the folder, hands it over.

'You live to climb again Dr Flanagan,' Mehmet Zorlu sneers. 'But not in Turkey! Leave and never return. This is a final warning.'

'What happened to Alanna? Tell me where she is. Please.'

'The Kurd woman is dead, Dr Flanagan. She was braver than you and took the step.'

'You bastard . . . *you bastard*,' he cries out, slumping to the ground.

'Leave Turkey Dr Flanagan or you will join her. You have 24 hours. After that the Muserin can no longer protect you. Good day.'

Suddenly he is alone and a swirling wind causes the gate at the top of the steps to rattle against the stone. Tears flow down Flanagan's cheeks, and a sobbing wells up that racks his whole being.

21

SINAN QUA NON

"Thou marble hew'st, ere long to part with breath:
And houses rearst, unmindful of thy death."

Horace • *Ode 18*

'Don't fucken' move!' Jack Dawson screams, moving with surprising speed. Gerrit Flatley and Ismâil are close behind.

Cormac McMurragh hesitates, looks at the oncoming men, looks at Rio, drops his fist and turning away from her rushes through the main restaurant past a panicked waiter.

Jack diverts to follow.

'*No!* Stop Jack,' she cries out.

Jack stops, looks at her and begins to walk back towards the table.

Gerrit Flatley has got there first. 'Are you all right, Rio,' he asks, gently taking her hand as reaches her. Her left cheek is reddened.

Jack tries to barge through.

'I'm ok, you two,' she says. 'Excuse me, I'm going to the toilet.'

Rio gets up. Jack makes to follow her but Flatley holds his elbow. He snatches it away and glares at the policeman.

'Let her be, Jack,' Flatley says.

'Yes, Mr Dawson. It is better,' Ismâil adds, slightly out of breath from the excitement. He lights yet another cigarette. 'Anyway you and I have business to attend to. My car is outside. Let us go now and complete the arrangements. We have to, what is it you say, strike while the hand is hot.'

Jack Dawson hesitates, growls, 'Iron. Strike while the iron is hot.'

'Whatever! We should go,' the bookseller says impatiently as he turns to leave.

Jack turns to Flatley. 'We'll all meet up back at the hotel. Say 6.00 pm.'

'Ok!' the policeman agrees.

Jack hesitates again, looks in the direction of the toilets and then at the departing Ismâil. 'Look after her, Gerry.'

'No worries, Jack! Of course I will.' Flatley smiles smugly as he watches Jack hurry to catch up with the bookseller. He is about to sit down when Jack shouts from the top of the steps.

'Oh, by the way Gerry! Look after the bill will ya. There's a good cop!' Jack's laughter follows him out of sight.

'Why did you bring me here?' Rio asks, hugging close to the wall to allow a battered truck, laden down with western style toilets and watermelons, negotiate the narrow street.

They had taken a taxi from the restaurant with the intention of heading straight for the hotel but Flatley had suddenly insisted on them being dropped off at Sirkeci railway station and then walking through the maze of streets to the rear of the Yeni Camii and onwards and upwards towards the magnificent presence of the Suleymaniye mosque that dominated the old third hill of Byzantine Constantinople. He took her hand.

'Whenever I come to the old city, I feel I have to walk amongst its streets, like a penitent seeking its blessing, breathing in its aromas, its resonance . . . its message. It has always had that effect on me.'

'But where exactly are we?' she asks.

'Just a little bit further,' he replies, striding forward, pulling on her hand.

They enter Mimar Sinan street from its southwestern end beside the hamam of the Suleymaniye and keep walking until they reach the small triangular apex at the head of the street where a small domed sebil stands. Behind this, at head level and difficult to see because of the high walls, was a marble sarcophagus with a turbaned tombstone at its head. She watches as Flatley reads the inscription on the southern facing wall.

'Well,' she demands.

'This is the tomb of Sinan the great, if not the greatest architect of all time. As modest in death as he was in life! He designed the Suleymaniye behind us and also most of the crowing architectural achievements of the Ottoman empire, without which it would not have been remembered, except for its brutality.'

'*Sinan qua non*,' she says and he laughs, hugging her. She likes the feel of his arms about her.

'And you are, Rio, a *sine quo non*, an indispensable person, like Suleyman's Roxelana, a person without whom I can do nothing, who for the first time in my life dominates much of what I think and what I wish for,' he whispers into her ear. 'That is why I brought you here, for the echoes of love built into the walls.'

She withdraws from him. 'You're serious, Gerrit. Aren't you?'

'Yes. Very! *Sine fraude*!'

'Thank you,' she says and leans forward to kiss him on the cheek. He turns his head slightly and their lips meet, tentative at first but then hungrily finding each other waiting and wanting. They eventually pull apart. Rio holds him tight. He laughs.

'I'm impressed,' he says.

'In what way?' she asks.

'I thought it was only us kids who were schooled – branded even – by the Christian Brothers, who could still quote their Latin.'

'There is much about me you have yet to learn,' she says burying her head into his shoulder, in a cautious tone.

'What do you suggest we do now?' he asks.

'What else is there?' she groans in need.

Walking hand in hand, stopping to kiss in darkened doorways and shadows, with desperate urgency they reach the hotel entrance, brush past the burly concierge and disappear into its silence.

Further down the street, a shadow hidden in a shadow watches and circling seagulls mask a cry of pain.

22

SPIRIT LEVEL

"We had caught the word handed down through the ages with secret laughter, that we ourselves are the inventors of the Game of Life."

Charles Johnson • *From the Upanishads*

They all met up at the airport to catch the 1.30 flight to Copenhagen with an onward connection to Dublin. There were enormous silences between them, for different reasons. Ahead of him in the queue, Flanagan thought that Jack Dawson looked pale, and suddenly quite old, as he stood close to Rio. He could see Jack's knuckles whiten as he held onto his bag tightly, casting furtive glances around the concourse, as if afraid that at the last moment someone would take the prize. Either of them, Flanagan thought.

'Quickest fucking round trip to anywhere, I've ever made, Jaffa,' Mac says. 'Just as well you were paying for it,' he says loudly.

'My pleasure,' Flanagan replies.

Rio doesn't look back in their direction but continues talking to Gerrit Flatley, who has decided to stay on in Istanbul for a few days.

'I'm a police officer, here as part of an international investigation. They might not help me, Rio, but they will not interfere.'

'Be careful, Gerrit. For my sake.'

'I will. That alone is worth the effort,' the policeman says sincerely without embarrassment.

'Thank you,' Rio says.

Flanagan watches her blush, a red hue to her beautiful blackness. The eyes widen and she leans forward to kiss Flatley. Not on the cheek but on the lips. It was the policeman's turn to blush; a brief display that they all notice. He tenses, Mac beside him is nearly rigid and Jack Dawson's knuckles whiten even more.

'I'll see you in Dublin, Tuesday. I'll phone when I get in,' Flatley says turning away. He sees that Jack, Flanagan and Mac have been watching. 'Have a good journey lads. Look after yourselves. Jerome, may I have a word with you.'

'Sure,' Flanagan says and walks with the policeman out of earshot of the others.

'You have a few questions to answer when you get home. However I've faxed my boss and the charge of obstructing our enquiry by leaving the jurisdiction is to be dropped. We just want your help in trying to track down any leads to finding Phyllis Andrew.'

'Sure Gerry. Thanks. I'll do all I can.'

'One other thing! I'll try my best to get some information for you on your friend Alanna.'

The man is sincere, Flanagan realises, no agendas or shadows just being himself. Lucky bastard, he thinks, knowing then that nobody else would have a chance, at least not at this moment in time. Rio had made her choice, and was going after it. In six months, or a year perhaps, he thinks, she will return to living dangerously, passionately, and Gerrit Flatley will have his work cut out to contain that passion. There is no point in warning him, Flanagan decides, let him enjoy the moment.

'Thanks Gerry. I really mean that. I hope we can catch up with each other in Dublin.'

'Yeah. Why not! See you Jerome.' He leaves after one more wave back at Rio.

Flanagan rejoins the queue.

Mac is seething. 'Smarmy git.'

'Afraid of the competition, boyo.' Flanagan tries to lighten the mood but realises he should have stayed quiet.

'I'm afraid of no-one except myself, Jaffa.' Mac's eyes deaden, like a shadow crossing over. It is followed by a deafening silence as they proceed to check-in.

The flight boards on time. Unseen eyes with penetrating presence watching them all the way, Flanagan suspects, making sure there were no last minute changes of mind. Rio and Jack were already settled in their business class seats by the time Mac and Jerome find theirs near the back of the plane. A large – very large – woman-with-enormous-breasts occupies the aisle seat of the row they are assigned to and as the plane is full, there is no possibility of sitting anywhere else. They wait for her to extract herself before sliding in. Mac takes the window seat, and Flanagan squeezes into the middle, instantly praying for the plane to crash and a quick end. The woman ignores his obvious discomfort; dons earphones and waits for take off.

By the time they reach cruising altitude, she is snoring.

Cormac Mc Murragh looks at his friend for a long time before finally asking, 'What's wrong with you, Jaffa?'

Flanagan knew he could no longer hide his illness. He had found it nearly impossible to lift his suitcase at the airport and had asked Mac to help. 'ALS,' he replies.

'What?'

'ALS. Amyotrophic Lateral Sclerosis or Lou Gehrig disorder! A disease of the nerves that control motor function.'

'Jasus! Is it serious?'

'Very.'

'Can anything be done?'

'Nope. Death in two to five years but some survive longer.'

'*What?* Are you sure?'

'I'm a fucking expert, Mac. 34,000 site hits on the Internet search engine. All say the same, including *retirementwithapurpose.com*, and my favourite: *AML products at shopping.com*. Two to five years to permanent retirement but the shopping is all planned out: bathroom rails, a neck brace, a walker, a wheelchair, a voice amplifier, a living will, a ventilator – in that sequence.'

'Any treatments?' Mac's voice was twitchy, like Flanagan's hand.

'Grape seed and *gingo biloba*, whatever the fuck that is. Oh! And minocycline in mice.'

'Shit!'

'Deep! Want to stick around?'

'Does Rio know?'

'No. Not the full story. She senses something is wrong but now . . . she doesn't want to know. About me . . . or anything. I don't blame her.'

'Shit!' Mac says again and goes silent.

The woman-with-enormous-breasts next to them wakes, not knowing where she is for a moment. She gets up with difficulty from her seat, rummages in the overhead storage, heads for the toilet.

'I want to ask you something, Mac,' Flanagan whispers.

'Sure.'

'Why did you let her go?'

'I haven't let her go, Jaffa.'

'But . . . What happened back in the restaurant? Jack said –'

'You disappeared off to do your thing, Jaffa. I was angry. Angry with you for getting us all into this mess, angry with myself for wanting her so much and angry with her for . . . being her.'

'Why did you hit her? What possible reason warranted that?'

Ever since Jack told him what happened at the restaurant Flanagan had thought about this, thought about how Mac would answer that question when it came. He had hoped the 'reason' word could be avoided yet knew, as Mac knew, it would come. What reason could Mac give? Had reason even come into it? Circumstances, accidents and metaphors are the shadows of reason, Mac had once said. Or Lou Gehrig blowing his trumpet with Coltrane, Flanagan thought, beautifying ALS to a jazz virtuoso.

The woman-with-enormous-breasts returns, smelling of Chanel.

'I was lonely,' Mac finally answers when Flanagan suspects he really wants to say, *I am afraid of being alone.*

Like me, he thinks. 'But you and Rio were great friends, Mac,' he says, trying to keep his voice low, trying to understand.

'Am a friend, Jaffa. Always will be. She forgave me for the slap, said she was sorry about throwing the hooker thing in my face. It's just that I . . .' Mac pauses, glancing across the aisle, knowing he needs to explain, needs to allay Flanagan's concerns, his confusion. 'This is strange thing to say but all the time I'm with Rio I'm lonely. The friendship is not enough. I need something else.'

'Like what? What was missing Mac? Was it . . .' he hesitates.

Mac laughs at the cynicism, and Flanagan notices that the woman next to him is listening and also waiting for the answer.

'Love, Jerome? Is that what you were going to say? What would you know of love? How would you recognise it?'

'*Sorry*,' he says defensively, stung by the truth, but not the whole truth.

There is a silence for a moment but then Mac speaks again. His voice has an urgent edge to it, as if he has to know. 'What *were* you going to say, Jaffa?'

'I was going to say a *lack of faith in yourself,* if you must know. Or conviction if you like; a certainty in your love for Rio.'

The woman-with-enormous-breasts coughs; her eyes look anxious, concerned. Mac stretches out his hand and lays it on Flanagan's arm. He engages her with a tender smile before looking at him. 'Wow. There are never any half measures in your questions, Jaffa. Let me think about that one.'

Flanagan nods, leans back and is content to let it rest for the moment. This had always been their way: a chess game never played against the clock but always played out, to checkmate, stalemate or fool's mate.

'I . . .'

'Go on, Mac.'

'I once tested that faith in me and found it wanting in the face of love; an available love, a gamble with virtue without real virtue on my part. As a result I lost most of the conviction in what I believed to be the truth; mine own, God's if you like, the truth of love, and what little was left clung like a ret rag to a drowning man in an ocean of deception. Because of that failure, my continuing failure to hold any virtue, I ultimately destroyed the love with Marie, and nearly destroyed our kids. I never wanted to test it again lest the last shreds would be stripped from me. But with Rio, I took the chance. I came out from under my own shadow and threw the dice. They landed on their edge and I moved to tilt them over. To no avail! I failed in that too. Failed in the simple task of convincing Rio of my love, the conviction of my love.'

'But –'

'But nothing, Jaffa! Rio did not reject me, I rejected myself and I hate myself for that . . . and in a way I hate Rio for forcing me into finding me out.'

They retreated into silence for some time after that. Shortly after the meal trays are cleared the woman-with-enormous-breasts hands Mac a card, behind Flanagan's back, as he levers past her to make for the toilet. Mac shows it to him when he returns. *Loneliness is the reward for true passion*, she has written on the reverse side of a business card printed with her name, and below this a mobile telephone number. Mac examines the card for a long moment, traces its gold-embossed invitation with his finger: his blessing finger, he calls it, then purses his lips, and looking up, thanks her, he hopes, with a smile of appreciation for her understanding.

'Has she deliberately thrown reason back in my face,' he whispers to Flanagan before winking, leaning across and asking of her quietly, 'Are you psychic?'

There is sudden turbulence and the airplane shudders. 'I am a woman and it is called intuition,' she says, matter-of-factly, appearing to want to continue but stopping short as the fasten-seat-belt sign comes on. This takes some effort on her part, and she begins to fumble with the straps.

Mac pockets the card with one hand while simultaneously buckling his own belt with the other.

Increasingly aware of other people's dexterity, Flanagan is envious. He thinks about all the women he has known in his life, and their intuition . . . and their intrusion. He also thinks about reason, and its intuition, and its intrusion. He had accused Mac, almost accused him, of losing faith and he would be sure to bring him back to this later, when his feet were not swelling up . . . or when he wasn't dying.

Mac must have sensed that Flanagan was thinking of him.

'If I can't have her, Jaffa, I don't know what I'll do,' he said quietly into the narrowing space between them.

Flanagan did not have an answer. What Mac and he had, he thought, as Pilate had, *in truth to do* was to accept what faith offered; K's collision of the finite and infinite, the merging of the improbable paradox and the passion, the release of subjectivity from the object and objectivity from the subject. *I am lonely . . . I am afraid of being alone*, he reminds himself, buckling the seat belt with more difficulty than the woman.

She looks at him and wonders why.

The turbulence eases and they relax. Mac turns to Flanagan and asks, 'Do you think much about good and evil, Jaffa.'

'No, not really, at least not in such concrete distinction.'

'I do, you know. Back in the seminary, in philosophical and theological discussion, Good and Evil always seemed so important. The polar coordinates of all belief systems. It was if they always existed, despite our friend Augustine's efforts to the contrary, even before the fall, justifying human existence because of the need to test their validity, their necessity. They were the Platonic life forces present from the very beginning. It was bullshit of course!'

'What do you mean?'

'The first and only life force is reward. Good and evil are secondary volitions, the response.'

'What do you mean?'

'Think about it. Born without sin, without knowing goodness or evil. As a unknowing child your understanding of good and evil is determined by the rewards attached to that understanding, either as self and a child's exploration of his environment, or from parents, teachers or persons or established values of authority. All your reason, all your behaviour, all your will, is determined by your perception of that reward system. Whether this behaviour is good or evil will depend entirely on the reward anticipated. Without reward there is no good or evil. That is the secret truth.'

'What's this got to do with you and Rio?'

'Goodness and evil are merged when I think of her. Whichever way I choose, and I will have to choose, she is the reward, Jaffa. She is the bounty!'

'But –'

'Ladies and gentlemen, this is the co-pilot speaking. We are now beginning our descent into Copenhagen. Please ensure your seats are in the upright position and trays stowed away. Cabin crew. Ten minutes to landing.'

As the plane drops through the clouds it hits another pocket of turbulence. An overhead locker opens and the woman-with-enormous-breasts' duty-free bags fall with a crashing, splintering sound to the aisle. The scent of Chanel fills the cabin.

Mac looks at Flanagan and says, 'Shit!'

The airplane banks and he returns to looking out the window. And beyond the window, Flanagan sees, there are windmills in the harbour, and the blue, blue sea on the horizon is shimmering in the sun and behaving like a spirit level.

SIROCCO

"And the 'Ãd, they were destroyed by a furious wind,
exceedingly violent . . ."

The Qur'an • *surat al-hãqqah* (The Catastrophe); 69, v. 6

23

WITNESS

"The fear instituted at the Retreat is of great depth; it passes between reason and madness like a mediation, like an evocation of a common nature. . ."

Michel Foucault • *Madness and Civilization*

"The psychotic 'loss of reality' does not arise when something is missing in reality, but on the contrary, when there is *too much* of a Thing in reality."

Slavoj Zizek • *The Metastases of Enjoyment*

Turning off the main road just outside the village, Ahmed al-Akrash stops, leaves the car engine running, turns on the interior light and once again checks his map and the directions that had been given to him. In the distance he can just make out a forest of pine, stretched across a low hill like a saddle. Not too far away now, he thinks, accelerating down the narrow, twisting secondary road.

He almost misses the forester's access and brakes late sending a spray of bark, moss and mud into the air. He slows, drives slowly along its pot-holed track, deeper and deeper into the forest, until finally finding what he is looking for. Two old crumbling stone pillars, the directions had said. He turns through their narrow gap only to find his way blocked by a modern steel gate. Turning off the engine, he opens the window and listens. He gets out, looks around and sees that the gate is locked. He climbs over the gate and begins to walk. It is an avenue of conifer and holly, standing sentinel behind crumbling perimeter walls, the stones tethered by clinging ivy. There is movement in the forest to his right. He strains to see. A large puck goat, horned and bearded stares back at him for a moment, before disappearing into the gloom. In the distance a square-tower type castle rises up above the canopy. He sees surrounding scaffolding and materials for a new roof.

Suddenly, he stops, frozen by the deep baying of two large dogs that are coursing down the lane towards him. He's hated dogs, ever since . . . He thinks about running, looks for a tree to climb but then picks up a rock from the ground and tests its weight in his hand; gets ready.

A sharp shrill whistle sounds and the dogs, a pair of Dobermans, instantly pull up, lay down with their paws forward, eyes locked on his every movement. He feels unable to move. The rock is heavy in his hand. A figure saunters down the track, smoking a cigarette, flicking it away as he approaches. The red tipped butt arcs through the night.

'They don't like visitors,' the figure says.

'Welcomes are sometimes worn out,' he replies, throwing away the rock.

The figure relaxes and immediately lights up another cigarette. He leans down to pat the two dogs on their heads. 'You must be Ahmed. I've been asked to give you every bit of help I can, by our friends. Malachy MacGaoth at your service.'

MacGaoth held out his hand and Ahmed takes it, keeping one eye on the dogs. 'I am Ahmed al-Akrash. It's good to meet you.'

'You look a bit worse for wear,' MacGaoth observes.

'I've been hiding out.'

'Come on in. I've some fish on the go. Are you hungry?'

'Yes.'

'Good.' He whistles sharply and the dogs bound up and run ahead of them towards the castle.

'What about my car?'

'Give me your keys? Gabriel will bring it up.'

'Gabriel?'

'Young fellow who helps me . . . with the building, don't you know. Thick as a goat . . . but he can drive.'

'I saw one.'

'What?'

'A goat! Big male . . . in the forest.'

'Did you now? Must have strayed from the farm down the road. They make cheese.'

They near the base of the castle. Ahmed looks up at the steel scaffolding surrounding the ramparts. 'How old?' he asks.

'From 1230AD. Used to be a monastery here as well. That lump of rubble over there.' MacGaoth points to an old archway and a collapsed wall. It takes all my time to keep it from falling out from under me. Quiet though, and private.'

They reach the main entrance. It's a low door. Ahmed begins to stoop but suddenly sees a strange carving in the capstone over the door. A female figure, legs wide apart, two hands coming down behind her thighs, separating the large labial folds of her sex. A finger-sized hole is between the folds, its lower edge smooth and worn. The figure's face is contorted.

His own face betrays his disgust.

'A sheela-na-gig,' MacGaoth says, watching.

'A what?'

'A sheela-na-gig, strange idol carvings that appeared in Irish churches and castles in the eleventh and twelfth centuries. No one quite knows the reason. "*Sile*" is the Irish for Julia and a "*ghig*" is an old hag or midwife. Midwives were often thought of as witches and perhaps these were put up on buildings to ward off the evil thought associated with them coming into the church or castle. Like al-Uzza perhaps.'

Ahmed says nothing, but is disturbed by the image.

'Put your finger in the hole there, and make a wish.'

'Allah preserve me, no!'

'Come on in then.' MacGaoth directs him inside. 'Gabriel!' he shouts.

A thin boy, sixteen or seventeen at most, Ahmed estimates, appears. He has a high forehead surmounted by red hair. Arabic red not Irish, Ahmed notes. The boy grins, and Ahmed watches fascinated as three metal studs planted in the skin below his lower lip seem to separate in different directions.

'There was a call for you, while you were down the lane,' the boy sneers, in a high-pitched rasp.

'Who was it?' MacGaoth asks.

'That cokehead wanker you set me up with, who was so spaced out he couldn't fucken do it. What was his name again?'

MacGoath's eyes narrow. They flick in Ahmed's direction and then back to the boy again. 'Watch it! No names!'

'Just telling you, dude. I'm pissed off with all that other fucken' shit you have me doing for the two of ye.'

'Go get your man's car, will you?' MacGaoth orders, tossing the youth Ahmed's keys. 'Remember to open the gate.'

The boy grunts, sticks a middle finger in the air close to MacGoath's face.

'What did he mean by that?' Ahmed asks, glad to see the back of the boy, whose voice irritated him.

'None of your concern, Ahmed!' MacGaoth says with finality. 'Come on in.'

The door closes behind them and they immediately turn into a narrow spiral stone staircase that takes them to the first floor. There is a large fireplace with carved heraldic inscriptions and a roaring fire. A large oak table, four high backed chairs, and two rocking chairs complete the furniture. There is a worn thick-woven carpet on the ground.

'Take a pew,' MacGaoth instructs, but sees Ahmed does not understand. '*A chair!* I'll get the food.'

Later, the food cleared away, they sit in the rocking chairs, nursing cups of coffee. Gabriel has been dispatched to town, money in his pocket, 'for a few pints'. They hear the sound of a motorbike disappearing into the silence.

'Mightn't see him for a week,' MacGaoth says, leaning forward stoking the fire.

The two dogs are sprawled out between them, their eyes always on Ahmed. He looks at them. 'What are their names?' he asks.

'Sam and Del . . . Samson and Delilah in full. Appropriate don't you think?'

'What do you mean?' Ahmed questions, confused.

'Samson, the first suicide-murder terrorist and what you're about to do.'

'Why do you say it like that?'

'Like what?'

'Suicide-murder, like it's a category?'

'It is. Part of a spectrum; suicide, suicide-murder, murder-suicide, murder, each with their own stimulus, purpose, goal, emotion, cognition and consistency.'

'It is not that easy to define,'

'On the contrary, *it is*, but perhaps not so easy to explain.'

'You sound knowledgeable?'

'I was a psychiatrist in a former life.'

Ahmed notices for the first time that MacGaoth's eyes are tinged yellow. 'And now this?'

'I told you. It's not easy to explain.'

'Try,' Ahmed said.

'I spent many years working with the victims of political torture, trying to heal their spirit, trying to understand why such evil existed, trying to erase that evil with goodwill, good intention, good . . .'

'And?'

'I realised it was pointless. Evil does not recognise the existence of good will or good intention, either in an individual being, or being in general and despite the claims of citizen sociologists and pragmatists has no capacity for justice, or charity, or reconciliation. Healing the spirit of tortured men and women was an exercise in futility when their spirit remained forever terrorized. I discarded my inward desire for truth in favour of an outward expression of that truth.'

'Which is?'

'Evil will only see its reflection when confronted by a greater evil, and is terrorised into submission.'

The image of the Sheela-na-gig flashed in Ahmed's consciousness. 'Are you prepared to die for that conviction?'

MacGaoth brought his hands up to cover his lips, and looked at his visitor for a long time. 'Good God, no.' He laughs. 'I am not yet that ambivalent. I still see death as the end of reason.'

'Your own or others.'

'My own, of course! I still hold out some hope for myself. Living is my challenge and I leave the business of dying to the martyrs and the martyred. '

'You have a strange sense of humour,'

'Somebody once said, Kierkegaard I think, humour is always a concealed pain but is also an instance of sympathy.'

'Is that it? Is that why you help me? Sympathy?'

'Perhaps but also because I believe that existence, each being's sense of being, lies within the individual and no one else.'

'Is it madness?'

'What you intend?'

'Yes.'

'Are you a fanatic?'

Ahmed thinks for a moment. 'Fanatics are full of doubts. That is what drives them. Me, I know the sun will come up tomorrow, I know what is in my soul.'

MacGaoth smiles. 'Do you believe you'll come back again and do this . . . do what you intend, another – what is it, ten times?'

'No.'

'Do you see it as a duty?'

'Yes.'

'To a political cause?'

'Not really.'

'To your faith?'

'No . . . well, perhaps yes, but in a very specific way, a conviction of right over wrong, a certainty of a greater good. As you have mentioned it's part of the truth in me, part of the reflection that is my becoming. Part of my witness.'

'Witness?'

'A conviction of righting wrongs. A true *shahid*: the original meaning of the word, not a martyr but a witness.'

'What drives it?'

'My soul.'

'Explain what you mean.'

'My soul is everything that I am. It penetrates my being. It has *ammâra,* whispering its breath in my ear, commanding me to evil because of my desire for revenge. But in sensing that desire it also has *lawwâma,* a righteousness returning me to the path from that evil so that finally I might achieve *mutma'inna,* tranquillity. It is everlasting.'

'Ah! The eternal soul of a martyr! An escape from the examination of the angels?'

'I am having it now, *Malaky.*'

'And if there was another way?'

'Are you a *djinn* sent to tempt me?'

'What happened, Ahmed?'

'My grandfather was a stonemason in the village of Deir Yessin. In 1948 the Hagana Jewish fighters entered the village and butchered men, women and children. My grandfather was paraded through the streets of Jerusalem then brought back to the quarry where he worked, and shot.' Ahmed stops, and looks at MacGaoth. 'It's ironic really.'

'What?'

'You and me, the coincidence of history?'

'What do you mean?'

'Deir Yessin is now known as Kfar Shaul, and the site of Jerusalem's main psychiatric hospital.'

'And what about you?'

'My madness?' Ahmed looks into the fire. 'I am . . . was a teacher of mathematics and geography, displaced in a distortion of both logic and location to Sabra refugee camp. On 15 September 1982, Phalangists instructed by the Israelis, stormed the camp. My wife and only child, a girl of seven, were butchered with a meat cleaver but not before they were both raped. I was unable . . . I could not save them. In my anger I drove out towards the border. Attacked a patrol with my bare hands, with rocks. They laughed at me, set their dogs on me.'

'I understand you now.'

'My fear of dogs!'

'Not just that! Everything.'

'My witness.'

'Yes.' MacGaoth studies his visitor for a moment. 'And what is the duty to your faith, that you touched upon?'

'I cannot go into that too much, for your sake more than mine, only to say it is a question of intercession.'

'I see. It's revenge so?'

'Retribution. It has always been our way . . . even before Islam.'

The two men rock back and forth in their respective chairs without speaking for some time. MacGaoth eventually gets up and Ahmed watches him pacing the perimeter of the room. His mobile phone rings and he answers it.

'Yeah. No problem. He's here with me now.'

There is silence for a moment as MacGaoth listens, his eyes flickering to where Ahmed is staring into the fire. MacGaoth's face suddenly contorts, his voice hardening to solid hatred, as he shouts into the phone. 'Listen to me when I talk to you. I know what I'm doing. That's done. It was all too easy to swap your sample. Security in the lab was shite, as they are in the middle of changing locations. You'll have no further problem from that quarter. Now fuck off and stop annoying me.' He hangs up.

'Problems?' Ahmed asks looking up.

'Nah!'

Their eyes meet and Ahmed feels he has to know. 'You never answered my question.'

'About madness?' MacGaoth moves in close and leaning on the armrests of the chair stares at Ahmed, their faces about six inches apart.

'Yes.'

'I have looked into the eyes of many "madmen", perpetrators and victims both, Ahmed. Whatever it is that they see, or feel, or imagine, is beyond my comprehension. It is for their eyes only.' MacGaoth withdraws and moves towards the stairwell where he turns and looks back. 'I became unable to discern a distinction between the inner reality of an individual "madman" and the supposed sanity of the external reality of civilisation and its endemic "madness". That failure is perhaps the real reason I stopped doing what I was trained to do.'

'What now?' Ahmed asks.

'Come, we will make Yihya Ayyash, proud of us.'

Ahmed's eyes open wide in surprise.

Malachy MacGaoth smiles, taking pleasure in catching his visitor off guard. 'You see? I also have my idols. Listen Ahmed. I'm very good at what I do, what I enjoy doing. I'll have you smelling of musk. I will show you the truth of the matter, how to strap it on, how do detonate it, how to focus its force . . . how to bear witness.'

24

ALCIBIADES

"The observer should be an eroticist, no feature,
no moment should be indifferent to him . . ."

Søren Kierkegaard • *The Concept of Irony*

Though little more than a light drizzle the cold wind whipping up
the dead-dark waters of the canal beside him funnelled the rain
droplets into sprays of icy needles that pierced into his skin and
froze one side of his face. They forced him into pulling the parka
hood tighter around his head as he gingerly stepped over the
detritus of earlier junkies to slide deeper beneath the shelter of the
bridge where, in the shadow cast by the streetlights, only his
exhaled frosted breath gives any sign of him actually being there.

Bloody typical, he thinks. *Defined by what we give back not
what we take in.* He digs deep into his pocket and pulls out the
bottle. Unscrewing the cap with fumbling numbed fingers he lifts
it to his lips and drains its last measure. He looks at the bottle in
distaste, before tossing it into the water.

From where he stands he is still able to see the door of her
ground-floor apartment in the expensive new development on the
opposite bank. Above him, at street level, the estate agent's sign
is rocking wildly in the wind, proclaiming the availability of

259

Phase 3 and the development's name, in big, bold letters: THE LACEWORKS. He knows that the name derives from the old canal-side building on the site and watches with some amusement as the letters are dissected by the wind into an open mesh of cardboard mush. He smiles at this, knowing also that inside Apartment 2, she is likely to be wearing lace. She likes to make love in it, leaving its invitation on, pulling them, him into the cobweb of her entrapment. He feels his testicles lift with the thought and hopes the drink he has taken will not interfere. *Should have popped a Viagra*, he thinks, before feeling his crotch.

Reassured he holds his hand out into the light to look at the face of his watch: 11.10 pm. Just then, from the corner of his eye, he sees the light over her doorway flickering into life. The door opens and the huddled figure of a man exits, stooping low before furtively walking away at speed. The door closes and the light goes out.

He waits for a few minutes, hoping to see her shadow, hoping perhaps that she would come to a window and would look out, look for him. Time passes as only the time of waiting does pass, slowly: defying physics with its laws of expectation. She does not appear and, disappointed, he steps out from beneath the archway, climbs the wet steps with some difficulty, crosses the bridge, approaches her glossy, blue door and presses the bell. Once, twice and then keeping his finger on it. The light overhead eventually flickers on and the door opens slowly, partially.

'Quit with the fucking noise,' her voice says through the gap.

He pushes against the door but it only opens inwards a small amount. The latch chain is still in place, he realises. An eye appears and then disappears again.

'Less me in, Angie,' he slurs.

'You're early, Mac. I said 11.45,' she says dismissively.

Smoke from a cigarette escapes through the gap.

'Jasus, girl. Only by ten minutes or so. Let me in, will ya. It's an awful night out here.'

'I don't want any of my clients bumping into one another. You know that! Those are my rules.'

'Fuck the rules, Angie. I saw your last trick leaving. Poxy looking character! Whatever do you do for him?'

'Wouldn't you like to know? How long were you watching?'

'Twenty minutes or so. Whass diff . . . difference does that make?'

'You sound pissed, Mac. I think it would be better if you went away.'

'Do you mind if we discuss this inside? It's fuckin' freezing out here!'

There is a long pause and then, 'Take your foot out of the way.'

'Sure,' he says and does. The door closes again and he hears the latch being removed. He pushes against it and it opens.

She retreats from the doorway and stubs out her cigarette in the ashtray on a small hallway table. 'Go on through, Mac, you know the way. Pour yourself a drink, if you must – though by the smell of you, you have probably had enough already. I'll be with you in a minute. I want to grab a quick shower.'

As he closes the door behind him she turns and walks towards a bedroom at the very far end of the corridor. He has never seen inside the room, as it is not the space she uses for clients. Tall with natural blonde hair falling onto her shoulders she is wearing a silk, embroidered night-jacket that just reaches the curve of her firm buttocks. She has Mickey Mouse slippers on her feet. A chain dangles below the hem of the jacket, disappearing into the cleft of her buttocks and a needle-worked dragon near her shoulders appears to be laughing back at him. He wants to follow her but turns right into the small living room and pours himself a vodka – neat – before sitting on the soft leather-covered couch. *Like a glove*, he thinks, moving his hand over the surface. Faces and smiles stare at him from across the room.

He stands up to look at the pictures in their silver frames on the mantelpiece. A first holy communion photograph with her parents and younger sister, all golden hair extensions of her; a school holiday photograph with friends, their faces gilded with the freedom of it; her eighteenth birthday party and long-legged exuberance; the night she received her degree in Philosophy and Economics and . . .

'It is so fuckin' normal,' he says aloud before downing the vodka in one. It sears his throat. '*What the fuck are you doing here*,' he asks himself, staring at the pictures.

'What the fuck *are* you doing here, Mac?' she asks, from behind him.

He almost jumps. He hadn't heard her come in and wonders how long she has been standing there. The silk gown is still in place but loosely wrapped to reveal a bodice of black lace. The slippers are gone and replaced by high-heeled red boots that lifted her higher, pushing her chest forward and bottom back.

'You star . . . startled me,' he says, slurring the words.

She smiles, a thin smile. 'What *do* you want, Mac? I'm already in enough trouble for coming forward to say that you were with me the night of the robbery.'

'I really appreciated that,' he says. He instantly sobers, knowing what is coming next.

'You didn't give me much choice, threatening me with telling my mother, about what I do,' she says coldly.

'I'm sorry about that, Angie. I was in deep shit and didn't know what else to do. I really am very sorry.' He moves to touch her but she pulls away.

'You're always sorry, Mac. For yourself and . . . Forget I said that.'

'No you're right. You are always right.' He slumps down into the couch. Tears course down his cheeks.

'Would you like a coffee?'

'No.'

'How about doing a line?' she asks, as if one was as convenient as the other.

'No.'

'Well I do. Excuse me a minute?'

'Sure,' he says watching her leave. He stares at the pictures until she returns. Her face is flushed and her eyes glisten.

'Anyway it wasn't all that bad. That cute detective, Flatley was very nice about it. I told him that you were my sugar daddy and that I only did it now and then to help with college expenses. More of a gift than a service, I told him, from desperation. He said that he understood and that if I cooperated he would not pursue it any further. Is he a man of his word?'

'I . . . I think so.'

'Good,' she says teasing him with her eyes, 'because I might just accidentally bump into him again, some day. He has a cute bum.'

'I didn't notice.'

She sighs deeply as she combs her hands through her hair to lift it before letting it fall again. Her chest rises higher and the loosely tied belt undoes spontaneously as she pirouettes in front of him. She stops suddenly, rests her hands on his knees.

'You've always said that you can only afford me once every two months or so. What are you doing here?'

'I don't know,' he says, leaning forward to pull her gown open and stare up at her breasts, crosshatched beneath the lace. He touches a pink nipple, which becomes instantly erect, before moving his hand down towards her crotch, where he knows the lace ends. 'I thought we –'

She pulls away from him and takes the glass from his hand. 'No freebies, Mac! You know that.'

'Yes.' He pulls out the envelope with the money and places it on the seat beside him. 'I thought we might just talk and then perhaps . . .'

She waits for him to finish and when he doesn't, she picks it up, opens the envelope, counts the notes and smiles. 'Up to you, Mac! It's your money and you can spend it any way you like. There's about an hours' worth of my time here.' She holds up the envelope, waves it in his face before putting it in the pocket of her gown. She moves back towards him and taking his hand guides it back to her crotch. She holds it there rubbing against his fingers. 'Oh God, that's nice. What did you want to talk about?'

'I . . . I . . .' Her rhythm against his fingers gets faster and faster, her breath coming in short fast bursts, blowing warm on his face.

She curls his fingers into a fist and presses against him even harder. She is laughing. He pulls his hand away and, suddenly interrupted, she looks at him. She keeps her own hand near her crotch, but the movements are disinterested. Her startled glare changes to a look of frustration, then annoyance.

'I'd prefer a fuck first, Mac . . . then we can talk,' she says harshly.

'What do you mean?' he asks, threatened by the demand and the brutality.

'I've had a really weird sort of day, all fetishes and S&M stuff. Distance fucking, I call it, most of it being in the head. It pays well but leaves me randy but frustrated, all that giving. What I'd like right now, Mac . . . What I'd really like right now is a simple straightforward ride, your kind of riding. Fast and furious! Besides which you have a dick the size of a donkey and I need that inside me right now.'

'Don't say that. Say it like . . .'

'Say what, Mac? Like I enjoy it?' She started to laugh. 'Come on, man. Get real. Of course I like it. I love fucking, any which way, size or sequence, and getting paid into the bargain makes it even better. This is not some Freudian fantasy, Mac and I'm not your fucking mother. I'm not some ideal, a random dream that you somehow hope we will both wake up from and think it never happened. This is what I am, Mac. This is my being and I love it, love myself for it. Either ride the wind or get blown away!'

'Shit,' was all he could say before getting up from the chair. He makes for the drinks cabinet on the far side of the room but suddenly and desperately unsteady has to lean heavily against the mantelpiece. His hand stretches out to anchor himself and pushes against one of the smiling faces. The picture of Angie in her communion dress and hair-extensions clatters to the ground. She stoops to pick it up, and then standing up replaces it, carefully lining the frame up with the others.

A chain-gang of smiles, he thinks.

She turns to him, her voice softening. 'Please, Mac. Fuck me first and I'll then give you two hours of my time. All the time in the world to talk.' She lets the robe fall from her shoulders and stepping forward quickly pulls at his zip until it gives before pushing her hand deep inside his trousers. 'There you are my donkey, come to mama. Mama wants to ride you so hard that you'll bleed.'

Mac watches as her eyes suddenly glaze over, the line of cocaine kicking in. She is looking at him and whispering the words but it is like she is staring at a nothingness, his nothingness, and that if she stares hard enough, for long enough, it will, he will, become a something; a reality whose focus is both before and beyond him. *Like Rio*, he thinks. He had come here looking for some sort of harmony, some sort of understanding, some sort of anything tangible and now, watching her, all he felt was indifference. It was as if she was, as Rio was, no longer there to sense.

'Fuck you,' he says, pulling away, pulling up his zip, and heading for the door.

There is a brief moment as she stares at the spot where her hand still is and he had been. Her pupils oscillate from side to side at first but then steady as she turns to him. 'Bu . . . but, Mac,' she slurs, surprised. 'What about the money?'

'Keep the money, Angie. You've earned it,' he says quietly, as the door opens and the light above flickers on.

25

NEY

"Inna li 'l-bulbuli sautan fi 'l-sahar
Ashghala 'l-'áshika 'an husni 'l-watar"
(The Bulbul's note, whenas dawn is nigh
Tells the lover from strains of strings to fly.)

Richard F. Burton • *Thousand Nights and a Night*

Rio waits by the window, alerted by Jack's call some ten minutes earlier. She watches the taxi draw up and moves into the hallway to open the door. Jack and a tall man exit the taxi and huddle under an umbrella trying to protect them from the driving rain as they make for the door. The tall man has a goatee beard and steel-rimmed circular glasses, which are fogging up.

'Welcome to Dublin, Professor Gilbert,' she says stepping back to allow them enter. 'I'm Rio Dawson, Jack's niece.'

'My pleasure, Dr Dawson. Excuse me!' He takes off his glasses and polishes the lens with a neatly pressed handkerchief he removes from and then replaces in an inside pocket. Although nearly equal in height he seems to have to lean back to bring her into focus. 'Thank you most sincerely for your kind invitation to examine the Book. I am most excited by the prospect.'

He replaces his glasses to sit low on his nose and holds out his hand. For the briefest moment she wonders how excited this man could ever actually get before extending her own. His handshake is firm and he has big hands, calloused and rough beyond expectation. She looks down at them.

Gilbert notices her surprise. 'Excuse the condition of my hands. Spent last week on assault manoeuvres. Some bloody awful climbing conditions.'

'Assault manoeuvres?'

'Yes, in Norway. I'm a reserve colonel in the Parachute regiment. Have to keep my "hand" in as it were. We were on winter training. Skiing and all that.'

'I see . . .' she mumbles, baffled.

Jack grins at her from behind Gilbert's shoulder, as if to say, *I should have warned you.* He closes the door behind him and starts to remove his coat. 'Sorry were late, Babs. Bloody rain! Made the traffic slow to a crawl,' he says, shaking himself down like a retriever.

'No problem! Let me hang up your coats and I'll put on some coffee,' she offers.

'Tea for me, Dr Dawson, If you don't mind,' Gilbert declares with unmistakeable finality.

'Of course.' Rio smiles. 'Milk or lemon?'

'Lemon, if you have it. Thank you.'

'Sure. You two go on in. I'll join you in a minute.'

Jack walks ahead but suddenly stops when he sees that Gerrit Flatley is already seated comfortably and smugly nursing a whiskey. The policeman smiles up at him.

'Gee! Hello, Gerry. Didn't expect you to be here.'

'Any chance I get, Jack,' the policeman replies, winking.

'Yeah,' Jack says under his breath before turning to introduce Gilbert. 'Gerry this is Professor Bertrand Gilbert from the Islamic Institute in Oxford. I've flown him over to appraise the Book, to see if it is what it is supposed to be. Professor, this is Detective Inspector Gerry Flatley of Dublin's homicide unit.'

Flatley gets up and offers his hand. The Englishman's eyes flicker as he takes it. 'My pleasure, Inspector. I gather it is still a very difficult enquiry.' The two men appraise each other, trying to estimate the others expertise in the handshake.

'Yes,' Flatley answers honestly.

Gilbert nods, releases his hand and turns to Jack. 'Might I see the book, Mr Dawson. I am rather anxious to proceed as I have to catch the evening flight back.'

'Sure.' Jack shows him to the table at the far end of the room where the book is sitting and hovers as the academic-paratrooper begins his appraisal.

Gilbert's face flushes as he inspects the exterior, tracing his finger gently along the faded embossed border of the leather binding. He teases out the horsehair tassels so that they lay in perfect alignment with each other. 'My-o-my,' he whispers repeatedly while opening the small briefcase he had carried with him and removing a small leather cushion. He places this under the book to elevate it at an angle before removing a length of material shaped like a string of sausages, a notebook, and a lead pencil from the briefcase. He leaves his magnifying glass in its padded place, as Rio's jeweller's angle-poise magnifying light is already available. He adjusts the poise so that it is centred precisely over the book. He then adjusts the poise of his own glasses.

'What's that,' Jack asks pointing to the sausage-shaped string.

'A reading sock filled with weighted pockets to hold down the pages, standard practice for dealing with old manuscripts. I always carry my own, one filled with ground pumice stone. Just the right weight, don't you know? Perhaps you'll excuse me, Mr Dawson if I get on with my work.'

Dismissed by Gilbert Jack returns to the settee to sit beside Flatley. 'What's happening Gerry? Any further leads on Phyllis Andrew?'

'No. Dead-ends all the way? If you excuse the expression.'

'Think that's the case?'

'Yeah. Unfortunately. No word. No contact.'

The two men sit in silence listening to Gilbert's excited breathing and the repeating 'my-o-my's'.

Jack whispers, 'What about the blood matches? Any problems with alibis?'

'No . . . well perhaps.' Flatley hesitated for a moment, wondering how open he should be. 'Mags Golden, Cormac McMurragh, Brigadier Crawford, Foley, the security guard, and the other trustee with Group A have all checked out fine. We also have their DNA back and they show no matches . . .'

'But?' Jack encourages him to explain.

'Professor FitzHenry's alibi of his whereabouts on the evening in question bothers me. It seems he was in the company of a friend of his who has subsequently disappeared.'

'Why?'

'Didn't like the thought of being questioned by police, it seems. This 'friend' is known to us and is involved with some very unsavoury characters here in Dublin. Obviously the attention was a bit too close for comfort. He scampered.'

'Unsavoury. In what way?'

'Drugs, prostitution.'

'Does FitzHenry know about this?'

'Apparently not! They are friends from college days. Always thought that he was a property developer. Shocked by the fact that your man is 'known' to the police. It's not that important as FitzHenry's DNA puts him in the clear but I hate loose ends in an investigation.'

Rio enters back into the room with a laden tray. None of the men seem to want to interrupt what they are doing to help. She serves Gilbert first before placing the tray down on the table in front of Jack and Flatley. 'What are you two in such deep conversation about?' she asks.

'I'm asking your uncle here, for your hand in marriage. I thought it was the best thing,' Flatley says with a deadpan expression.

Jack splutters. 'What the fuck,' he almost shouts.

Bertrand Gilbert coughs reprovingly in the background.

'Relax, Jack. Gerrit is only teasing you.' Rio laughs with Flatley at Jacks' obvious fluster.

'I'm not the marrying kind,' Flatley adds.

'Why? Are you gay or what?' Jack is bothered – pissed off –

with the policeman's apparent – and casual – dismissal of Babs and her possible needs. *Not that she needs anyone else*, he reminds himself.

'No. It just scares the bejasus out of me. I'm too selfish for any meaningful relationships and I run scared.' Flatley looks up at Rio. This understanding has already been reached between them.

Jack Dawson notices and is even more concerned.

'Doesn't stop you having fun though,' Rio confirms, sitting down beside the policeman.

'Live for the moment and let it go. No history, no legacy, no responsibility . . . no bullshit,' Flatley says without expression.

'Few men you can say that about, Jack. Don't you agree?' Rio asks.

Jack moves uncomfortably on the couch suffocating in the simplicity of the accusation. 'I think that's a fucken cop-out. I think –'

'I agree as it happens,' Gilbert interrupts from the far end of the room.

Jack jaw angles sharply. 'Whaddya mean?' he growls at the academic before regretting his over-reaction.

Gilbert leans back in his chair, removes his glasses, lifts his cup of tea to his lips, half-turns to look at Jack and smiles over the rim of the cup before placing it back in its saucer. 'Just that! Moments do not demand responsibility just response.'

'But surely history, and its legacy of moments and the sense of that legacy dominate your entire work?' Jack demands. He gets up, and walks to the table followed by Rio and Flatley.

'History as we understand it, is simply memory, a sequence of someone's idealization. As such it is an imperfect legacy, and a poor basis on which to hang responsibility of any kind. Take this book for instance. Look at the penmanship. No don't just look at it. Listen to its song. Think of the reed pen in the hand of the calligrapher and the strokes he made. Then think of wind rustling through reeds and how both pens and flutes made from those reeds try to capture the beauty and music of that wind. This . . . this book captures the moment in time just after the writer truly believed that he had been given the message, been shown the truth in all the confusion of history. When the flute and pen, the song and sign, were in complete harmony. He is excited and is desperate to have that clarity recorded, a clarity, which has only been in existence, in his own mind, for the shortest time. For all of us a thought comes to mind and an instant later it is both history and legacy. That beautiful moment of transcendent clarity, in which the clarity is the moment, is soon betrayed and its history and legacy become weapons of both certainty and of confusion: chaos.'

Gilbert stops talking, sips his tea again and gently closes the book, resting his hand on the cover as if giving a solemn oath.

'Does the text give an explanation for the strange symbols at the beginning of some of the sura, Professor?' Rio asks, a little breathlessly. Gerrit Flatley is deliberately pressing up close against her as they crowd in around the chair of the academic. She senses his crotch bulging against her and pushes back against him every so slightly.

'Don't know, I'm afraid,' Gilbert says slowly, shrugging his shoulders apologetically. 'But the book is so very special. That I am certain of! The binding is, I think, seventeenth century Ottoman and the colophon most certainly is, but as for the script, there I am stumped.'

'What does the colophon say?' Jack asks, turning to glare at Flatley.

'*We send forth the messengers as bearers of glad tidings and as Warners.* It's from the Qur'an, from Al-An'am, the sixth sura. It is signed by your friend Karabatakzade, 1080AH or 1669CE,' Gilbert explains.

'The year he died,' Rio adds.

'And the script?' Flatley asks moving to Rio's side, red-faced.

'I'm not sure Inspector but am fairly confident that it is very ancient and much older than standard Kufic or even the more rare Hijazi. Much closer in fact to Nabatean, I suspect: only consonants and no *hareke* or diacritics to indicate vowels or sounding. Leaving aside its scriptural significance for a moment I am near certain that as a complete example of the transition from Nabatean to Arabic script it has no extant equal. That said, because of its age of origin, I am having great personal difficulty interpreting it and I would suggest, perhaps, that the book should be sent to the world's best Arabic palaeographers at Saarland University, in Saarbrüken.'

'I'm not keen on letting it out of my sight,' Jack said.

'I can understand that Mr Dawson. In any event it would be better to have it photographed and you could send a copy of these on microfilm to Germany,' Gilbert says, nodding his head.

'I'll organise that with Mac,' Rio offers. She feels Gerrit pulling away from her and suddenly notices Jack's glare. 'Whoa! Easy lads. Less of the possessive posturing, please! Mac and I have worked things out. I said some things I should not have and he is sorry for what happened.'

'You're not to –'

'For the final time, Jack, I make my own decisions,' she says emphatically.

'Its my book now and I'll make the decisions.' Jack felt hurt and didn't care if he showed it.

'With respect, Mr Dawson,' Bertrand Gilbert stood up, and started putting his equipment back into his briefcase, 'It is not *your* book, never can be. You might have possession of it but it is not yours. You might contribute to its history and legacy but you will never own its moment. Like with people, perhaps . . .' His eyes flick to Rio and back again to the briefcase. 'I think, if it is all right with you, Dr Dawson that I might call into the museum. There is a Ruzbihan al-Shirazi Kur'ān I want to look at before heading for the plane.'

'Sure. I'll call the librarian to have it ready for you,' Rio offers as she picks up the phone.

'My thanks.' Gilbert turns to Jack. 'I'm sorry that I cannot be of more help. Your friend Dr Flanagan was right, Mr Dawson. This –'

'He's no friend of mine!'

'Whatever. This book is a Holy Grail and sometimes the

silence that erupts in the finding of such a wonder is because you realise there cannot be any other sounds. It is both an end and a beginning, a singularity.'

'A big bang!' Gerrit Flatley blurts out, winking at Rio.

'Exactly, Inspector. Exactly!'

26

BIRDSONG

"There is enough evil in the crying of wind."

William Butler Yeats • *He Reproves the Curlew*

She could hear him moving around in the background, filling a kettle, pulling plates from a cupboard, searching in a drawer for cutlery. This bothered her, the man searching amongst knives and forks. Unable to see she tries to stop imagining a knife in his hand, his finger running along its edge, testing the sharpness, him stealing closer to her, behind her, pulling its edge across her neck . . .

'Would you not take off the hood?' she asks, anxious to see his hands.

'No.' The voice is metallic, high pitched, slurred. It reminds her of her own father's voice, only much younger. Her father's throaty voice, transmitted through a small handheld microphone he had to hold close to where his vocal chords had once been, before they were destroyed by cancer.

'Please,' she pleads, tears forming.

'*Shut the fuck up,*' he rasps.

The words cut through any hope she felt. Why now, she wonders. The room feels icy all of a sudden, and his words echo and echo against its walls. She feels frightened, more frightened that she has ever been. Her wrists are sore, bound down too tight by the plastic or thin rope cords to the armrests of her wheelchair.

She remembers waiting in the lobby of the museum, a movement behind her, a cloth pressed against her face, her gagging, her wanting to be sick, and then nothing. She remembers regaining consciousness in the car, being lifted out and tied into her wheelchair, her head covered in a hood noosed tightly around her neck. She remembers that first day, the silence of the man, the silence broken only by the twittering of early season wagtails. She remembers listening to the kettle boiling; its whistling; its water being poured; the stirring sound of a teaspoon inside a cup. She remembers trying to imagine what he is like.

That first day as his footsteps got closer she had tried to turn away. Suddenly she felt her left hand fly free and automatically brought it up to pull at the hood. He slapped it down. He placed her hand around a hot liquid-filled mug, and got her to hold it against the still bound right. He pulled at the hood just about where her mouth was. Suddenly she felt the point of a knife glance off her teeth. She pulled back but he put a hand on her neck and pushed her head forward again. A tube, a straw, came through the hood, up into a nostril before finding her mouth. He had pushed her head down further, toward her hands and the mug they held. "*Suck*" he had said, his first word, his only word: until now. All food that first day was given the same way; liquidised through a straw. That first day, he was attentive, bringing her to the toilet, lifting her onto the bowl, watching her while she placed the metal catheter she carried in her pocket, waiting close by until she cleaned herself.

Now she is hungry, thirsty, wishing for the straw to come in. Now she is sitting in a pool of her own urine, her bladder overflowing having been left un-emptied all night and most of day.

'What *do* you want with me?' she asks again, desperate to engage him.

Silence.

She had thought about this when left alone, tried to imagine her surroundings, her existence. She had thought about Joe and wondered what had happened to him? Was it bad luck or fate that she happened to be in the Museum when they came to rob it? Was it bad luck or fate that her back was broken all those years ago by a drunk in a car? She had fulfilled her duty to herself, to survive, to desire happiness, to achieve happiness, thinking she was in control; luck or fate had nothing to do with it.

She had often thought about death, her own death. Each year the difficulties were getting worse, and she knew she needed to make plans. She had considered moving to Holland, taking up the offer of a job in Amsterdam. She had followed the arguments on euthanasia and how the Dutch Supreme Court had determined that in order to assess suffering it must be abstracted from its cause: from bad luck or fate. How it had held that *unbearable being*: existential suffering, the absence of any perspective on the duty for happiness, could not be entertained as a legal justification for assisted euthanasia because no doctor, no person, is an expert on the true existence of another.

Always practical she had many times, on dark nights, driven to the old docks and after getting out, wheeled to the edge, always at the same place, an old disused quay that had once berthed the coffin ships. She had gone there so often she knew the sounds and smells of the place and the rhythm of the tide that slapped against the disintegrating wooden piles. She had become part of those rhythms, no longer an intrusion and looking down into the waters she knew what she wanted to do was neither selfish nor selfless. She had changed her mind when Joe had asked her to marry him. She had said yes. It had been their secret for two months.

'What are you going to do with me?' she asks, quietly.

'*Shut the fuck up.*'

She does. Listens to the kettle boiling, whistling, water being poured, then, a stirring sound – a teaspoon inside a cup. Tries again to imagine what he is like.

'Please let me go,' she whispers.

His footsteps get closer. Suddenly she feels her left hand free and the mug in her right. The straw comes through the hood. She starts to bend down but then suddenly throws the cup, in the direction she thinks he is at. She spits out the straw.

'*Do that again and I'll stick you.*'

'Please let me go,' she pleads.

Silence as he ties her hand to the wheelchair again.

'Oh God no. Please don't,' she whispers.

A mobile phone rings. Keeps ringing. The footsteps recede, a door opens, closes.

'Don't go. Don't leave me here,' she shouts.

Silence apart from . . . Somewhere above her head is the sound of birdsong. Two wagtails calling out to each other, familiar. And in the distance she hears a voice talking. It's muffled but also sounds familiar.

'Please come back. I'll do anything,' she shouts again. 'Please.'

A car engine starts up.

'Please come ba . . .' Her voice is breaking and tears begin.

The door opens. She cries out, 'Oh. Thank god. What's happening?'

Footsteps move closer to her. She feels him beside her, very close; feels his breath near her ear.

'My name is Malachy MacGaoth and I have a message for you.'

The voice is different, almost caring. 'What? Who are you? Are you letting me go?'

'In a matter of speaking, yes.'

'Oh God. You're going to kill me.'

'Yes, but as kindly as I can.'

'Why?'

'Because I choose to.'

'Why do you want to kill me?'

'Your living or dying makes little difference to me. Somebody else wants you dead.'

'Who? Why?'

'No reason that I can think of but that I'm being paid for it. And his name is irrelevant, as he has not the balls to be here himself. He is nothingness. Only you and I matter now, Phyllis.'

Suddenly, something that she had increasingly desired was now being offered, but it was not of her choosing. She starts to cry. 'Please get a message to Joe Reilly. Tell him I love him.'

'Joe Reilly is dead, a heart attack, as unfortunate as you are, Phyllis. Bad luck or fate, who knows which!'

'Oh Christ!' she whispers, and the tears flow.

'I'll try to make it as easy as I can.'

'I want . . . want to see your face,' she sobs.

'No point! There is nothing to be seen.'

His words are not harsh but understanding. She knows then that he knows and that he has given her back the choice. 'In that case do what you have to Malachy MacGaoth . . . and God save your soul.'

'Unlikely!'

His footsteps move behind her. They shuffle and suddenly there is pressure on her face again, pulling her head back. The hood over her nose feels wet, a liquid dripping onto her skin. She tries to pull her hands up. The ties cut into her wrists. She thinks of the waters of the old dock and drowning. She keeps her mouth closed trying not to breathe the wet. He pulls up against her jaw, forcing the wet against her nostrils. Nausea begins, and gagging against the cloth she begins to retch. She inhales deeply. At that moment she hears the wagtails again, but this time they are urgent calls, their ecstatic song variant as if mobbing a sparrow hawk. Feels dizzy and then . . .

27

THE VANISHING POINT

"This sacrifice, in essence, of two things
Consisteth; one is that, whereof 'tis made;
The covenant, the other."

Dante • *Paradise*; canto v

"Every instant is autonomous. Not vengeance nor pardon nor
jails nor even oblivion can modify the invulnerable past."

Jorge Luis Borges • *A New Refutation of Time*

DI Gerrit Flatley stands near the door, watching. Many of the
invited diplomats are already inside, gathered in the foyer drinking
champagne and coca-cola. From where he stands he can see
Brigadier Crawford, on the margins of the crowd, ghostlike. Also
Aengus FitzHenry, looking flustered, his check jacket flickering in
the forest of sombre suits and floral dresses. Joyce Holden and
James Somerville are standing on the lower crosswalk, listening
to Albhar – a traditional group composed of Moroccan, Galician
and Irish musicians – entertain with songs from their *Atlantic
Shore* suite. His mobile phone rings.

'Hello. Flatley here,' he says quietly, moving to a small seating
area, near the entrance. A group of laughing and giggling
schoolgirls, on a tour of the Castle, walk past him. One is licking
an ice-cream, with real relish. He smiles at her.

'Gerry, it's Paddy. We've found her.'

'Phyllis Andrew?' he asks, feeling more disappointment than he usually did.

'Yep! The sub-aqua unit dredged her up, still strapped into her wheelchair, from the reservoir.'

'Shit!'

'The post-mortem is scheduled for 02.00 pm.'

He looks at his watch, 11.30. Presentation due to start any minute. 'I'll be there.'

'Right. Oh. Gerry.'

'Yes.'

'What about your man, Flanagan? He's still in the holding cell. We cannot hold onto him much longer without a formal charge being brought. What do you want to do?'

Flatley had brought Flanagan in for further questioning 24 hours previously, more out of frustration with a lack of progress in getting any leads to the missing Phyllis Andrew than anything else. It was the second time since their return from Istanbul. Flanagan had realised this, cooperated, yet still accused him of it.

'Let him go, Paddy. But hold onto his passport.'

'Right. See you at 02.00.'

Flatley hangs up and walks back through the glass doors into the museum, pauses. He looks for FitzHenry wanting to inform him about finding Phyllis Andrew as soon as possible. He sees Jack Dawson and Rio exiting, from the corridor where her lab is, onto the upper crosswalk. He realises then, that even when out-of-sight from him, he can sense her movement, her presence. He tries to attract their attention but they don't see him. He watches as they abruptly stop, gesturing to each other as if they have forgotten something. The Durer etching for the presentation, he suspects. He had delivered it back to Rio earlier. She quickly turns and retraces her steps. Jack waits, his body only half visible, holding the outer door open.

Flatley goes deeper into the atrium. He sees FitzHenry mounting the small podium in the centre and testing the microphone. There is polite applause and then silence.

'Your Excellencies, ladies and gentlemen,' FitzHenry begins. 'Once again I wish to extend my sincere gratitude to members of the diplomatic community and their continued support of the Library. In particular on this occasion I would like to acknowledge the magnificent generosity of the Embassies of the Kingdom of Denmark and the United Kingdom for helping us to mount an exhibition of legal and ecclesiastical manuscripts associated with Viking Dublin and the Danish kingdoms on the east coast of England.'

There is more polite applause which FitzHenry allows to subside before continuing, 'No doubt as many of you are aware it has been a very difficult time for the Library lately but it gives me great pleasure to announce a recent discovery . . .'

Flatley holds back. FitzHenry's speech fades into the background as suddenly, to his right, an unusual movement catches his eye. The door of the toilet for disabled visitors opens and the figure of a man steps out, dark skinned, with a red chequered scarf around his neck. The man is smiling – *a detached frightening smile*, the policeman thinks. The man begins to move forward towards the podium but then hesitates by the door of the museum shop. He seems to be having difficulty opening the zip of his jacket.

Gerrit Flatley looks up, waves urgently in the direction of Rio. Behind him, projected on the atrium screen, the image of the Dürer etching appears.

FitzHenry drones on in the background, 'Thanks to the conscientiousness of one of our staff members, Dr Rio Dawson, a new, previously unrecorded Dürer etching entitled the Paraclete has been identified and validated. We are deligh –'

There is an abrupt pause in the flow of words. Aengus FitzHenry has looked up from his notes, and suddenly seen the man standing by the shop.

Flatley throws a quick look in the direction of the podium.

The colour has drained from FitzHenry's face. His mouth is open but no words come out. He is holding out his arms, flapping them wildly.

Then a scream comes, a scream that reverberates around the enclosed space of the atrium. 'Oh, God! No, Ahmed. *No!*'

The audience turn as one in the direction of FitzHenry's extended arms.

Everything appears to be happening in slow motion. A gust of wind blows through the doors behind Flatley and he sees the tassels on the red-chequered scarf flutter. He lunges forward.

He sees the man's hand move towards his chest, pulling open his shirt. He sees him tugging at a silver-coloured draw-ring.

He is nearly up to him.

'*Al-Awda, I am witness,*' Ahmed Al-Akrash shouts, and looking directly at the onrushing policeman tugs down on the ring once more.

There is a blinding flash, and then a blast of wind roars from within the museum shattering outwards the doors of the entrance. And some 50 yards away, the schoolgirl licking the ice-cream is impaled by a sliver of double-glazed glass to one of the park benches. And then the screaming starts . . .

28

THE CAT WALKS

"After realism, decide on the illusion."

Marie Helvin • *Catwalk*

Rio push-opens the door quietly. The nurses had told her to go
on in and that Joyce was anxious to see her. Joyce is turned away
from the door, looking out the window. A thin-legged nurse with
her back to Rio is leaning forward adjusting an intravenous
infusion. There are no flowers apart from a pink-petalled orchid
sitting on the windowsill. The room is spartanly furnished, save
for a television high on one wall. It is tuned to Fashion TV. For a
moment Rio's attention is diverted to anorexic models parading
down catwalks, black pools for eyes; dead light, zombie-like.
One life not nine, she thinks, and coughs.

Joyce turns. 'Rio, thank God. How did it go?'

Rio stared at her. She had just returned from Phyllis Andrew's
funeral and it was hard to describe the devastation, the
desolation, she felt inside. Too many funerals; Gerrit, Crawford,
the American and Israeli Ambassadors and their wives, the
Danish cultural attaché, one of the library volunteers – Angie's
mother – two of the musicians . . . the list went on and on. She
was so tired of it. Joyce looks impossibly thin; her face gaunt, and
left eye covered by a bandage.

Rio gasps, 'Joyce . . .' She starts to cry; uncontrollable crying.

Joyce holds out her hand. 'You poor thing! Come over here.'

The young nurse looks concerned, moves out of the way. 'Is there anything I can get you, Miss?'

'No, thank you.'

'This is Vicky, my new nurse. We were watching to see what bikinis we should wear this summer.' Joyce laughs.

The nurse smiles thinly and then leaves.

'Oh Joyce. I don't know what to do.'

'Common. Sit down here beside me. Talking about it will surely help.'

Rio is not sure about that but she obeys, and sits on the edge of the bed, holding Joyce's hand to her face. 'I'm so sorry, Joyce.'

'It's not your fault, Rio. Phyllis would never have wanted you to believe that.'

Rio looks at her, admires her courage. In a coma for four days, following the explosion, and then operated on to remove her damaged eye, she still remains caring, concerned. She notices the flower again. 'Nice orchid.'

'Jerome sneaked it into me, past the infection-control sister. *Cymbidium* he called it. Nice of him.'

'Yes,' she answers blankly.

'How are the others? I've had no other visitors today to tell me anything.'

'James is doing ok. Lost a good deal of blood, and his spleen, but doing ok.'

'What about Aengus FitzHenry?'

'It's now unlikely that he will come out of his coma. His family, I think, are considering withdrawing intensive care. Probably for the best! It seems . . .'

'It seems what?'

'Paddy Crehan, Gerrit's second-in-command, called to see me yesterday. It seems that it was FitzHenry and Ahmed Al-Akrash who planned and executed the original robbery. FitzHenry was being paid by some fundamentalist Pakistani organisation to keep an eye out for the Book, and also on Ahmed, who was considered a loose cannon. It was also FitzHenry who drugged Phyllis with chloroform from my solvent cupboard and who probably killed her.'

'Oh God. Not Aengus.'

'Needed the money. Had a secret life. Being blackmailed; a large cocaine habit and a liking for rent-boys it transpires.'

'Christ!'

'Ahmed Al-Akrash was supplied with explosives by a dissident terrorist group and the main reason for his suicide-bombing, it seems, was revenge.'

'How do they know all this?'

'Ahmed left a note for Mac, along with the missing page of parchment, explaining his reasons, his involvement with FitzHenry and the terrorists, and finishing with a verse from the Sura 6 of the Qur'an: "*We have witnessed against ourselves.*" It turned up yesterday. Found amongst the last bit of rubble being cleared from the café.'

'Why Mac? Why should he send him a note.'

'They were friends in a way, although the police now suspect, from information Jerome has given them, that following old Prof Symmonds' death, the word was out about the Book of the Messenger and Ahmed was put in place in the museum to keep watch. He befriended Mac to glean any information he could.'

'Where is Mac? He hasn't called to see me.'

'No sign of him! Not since the explosion, anyway. He was uninjured, as I was, because we were in my lab at the time. We had both turned back to get the Durer for the presentation. I hope he's not drinking. Marie hasn't heard from him either.'

'Poor Mac!'

Rio hesitates for a moment. 'We all pity the pain of alcoholics yet never stop to ask what made them drink in the first place. Was it pleasure or pain that drove them there? And if it was pleasure do they then deserve our pity? We all have ways of separating ourselves.'

'You're right. For me, right now, it's trying to decide what bikini to wear with an eye-patch.' Joyce smiles.

'I love you, Joyce.' Rio leans forward and hugs her tightly.

'How's your uncle by the way?'

'Always in the right place, that man! He was protected from the main force of the blast because he was waiting in the doorway for us. Some deafness only.'

'A little good-luck, at least. Give him my best.'

'In the chaos the Book has gone missing,' Rio says, shaking her head, but not really caring.

'Good riddance,' Joyce almost spits. 'What will you do now?'

'I'm not sure. As you know, the building is badly damaged. Thankfully little or no damage to the exhibits from the explosion, but the fire brigade managed to inflict some serious destruction with their water hoses in the archives. Once I am happy that is being taken care of, I'll head away, with Jack.'

'Probably for the best.'

'What about you, Joyce?'

'Another week or so here, then home. You never know, they might want me to act up as Director, supervise the rebuilding.'

'No better choice. Take care, Joyce. I'll call again.'

'You too, Rio.'

Rio gets up, turns and heads for the door. On the TV sees a model's legs go on forever, down the catwalk. One life, she thinks again, and leaves.

29

THE APPROXIMATE LIKENESS
OF BEING

"The metaphysicians of Tlön are not looking for truth, nor even
for an approximation of it; they are after a kind of amazement."

Jorge Luis Borges • *Ficciones*

"It is the egotism of love that disregards the woman, and
cares nothing for her real inner life . . .
Love is murder."

Otto Weininger • *Sex and Character*

Passing the open door of his bedroom Flanagan hears the
branches of the plum tree rattling against the window. He stops
and has a glimpse through the window, of a shadow moving
through the branches. He waits. Soon the intercom buzzes, and
he presses the lock release without enquiring, knowing, expecting
the visitor. He waits by the opened apartment door. The high-
heeled shoes tap along the corridor. Cohen and Kremer's *Zohar*
is playing on the CD. He sees her shadow first and then the shoes,
red pointed high-heeled shoes.

'Hello Rio,' he says, looking up.

'Jerome,' she replies, quietly, staring into his eyes.

He leans forward to kiss her, but she shakes her head, and he watches as a curl of distaste – or pity, perhaps – pulls her lips away, past him. He follows her into the room.

'It shouldn't have ended this way,' he says, to her back.

'Nothing is ever ended, Jerome. You know that,' she says, looking around the room.

'What are you planning to do?' he asks.

'Jack and I are heading for Eleuthera. I might not leave this time.'

'It's not right, Rio.'

'What's not right, Jerome?'

'Running away.'

'Running towards something, more like,' she says, dismissively. 'He needs me. I need him. Anyway, I've been down the road before.'

'What do you mean?'

'May I sit down?'

'Of course! Excuse my manners. Would you like a drink?'

'No thank you.'

He watches as her skirt rides up her slender thighs as she settles into the chair. 'Do you mind if I do?'

She nods her head and waits as he crosses the room and fills his glass with malt. He takes a seat opposite her. 'What do you mean about having been down the road before? he asks, fingering the glass.

Her eyes flash a warning of what is to come.

'Jack and I. . . we were . . . are lovers –'

'What? *When?*' he sputters.

'It started, at least the adult version did, when I was 19, on Eleuthera. Four months of hedonistic fun, unquestioned, without regret, without obligation. On and off since then, whenever he felt the need and I felt like giving. '

'Jesus!'

'Does it shock you?'

'Of course it does! But why? You are one of the most desirable women I have ever encountered. You could have anybody you want.'

His hands begin to shake and he feels the tightening in his

throat begin. He puts the glass down, awkwardly, on the small table. She leans towards him and he has difficulty focusing on her face. The nearer she gets, the more difficult it becomes.

'*Desirable!*' she dismisses.

The word ripples over the skin of his face with its scornful vibration.

Receding from him a little she continues, 'That's your fucking problem, Jerome. Desire, love even, is an approximation. It's a need to create something, an illusion of being instead of being something.'

'It's close enough for most people,' he says and senses immediately that this irritates her.

With an abrupt movement she stands, walks to the centre of the room, keeps her back to him and begins to remove her clothes. He is mesmerized by the revelation and what is revealed, and wonders if it is really happening. She turns, comes back to him, stands over him, and straddles him in a hazy nakedness.

'Is this close enough for you, Jerome? Why not accept the reality that I actually exist beyond your desire. Fuck me here and now. Express your need.'

He says nothing, is too stunned to say anything, but leans forward to touch her skin just above her hip and moves his hand slowly towards her breast. Her skin goose-pimples beneath his touch. He stops and looks up at her.

'It's something I cannot be,' he says.

He leans down to pick up her shirt and hands it to her. He watches her shrug, then turn to dress in silence. She is neither disappointed nor embarrassed, he realises.

'Thank you all the same,' he says when she is fully clothed, moving sideways on the chair to make room for her.

She sits down and her voice softens. 'Remember in the Church in Istanbul I said I was not very good at love but passionate about loving.'

'Yes.'

'I just want the expression not the reason.'

'Is that why you took up with Flatley? No reason?'

'It's what I am, Jerome. Its what I need to be me. Loves, hate, like, affection, attraction are simply volitions, the exercise of my will and are too easily modified to suit that wanting, that need. What I want to experience is not the sense of will, but the sensation. That sensation is my reward. That for me is *being*, and the *uncontainable*.'

'But why Jack . . . your *fucking* uncle of all people. What is it he holds over you, Rio?'

'That's easy! Jack's passion for me is stronger than my passion for me. Also . . .' Her voice trails off and her eyes close.

'Also what, Rio?' he asks softly.

She is suddenly somewhere else in her thoughts and does not answer.

'Also what?' he demands.

Her eyes open. 'Passion! Jack has it, Mac also – in a way, but not you, Jerome. Not you.'

His focus returns and he sees the intensity, the truth in her eyes. 'Yes, perhaps you're right.'

'Did you ever want me, really want me, Jerome?'

'The truth?' he asks, staring right at her.

'The truth!'

'Someone once said that in life, love and even suicide a woman will think of others, and the effect on others whereas a man thinks only of himself. When I think of you, when I think I really want you, I am not thinking of myself and that bothers me, gets in the way. There is something about you that I cannot put my finger on, cannot get passionate about if you like.'

She laughs, a laugh without vibration. 'There is "something" you should know, something I have never told anyone.'

'Why me?' he asks.

'I'm not sure. Some sort of premonition, I think. It's part of the reason I came here tonight. I can't explain it.'

He raises an eyebrow. 'What is it?'

She looks at Flanagan with tired eyes, then at her hands, which are rubbing back and forth across her knees, and then at him again. 'Jack is also my natural father . . . only he doesn't know it.'

'Christ!' Flanagan rocks back in his seat.

'He and my mother were lovers and when she became pregnant she made up a story about a wandering musician. He might have suspected but he never knew for sure. Nan, my grandmother, instinctively knew and told me as she lay dying.'

'So why the fuck do you do what you do?' he asks.

'I like it! I like the rotting depravity of it and its aroma of inevitable extinction. An orgasm with Jack inside me is asphyxiation. Sometimes I reach a level of arousal so intense I feel nothing, sense nothing, am nothingness.'

'Christ!' He looks at her for a long time.

'I'm sorry to shock you.' She leans forward to touch his hand. He pulls away. 'I now understand.'

'Understand what?'

'You, the unforgiving you, Rio! Does Mac suspect about you and Jack?' Flanagan had difficulty swallowing the spittle that was building up in his mouth, and its bitter taste.

'No, of course not! I told him that I was going to take up with Gerrit after we all came back.'

'Why, for God's sake?

'Mac wanted me to marry him.'

'And?' Flanagan's hands were beginning to shake; she stared at them.

'I said no, of course. I'm not the marrying kind, Jerome and right now Mac's passion for me is dangerous.'

'Shit! How did he take it?'

'Badly but I didn't have a choice. Not after what happened in the restaurant.'

'I don't think you ever had a chance to choose, Rio . . . and Jack has taken advantage of that – again.'

'I took advantage of him, if you must know.'

Another silence creeps up and settles between them. The music finishes and, glad of the excuse, Flanagan stands up and moves to the stereo. He feels they are dancing a tango, with their emotions. If only I could dance, he thinks, and seeks out Astor Piazzolla's *Exile of Gardel* in the rack. He finds it but his hands are cramping and cannot open the box. Easier to rerun *Zohar* again, he decides, and so he touches the play button. A thought suddenly dominates. *Bloody weird*, he thinks and turns to look at her.

'Poor Mac, castrated, metaphorically of course, by the uncle Fulbert,' he says quietly.

'What?' Rio is only half-listening.

'The *Historia Calamitatum*,' he says more emphatically, 'Abelard's classic medieval tale of the love affair between Heloise and himself and of their overpowering passion for each other. And of her Uncle Fulbert, Heloise's *guardian*, who couldn't abide that passion and had Abelard castrated. It's ironic in a way.'

'What is?'

'Abelard's Heloise was officially known as the Abbess of Paraclete, after the oratory where her order of nuns was based.'

'*Paraclete?*' she questions, surprised.

'Yes. Weird isn't it? A closure of the circle you might say.'

Rio looks at him for a long moment. The opal irises dilate then narrow and her words, when they come, are brittle, 'I'm not sure that I believe in closure, Jerome – ever!'

She is beautiful, truly beautiful, he thinks, her lower eyelids rimmed with the beginning of tears, like small pearls on the rim of an oyster-shell. 'What do you mean?' he asks holding out a tissue from his pocket before retaking his seat.

She dabs at her eyes with the tissue. 'Nothing is ever fully resolved. Our loves, hates, desires, satisfactions, retributions even, might approximate enough to accept but examined carefully you know deep down that "closure" has not happened, is not likely to happen and can never really happen. That is why, I think, I prefer the sensation and not the sense. In the pond of life, once the rock is thrown, so to speak, those same circles, like passion, spread out like ripples, carrying the closure somewhere else.'

'What are you not telling me, Rio?' he asks.

She hesitates for a moment but then explains, 'The Book is still missing. I think Mac might have taken it but I'm not sure.'

'Why do you think that?'

'He was nearby at the explosion and also . . .'

'Also what?'

'A more personal thing! A computer disc with a diary of mine on it is also missing. I think he has them both but I cannot track him down. I want you, need you, to get them back for me.'

'I don't know about the book, Rio. It has cost too much already. I'm not sure that it is necessary anymore. Not for me anyway. So what if Mac has it.'

'Right now I think Mac is unstable . . . drinking again and all that. Joyce told me that you are the only one he really trusts.'

'Did she now? What else did she say?'

'That you helped him before.'

He looks at her, not sure that he really wants to know her reasons. 'I'll try Rio. Not for the Book or your diary, but for Mac.'

'What do you mean? I thought that finding the Book was your life's quest.'

'Which you wanted a piece of? No . . . forget I said that, Rio. The Book for me, I know now, was no more than the dreaming of something that can never be. What did you call it earlier? An approximation! I think that's true for the Book. It's an illusion from the past. Alanna's death taught me that. The present has enough history already.'

'Then it was all a waste . . . you and I, Phyllis, Gerrit, Ahmed . . . all of the pain and hurt.'

'Nothing is a waste. Not in your case anyway. It's the price and pleasure of your being!'

'What do you mean?'

'In the sum of things we are sometimes fortunate to have our misfortune become significant enough to warrant attention to our living . . . our continued being in which it is forbidden to forget that we exist . . . still exist, Kierkegaard's paradox.'

'What has that got to do with me?'

'What you said earlier about passion! You are right. Existing, the expression of "I" should be passionate and I just don't seem to have that capacity anymore. I've settled for liking myself, my approximate likeness of being.'

'Why –' She begins to ask but stops when she sees his hands begin to shake again.

Qum Kalthoum's voice on "Angel" suddenly fades. Frog sounds and Cohen's trumpet give way to "The Merciful One". They look at each other for what seems an age. She finally decides against asking about the shaking. The thoughts are crowding in on her: Gerrit's death, Jack's needs, Mac's disappearance, her behaviour earlier, her diary, the Book, the Paraclete . . . Jerome's shaking hands and his *fucking* paradoxes! *I can't deal with any more shit right now*, she thinks and stands up.

'Goodbye, Jerome.'

He follows her to the doorway, and this time she allows him to kiss her cheek. 'I'll try and find the Book, Rio. And Mac as well!' he says this, meaning it but knowing it's impossible . . . for him.

She nods her head and is gone. He pushes gently against the door to close it quietly but it suddenly accelerates and slams shut loudly. Behind him the calico curtains billow in a breeze that suddenly wafts through the half-opened patio door to lift the hairs on his neck. He turns to make for the far end of the room but something stops him. He hears her footsteps on the marble corridor. *They are so confident*, he thinks; *striding forward without a backward glance*, he imagines. Then they stop. He hears voices, muffled at first but then louder: two distinct voices. He wonders what is happening and decides to find out. His hand is twitching badly as he tries to pull at the security latch. He hears a scream, a woman's screaming. He fumbles at the latch.

'Oh God, nooooo!' He hears a wail.

Suddenly there is loud bang, a thud, a moment of silence and then, yet another bang. The walls around him vibrate.

Then he hears the creak of Felicity Fellows' door opening and yet another scream, a piercing, despairing scream. Felicity, he realises, is screaming out his name. Finally managing to release the latch and open the door, he rushes out and nearly falls over her. She is kneeling, keening almost, collapsed to her knees in the middle of the corridor, her hand outstretched, pointing. A stream of blood is tracking towards her over the polished marble, mingling with the fine layer of red dust that had been brought in on the wind.

Flanagan follows the compass of her hand. Sees Rio's body slammed at an angle against the wall, her blackness bleak against the brilliant white gloss paint. On the wall a splatter design surrounds a picture of a Connemara bog, blood and pink tissue, dribbling down the glass picture frame like melted ripple ice cream. Rio's hand is jerking, her left eye staring, her right eye replaced by a hole with black, rimming powder burns. The back of her head is missing. He recoils for an instant but then rushes forward – clutches at her hand.

Already Rio's skin is cooling. He tries to cradle her head but there is no strength in his arms and she flops down again. The head, what is left of her head, smashes against the marble floor tiles with a crunching sound. He looks back towards Felicity, looking for help; looking helpless.

But Felicity's mouth is open in yet another – this time silent – scream, and she is pointing again, this time over his shoulder towards the main doorway.

Flanagan looks behind him. Beyond where the glass inner partition should have been, another slumped body, another half missing head, lays bent over backwards, covered in shattered glass. He sees a clump of blood and tissue on the ceiling, shaped like a butterfly. He thinks of a Rorschach blot roaring out an interpretation of madness before his eyes are drawn back down to the body. He sees that there is no lower jaw, and what remains of a rendered face is staring in his direction.

Mac's fingers are still curled around the trigger of a shotgun, jerking, as if trying to fire again . . .

BECALMING UNSCIENTIFIC
POSTSCRIPT

"Then even 'he' disappears and only the dream of
himself remains with himself in it."

Robert M. Pirsig • *Zen and the Art of Motorcycle Maintenance*

"When numerous people have the same type of dreams and what they
have seen in their dreams actually happens – to call these kind of
dreams as only dreams, this is said by the people that have no sense."

Hafidhh Ibn Qayyim al-Jawziyya • *Kitab al-Rûh (c.720AH/1320CE)*

The music surrounds Flanagan, gusting through the room, and
the cracks between his fingers. It is not music for lovers, he
thinks, at least not in the shared sense, unlike that first night with
Alanna long ago in Corsica; a night like this, on a blanket thrown
down beneath the stars in the middle of a mountain chestnut
grove, and the urgent, passionate love made to a stranger, a
stranger more intimate than many he had known forever, to the
strains of a shepherd's lament, rising within and without the song
ever upward *a paghella* from the village square below. 'Music of
the wind,' the stranger'd said. 'Breath in my breath,' Alanna'd
said.

   He lifts his head from his hands and types: *The journey for all
of us is finding the music of the wind, the chant of being!* He
rereads the words, shivers, gets up from the chair and stares at the
moon and a star-filled northern sky. He thinks he sees the silhouette

of an airplane cross in front of the moon and realises that Jack Dawson must be nearly landing in Miami by now, with Rio's hermetically sealed coffin in the cargo bay. Probably drunk too, he supposes, as he had been when he came back to the apartment:

'Did you know what your fucken' friend was capable of?' he immediately asked, before the door was half-open. 'Did he give you any hint of what he was going to do?'

'Who knows what any of us are capable of?' he replied, accusing Jack with his eyes.

'Whaddya mean?' Jack slurred.

'Nothing, Jack! I meant nothing. I'm just tired. Mac's funeral is on Thursday in Connemara.'

'He can rot in fucken' hell . . . and you too Flanagan!'

'I'll be there soon enough Jack,' he said.

'Whaddya mean?'

He thought about explaining but then decided it was pointless. 'A package was delivered yesterday with the Book in it. That's why I left a message for you to come over,' he had said.

'Did he send it?'

'Don't know.' He lied easily. 'There was nothing else in the package. It's over there on the table if you want it.'

Jack crossed the room and picked up the Book. He immediately checked the postmark on the outside. 'Posted four days ago, a day before . . . Are you sure there was nothing else in this,' he said, ripping back the paper.

'Certain!' He replied. Jack is not getting either the note or the diary, he had decided. Those he had destroyed.

'What did Babs want when she came here?'

He said nothing for a long time and watched as Jack stood, ashen-faced, waiting. He took no pleasure in it. 'She wanted me to keep looking for the Book. She was happy about going back with you to Eleuthera and intended to be there for a long time,' he finally said.

'Was she?'

'Yes, Jack. She was.'

Jack Dawson slumped at that stage, and great sobbing tears had flowed down his cheeks.

Flanagan waited until they subsided. 'What will you do with the Book, Jack?'

'Dunno! I want fuck-all to do with it. I'll probably give it to the Oxford crowd; perhaps arrange a rotation with Dublin every five years or so. Whaddya think?'

'I think Rio would be glad of that?'

'Yeah.' Jack Dawson said without conviction before heading for the door. 'I'm flying home Friday afternoon. Taking Babs' body with me, to bury her on the island.'

'That's the right thing,' he said.

'Don't bother ever looking me up, Flanagan. You will not be welcome.'

'Right. Goodbye Jack.'

And the door had closed with a bang behind him.

After a few moments, Flanagan shivers again, closes the patio-door and shuts out the breeze. He touches the orchid, fondling one of its blooms, remembering how Alanna had known how to find the wind and journey with its power. She had shown me how, he thinks. Mac on the other hand knew instinctively where that wind would take him, tried to warn him but was now gone.

'I'm so sorry,' he howls, suddenly, violently at the moon, ashamed at his inarticulate sense of grief – grievance even – the previous day when he arrived late at the small church where the funeral service was taking place. The church and the occasion had really bothered him, unsettled him. Mac would have appreciated that, he thinks.

Later – three whiskeys later – Flanagan sits down at the computer again, fires up the sleeping keys and begins to type:

The church nestled in a hollow, sheltering behind bent mystical hazel, *coll*, and a single fairy hawthorn, *sceach gheal*, at the bleak, bog-end of an Atlantic estuary; also some alder, *fearnóg*, its soft wood white in life, blooded in death. Built during the famine period the church somehow, had never shrugged off its blighted, shrivelled appearance and given present-day vocational and spiritual rationing denying it pastoral or communal sustenance, now only opened sepulchral doors: the consolation for a departing soul, conducted from his temporal way by a temporary priest and temporising congregation.

There was a big turnout. Arriving late I found the church's car park, and narrow access road, full to obstruction with haphazardly parked cars and about the doorway, overflowing groups of mourners gathered; some by choice and some by exclusion. Men in the main, they stood with flat-capped heads, ruddy faces, impassive eyes and solemn stoop in occasional and ill fitting suits; collars unfurled high against the wind, and intrusion. Some looked up as I approached; a nod of recognition here, a shrug of resignation there, and then quickly returned to their stoop.

I didn't feel like pushing past these men to seek the warmth of the church but in electing to remain outside had to listen to the service as it was relayed by the small, single speaker mounted near the door; its rusted brackets threatening to disintegrate with every squall.

The priest's words struggled to be understood; their pitch and volume sucked here and there by that same wind: ' . . . and as human beings we are distinguished in . . . by the gift of reason. That is our gift from God . . . and faith is the duty of that reason; the covenant with . . . and that draws us to His Being. In death faith is . . . but it is that faith . . . goodness rewarded and we become One with Him: one truth, one being. Cormac McMurragh had such faith . . . will get . . . reward. He –'

What faith, what reward, I wondered, as the words from the speaker death-rattled and then ceased completely. Bothered by this version of the truth, I suddenly felt very tired; tired of funerals; tired of waiting; tired of the search for truth and, turning away from the church, returned to my car to drive back towards the city.

About halfway to my hotel the tiredness overwhelmed me and after a near miss with an articulated truck – piled high with plastic-wrapped bales of winter silage – I pulled into a small lay-by that overlooked breaking green-black waves as they pounded a salt-marsh shoreline. Turning off the engine, my thoughts idled on being nearly foddered to death as I watched the scurvy grass, reeds and sedges protest the wind and spray. After a while however, the land, sea and sky began to merge and as the waves receded I receded, hopes ebbing out of me. Good and evil merged into being, and that *being*, being reward enough.

Dreamt of crossroads again, a recurring theme. Strange the topography of the mind when confronted by an image of crossroads: conjuring up dust bowls of mid-continental drifting, centrifugal and centripetal emotions, being somewhere and not being anywhere, harmony and discord, certainty and confusion, entrapment and escape, an end and a beginning . . .

It was nearly two hours later that I awoke, disturbed by the fierce alarm of wading curlew: *vi-vi-vü, vi-vi-vü!* I felt stiff and sore in the cold car; the windows misted over by my moistened breath.

Flanagan straightens, easing an aching back, and looks down at what he has typed. *I'm a romantic*, he thinks, interested, as Robert M Pirsig would have it, in the imagery and 'pleasure-seeking' of the words. Pirsig, he remembers, was an important ghost in their discussions, before the Messenger changed their lives – all our lives. What would the classicist have done, he wonders and then begins typing again:

Small church, isolated, nowadays only opens for funerals. I arrive late; groups of men standing around; listen to service on small outside speaker; hard to hear the words of the priest but he is talking about reason, faith and reward. I'm bothered by this version of the truth, Mac! I don't really want to be there and head for the city; nearly killed by a truck because of tiredness; pull into a lay-by to rest; fall asleep thinking about our discussions.

Dreamt of crossroads. *Good and evil merged into being*, and that *being*, being reward enough.

Wake up cold and stiff.

Or something like that, Flanagan thinks, before pressing *save* and moving the pointer towards *quit*. He hesitates. If only there had been more time to right the wrongs, to wrong the rights, to . . . He feels the fatigue, and the tightness in his throat. Suddenly there is an even greater urgency. He types furiously, pounding down on the keys, which offer little resistance:

Time is the messenger, and killing time, an illusion: as if there is an end to it . . .

Time to quit, he thinks, and does. His fingers cramp and he lets his hand rest on the closed lid for a moment, feeling the heat leave its ceramic heart, waiting for his twitching to ease before heading to the door of the study and turning off the lights. In the small garage to the rear of the apartment building, he knows everything is prepared: the fresh bottle of whiskey from the Isles; Joe Cocker in the tape-deck of his old Capri; a hosepipe connected through a bored hole in the floor to the exhaust; the tablets; the letters of instruction . . .

He hears the wind rising again behind him, causing the branches of the plum tree to drum against the glass of the bedroom window. *Did I lock the patio door*, he suddenly wonders. Turning around, he imagines – no, he sees the orchid dancing in the moonbeams. *But* that's not possible, he thinks, staring into the darkness. 'No *buts*, Jerome,' he says aloud, thinking of what K had written: *The least trace of a 'but' and the beginning has already gone wrong.*

It is dark when he finally hears the creak of Felicity's door and the clip of her high-heeled shoes exiting the building. He gets up, picks up the envelope from the coffee table, and then quietly opens the door of his apartment. He hesitates there for a moment, his hand resting on the doorknob, before moving out and pulling the door shut behind him. Standing in the middle of the corridor he stares down at its polished marble floor before letting his focus drift upwards to the picture of the Connemara bog on the wall. It had been replaced earlier that day by the caretaker and is hanging, he notices, at a slight angle. Instinctively he moves to straighten the frame but then, suddenly stops, smiles, shakes his head and ignores the urge. Jerome Augustine Flanagan drops his key into the envelope he is carrying, seals it, and then bends down to slip the envelope under Felicity Fellow's door. He stands erect again, looks in the direction of the front door for a moment before slowly, stiffly, turning to walk towards the rear exit.

And the three-cornered light awakening
So strong as to take your breath away…

APPENDIX

A Brief Explanation • The Language of Being.

HEBRAIC SOURCES

Ruah: In Hebrew *ruah* is used interchangeably to indicate breath, wind and in particular the life force given to mankind. The receptacle of that life-force is the soul or *nephesh*. *Neshamah* is also used to describe breath.

> "In his hand is the soul (*nepesh*; Gr: *psyche*) of every living being, and the life-breath (*ruah*; Gr: *pneuma*) of all mankind."
>
> Job 12:10

In general in the Old Testament breath is life and inspiration is the in-breathing of the life-force or spirit of man. In contrast, in Job 4:9 the wind (*ruah*) of God is judgemental and destructive whereas in Job 26:8 the *ruah* is seen as the spirit, breath or life-force within mankind and the breath of God is *neshamah* and is described as a source of wisdom.

> "But it is a spirit (*ruah*) in man, the breath of God (*neshamah*), that gives him understanding."
>
> Job 26:8

ARABIC SOURCES

Rûh: In Arabic *Rûh* is used in all the possible meanings of "spirit" but in particular means the non-individual aspect of the soul, the intellect or *nous*, in Arabic *al 'aql al-fa'âl* (active intellect), as opposed to the lower individual soul, the psyche, in Arabic *an-nafs*.

The Spirit (*al-rûh*) in the individual is continuous with Being itself . . .

> – Cyril Glassé, Concise Encyclopaedia of Islam,
> Revised Edition, Stacey Int. 2001

Nafs, in the early Arabic poetry is used reflexively to refer to the self or person, while *rûh* meant breath and wind. Beginning with the Kur'ān *nafs* also means soul, and *rûh*, means a special angel messenger and a special divine gift. Only in post-Kur'ānic literature are *nafs* and *rûh* used interchangeably and both applied to the human spirit, angels and *djinn*.

> – Shorter Encyclopaedia of Islam,
> E.J.Brill, Leiden 1953

"*Rûh* is an entity which differs totally from the physical body. It is a subtle, ecclesiastical, enlightened living and moving body which penetrates into the depths of the organs and flows into them like the water in the rose or the oil in the olive or the fire in the coal. As long as these organs remain able to accept the impressions of this subtle body, the 'Rûh' remains attached to these organs and provides them with feeling and movement. But when these organs are spoiled because of the dominance of diseased elements upon it, and they are no longer able to accept the impressions of the soul, it leaves the body and heads toward the world of souls."

> – Hafidhh Ibn Qayyim, *Kitab al-Rûh*

GREEK & LATIN SOURCES

In the Greek version of St John's Gospel the same word *(pneuma)* is used for wind and spirit:

> "The wind *(pneuma)* blows where it chooses, and you hear the sound of it, but know not where it comes from or where it goes. So it is with everyone who is born of the Spirit *(pneuma)*."
>
> John 3:8

Anemos in Greek is also a term for breath or wind, and sometimes *anemoso* was an archaic term used for the Holy Spirit. In Latin usage *anima* is the breath of life, or soul (i.e. animal – having breath) and *animus* the mind or soul. *Spiritus* is breath or spirit as in inspiration or expiration.

THE WINDS

The Mistral
   (It., *maestrale*) are the cold, northerly winds blowing down the Rhone valley and called as such for their force. (It., *maestro*, master)

The Meltime
   (Turk. *Melteme*: from the shore) winds are the annual Northeasterly Aetesian winds in the eastern Mediterranean.

The Sirocco
   (Scirrocco scillocco **sirocco** It., Sp. siroco xaloque, Pg. xaroco, Pr. Fr. siroc, sirocco South-East wind; from Ar. Schoruq, *scharq*: east. – An Etymological Dictionary, T.C. Donkin, 1864) is a hot, oppressive, and often dust-laden wind blowing from North Africa across the Mediterranean to southern Europe. Known locally as the *khamson*, Horace called this wind the *plumbeus Auster*, heavy as lead.

The Author

Roger Derham was born in Dublin, 9 October 1956. He graduated in Medicine from University College Cork, Ireland in 1981 and pursued postgraduate specialist training in Obstetrics and Gynaecology in Ireland, England, and Australia. Living and working as a gynaecologist in Galway, Ireland since 1991 he helped establish, with Brenda Derham and Valerie Shortland, the publishing company Wynkin deWorde in 2001 to promote literary fiction.

His first novel, *The Simurgh and the Nightingale* was published by Collins Press, Ireland in April 2001 and this was followed by *The Colour of Rain* (2002), a novel for children under the nom-de-plume, Alex Skalding, and *When Twilight Comes* (2003).

Other interests include maritime maps, the frontiers of language and religion, and sport. An active Irish Rugby Football Union referee and golfer he is married with three adult children.